DARK
DEEDS

DARK DEEDS

KEIKO BOOK THREE

MIKE BROOKS

SAGA PRESS

LONDON SYDNEY **NEW YORK** TORONTO NEW DELHI

SAGA PRESS
AN IMPRINT OF SIMON & SCHUSTER, INC.

1230 AVENUE OF THE AMERICAS, NEW YORK, NEW YORK 10020

★ Text copyright © 2017 by Mike Brooks ★ Jacket illustration copyright © 2017 by John Harris ★
For information address Saga Press Subsidiary Rights Department, 1230 Avenue of the Americas, New York, NY 10020. ★ SAGA PRESS and colophon are trademarks of Simon & Schuster, Inc. ★ For information about special discounts for bulk purchases, please contact Simon & Schuster Special Sales at 1-866-506-1949 or business@simonandschuster.com. ★ The Simon & Schuster Speakers Bureau can bring authors to your live event. For more information or to book an event, contact the Simon & Schuster Speakers Bureau at 1-866-248-3049 or visit our website at www.simonspeakers.com. ★ Also available in a Saga Press paperback edition ★ The text for this book was set in Adobe Jenson Pro. ★ Manufactured in the United States of America ★ First Saga Press hardcover edition October 2017 ★ 10 9 8 7 6 5 4 3 2 1 ★ Library of Congress Cataloging-in-Publication Data ★ Names: Brooks, Mike, 1982– author. ★ Title: Dark deeds / Mike Brooks. ★ Description: First Saga Press hardcover edition. | New York : Saga Press, 2017. | Series: Keiko ; 3 ★ Identifiers: LCCN 2017013964 | ISBN 9781534405462 (eBook) | ISBN 9781534405455 (hardcover : acid-free paper) | ISBN 9781534405448 (pbk) ★ Subjects: LCSH: Space ships—Fiction. | Smugglers—Fiction. | BISAC: FICTION / Science Fiction / Space Opera. | FICTION / Science Fiction / Adventure. | FICTION / Science Fiction / General. | GSAFD: Adventure fiction. | Science fiction. ★ Classification: LCC PR6102.R6633 D36 2017 (print) | DDC 823/.92—dc23 ★ LC record available at https://lccn.loc.gov/2017013964

```
        *              *
     *     *        *     *
  *     *     *        *     *     *
```

This book is for everyone who
looks out for those closest to them,
and for everyone who's just trying to get by.

ACKNOWLEDGEMENTS

Well, who'd have ever thought I'd get this far?

First to be thanked is, of course, my wife, Janine, for the support she's shown me by giving me the time and space to write stuff, being encouraging about it, and not getting too envious over the fact that I now have an extra day on my weekend to Be an Author. Thank you. I love you.

Next is my agent, Rob Dinsdale, always patient and determined, and thankfully tolerant of my tendency to say things like "Now what if I do this?" or "Yeah, I've started writing a young-adult portal fantasy; thought it'd be a laugh." I salute your sterling efforts on my behalf.

And then of course thanks are owed to Joe Monti and all at Saga Press for wanting to see more of the adventures of this motley crew of miscreants and putting in the hard work to make it happen—from commissioning yet more amazing artwork to running the Mandarin past a freakin' Hugo Award winner (!) without me even asking them to, just to make sure it's all okay.

So on that note, I should thank Ken Liu (even though I've never met him; it's not like I hobnob with important people) for checking the Mandarin, and give thanks again to Ande for Drift's Spanish. Tying in on this, I'd like to thank Muhammed Aurangzeb Ahman at @IslamSciFi on Twitter, who put me in touch with a couple of people (whose names

I am ashamed to admit I can no longer recall) to address some queries I had about Alim Muradov and the appropriate behaviour for a space-faring Muslim. Any errors in any of these respects are not due to them but to me. Or, if I can get away with it, the centuries between us and what happens in these books.

Thanks again to Blaise, who's always there for me to bounce ideas off when she's not busy keeping the country safe.

Thanks also to Magic Tom for my ubercomfy new writing chair of awesomeness, from which I wrote most of this. My back thanks you.

I would like to thank anyone who gave me information or advice that helped me write this book and whom I have forgotten to thank. I foolishly didn't compile these acknowledgements at the time of writing, and it's been something over a year since it was finished so I've undoubtedly forgotten some people. My humble apologies to you, whoever and wherever you may be.

DARK
DEEDS

PROLOGUE: TEN YEARS AGO, IN A STAR SYSTEM FAR, FAR AWAY

She'd nearly reached him when the brawl started.

The man who had to be Captain Drift—tall, dark, and, she supposed, probably handsome—was standing outside a coffee bar, although instead of sampling its wares, he was sipping from the disposable cup he'd got from the urn off a street vendor's back. She knew that because that same vendor had told her where to look for the man she'd described, for the cost of the somewhat overpriced coffee she held in her own hand.

"*Drift!*"

The voice was an enraged roar that cut through the hubbub of the Grand Souk's marketplace. Drift jumped and turned towards the sound for a moment, then clearly decided that he didn't like what he saw and pivoted away to presumably make a run for it. Which would have worked wonderfully had a large man with a bristling beard not stepped smartly out of the crowd in front of him and landed a thunderous left-handed punch to his jaw.

Drift stumbled to one knee, sending the other market-goers scattering in alarm, and his attacker closed in on him with beefy hands extended. The starship captain wasn't knocked as silly as it might have appeared, however, as he lashed out with his own punch directly into the other man's testicles. The bearded man's eyes bulged, and he let out a choking

I

sound that was cut off abruptly when Drift stood up, deliberately unfolding his long frame to drive the top of his head into the other man's jaw. The impact didn't seem to do a great deal for Drift's already shaky equilibrium, and he might have made it away had two more men not emerged from the swiftly receding crowd and grabbed him by the arms.

"Where's my *cargo*, you son of a whore?" one of them shouted; clearly the man who'd yelled Drift's name to begin with. Both of the new arrivals were also bearded, and what could be seen of their faces bore a strong resemblance to that of the man currently lying on the ground holding his crotch with one hand and his jaw with the other.

"You got what Tanahashi gave me!" Drift protested desperately. He was trying to squirm free of their grip but was only wearing a sleeveless armavest on his top half, and they had hold of his flesh rather than a jacket he might have been able to slip out of.

The man who'd spoken before, the older one judging by the greater presence of grey in his beard, spat an unfamiliar but doubtlessly uncomplimentary phrase in Arabic and then motioned with his head to the man who was presumably his brother. Each of them swept one of Drift's legs out from under him and brought the struggling starship captain down to the ground with a thud. The older brother then reached one hand towards Drift's face.

Drift began to scream.

At this point, she would normally have withdrawn. All her training had drummed into her that a field agent shouldn't draw attention to themselves and should abort and try again another time rather than press ahead with a compromised mission.

The thing was, she wasn't a field agent for the Galactic Intelligence Agency any longer, and this Captain Drift was the only likely way she'd found off this waystation orbiting New Dubai in the month that she'd been here. So her training could go hang.

She stepped out of the circle of shocked bystanders and kicked the younger of the two attackers in the side of the head as hard as she could.

He toppled sideways into his brother, who pushed him away and came up to his feet with a snarl directed at this new and unexpected threat. He reached for her with the bloodstained fingers of his right hand while his left dived into his clothes, probably for a weapon, but she threw her coffee into his face. It wasn't particularly hot any longer, but it blinded him for a critical second and allowed her to duck past his groping fingers and slam a heel kick into the knee of his planted front leg. With all his weight on it, the limb had nowhere to go, and his patella gave way with a sickening crack. He stumbled forward onto his knees with an agonised cry: She reached down, grabbed his hair, placed her foot on the back of his head, and stamped down as hard as she could.

She was a long way from being the heaviest person in the galaxy, or even in the surrounding ten metres, but the impact of his head onto the metal deck was sufficient to incapacitate him. The younger brother was only now rolling up into a sitting position after her first blow, so she took a one-step run-up and kicked him in the face again. He went over backwards, howling.

Drift was staggering to his feet, cursing a blue streak in Spanish and clutching the right side of his face. Blood was leaking from between his fingers.

"Captain!" she shouted, grabbing him by the elbow. "Come on, we're getting you out of here!"

It worked. The use of his title, the implied companionship of "we," and most probably the definite assertion that she was taking him away from the place where he'd just been attacked meant that he followed her instead of snatching his arm away and treating her like another aggressor. She aimed a kick at the man Drift had chinned as they passed him too, which probably didn't damage Drift's view of her intentions.

3

They got two streets away before Drift staggered to a halt, still clutching his face. "I can't see properly!"

"Let me look." She reached up and prised his hand away, then sighed grimly. Drift's warm brown left eye was untouched, but there was only a bloody hole where his right eye had been. "Well, that's because you've only got one eye now. Sorry."

"*Me cago en la puta!*"

"Hold up." She unslung her pack and reached into it. The GIA had offered her a few things upon her discharge from active duty, including yet another false identity (which she'd refused), but that hadn't included this small stash of medical drugs. So far as she knew, they were a secret between her and Dr. Grazioli, who'd always liked her.

She selected a low-dosage intramuscular painkiller: There were few nerve endings in an eye socket, so Drift wouldn't be in agonising pain. But he would be a long way from comfortable, and something to settle his nerves probably wouldn't go amiss. "Now hold still a second."

She jabbed the hypodermic through the fabric of his pants and into the side of his glute. He let out a strangled yelp but didn't pull away, and she was able to withdraw the needle without it snapping off. He stood there for a couple more seconds, taking deep breaths, until his breathing slowed slightly and a little of the tension dropped away as the drug started to take effect.

"Okay." He exhaled hard. "Okay." He turned his one remaining eye on her, seeming to see her properly for the first time, and narrowed it. "Right. Now, it's not that I'm not grateful, because I am. But who the hell are you?"

"Tamara Rourke." She tucked the hypodermic away, in case she got the chance to change the needle and refill it for use another time. "We spoke over the comm about the pilot job."

"The pilot job. Right." Drift looked back the way they'd come. "Not the knocking-people-the-fuck-out job. Because you seem pretty good at that, too." He was clearly North American, like her, and judging by his appearance and his accent, he'd grown up on a planet with a population of mainly Mexican origin.

"I have a few talents," Rourke said. "But speaking of knocking people out, shouldn't we be moving again?"

"Yeah," Drift agreed with a nod. "Yeah." He set off at a fast walk, his longer legs meaning she had to nearly jog in order to keep up. "Answer me one thing, though: Do we know each other?"

"No," Rourke said cautiously. "Why?"

"Because I was just about to get taken apart by the Al Shadid brothers, and you stepped in," Drift said. "That's a hell of a thing to do for someone you don't know, on the chance of a job he hasn't offered you yet. Might make a man a bit suspicious, if you know what I mean."

Rourke raised her eyebrows. "Captain, I've been stuck on this thing for a month, and the only jobs I've been able to find have been junior crew posts on big corporate freighters. That's not the sort of work I'm looking for. Yours is."

Drift stopped in his tracks and stared at her. "And how do you know what my work is? All we discussed over the comm was where to meet."

"Captain, your advert was for a Grade III pilot," Rourke said quickly and quietly, "and specified extensive experience with atmospheric manoeuvring. It required familiarity with Jubilee Beta nav computers, which are an old model not used by any commercial shipping line that I'm aware of. You also included a requirement for 'professional discretion.'" She spread her hands. "Put that all together, and you get 'freelance captain.' And most of the time that's just a nice way of saying 'part-time smuggler.'"

Drift narrowed his eye again. "You got any references? Anyone I'd know?"

Rourke kept her face smooth. "No."

"No one at all?" Drift shook his head, possibly in disbelief or possibly in response to a jab of pain getting through. "So you're, what, a pilot in your midthirties with no employment history who wants to make a living flying on what she thinks is a smuggling boat?"

Rourke resisted the urge to smile a little. She knew she looked younger than her age, but he'd undershot her by about a decade. And she didn't think he was trying to be flattering. "I'd rather answer to one person than a faceless organisation, Captain, and that's all I have to say on that. I've demonstrated I've got other skills that might be useful to you. What do you say?"

Drift chewed the inside of his cheek for a second. "I . . ."

There was a commotion behind them that rapidly turned into screams. Rourke was running before she even heard the gunshot, and she was pleased to note that Drift was beside her. Clearly, the Al Shadid brothers had found them.

"Bay Forty-Two!" Drift yelled at her, one arm stretched out in front of him in a crude attempt to compensate for his enforced lack of depth perception. "If you can fly us out of here, you can have the job! Deal?"

"Deal!" Rourke shouted back, doing her best to keep pace. She knew she was as fit as someone half her age, but Drift was nearly a foot taller than her. And most of that was in his legs. "Who *are* these clowns, anyway?"

Drift snatched an incredulous sideways glance at her. "You've been on the Grand Souk for a month looking for smuggling work, and you don't know who the Al Shadid brothers are? Did you just drop out of the fucking sky or something?!"

"More or less!" Rourke snapped, then grabbed his arm as she saw a disturbance in the crowd ahead that might just have been caused by people retreating from a man with a gun. "Left!"

This was a smaller alley, with stalls pressing in on both sides, and Rourke wondered if she'd made a mistake: They had less room to move here, and if someone started shooting without regard for collateral damage, then they'd be like the proverbial fish in a barrel. She slipped around Drift so she was on his blind side. "Do you have a gun?"

"Firearms aren't allowed on the station," Drift grunted, shoving an elderly man aside.

"Hasn't stopped them," Rourke pointed out.

"They're the fucking Al Shadid brothers," Drift bit out. "I'm a two-bit starship captain who didn't want to be thrown into jail for carrying a weapon and didn't know that anyone would be coming after him because it seems Enrique Tanahashi was playing silly buggers with their cargo!" He nearly pie-faced an overly keen vendor offering genuine vegetables. "That's the last time I carry a cargo without knowing what it is, unless someone's paying me *very* well and in advance!"

They made it out of the other end of the alley onto a larger thoroughfare, and Rourke realised with relief that they'd reached the edge of this level of the waystation. Pedestrian walkways ran alongside a wider space for cargo crawlers, small personal maglevs, and buzzing courier drones. On the far side she could see small portholes that gave glimpses of the stars beyond and, at the moment, a sliver of New Dubai.

"Is this the right level?" she asked Drift, scanning for the nearest docking bay.

"Yeah," he replied, pointing to their right. "That way. At least these bastards don't know where my ship is. I hope." He tapped his comm as they began to run again, then huffed into it between steps. "Pieter? It's Drift. Get everything ready: I've found us a pilot, and we're leaving. It sounds like Tanahashi stiffed the beardy brothers on the cargo, and they're taking it out on us." He paused, then began shouting so loudly that Rourke nearly stumbled.

"Yes, I tried fucking talking to them! I've lost an eye; I'm hopped up on painkillers; and if you want to make friends with them so badly, you can sit outside the fucking air lock and wait for them to show up!" Rourke heard him tap the comm again to disconnect it, and hiss in frustration. "*Jesu, Maria, madre de Dios,* this is not one of my better days!"

"Glad to hear it," Rourke told him fervently. "If it were, then I'd be reconsidering signing on." She pointed at an upcoming air lock. "Is that it?"

"It's after Forty-One, so it had better be," Drift muttered. He shifted direction without warning, running out in front of a cargo crawler big enough to crush him but making it across to the other side before the wheeled behemoth could do more than start to sound its horn. Rourke followed more cautiously, slipping around behind the crawler and waiting for a moment to let a tuk-tuk scoot past before she followed her new captain. By the time she caught up with him he was placing his palm on a scanner next to the air lock door, which hissed open.

"Come on through!" Drift barked at her, and she obliged. He followed her and slapped the closer, then slumped against the wall breathing heavily as soon as the door had ground shut again. "Seriously. Today can piss off."

"Come on, Captain," Rourke said, eyeing the second air lock at the far end of the corridor that would lead to his ship. "Let's get out of here before we get any further surprises. What kind of ship do you have, anyway?"

"StarCorp *Kenya*-class freighter," Drift replied, levering himself fully vertical again with a groan. "Twenty years old if she's a day, but the Alcubierre ring's practically pristine. And I had the thrusters redone last year. I call her the *Keiko*." He set off down the corridor, his tread significantly heavier now he didn't need to move quickly. "You flown anything like her before?"

"I'm sure I'll be able to handle her," Rourke said calmly, although in truth she was anything but. Her piloting experience was nowhere near what Drift's job advert had wanted, and this was something of a desperation move on her part. "I'll take it slowly to start with though, to make sure I don't shake anyone up."

They'd barely got through the second air lock and onto the *Keiko* when a tall, fat man so pale he was virtually albino and with white-blond dreadlocks to match rounded a corner and stopped with a horrified expression on his face. "Cap?"

"Pieter, this is Tamara," Drift grunted, indicating her with a jerk of his thumb. "She's our new pilot. Now, I'm gonna—"

"Cap," Pieter broke in, and Rourke suddenly realised that his horror wasn't anything to do with seeing Drift's ruined eye socket. "Cap, we've just been hailed. There's a customs boat on its way to block us in, and they say we should expect a boarding party any moment. We're being accused of smuggling."

"For *fuck's* sake!" Drift spat furiously. He shoved Rourke in the back. "Go on, get us out of here! I'm not going to some New Dubai jail to wait for an Al Shadid goon to walk in and execute me!"

"Bridge, now!" Rourke snapped, grabbing Pieter. He gaped at her for a second, then towed her round a corner and slapped the door open, revealing the *Keiko's* cockpit. She stared at it for a second, trying to make sense of the layout, but her eye was mercifully caught by the nav computer. And she gravitated to that on the basis that the chair next to it must be for the pilot. A speaker crackled as she hurriedly sat down.

+*Attention,* Keiko. *Acknowledge this transmission, and prepare to be boarded, over.*+

It was a pleasant, neutral-toned female voice: The ship's autotranslation protocol was dealing with the incoming Arabic communication. Rourke glanced at the speaker for a moment, then went back to trying to decipher the controls. She'd never flown anything like this freighter before—a small, two-person shuttle was the limit of her experience—but the theory was the same. The ignition codes had already been entered, so all she had to do was power up the drive. . . .

"You've got to disconnect us from the air lock!" Pieter snapped, reaching across her and jabbing at a switch. She felt a slight judder as they unclamped and began to drift very slightly away from the station. "Are you sure you're a pilot?"

"Are you sure you shouldn't be strapped in?" Rourke replied nastily, and rammed the drive to full. The freighter lurched forward like one of the racing camels she'd seen when she'd been on a mission down on New Dubai itself once, many years before. If said racing camel had been drunk. The *Keiko* wallowed, sending small items careering across the cockpit, and Pieter tumbling sideways into something that sounded hard.

"Are you mad?!" the fat man bawled at her.

"Just get in a chair, and tell me where that customs boat is!" Rourke ordered him, trying to make sense of the scanners. The speaker squealed as another transmission came in.

+*Freighter* Keiko, *power down your drive at once, and hold position,*+ the autotranslated voice said; far more mildly than the original speaker had, if Rourke was any judge. +*I repeat, power down or we will fire.*+

"*Keiko* to customs," Drift said, appearing at her shoulder and taking the comm, "we have experienced a full drive malfunction, and our pilot is trying to bring us under control. Please hold your fire, and we *will* submit to boarding as soon as possible." He killed the transmission and grabbed her shoulder. "What the hell are you doing?"

"Trying to get us out of here," Rourke bit out, jabbing at the nav computer. Jubilee Betas were reliable enough—nav computers that weren't reliable tended to send you through stars or into planets, which limited their marketability—but they weren't the fastest to boot up. She searched for a previous destination rather than wasting time trying to programme in a new one, and hissed in frustration as she saw that most were out of range of their current fuel stocks.

"Look out!" Drift yelled, pointing out of the viewshield, and Rourke's heart flew into her mouth as another ship attached to an air lock loomed up ahead of them. She veered them to one side, feeling Drift's hand weighing down on her shoulder as she did so.

"Have you even flown before?" Drift demanded. "Get us away from the station before you hit something!"

"Wherever that customs boat is," Rourke snapped at him, looking pointedly over her shoulder at Pieter for a second, "it won't shoot at us if there's a risk of hitting the station! If we head out into space, it'll light us up no matter what you tell them!" She knocked Drift's hand from her shoulder. "Besides, I'm the reason you still have *any* eyes left, Captain, so I'd appreciate it if you cut me a little more slack!"

"Slack be damned," Drift spat. "Do you know what happens if you damage the Alcubierre ring?"

"We're stuck here," Rourke said, finally finding a viable destination from the nav computer's memory and selecting it. The Alcubierre ring surrounding every interstellar craft bent space-time and allowed ships to travel at speeds that were objectively faster than light: Without it, the *Keiko* would be left lumbering around until the sublight engines ran out of fuel or, more likely, they were shot down by New Dubai customs.

"Missile lock!" Pieter yelped as a klaxon went off. Missile lock alerts weren't standard fit on freighters, Rourke noted absently: Drift wasn't without some foresight, at any rate.

"No," Drift snarled at her, leaning down until his face was level with hers, "if you damage my ring, I throw you out of the damned air lock!"

"Is that what you tell all the girls?" Rourke snorted, pulling the *Keiko* up sharply, or as sharply as the sluggish freighter could manage. She didn't usually take refuge in sexual innuendo, but she was either about to pull off a heroic escape or be blown to pieces. So it seemed as good a time as any. She waited for the green light to appear on the nav computer, flicked the switch to transition from sublight power, and hit the Alcubierre activation button.

"Hold on to your butts!" Drift yelled as the *Keiko* juddered . . .

. . . And abruptly, the pinpoints of light that were the innumerable stars of the cosmos were replaced by the eerie, mottled expanse that was all that could be seen when travelling inside an Alcubierre field's distortion bubble.

They'd done it.

Rourke turned in her seat and looked up at Drift. "Hold on to your *what?*"

Drift's one remaining eye studied her for a moment, and then he sighed. "Honestly. Does no one study the classics anymore?" He looked over his shoulder. "Pieter, go check on Sam, and make sure she wasn't thrown about too badly. Probably didn't even have a chance to strap in."

"Yes, boss," Pieter muttered, exiting the cockpit with a glare at Rourke. Drift waited until the door had hissed shut behind him, then turned back to her.

"You're not a Grade III pilot."

"No," Rourke admitted, leaning back in her chair.

Drift pursed his lips. "So we need to get a new pilot."

Rourke sighed, feeling her heart sink. She tried to look on the bright side: At least she wasn't stuck on the Grand Souk anymore. "Can I assume that you won't be throwing me out of an air lock until we at least reach somewhere I can breathe on the other side?"

"Huh?" Drift frowned. "Ah, that's not quite what I meant. I said 'we.'" He pointed between himself and Rourke. "I'm not hiring you as a pilot, but you can take down the Al Shadid brothers single-handedly. Besides, and don't tell them I said this, but right now you seem about as capable as the rest of my damned crew put together." He drummed his fingers together for a moment. "You got any funds?"

Rourke frowned up at him, damping down the momentary hope in her chest. Was he looking to rob her? "Why?"

"Haulage work for other people is fine, but there's not much profit margin in it," Drift said, glancing out of the viewshield. "If we could find our own cargos and pick the market to sell to, we could make much better money, but most of my capital's spent on keeping this ship and her shuttle in repair. And none of my crew can keep money in their pocket once they see a bar or a brothel." He looked back to her. "I've got the ship. If I could find someone to invest in a cargo and get us moving, we could take it from there."

Rourke looked at him, weighing him up. She had a payoff from the GIA: Not a huge amount, but it might be enough for what Drift was suggesting. The question was, did she trust him?

Then again, she'd lost count of the number of times she'd been working undercover and had needed to trust her gut on someone else. Would they pull through? Were they actually a double agent working for the other side? Besides, she'd gone looking for work with someone she'd never met, hoping to blag her way into a job she wasn't qualified for, and had got it by way of kicking three men hard in the head. Nothing was certain except death and taxes, and she figured that Drift was looking for a way to avoid at least one of those.

"A joint venture, then?" she said. "Business partners?"

"I'm not saying definitely, not yet," Drift said, raising one hand. "Let's see how we go. But you saved my life when you had no reason to do so. I figure I can extend a bit of trust here." He extended his hand. "We were never properly introduced. Ichabod Drift."

Rourke took his hand and shook it. "Ichabod. From the Bible.

Hebrew origin, meaning 'inglorious.'" She looked up at the tall, wiry Mexican. "And is that your real name, Captain Drift?"

Drift snorted. "Is Tamara Rourke *your* real name?"

Rourke smiled wryly. "I have the ident to prove it. But let's get you to the infirmary, Captain, before those painkillers wear off." She stood up. "I set course for Akallabeth; it was about all we could reach. Does anyone there want to kill you?"

"Not that I know of," Drift said, turning to head for the cockpit door. "I'm going to try to avoid that sort of thing from now on, I think."

SHIP HIGH IN TRANSIT

A Harja Logistics standard small shipping container was a mainstay of commerce, used galaxy-wide and across governmental boundaries. Produced from high-grade steel in huge quantities, it was precisely two metres long, a metre wide, and half a metre deep.

It seemed a lot smaller from the inside.

Ichabod Drift knew precisely how long it had been since he'd been forced into one with a hood placed over his head and anchored around his neck by a collar that his fingers couldn't loosen, because his mechanical right eye could call up a chrono display. It had been seventeen hours and twenty-six minutes, and that information wasn't reassuring him at all. He'd tried to batter his way out at first, but that was futile. He had very little room for leverage, and besides, standard shipping containers were sturdy things. All he'd managed to do was hurt his hands. He'd yelled as well—for someone, anyone—but all that had got him was a dry mouth and a sore throat.

He hadn't had a drink since, and he was so thirsty his hands were shaking. He'd been unable to restrain his bladder any longer at about the twelve-hour mark. Half of his right thigh was still damp, and the container stank of piss, which was aggravating his throat further. Most of his body was damp, in fact, because although the hood was porous and airholes must have been added to the container before his incarceration, the limited airflow didn't have a chance of counteracting the accumulated water vapour from seventeen-and-a-half hours of respiration by a six-foot-four, two-hundred-pound adult male.

A six-foot-four, two-hundred-pound adult male who was, by now, scared so bad he could hardly think straight.

What if they never let him out, whoever they were? What if his container's current resting place was to be *his* final resting place? At first, when he was still capable of rational thought, he'd tried to work out who'd grabbed him and where they might be taking him. After a few hours of imprisonment, though, he'd lost his grip on that thread of speculation. He'd started to fear that he wasn't being taken anywhere, that the container he'd been trapped in had simply been dumped somewhere out of the way, for someone to find days or weeks or months later when he'd long since expired of thirst.

His mind worked away feverishly, focusing on the problem like a hypochondriac with a chest pain. He'd heard that a human could go about three days without water, and the glowing chrono display in his right eye was starting to feel like a clock counting down towards his own end. Yet he didn't dare turn it off, for fear that abandoning the one constant he had left to focus on would see him pass into a state of true madness. He'd tried sucking the hood to recover the moisture his breath had lost to it; it didn't seem to do a thing. How badly would he have decomposed by the time someone wondered what this container was and opened it?

Ichabod Drift had made enemies during his career as a smuggler, bounty hunter, and entrepreneurial starship captain; it was true. But this seemed extreme. What if whoever had trapped him in here wasn't after Ichabod Drift? What if they were after Gabriel Drake, the name he'd adopted when he'd been young and desperate and had agreed to a career of piracy in service to the Europan Commonwealth in exchange for not being executed for a mutiny that he'd only technically led?

Well, in that case, his captors would likely be from the Federation of African States, and their government would undoubtedly be very interested to hear that he wasn't as dead as they'd thought. The fate that would await him at their eager, vengeful hands might make dying of thirst over the course of a couple of days in the forgotten corner of a cargo hold somewhere look positively idyllic by comparison. He'd cost them an awful lot of money when he'd repeatedly hit their shipping over several years.

Of course, he'd also caused the deaths of a fair few of their people on the occasions that the crews had tried to resist his boarding parties, but in Drift's experience, governments mainly cared about money.

There was a jolt. He cried out involuntarily in shock and sudden fear, but his throat strangled it down to barely a whisper. More jolting, and a disorientating swaying motion. He was being moved.

There was a brief sensation of increased weight—being lifted into the air?—and then an impact hard enough to knock the back of his head against the container's bottom as it landed on something. He groaned, then threw his hands up reflexively and as best he could in the confined space as something hammered viciously on the metal, scant inches from his face.

He might have whimpered. He wasn't sure if any noise made it out or not. However, the hammering broke off after half a dozen or so impacts and was replaced by harsh laughter that filtered dimly in through wherever the airholes were.

Another faint sensation of movement, this one rather smoother. He forced himself to ignore the burning pain in his throat and concentrate. Something was happening, enacted by people who knew there was a human inside this container, and that meant he wasn't just going to be left to rot.

So *what* was happening?

He was still horizontal but apparently moving, and moving smoothly. So perhaps his container was being transported on some sort of maglev bed? That meant a spaceport, presumably. There was certainly some sort of noise from outside his container, but it was hard for him to tell what, exactly.

He didn't get a quick answer to his question. His right eye's chrono told him that it was a further twenty-two minutes, containing various other jolts and knocks, before he came to a final halt.

He sniffed. There was a very unsettling smell starting to seep in through the airholes. It smelled like . . .

Meat? Lots of old meat?

Oh, that's not good. That's never good.

UNWELCOMING COMMITTEE

The catches disconnected with a snap. Drift felt the lid being lifted free from above him and new air—"fresh" would have been pushing it, given the charnel stink—rushed into the crate. The temperature around his body dropped a few degrees instantly, and his clothes and skin suddenly felt clammy. Nonetheless, he could have cried in relief; he wasn't going to be left to rot in a mass-produced coffin after all.

A male voice spoke in Russian. Drift didn't have either his comm or his datapad, and so didn't have the benefit of the instant translation they could provide when he linked them up. But he knew enough of the language to get the gist.

"Get him out."

Strong hands reached down and hauled him up, not gently. His muscles wouldn't support him, and he would have fallen had he not been held, although the muttered curses from either side of him indicated that this wasn't done gladly. There was a momentary pressure at his neck as a hand unlocked the collar, then the hood was pulled free and he could finally see where he was . . . sort of. His left eye was useless after so long in darkness, but his mechanical right one adjusted almost immediately.

He wasn't a big fan of what it showed him.

He was in what looked to be a warehouse. The floor was concrete, with various safety marks emblazoned on it indicating restricted areas and safe distances from machinery. The machinery itself consisted of conveyor belts, rows of hooks hanging from the ceiling, and a couple of visible band saws.

Not a warehouse. A slaughterhouse. Which would explain the smell.

Worrying though that was, it wasn't as alarming as the man who stood directly in front of him. He was white and middle-aged, with dark hair cut short at the sides and longer on top, and was dressed in a midnight-blue suit of the type popular in the Russian systems, with a breastplate-like frontpiece buttoned at the right side of the chest. His physique was a few steps from athletic but a long stride from actually being fat, and he had unremarkable features—the sort of face you might walk past on the street on half a hundred worlds and think nothing of it. He had an undeniably commanding presence, however. Admittedly, that was probably helped by the half a dozen thugs standing around ready to do his bidding.

Drift nearly pissed himself again.

"Captain Drift," said Sergei Orlov, his tone arctic.

Sergei Orlov. Crime boss of New Samara, gang lord, powerful businessman, and the most influential person for five star systems, and someone for whom Drift and his crew had failed to complete a theoretically simple job just over a month ago. Suddenly, the crate was looking very appealing.

"And your business partner, Miss Rourke," Orlov continued, glancing to Drift's left. Drift followed his gaze and saw a second container the same size as his being cracked open. The lid was pulled aside by another of Orlov's men while his colleague reached in for the container's occupant.

It had long ago been theorised by a physicist whose name Drift couldn't remember that a cat in a box could either be alive or dead, and you couldn't know for certain until you opened the box, or something similar. He'd heard that the theory had later been amended by a popular author to "alive, dead, or bloody furious."

It turned out that, in this case, what was true for cats was also true for Tamara Rourke.

Drift watched in astonishment as two dark-skinned hands reached up with a thin, glittering strand wound between them—Rourke's garotting wire, sewn into one sleeve of her bodysuit—and hooked it around the back of the stooping thug's neck. He was pulled down face-first into the edge of the container before he could react, and rebounded off to collapse backwards onto the floor. His colleague threw the lid aside and fumbled at his belt for his gun, but Rourke sprang up and pivoted on one arm to send both her legs around in a scything motion that cut the thug's out from underneath him. She ended up in a crouch outside the container, collar still in place around her neck but the hood cut away, presumably by the short, thin knife she now held to the second thug's neck from behind as she wrenched his gun from its holster and raised it in the direction of Sergei Orlov.

Two goons jumped between Rourke and their boss, while Drift suddenly felt the gun barrels belonging to the pair holding him upright pressed against his head from different angles. He tried to struggle free, but only managed a vague spasm. Rourke's eyes flashed to him, then back towards Orlov.

"*Ms.,*" she spat at the crime lord.

Orlov's face, which a moment ago had been a picture of shock, resolved into an expression of consternation. Drift had never found out Tamara Rourke's exact age, but she had to be over forty and was possibly older than that. She was short and slight and wore her pure black hair cropped close to her skull, and even in one of her bodysuits she still looked like a boy in his early teens. And yet she'd just taken out two of Orlov's thugs without even breathing heavily, after presumably being stuck in a crate for seventeen and a half hours.

"What?" Orlov asked, apparently unable to believe his ears.

"Ms.," Rourke repeated levelly. "If you're going to kidnap and incarcerate me, at least have the decency to give me the correct damn honorific."

"*Ms.* Rourke," Orlov said, perhaps a little tightly, "put the gun down or your business partner gets two holes in his skull."

More like four, Drift thought manically, *both bullets will leave entry and exit wounds, assuming my head doesn't just get blown apart. . . .*

Rourke snorted. "The only reason you're not dead right now is because Ichabod isn't."

"Do you really think that you can fight your way out of here?" Orlov demanded.

"Are you one hundred percent sure that I can't?"

Orlov tilted his head sideways slightly, as though conceding a point. "I must confess, I am impressed. You are *supposed* to be in the same state as the good captain here."

"I keep telling him he should try yoga," Rourke said dryly. At that moment the man she'd pulled down into the crate pushed himself up onto his knees, clutching at his face. Drift couldn't see his expression from behind, but the sulphurous cursing the thug let rip with as he reached for his own firearm made his feelings towards Rourke fairly clear, nonetheless.

He cut off and froze abruptly as she calmly brought her stolen pistol across to point at his head.

"Manners."

There was a moment's silence. Then Orlov exhaled in apparent exasperation and spoke clearly in English. "Gentlemen, if Ms. Rourke places her gun on the ground and releases Alex in the next five seconds, then do not harm her or Captain Drift further. If she does not, shoot her and then send the Captain face-first into the band saw. Then get the rest of their crew and do the same to them." He shot a glare at Rourke. "Even if she manages to kill me in the meantime."

Rourke pursed her lips. Drift could practically see her doing the math of combat in her head. He honestly wasn't sure what conclusion he wanted her to come to. He didn't want to be left to the mercies of Sergei Orlov, of course, but he *really* didn't want to be sent face-first into a band saw.

His eye's chrono display suggested four seconds had passed before Rourke sighed and lowered her captured pistol, then slid it across the floor to come to rest at the feet of the thugs standing guard on Orlov. She then stood up and stepped back from the man apparently called Alex in one smooth motion, allowing him to fall backwards onto the floor with nothing but the faintest of scratches on his throat from where her knife had nicked him. The man she'd been holding the gun on relaxed from his frozen crouch to sit back in relief.

Sergei Orlov picked the discarded weapon up from the floor and shot both of the thugs Rourke had taken out, one after the other. It was Rourke's turn to look surprised.

"I do not take kindly to failure," Orlov said matter-of-factly, while Drift tried to process what he'd just seen. "Especially not from those I charge with guarding me. Expectations of your condition should not have prevented Alex and Yegor from doing their jobs. It is, however, *my* place to deal with such failings, not yours." He whistled a shrill, pure note, and more thugs stepped out from behind machinery, all aiming their guns at Rourke. "You made a wise decision."

"Lucky me," Rourke muttered. Drift wasn't feeling particularly optimistic himself: If Orlov was prepared to shoot two of his own employees for failing him, what chance did a freelance crew have?

"Captain," Orlov said, turning to address Drift for the first time since Rourke had made her startling appearance. "I hired you to do a job for me. You agreed of your own free will. I, at least, was dealing in good faith, but instead of bringing me the information I requested, you instead left the system altogether." He clasped his hands in front of his chest, steepling his index fingers and tapping them together. "I hope you can understand my disappointment."

Drift figured that this was where he should start to contribute to the conversation, but his mouth wouldn't form sounds. He tried to moisten it, to little avail. Orlov watched him expectantly for a few long seconds, then sighed and gestured. One of his men stepped forward with a flask that he unstoppered and held to Drift's mouth.

It was water, and it was stale, but right now it tasted better to Drift than any twenty-year-aged whiskey. He slurped eagerly, not caring that he was spilling some down his chin, but the thug still withdrew the flask too soon for his liking.

"A revolution tends to make things trickier," he rasped, when it became clear that no more fluid was forthcoming for now. He was still shaking, but he started to feel a bit more human almost immediately.

"I have no doubt," Orlov acknowledged, "but I was hoping to have hired a resourceful crew that could cope with such pressures. It appears I overestimated your ingenuity."

Drift grimaced. The job had seemed simple, but their entire crew had been arrested on charges fabricated out of spite by one of Drift's old smuggling rivals who'd happened to be there on illegal business of his own, and then a revolution had kicked off that had required all their efforts merely to survive. Sometimes the galaxy really was not on your side.

"Okay," he said, trying to marshall his thoughts. "You're a businessman. If you wanted us dead, we'd have been dead where your men found us on Medusa II. You brought us here like you did to make a point, and believe me—" He coughed, swallowed, coughed again. "Your point was well-made. So that all begs the question: What can my crew do for you?"

"I am indeed a businessman," Orlov agreed. "I am, as it happens, a very rich businessman who will not shy away from spending money if it will assist in a necessary object lesson. Such as what happens to those who accept a contract from me and do not fulfil it."

Drift prided himself on his ability to talk his way out of pretty much any sort of trouble, but he was tired, weak, and still rather dehydrated. His well of words had pretty much run dry.

"Oh, come on," he managed, his voice little more than a whine even to his own ears. "The revolution meant those shipments never took off. The information would have been worthless anyway!"

"You were not hired to make that decision!" Orlov snapped, stepping close to him. Drift was taller than the gangster, but he wasn't exactly drawn up to his full height at present, and so Orlov's nose was level with his. He tried to sway backwards, but he was held in place.

"You were hired to do a job. Had you brought the information back to me, I would have paid you the agreed fee, even if the information had proved useless," Orlov said, his voice tight and cold and deadly. "I am a businessman, and businessmen do not become successful by breaking deals. But due to the nature of business I am involved in, I have a certain reputation to maintain when people run out on a contract."

That didn't sound good. With reason failing him, Drift fell back on bribery. "How about we recompense you financially? We have an account here that—"

"The account we spoke about when I hired you? The account belonging to Nicolas Kelsier, the terrorist whom you tricked the Europan government into helping you bring down?" Orlov asked. "Captain, please. I would have seized those assets myself, had someone not beaten me to it."

Drift blinked, his hastily constructed plan already disappearing from under him. "Er, what?"

"I thought you might mention this," Orlov continued, pulling out a datapad. "I have access to the security feeds from the bank in question. Someone entered the branch the day after you left for Uragan. You may have had the access codes, enough to draw money out bit by bit, but this person had full authority—enough to close the account and transfer the balance to a universal credit chip, it seems."

He turned the pad so that Drift could see the screen. "Here. A friend of yours?"

Drift watched someone wearing a niqab approach a counter and tap instructions into the terminal, then provide a palm-and-retina scan before taking the simple plastic slip that was dispensed in response. That was a universal credit chip, a piece of plastic that was allegedly unsliceable and that undoubtedly meant that the lucrative account he'd been counting on to help buy their way free of Orlov was now emptier than a politician's promise.

"I wouldn't say she was a friend," he replied weakly. One black niqab looked much like another, of course, but he was fairly sure who was underneath that particular piece of clothing: Sibaal, the woman who'd seemed to be acting as Nicolas Kelsier's second-in-command. He'd hoped she'd been picked up by the Europans, but it appeared they must have missed her.

This day was just getting worse and worse.

"So tell me, Captain," Orlov said. "How will you repay me?"

"Offhand? I don't know," Drift admitted, taking refuge in what he hoped was disarming honesty. "But I'm an ingenious sort of guy. Give me a bit of time to discuss things with my crew when I've had some rest and I can stand up on my own, and I'm sure we'll come up with something."

Orlov just looked at him for a few seconds, then broke out into what seemed to Drift to be a genuine chuckle. "Captain, I must confess, you are good at this. Being held upright, barely able to speak and stinking of your own urine, and you can still sound convincing with a bit of fast talking. I almost like you. But where would I be if I allowed men who had failed me to just walk away?"

He tapped one finger on his lips as though considering, then smiled. "I have it! You and your crew may go. My men piloted your ship back here: I will take your ship and shuttle as recompense for your failure to honour our contract."

Drift felt like he'd been punched in the stomach. "You've gotta be kidding."

"You do not like this offer?" Orlov frowned. "You get to walk free, alive and in one piece."

"And marooned here," Rourke put in. Drift couldn't help but agree. He doubted any of the crew had much money on their person, which ruled out buying passage off New Samara. And even if they did, what then? What sort of employment was available to a starship captain with no ship? No, in a galaxy where freedom depended on your ability to travel and find work, this was no merciful offer.

Orlov gestured to his thugs, who stepped away. Drift wobbled as their support was withdrawn, but found himself just about able to remain upright without them. The fact that he had to consider that something of a triumph was somewhat depressing.

"You do not seem interested in my proposal, Captain," Orlov mused. "Very well: I withdraw the offer. You have previously shown yourself to be a gambling man. Perhaps I should give you a second chance, but if I do, then the price for failure this time must be high indeed."

"Go on," Drift said, feeling his bile rise.

"Tamara Rourke will remain with me," Orlov said, his head tilted slightly as he studied Drift's reactions. "You will have . . . let us say two standard months to deliver to me five hundred thousand stars, or an equivalent value in other currency. If you do not do this, I will post a bounty on your head. I will also kill Ms. Rourke slowly and painfully, document it, and send footage to everyone I think you may possibly attempt to deal with in the future. Even if you avoid the bounty hunters, you will starve when your contacts learn how you abandoned your own business partner to me. After all, what will that say about your trust-worthiness or loyalty?"

Drift's throat was tight, and not just because of his returning thirst. "Hold on a second. Tamara is a vital part of my crew. I've got a much better chance of getting you your money if—"

"'Vital'?" Orlov frowned. "Perhaps I should keep you instead, then, and leave her to raise the money?"

Drift looked sideways at Rourke, torn by indecision. It wasn't that he didn't think they could get the money—of course he did—it was just that . . .

Well, half a million stars *was* an awful lot of money to raise in two standard months with no current plan.

"Ichabod, don't be an idiot," Rourke sighed, and then hesitated. "You're better at thinking up schemes than I am."

"Well, you're better at enacting them."

"Then I suggest you start improving, fast." She turned to Orlov. "I accept your terms. So does he."

Drift blinked. "I—"

Orlov nodded. "I appreciate decisiveness when doing business. Very well."

"Hold on a—"

Rourke glared at him. "Ichabod, stop wasting time and get moving. I'll be fine. You'll make sure of that."

What else could he do? He allowed himself to be led away from his business partner and the most powerful man in a five-system radius, back towards his crew and his ship, and a very, very tall order.

"Tick, tock, Captain Drift," Orlov called from behind him. "Tick, tock."

THE ONE LEFT BEHIND

The slaughterhouse door had just banged shut behind Ichabod and his escort, leaving Tamara Rourke alone. If you could count being in the same room as a dozen thugs, a ruthless gangster, and two cooling corpses as "alone."

She turned to face Sergei Orlov again, and found him watching her. She raised an eyebrow. "So, what happens now?"

"Now, we talk about your behaviour while you are my guest," Orlov said. "You will have a room, food, and drink. If you try to escape, you are cancelling my agreement with your captain, and I will proceed as though they had failed to raise the money. Which means you die, and when your crew returns to buy you back from me, they also die."

Rourke nodded, choosing not to rise to the description of her as property. "At least I know what to expect. Anything else?"

Orlov gestured at her, up and down with one hand. "You remove the suit. The wire is retractable from one of the sleeves, yes? And I suspect the blade in your hand was concealed in it as well. I do not wish to find out what other surprises it may hold."

"Water reservoir," Rourke replied, tapping the top of her suit's collar and pulling out an inch or so of thin, clear pipe. "It's spread thin, but it's better than nothing. It recycles and purifies waste water, too."

"Which would explain why you were not dehydrated after your journey," Orlov said in understanding. "And I am curious. . . . No cramp?"

"I'm a bit stiff," Rourke admitted, "but there are ways to keep your muscles relatively limber even when your movement is restricted. Besides, I'm smaller than Ichabod; I'm sure I bounced around more, but I had more room to move."

Orlov nodded as though it made perfect sense. "You are most resourceful. Lose the knife."

Rourke tossed it to the floor, where it made a tinkling noise as it struck the concrete. "I don't think even I could get you with that from here."

"I prefer not to take chances with my own safety," Orlov replied, smiling slightly. His smile faded when Rourke snorted. "Is something funny?"

"It's always funny when someone thinks they're safe."

Orlov gestured to his bodyguards, most of whom still had their weapons at least half-trained on her. "I think you are in more danger than I."

"I could have shot you five minutes ago," Rourke said flatly, folding her arms. She nodded down at one of the bodies. "You arm the people around you without making sure that they're good enough to prevent themselves from being *dis*armed. If you weren't taking chances with your safety, you wouldn't have been present when the crates were opened. Hell, you wouldn't have had us brought here at all."

Orlov frowned at her, as though she were a puzzle to which he was missing a piece. "You did not shoot me, though, as otherwise Captain Drift would have died. I had the necessary . . . leverage."

"Accidentally," Rourke countered. "You weren't expecting me to come out of the crate fighting. You didn't know that I wouldn't shoot you anyway, and the consequences be damned. I could have figured that we were going to die so I might as well take you with us." She shrugged. "I'll be honest, I nearly did."

"But you did not," Orlov said softly.

Rourke shrugged. "So you got lucky, this time. But you're a powerful man, and you make a living out of stepping on people. That makes enemies. Hell, sometimes your employees don't fare too well either." She nudged one of the corpses with her foot. "Who's to say Alex here doesn't have a sibling or a partner that's going to come after you now?"

Orlov actually laughed. "I would like to see them try."

She smiled, deliberately. "Perhaps you will."

The crime lord studied her for a moment, as though expecting her to say more. When she held her tongue, he shrugged and waved a hand at her. "Take Ms. Rourke to a guest suite and provide her with a change of clothes."

"I'm just going to walk out of here into the street at gunpoint?" Rourke asked. "You don't think people will notice?"

"This is New Samara, Ms. Rourke," Orlov replied levelly. "This is *my* city. People only notice what I want them to notice." He smiled thinly. "But no, you will not be at gunpoint. You know what will happen to you and your crew if you try to escape. I think we may need to secure you, though." He nodded at one of his thugs, a thickset man with an overlarge nose and a brown ponytail. "Tie her hands, and get her out of here."

Rourke couldn't help herself. She centred her weight just enough to be noticeable, and held her arms ready slightly away from her sides.

Orlov narrowed his eyes. "Wait."

The thug dutifully halted before he'd taken two steps.

Orlov's eyes bored into Rourke. She stared back at him as blankly as she knew how. She'd gone through the Galactic Intelligence Agency's counterinterrogation training back in her old life, and she could make a steel wall look emotional and expressive when she wanted to. After a couple of seconds a muscle in Orlov's cheek twitched, and he switched to Russian.

"Leave your gun here."

The thug dutifully passed his pistol to his boss, then approached Rourke with wrist binders in his hands. She sensed a slight ratcheting up of the tension in the room around her, shifts of movement indicating that weapons that had loosely been covering her before were very definitely covering her now.

She held her hands out in front of her and watched the ponytailed man flinch backwards, ever so slightly. He recovered himself after a split second and fastened the binders securely around her wrists. She didn't smirk at him, and didn't look past him to smirk at Orlov. She didn't smirk at all. She simply turned when Orlov's man took her arm, and allowed herself to be propelled towards the door. Footsteps from behind told her that one . . . no, two more thugs were following them out, but she wasn't overly concerned with them. Orlov wasn't speaking, which probably meant he was watching her. If he was watching her, then he was probably thinking about her or what she'd said, which was exactly what she wanted.

Rourke trusted that Ichabod and the rest would do their utmost to come up with what essentially amounted to her ransom, but she knew as well as anyone that the galaxy didn't always play fair. It was no one's responsibility other than her own to keep her safe, and she was already working on ways to achieve that.

It was nighttime, and the air was thick and close with a promise of rain, but for now the streets were still dry. A gust of wind, funnelled between the identical, dark-windowed warehouses blew fine bits of dust and detritus into Rourke's face. There was a distant roar, and she looked up to see a star rising into the sky: a shuttle taking off and heading towards orbit. She knew New Samara's spaceport was on the city's northern boundary, which meant that—she quickly orientated herself—she must be somewhere in the southwest. The simple act of stepping outside had confirmed that she was definitely in New Samara; the planet's capital was the only urban area in the temperate zones of this naturally habitable world of the same name. Every other farmable inch was given over to the cultivation of food, with the other major population centres relegated to the desert or tundra, save the small farming settlements scattered here and there.

One of her guards, bald as an egg, spoke briefly into his comm. Another one, a handsome man with short blond hair but oddly crooked eyebrows, put himself into her line of sight.

"*Do you speak Russian?*" he demanded, in the same language.

Rourke allowed a slight frown to crease her forehead. "What?"

"*When the car comes, get in the back,*" he said. Rourke heard the faint whine of an aircar but kept any comprehension from her face.

"I don't . . ."

The thug armed his pistol with an audible buzz and raised it to point it directly at her head. She saw the ponytailed man stiffen; he at least was smart enough to realise that, with her hands bound in front of her, she could potentially snatch the weapon, but she did nothing other than sway back slightly.

The whine grew louder and the aircar rounded a corner, then settled down beside them with a blast of downdraft. The handsome man raised his voice.

"*Get in the car, or I'll shoot you dead.*"

Rourke let her expression harden. "If you want to threaten me, try speaking a language I can understand. *Hablas español?*"

He held her at gunpoint for a moment longer, his eyes hard, then smiled and spoke in accented English. "Get in the back."

"Not so hard, was it?" Rourke muttered, turning to pull the door open and climb inside. It was a midrange Excelsior, sturdy and reliable, and large enough to ferry several people of reasonable size from one place to another. The handsome one got in to her right, the bald one to her left. The ponytailed man sat in the passenger seat next to the driver, but turned around to look over his shoulder.

"*Put your gun away, Sacha. You saw what she can do.*"

The handsome blond man, apparently Sacha, snorted. "*Mr. Orlov made a deal with her, right? She just has to play nice and no one hurts her, or her friends.*"

"*What do you think she's going to do, Andrei?*" the bald man asked with a chuckle. She could smell old alcohol on him, stale and sour. "*Take his gun and kill us all in midair? If she shoots Boris, then we crash and she dies anyway.*"

Andrei grimaced and turned to face the windshield. "*I just don't want to take chances. Mr. Orlov didn't want me to have my gun on me around her, remember?*"

"*Yeah, when her hands weren't tied,*" the bald man replied.

"*And besides, she probably could beat you up,*" Sacha added. "*Boris, you getting us moving or what?*"

"*Just waiting for you ladies to stop babbling,*" the driver growled in a surprisingly gravelly voice. "*Do you always bicker like this in front of Mr. Orlov's guests?*"

"*She can't understand Russian,*" Sacha told him, his tone one pace back from outright patronising.

"*How do you know that?*" Boris demanded, engaging the lifters. The car began to rise smoothly, despite the weight on board.

"*You saw me with my gun to her head, right?*" Sacha asked. "*I was telling her I'd shoot her if she didn't get in. She just asked me to find someone who spoke her language. Didn't have a clue what I was on about.*"

"*She could have been bluffing,*" Andrei pointed out, turning around again.

"*You worry like my mother, Andrei,*" Sacha snorted. The bald man shifted and shot Sacha a glare, which he ignored.

Andrei was studying Rourke, and she stared back at him. It was hard work, putting on a performance this nuanced. Any idiot could pretend not to understand what was being said around them, although it took a bit of practice. However, the Tamara Rourke that these men had seen in the slaughterhouse would be doing her best not to look unnerved despite the fact that she couldn't understand them. So she had to pretend not to understand them, but also pretend that she was pretending not to be nervous at the fact that she couldn't. But she *was* a little nervous, because she was only human.

The main thing was, she could understand them and they didn't think she could. She'd settle for that, for now.

A REDISTRIBUTION OF WEALTH

The *Keiko* was the closest thing to home Jenna McIlroy had.

There could be those who'd disagree with that assessment, of course. She still had a family back on Franklin Minor, so far as she knew, but she'd left in a hurry. She might have been able to travel faster than light, but communications couldn't. Alcubierre jumps were illegal too close to inhabited planets due to the risk of collisions between ships, so across the space of a solar system, it might be quicker to send a radio wave, but otherwise nothing could travel faster than the person carrying it. She'd been able to send messages home assuring them that she was safe, but there was no way for her family to send a reply that would reach her. Or even for her to know if they'd actually heard from her at all.

However, for all that, the *Keiko* was where Jenna now felt most comfortable, the ship had seemed strangely empty since Drift had returned alone from New Samara. Tamara Rourke wasn't big and she certainly wasn't loud, but there was a noticeable gap where she should have been. Jenna's eyes kept getting drawn to the bare space by the canteen door where Rourke usually leaned during crew meetings, and the Captain kept pausing as though subconsciously waiting for her to clarify or confirm something he'd just said.

"So, what we gonna do?" Apirana Wahawaha rumbled from beside

Jenna when Drift had finished recounting his conversation with Sergei Orlov. The big Māori was sitting in the huge armchair that he'd brought aboard years ago, for the simple reason that the standard canteen seats were on the small side for him. Jenna was perched on one arm of it, leaning against his shoulder. One of the very few good things to have come out of their disastrous trip to Uragan was that she and "Big A" had, after some misunderstandings, embarked on a relationship. They were still feeling their way through the first few weeks, and the crew's capture by Orlov's thugs hadn't exactly been the best start to it, but she didn't have a regret in the world.

"Even if we get the money, what are the odds Orlov lets us go?" asked Kuai Chang, the *Keiko's* mechanic. The little man was fiddling with his dragon pendant, as he tended to when uncomfortable or nervous. "How do we know he won't just take it, then kill us anyway and laugh?"

"Ain't the point, is it?" his sister said. Jia was somewhere in her midtwenties, a few years younger than Kuai and a few older than Jenna, and was the *Keiko's* pilot, a role at which she was spectacularly gifted. She was also staggeringly egotistical, incredibly foulmouthed, and almost pathologically anti-authoritarian.

Kuai scowled at his sister. "I think us being killed is a good point."

"We don't go back with the money, Rourke dies. Not fuckin' happening," Jia said firmly, crossing her arms and glaring at him.

"I just—" Kuai glanced around for support, but found none in the rest of the crew. He subsided. "Fine. We go get money for the mad gangster. So how are we going to do that?"

"I've still got about twenty grand of the money I won in Orlov's casino right before he hired us in the first place," Drift said, looking around, "so at least that's a starting point. Anyone else got any sizeable amounts?"

There was a gloomy shaking of heads.

"What about Kelsier's other accounts?" Jenna suggested hopefully. In taking down Drift's former-boss-turned-terrorist the *Keiko*'s crew had gained details of the ex-politician's secret funds. "There'll be enough if we combine some of those."

It was Drift's turn to shake his head. "There's two problems with that. First, it would take too long: They're widely scattered, and I don't think we'd be able to hustle fast enough to get what we'd need together and get back in time. Second, Sibaal cleaned out the account on New Samara, but she'll know that some money's missing, and she'll guess who's to blame. We have to assume she'll go after the other accounts to prevent us from getting them. We won't know which ones she's reached. So it would be a gamble in any case, and I don't fancy gambling with my business partner's life."

"That limits our options," Jenna said, grimacing. It wasn't like the *Keiko*'s crew hadn't made some big money in the past, but half a million stars sounded like a lot even with her uncertainty of the exact exchange rates.

"It surely does," Drift acknowledged grimly. "We need something close—I'd say two weeks' travel time, tops—if we're to have any chance of pulling off a scheme to get what we need. And I can't think of anything legal that will net us that much in the time we've got."

"There's always piracy," Kuai suggested blandly.

"No!" Drift snapped, rounding on the little mechanic.

Jenna felt Apirana stir beside her, and the big man leaned forward to glare at his crewmate. "Can't believe you suggested that, bro."

"Piracy, theft, fraud, what difference is it?" Kuai protested, looking hurt.

"The most obvious difference is that to go pirate you need to knock out a ship's Alcubierre ring to prevent them from jumping away, and we have *no damn guns* on this boat," Drift snapped at him. "You also need up-to-date information on shipping routes, cargos, and local law enforcement patrols, as well as a fence to sell hot goods to, none of which we have here." He scratched the skin next to his metal eye. "Besides which, I'm not doing that again. Not even for Tamara."

Jenna breathed a little more easily. She'd done quite a few illegal things with the *Keiko*'s crew, but piracy was not something she ever wanted to get involved in, judging by the vague details the Captain had been willing to share about his former career. Margins for error were very fine when the crew of one pressurised tin can was trying to board another pressurised tin can in the depths of space. Even if the victims were left alive, their ship was probably crippled and unable to get back to port. They would be reliant on rescue, which was always an uncertain factor in the big black. Jenna wasn't sure if she could be party to leaving a boatload of human beings adrift with their hope of survival coming down to a mix of blind chance and the goodwill of others.

Kuai threw up his hands. "Do you have a better idea? Because right now the only one I see is running and hiding, and saying sorry to Rourke's spirit if it ever comes to haunt us."

Drift looked sideways, to where the last and newest member of the *Keiko*'s crew—and how strange it was for that to not be Jenna anymore— was sitting quietly at the canteen table.

"Chief?"

Alim Muradov looked up. Up until the revolution he had been Uragan City's Chief Security Officer, but then he'd shot the planetary governor to prevent the man from using Uragan's toxic atmosphere to poison the rebelling population. He'd been quiet and withdrawn in his short time with the crew so far: Jenna wasn't sure if that was his natural demeanour, or a result of his coming to terms with the fact that the government he'd served for his entire adult life had been ready to kill a couple million of its own people to keep hold of a valuable mining asset. She suspected it was a mix of both.

"Captain, my experience is as a soldier and an officer of the law," Muradov said soberly. He scratched at his moustache, looking a little uncertain. "I am not sure how I can help you here."

"Who knows better how to break the law than an officer of the law?" Drift asked.

Muradov shrugged. "A criminal, perhaps?"

Kuai snorted, but the Captain's natural eye narrowed in a way that Jenna had seen before, which usually meant he was starting to fit pieces together. He sat down opposite Muradov and looked at him thoughtfully.

"You know this system better than us," Drift began. "Where's the money here?"

"Here? In Sergei Orlov's pockets." Muradov held up a hand placatingly as Drift's face stiffened. "That was not a facetious answer, Captain. The man owns or has an interest in practically every industry in the Rassvet system, as well as most of the political figures."

"He didn't own you," Drift pointed out.

"I was not important," Muradov replied dryly. "He had no interest in Uragan other than to ensure it kept producing minerals so he could make money on the stocks. Most of the population were too poor for him to profit much from drug-running, and such activity would have disrupted the workforce in any case. The rebellion there will have hurt his interests more than I ever did, for all that I did my best to uphold the law."

Drift sighed, clearly frustrated by Muradov's statement. "So if we were to . . . acquire . . . a large sum of money in the Rassvet system by nonlegal means, we would almost certainly be taking it out of Orlov's pocket in the first place?"

"I am hardly his accountant," Muradov said, with a shrug, "but that is my guess."

"So Rassvet's out," Drift muttered. "But Orlov has rivals. He told me so himself; the reason he hired us in the first place was because he thought anyone he sent to do the Uragan job might sell the information elsewhere. He knew I wouldn't know his rivals, and so wouldn't have time to find out who else I could sell the info to before it became outdated. Anyone who could afford that has to be a major player."

Muradov pursed his lips and tapped one finger on the tabletop. "You think to pay one criminal by stealing from another?"

Drift shrugged. "It sits better with me than mugging old ladies."

"I do not know what rivals Orlov may have here, but perhaps we should try Zhongtu in the Guangming system," Muradov said. "It is also Red Star; mainly Chinese. It is not the closest, but I have a former army colleague there who went into the *politsiya*, as I did. I have heard from her that the Triax has ensured it is as corrupt as Rassvet." He grimaced. "I cannot say I relish the thought of attempting to steal large amounts of money from any form of organised crime, but at least we should not be short of targets there."

"How far away?" Drift asked.

"I believe no more than ten days' travel," Muradov replied, "although I have never been, myself. I believe I met Security Chief Han at a conference once, but that was held elsewhere."

"Then we have the beginnings of a plan," Drift said. Jenna was sure she didn't imagine him glancing towards where Rourke habitually stood, but it was only for a split second before he looked around at the rest of them in turn. "Are we all on board with this?"

"You don't even have to ask, bro," Apirana said firmly. "There ain't a one of us whose life she ain't saved at some point."

"You want us to go to a Chinese system and rob the Triax?" Kuai asked incredulously. "What sort of *shén jīng bìng* is this?" He looked over at Jenna. "How about you slice us half a million into a bank account?"

Jenna rolled her eyes. "Because it's that easy."

"Gotta be easier than robbing the Triax," Kuai insisted. "You're some sort of tech genius—why not?"

"Okay." Jenna started counting points off on her fingers. "One, banking security systems are usually the tightest in the galaxy, because they're the most obvious targets. Two, even if I *could* break in and just fabricate half a million stars, which I don't know if I could, there wouldn't be any trace of where it had come from and that would set off other alerts. Three, have you ever tried to draw half a million stars out of a bank account?"

Kuai snorted. "You think I'd be here if I had?"

"Exactly," Jenna told him. "The reason we were taking money from Kelsier's account a bit at a time is we didn't have the authorisation to make a bulk withdrawal. To get an amount of money that large, you're talking fingerprints, retina scans, and so on, which we'd have to give in the first place to open the account that we'd then mysteriously deposit half a million in from no identifiable source, and *then* try to withdraw it all." She shook her head. "You might as well walk into the bank carrying a large sign that reads FRAUD IN PROGRESS."

Apirana glanced around at her. "You looked into this, then?"

She felt her cheeks heating a little, and not from irritation at Kuai. "I may at one point have been an oversmart teenager with a get-rich-quick scheme that other, more experienced people thankfully talked me out of."

"Still reckon it's a better plan than trying to steal from the Triax," Kuai said sulkily.

"You scared?" Jia asked her brother scornfully.

"Damn right!"

Jia stood up, looking at the Captain. "Ignore this *nǎozhǒng*. I'll get us there; you come up with a plan. Best leave him out, though, case he shits himself!" She stormed out of the canteen and turned right to head for the cockpit. Kuai bolted after her, shouting angrily in Mandarin. Drift watched his departing back for a moment, then sighed and turned back to Muradov.

"Do you have any siblings, Captain?" the Uragan asked.

"No." Drift shook his head. "From what I've seen of the Changs, I didn't miss much."

"Likewise." Muradov took a deep breath and exhaled. "So. We have around ten days to steal more money than I have ever owned in my entire life from one of the largest criminal organisations in the galaxy. I am wondering if remaining on Uragan would have been less painful."

"That's cos you're thinkin' about it wrong," Apirana said, heaving himself to his feet. "An organisation ain't a thing; it's all made up of people. People make mistakes, get careless, get sloppy. Plus, criminals can be bribed just as much as anyone else. There's always a way in." He looked at Drift. "You need us, Cap?"

"I'll pick your brains over the next day or two, see if there's anything we can put together as a starting point," Drift replied, waving a hand. "Go on; run along. Grab some time together while we've got it."

Jenna raised an eyebrow as she stood. "'Run along'?"

Drift snorted. "Well, 'limp' in A's case." He looked over his shoulder and down at Apirana's ankle, which had been broken in a stampeding crowd on Uragan. "How's the leg holding up, anyway?"

"Still sore, bro," Apirana said, "but I can tell it's mending well. Those circuitheads knew their stuff, I'll give 'em that."

"Glad to hear it." Drift glanced up at Jenna. "Don't tire him out, you hear? We might need him at the other end."

Jenna felt her cheeks burn. "Excuse me?"

"I heard what you were up to the other night before we reached Medusa II; that's all I'm saying." Drift shrugged, turning back to Muradov, who looked decidedly uncomfortable. "Remember that I've got the cabin next to his."

"We were *watching holos!*"

"Yeah, for like nine hours straight," Drift groused. He looked back around again and Jenna caught the mischief in his natural eye. "With the volume right up too. I've never known A to watch them for that long in one go before. You're a bad influence on him, young lady."

So it was going to be like that, was it? Jenna leaned down until she was nearly nose-to-nose with him and tucked the strand of her red-blonde hair that always seemed to be misbehaving back behind her ear.

"Did you ever wonder *why* we had the volume so loud?" she asked quietly.

Drift's left eye opened slightly wider, flicked up to where she knew Apirana was standing, then back to her face. Then he turned away from her again.

"This conversation is over."

Jenna couldn't help but laugh. "C'mon, A, let's go *watch some holos.*" She turned and left the canteen, Apirana's lopsided tread on her heels. It wasn't until they were a few paces away down the corridor that she looked up at him. "Sorry, was that weird?"

"I, uh . . ."

Jenna couldn't stifle a giggle. "Oh my god, are you *embarrassed?*"

The big Māori's mouth moved for a moment before he gave an awkward, one-shoulder shrug. "Yeah, okay. Kinda."

Jenna stared at him in amazement. "*Why?* You and I both know that we really were only watching holos." She frowned. "You're not embarrassed of *me*, are you?"

"Wha—wait, no, that's not . . ." Apirana stopped in mid-protest, eyes narrowing in his heavily tattooed face. "Wait, you having me on?"

She smiled. "Yeah, sorry. I don't really think that." She looked back at the canteen door, now shut behind them. "I have to say, I'm surprised that the Captain, of all people, got all twitchy about the notion of someone having sex."

"To be honest, I'm kinda shocked he's never made a pass at you himself," Apirana admitted. "Young, pretty blonde girl, you're his type." He frowned. "Hang on. . . . He *didn't*, did he?"

"What?" Jenna hoped her face sufficiently expressed her surprise and mild nausea. She liked the Captain well enough, but . . . "No, definitely not. I didn't think he'd go there with crew."

"He hasn't recently," Apirana allowed. "Ain't always been that way, though."

"Huh." They'd reached the door to Apirana's cabin, and Jenna stood aside to let him open it. "I like how you say I'm his type. So far as I've seen, the Captain's type is pretty much any woman, ever."

"To be fair, most of that's what you might call tactical flirting," Apirana said, punching in his access code. The door hissed aside and he stepped through. "He's good at it. Greases the wheels. But you're *sure* he's never come on to you?"

Jenna laughed as she stepped in after him. "Truly, never. To be honest, I think he almost feels kind of fatherly about me." She gave Apirana a level look as he looked around incredulously. "I said 'almost.'"

"Yeah, I was just remembering that I'm actually older than he is," the Māori muttered. "Which don't make me feel too good, given that comparison."

Jenna rolled her eyes as he sat down onto his bunk, which creaked in protest. "Are you seriously still hung up on that?"

"Ain't gonna lie: yeah," Apirana mumbled. "I'm twice your age, about three times your weight, and I'm half as smart as you. Don't get me wrong: I think I came out ahead on this one, but—"

"First of all, you are *not* half as smart as me," Jenna told him crossly. She was acting most of it, but there was a kernel of irritation at the core of it: Apirana wasn't the sort to seek out pity, and the notion that he didn't think he was good enough for her genuinely upset her. "Secondly, if I *am* twice as smart as you, then trust that I know what I'm doing!"

"Can't argue with that, I guess," Apirana chuckled, then sighed. "Thinking of smart people, and I hope you ain't gonna take this wrong what with me thinking about another woman, but I sure hope Rourke's gonna be okay."

Jenna sat down beside him and put an arm around his shoulders as best she could. She wasn't short, but Apirana was closer to seven feet than six, and broad with it, so it wasn't that easy a task. "Yeah, me too. But if there's anyone in this galaxy who can look after herself, it's Rourke."

He looked at her, their faces only inches apart. When she'd first met Apirana she'd barely been able to see beyond the moko, the tribal tattoos that covered his shaved head (and, as she'd more recently found out, much of his body as well). She barely noticed them now, and his face was as easy to read as anyone else's—easier, in fact, because he usually wore his emotions close to the surface. He was worried, deeply worried.

"It ain't what's gonna happen while we're away, so much," he said slowly. "Tell me true: Do *you* see us coming up with a plan to pick up half a million stars, from scratch, in under two months?"

Jenna took a deep breath. "I don't think it'll be easy, but . . . we took down an intergalactic terrorist with not much more than bullshit and bravado. And that was even with me getting accidentally abducted. If the stakes are high enough, the Captain finds a way."

"He has so far," Apirana conceded, "but he's had Rourke with him, always, even before I was on the crew. What are we gonna do without *her?*"

WORKING THE OTHER SIDE

Alim Muradov had grown up in the mining tunnels of Uragan. It had been seventeen years before he'd left that planet and gone into training to join the Red Star military, and another year before he'd stepped out of a hermetically sealed environment to stand, for the first time, under an open sky.

He'd hated it.

The roofs of even the largest of Uragan's chambers had been a virtually uniform seven metres high. The military training halls had rarely been as tall, and nor had those in the orbit facility where they'd been taken to practice zero-G movement and combat. When he'd finally donned a rebreather mask and burst out of an air lock with his fellow cadets onto a reddish, rocky plain, he'd nearly stopped dead in his tracks at the sensation of emptiness above him. Throughout the rest of his training, and the twelve years of active service that followed it, he'd never been properly able to shake that unease. He'd learned to suppress it, though: You didn't become a successful sniper if you were twitchy or unfocused.

All the same, he still didn't like the dark-blue void that was now above him, despite the brightly lit skyscrapers that crowded the streets and minimised the sky overhead to a letterbox-like window. The *Jonah*, the battered *Carcharodon*-class shuttle that serviced the equally battered freighter he now found himself living on, had touched down on Zhongtu, the middle of the three planets around Guangming Alpha. Guangming Beta, the smaller and dimmer star of the binary system, was currently opposite its sister star in the sky, and as a result even Zhongtu's nights were currently little more than twilight.

"*It's good to feel the wind again,*" McIlroy the slicer said in English from next to him, smiling happily. Alim couldn't agree. They'd landed in Zhuchengshi, the planet's capital city, which sat several hundred metres up a mountain range in one of the desert zones. The planet's original settlers had apparently decided that they didn't want the scorching temperatures and frequent dust storms that would plague them at ground level, but also didn't want to sacrifice any of the potentially cultivatable ground in temperate climes. Their compromise had been to construct a city between two towering peaks, and to get around the lack of flat ground by setting most of it on a huge level platform of superlight carbon fibre with plentiful bracing and support struts anchored on the rock a long way (sometimes a very long way) below. However, the altitude meant that the wind was not only strong but very chill, and Alim suspected it would remain so even when the primary star rose again and started to heat up the ground below once more.

"*Did you grow up on a planet like this?*" he asked. McIlroy turned her face to him to answer, and he was struck again by how young she looked. He still wasn't certain what would drive such a clearly talented young woman to fly with this rather desperate crew barring some form of compulsive criminal psychological trait, but then he was hardly in a position to judge. One month ago he'd have been concerned with preventing large-scale thefts, not performing them.

"*It had a breathable atmosphere, yes,*" McIlroy was saying. "*It wasn't an agriworld, though. It was a bit more like Old Earth, I guess; some farming, but also lots of cities and industry.*"

Alim frowned. *"How strange, I had heard that the USNA was running short of farm space. I fought in a small war because of that, actually. I would have thought any suitable world would have been turned over entirely to agriculture."*

"The Franklin system was one of the first we colonised," McIlroy said, *"and I think back then we weren't expecting to have to fight anyone else for what we wanted. By the time we realised we didn't have the whole galaxy to ourselves, the Franklins had already been widely settled."*

"You are from the Franklin system?" Alim asked, his curiosity momentarily piqued. *"Where the Universal Access Movement started?"*

McIlroy's face went from animated to stony so quickly that for a moment Alim thought he'd only imagined her previous chatty demeanour. The young slicer mumbled something that sounded vaguely affirmative and glanced around, then saw something that apparently required her attention and hurried off. She was almost immediately replaced by the towering presence of her boyfriend, if that was the correct term for someone about twice her age.

"Jenna really don't like the Circuit Cult, bro," Wahawaha said neutrally. *"Not having a go at you, just making you aware. Y'know, for future reference."*

"I appreciate it," Alim replied with a nod. He'd decided he rather liked the big Māori. The other crew members were a diverse, somewhat chaotic, and often rather forceful mix of personalities, but Wahawaha seemed sober and grounded. He was clearly aware of his size, too, and seemed to make a conscious effort not to loom over you. Alim wasn't a tall man, and he appreciated the consideration.

He realised Wahawaha was looking at him curiously. *"Is there a problem?"*

"No problem," the Māori replied, *"but by now most people would be asking me what Jenna's problem is with the circuitheads, that's all."*

Alim shrugged. The Universal Access Movement and their provision of cheap, reliable prosthetics to the disabled or injured were not just necessary but widely welcomed on mining planets like Uragan. However, he could understand how their sometimes rather evangelical approach could be off-putting to outsiders. *"I rather think that is her story to tell, should she wish. Given how quickly she ended that conversation, I do not think she does."*

Wahawaha's heavily tattooed face cracked a grin. *"Chief, I think you're gonna fit in well around here."*

Alim nodded, scratching his moustache. *"I must ask: Does it not bother the crew, having a former officer of the law on board?"*

"Yeah, but 'former' is the operative word, right?" Wahawaha said. *"It's what you're doing now that matters: We all got something in our pasts we don't wanna be carrying with us anymore. Except maybe Kuai,"* he added, *"but he's just a sourpuss because he promised his parents he'd take care of his sister and . . . well, you've met her."*

Alim snorted. The younger Chang struck him as someone who would deliberately make her brother's life hard for the sake of it, but even a groundrat like him could recognise her natural piloting skill. It went against all his military and policing instincts to let someone with such a toxic personality remain on a team, no matter what their nominal individual value, but he was rapidly coming to realise that his new life carried different necessities. For one thing, instead of being part of a chain of command that theoretically stretched all the way back to the Red Star government in their seat of power on Old Earth, his only superior now was a flamboyant, one-eyed Mexican with a fondness for whiskey.

Ichabod Drift materialised at Wahawaha's shoulder, a few inches shorter than the big Māori and half his width, smiling the ready grin that seemed to be his default expression. Alim still hadn't worked out if the Captain's spontaneous, mercurial persona was a front designed to dazzle, a true reflection of his character, or somewhere in between. Alim prided himself on being able to read people, and the fact he couldn't pin Drift down was annoying him.

"Are you ready, Chief?" Drift asked in heavily accented but understandable Russian. Alim blinked at him and responded in his mother tongue.

"I didn't think you spoke Russian."

"I used to not well," Drift acknowledged, "but I more learned on way here. I thought would need it I."

"You decided against Mandarin, then?" Alim asked. Since it was a Red Star planet the population of Zhongtu would speak both Russian and Mandarin, so it made little difference. However, it was generally accepted that you spoke the language of the branch of government that controlled a particular world.

"You ever heard him trying to talk this shit?" Jia asked in Mandarin, pushing past. "I swear, he'll learn to jump into orbit before he works out the fucking intonations."

"It's good to know you can sound uneducated even in your native tongue," Alim told the back of her head.

"Fuck you, copper."

Alim sighed, turned back to Drift and reverted the conversation to English. "*I am ready.*"

"*You're sure?*" the Captain asked. "*I'm taking a guess that you haven't done much undercover work before.*"

"*It is hardly undercover,*" Alim protested. "*I am a former security officer who is meeting an old army colleague and pretending to be an undercover security officer. It does not require much acting skill.*"

"*Well, just shout if you need us,*" Drift said, tapping the commpiece in his ear. "*We'll be listening.*"

Alim nodded and watched the rest of the crew file off towards a nearby bar. Zhongtu had a day of roughly eighteen standard hours, which didn't bother the crop plants any but was too short for humans to easily adapt to. As a result, Zhuchengshi, like the other population centres, largely operated around the clock.

He looked down at his pad, which provided him with a street plan courtesy of the local Spine, Zhuchengshi's hub of electronic information and communication. His destination was a different bar on a different street: A quick glance and the map was memorised, a throwback to his military days when information had to be absorbed and retained quickly. He made his way through the small tangle of pedestrian walkways without any of the hesitation that might have marked him as a tourist or newcomer. The last thing he wanted to do was attract attention.

He walked past gambling dens and flesh houses without a sideways glance, and skirted the doorways of garish drinking establishments where every surface was a vidscreen. Drones whirred by overhead, transporting small packages or messages too sensitive to be entrusted to the Spine. Advertising holos reached out from the surrounding buildings, their pulsing messages blindly imploring passersby to drink Star Cola, or buy a diamond bracelet from Yang & Sons Jewellers, or take out travel insurance and visit the luxury void station resort of Cosmic Parcs.

Music thudded out of shop doorways and drifted down from windows above street level, faint snatches of song or tune that tugged at a memory of something he'd heard once, before fading into the surrounding cacophony as he walked on. People talked and laughed and shouted, a child's scream of laughter or pain cut through the babble for a second, and somewhere he could hear the rumbling engine of a wheeled truck crawling through the streets. It was an almost overwhelming sensory stimuli, particularly for someone who had grown used to the relative quiet of Uragan City's subterranean passages, and he nearly missed the doorway of the Lemon Tree. However, he spotted the sign at the last moment and turned into a very different manner of bar.

It was much darker, and subtly lit by rustic-looking lanterns. A quick glance at one showed that it was a holographic source, but with the appearance of a filament bulb. The furniture was replica wood—the real thing would have cost a small fortune—and the door that swung shut behind him blocked out most of the bustle of the street outside. It wasn't silent, but it was quiet, and reserved.

He paused, looking around. A woman in a nearby booth raised one hand in greeting, and Alim walked over to her as casually as though they'd seen each other the day before. In fact, the last time they'd spoken face-to-face had been over a decade ago.

He swung himself into the booth. "Mariya."

The seats were comfortable, but well-worn. She had taken the seat facing the door, which meant he could see down the bar but couldn't watch who came in without turning his head. In these circumstances that made him feel a little vulnerable, despite the pistol riding in his inside jacket pocket.

"Alim." Mariya Li smiled, and swirled an unfamiliar bright-red drink around the glass in her right hand so the ice clinked. Her hair was its natural dark colour, and cut so short that it barely covered her ears. Her role in the security force didn't seem to have affected her physical fitness, since so far as he could see she had the bulky shoulders and lean waist she'd had in the military. "It's been a while. What will you have?" she asked in Mandarin

He tapped the tabletop, which instantly became a menu, and selected a flavoured water. He winced internally at the cost: Zhongtu's status as a breathable world meant it attracted the rich, and the prices matched the expected clientele. There was the additional problem that he didn't have any money of his own, as he'd left every single personal possession other than the crescent moon pendant at his neck on Uragan, so he'd had to take a loan from the Captain.

"No drinking on duty, of course," Mariya commented. Her tone was neutral, but her eyes held a faint hint of a question.

Alim looked at her levelly. "I'm Muslim, if you recall. Who's on duty?"

"I'm not a fool, Alim," Mariya sighed. "Sure, we've thrown a few messages back and forth over the years. And it's been nice to stay in touch, but when you suddenly contact me from low orbit and ask if we can meet up? I doubt this is a social call."

Alim smiled ruefully. He'd wondered how to approach this, but luckily it seemed that Mariya had already done most of the groundwork for him in her own head. "And how do you know I'm not fleeing the rebellion on Uragan, down on my luck and desperate for help?"

"Offhand?" Mariya took a sip of her drink. "You'd have gone to a cheaper planet."

Alim couldn't help but laugh. "You may be right." A robotic waiter rolled up with his water and waited for him to drop coins into it before it released the clamp. He watched it trundle away, then turned his attention back to his former regimental colleague. "Your first guess was accurate. I'm here on business. My employment on Uragan ended just before the government lost control of the planet, as it happened, and I was reassigned." *Technically true, more or less.*

Mariya's eyebrows raised. "Interesting. I bet they regretted that decision when everything went to hell."

Alim tried not to let his feelings show on his face. He still blamed himself for not giving more credence to the occasional whispers of discontent that had made their way to his office, and couldn't help the feeling that perhaps another person might have been able to stamp out the revolution before it had taken hold. He grimaced instead and took a sip of his drink, which was at least cold and refreshing. He couldn't help but ask after his homeland despite the pressing purpose of this meeting, although he privately dreaded the answers. "I've been out of the loop for the last few weeks. How have things progressed there?"

Mariya swallowed her mouthful and puffed out her cheeks, somehow managing to indicate a whole planet's worth of chaos and confusion in one exhalation. "The government tried to take back Uragan City from the rebels and found that a lot harder than they expected. I don't think they got beyond the first level, although you know as well as I do that they don't let many details out when things don't go well. Then some envoys from the Free Systems turned up and tried to get all diplomatic about things, saying Uragan had declared for them now and they wanted an independently moderated referendum on secession. The last I heard, it was rumbling on as a whole load of interplanetary trash talk and not much else, but you know anything could have happened in the last week and we wouldn't have found out yet."

Alim sighed. Better than he'd feared, although he suspected a government-sponsored genocide had merely been stalled. "Well, for better or worse, Uragan is not my problem anymore," he said, trying to convince himself as much as Mariya. "There was precious little to tie me to the place anyway, since my mother died."

"So what brings you here?"

He leaned forward. "Corruption. You've mentioned the Triax here to me before, but it seems our paymasters have finally caught up with the situation. I'm on a fact-finding mission, getting an outsider's perspective on . . ." He trailed off as Mariya's face went stony, and resisted the impulse to look over his shoulder. "Is there a problem?"

"I never mentioned anything of the sort," Mariya said. She was sitting stock-still in her seat, and her knuckles were white where she gripped her glass. "You must have confused someone else's messages with mine."

Alim opened his mouth to remind her of what she'd said, but thought better of it. Mariya had always been possessed of a certain gallows humour even in their most stressful combat situations, and he'd never seen her this alarmed. He sat back slowly. "Perhaps I have. I apologise."

She drained her drink in one swift motion and set the glass down on the table. "It was good to see you again, Alim, but I should be going." She got up before he could protest and took a step towards the door, then bent in towards him. It was his turn to freeze—a kiss on the cheek had certainly never been on the cards between Mariya and him—but she stopped a fraction before her lips made contact with his skin. Her whisper was barely audible.

"Street market. Five minutes."

Then she pulled away and turned towards the door. Alim watched her go, not bothering to hide his confusion, then returned to his water with his thoughts in a whirl. Two options quickly presented themselves. One, Mariya was very concerned about being overheard, even in this place, and wanted to go somewhere far noisier and more chaotic to continue their conversation.

Two, Mariya was now in the pay of the Triax, and wanted to go somewhere far noisier and more chaotic to ensure the person she thought was a Red Star Confederate anticorruption agent could be made to disappear quickly and easily.

He tapped his pad and opened a channel to Drift, using the *Jonah*'s communicator to avoid having to go through the local relays.

+*Chief?*+

He switched to English, scanning the Lemon Tree to see if anyone else was taking an interest in him. He couldn't see anyone acting particularly suspiciously, but subterfuge had never really been his stock in trade. "*Captain. We may have a problem.*"

WORD ON THE STREET

Zhuchengshi's street market was what Alim imagined mining must be like if the rock was made of people and his face was the drill. The crush was oppressive and the noise little better, and there was simply no way of making progress without shouldering or elbowing people aside. He went with it, keeping one hand on his wallet and the other close to his gun. He didn't want to lose either of them to the eager fingers of the pickpockets he knew would frequent this place, and he might need both before this night was out.

How was he even supposed to find Mariya in this? Was that the point? Had she made this suggestion so he wouldn't follow her straight out of the bar, so he would instead waste time floundering through this mess of people until she was long gone?

He gritted his teeth. He held no love for Sergei Orlov and didn't want to enrich the mobster further, but he needed to prove his worth to Drift in order to keep a place to live, at least for the time being. That meant not falling at the first hurdle of this scheme to save another member of their crew, no matter how crazy that scheme might seem.

A waft of scent from one of the food stalls grabbed his throat, and he paused. He was hungry; there was no denying it, and the fresh, vibrant flavours promised by the market held great appeal for someone whose meals had mostly consisted of long-life military rations and Uragan food imports. Besides, he reckoned that stopping to eat on a corner would look less suspicious than just standing still and scanning the crowd for no good reason. A win all around, then.

He handed over a few stars and got a foiled container of rice, mushroom-based protein, and miscellaneous vegetables along with a disposable fork, which he put to good use as he found a place to lurk between a woman hawking candles and a stall offering fancy chocolates. The food was some Mexi-Szechuan concoction, all ferocious spices and deep flavours, and was simultaneously one of the most delicious and most painful things he'd ever eaten.

He was halfway down the container without having seen any sign of Mariya when something hard dug into his back and he felt breath on the nape of his neck.

"Don't move," a woman said in Mandarin.

He swallowed his mouthful. "Mariya? Is that a gun in my back?"

"No, it's my cock." She pressed it into his spine a little harder. "Of course it's a gun, you prick! And do you think I'm some kind of idiot?"

Alim tried to think clearly. Things had taken an unexpected turn: Mariya sounded desperate, almost scared, and he was not fond of the idea of a scared person with their gun in his back. Stall for time, keep her talking, try to de-escalate the situation. All good policing tactics, and currently rather more viable than the military way to resolve the problem, which would have been to shoot her in the head from half a mile away.

"Why do you say that?"

He heard her hiss in frustration. "You expect me to believe that you're here to address corruption on this planet? That you're here to get an 'outsider's perspective' on it? You wouldn't have made it to the ground!"

Alim frowned. "Why . . . What? You're saying the spaceport staff are corrupt too?"

"The entire damn *system* is corrupt, from the chief on downwards!" Mariya snapped. "We might fly the flag, but this isn't the Confederate's planet anymore."

"So if you know this," Alim said slowly, "why doesn't anyone do something about it?"

"Like who? The force?" Mariya snorted. "I think there's about three other cops I know who definitely aren't on the take, and two of them are rookies who just haven't been cozened into it yet. We're the goddamn Dragon Sons' pets so long as they pay us to keep us sweet, and no one's looking to change that. If I start even trying to make trouble, I'll end up dead faster than a blind woman in a gunfight."

Alim nodded slowly and visibly. "I had no idea it was that bad. In that case, I can see how my conversation could have endangered you. I apologise."

"You apologise." Mariya's tone was bitter. "How nice. That'll help a lot."

"It's all I can do," Alim told her. "So where do we go from here?"

"Excuse me?"

"You're holding a gun on someone in a busy market," Alim pointed out, carefully resting his fork in his food container and trying to edge his right hand towards his concealed pistol without telegraphing the motion to her. "You might be tucked away back there, but someone's going to notice you at any moment." He hesitated for a moment, then added, "Also, my food's getting cold."

"Fuck your food," Mariya snarled. "How about you tell me what you're *actually* doing here?"

Alim smiled a little wryly to himself, despite the gun in his back. "Even if I told you, I doubt you'd believe me."

+Chief.+

He managed to prevent himself from stiffening in surprise as his comm clicked on and Kuai's voice whispered in his ear. Every crew member's personal comm was set to automatically receive incoming calls from every other member while in range of the *Jonah*'s transmitters, effectively giving them their own (fairly) private radio network. It could doubtlessly be handy, but was also potentially disconcerting.

+*Duck when I say 'now.'*+

He'd asked the rest of the crew to be available, but hadn't known that they'd been watching him. Then he realised that Mariya had said something just as Kuai had spoken again, and he felt his pulse rate suddenly soar because the last thing a person with a gun wants is to feel like they're not being listened to. He turned his head, keeping the ear with his commpiece in it facing away from her, and looked over his shoulder at her for the first time. She was frowning at him, her mouth tense and her face stern.

"I'm sorry, what did you say?" he asked, keeping his voice as level as possible. "It's so noisy here." Something caught his eye in the street, and he had to prevent himself from groaning aloud as he saw the Changs making their way towards his position through the press of people. Of all the people he'd trust to get him out of a tight spot, the bickering siblings were pretty much at the bottom of the list.

Mariya's eyes narrowed into a glare that could have cut granite. "You've heard everything else I've said, Alim."

"I—"

+*Now.*+

He hadn't truly known, up until that moment, exactly how far he trusted his new crewmates. In that split second when he heard Kuai's voice in his ear again, his body decided for him, as he threw himself downwards and tucked his head in. Apparently he at least trusted that they would take potentially precipitous action without his involvement or consent, and that he should shield himself as best he could from the consequences.

There was a muffled squawk from behind him, but no hammer of a gunshot. He looked back and saw the massive shape of Wahawaha behind Mariya, hood up and rebreather mask over his face to hide his distinctive tattoos, his fingers wrapped around her gun and pointing it skywards while his other huge hand covered her mouth and nose. The big Māori was already stepping farther back into the narrow, shadowy spaces between the backs of the stalls, dragging Mariya with him. Alim got back to his feet to follow them in, then looked around for a second as loud shouting in Mandarin arose on the other side of the avenue where he had been standing. Kuai and Jia were engaged in a furious and, if he was any judge, entirely fake row. Any passersby capable of paying attention to anything other than fighting their way through the crowds were focusing on the noisy Chang siblings instead of the casual and near-silent abduction of an armed woman taking place opposite.

Alim sighed. The ease with which his new colleagues could pull off something like this said a lot for their character, and not in a good way. Then again, what he was about to do was hardly to be applauded.

Come now, Alim. Even if she's not exactly crooked herself, she's still taking pay to protect this city but is letting the Triax run it as they please. She's no paragon of virtue either.

He grimaced, remembering Governor Drugov reached for the controls on his desk. That would have opened the vents in Uragan City, flooding the subterranean metropolis with the planet's toxic atmosphere and killing the population rather than let the rebellion get control of its mining facilities.

Also, the government she's meant to be serving isn't much better than the Triax anyway.

He'd shot Drugov in the head to prevent that atrocity from taking place. Up until that point, he'd considered the man to be his friend.

"Mariya," he said softly, stepping up to his panicked former sister-in-arms, "he can break your neck with his bare hands. I would suggest letting him have the gun."

She stared back at him, her eyes wild and furious, but didn't let go. He sighed again and pulled out his own weapon, then set it against the side of her ribcage. If he pulled the trigger, it would go right through her body crosswise, without any risk of hitting Wahawaha.

Of course, he had no intention of pulling that trigger. He'd meant every word when he'd told Drift that he wouldn't kill except in defence of a crew member's life. But Mariya didn't need to know that.

"Mariya? Do not make me ask again."

She struggled for a moment—Wahawaha's grip was hard to escape even when she'd let go of what he wanted, it seemed—and then let her hand fall, empty. Wahawaha pocketed the weapon while still keeping one huge hand wrapped around Mariya's mouth and jaw. Alim had to concede that the big Māori took on a new and frightening aspect as this silent, hooded, and masked giant instead of the affable character Alim had started to get to know over the past few weeks.

"Thank you." He lowered his gun. "Now, Mariya; in a moment I'll ask my friend to uncover your mouth. Please don't try to draw attention to us. Just answer my questions and we can all go home afterwards." He looked up at Wahawaha and switched to English. "*Let her speak, please.*"

The big man didn't reply, but his hand slipped downwards, leaving Mariya's mouth free and settling almost gently around the base of her throat. Mariya's lips were pressed tight and her eyes were wide. Alim could see her breathing fast.

"What is this, Alim?" she asked in Mandarin, her voice barely more than a whisper. "What the hell are you doing?"

Alim shrugged. "What I need to. I'm no friend to the Triax or your corrupt colleagues, I can assure you of that. You said the Triax here are the Dragon Sons?"

Mariya's lip twisted. "They came in force about ten years ago, it seems. Drove out the other clans and took over their interests. The Long Street

Men and the Small Room Circle are still in other cities, but Zhuchengshi belongs to the Dragon Sons now."

Alim nodded slowly. "And the corruption extends all the way up the force?"

"It feels like it," Mariya replied bitterly. She glanced from side to side. "Listen, Alim, it's not safe for us—"

"The last time I took advice from you on where to talk, you stuck a gun in my back," Alim cut her off bluntly. "If you don't want to be here, speak quickly and stop stalling."

Wahawaha ever so slightly flexed the fingers he still held around Mariya's throat. She swallowed noticeably, her eyes widening again for a moment.

"Most of my colleagues are on the take; it's part of the culture. Our wages aren't high, so most people take a cut from the Triax and look the other way when they're supposed to."

"How do the bribes get paid?" Alim asked carefully. Mariya hesitated for a moment, but clearly whatever reservations she had about informing on the city's mobsters were outweighed by her current predicament. And perhaps, Alim thought, her own morals.

"Regular cops send their uniforms to Triax-owned laundrettes to get cleaned. Arena Street, Northside Laundry, any branch of Wu Hao Cleaning . . . The clothes go back to the owners with money in the pockets, sometimes a slip of plaspaper with additional instructions." She snorted. "They call it 'second payday.'"

Alim nodded again. "And the senior officers? The detectives?"

Mariya grimaced. "I don't know. Maybe some do it the same way. Others might have something else set up. The Dragon Sons have their fingers in half the businesses in this city; backhanders could come from anywhere."

Alim frowned. "How can they just operate with this sort of impunity? Is the planetary governor in their pocket too?"

Mariya shrugged helplessly. "Perhaps? Personally I suspect that just enough progress is made to keep the higher-ups content, although it's all a sham. Every now and then we shut part of the operation down, or make a high-profile arrest, but it never seems to do much. It's probably a sacrifice the Triax make, letting us take something they're about to stop using, or can easily replace. Any significant arrest is probably either taking one for the team or has been set up as a fall guy. The second sort usually die in custody, too, to make sure they don't talk: The PR department plays it up as proof that we got someone big enough that the Triax had to take 'desperate measures' to shut them down, but really it's just them dumping someone out of favour with us, and then their puppets in the force arrange an accident to get rid of them."

Alim fought down the anger rising in his stomach. This wasn't his world, not his government anymore, and certainly not his fight; but he still struggled to listen to Mariya's description of endemic corruption in an organisation that should be protecting the population it served. Forget ransoming Rourke: He was now quite happy to do what he could to harm the Triax's operations here simply out of spite.

However, it was quickly becoming clear that he and his new crewmates were going to have to tread very, very carefully.

LINES OF ATTACK

"'I live through risk. Without risk there is no art. You should always be on the edge of a cliff about to fall down and break your neck.'"

Jenna looked up from her seat in the *Jonah*'s cockpit. "Sounds dangerous."

Drift sighed. "What we're trying to do isn't exactly safe. Besides, I was quoting. What do they teach you in school these days?"

"In my case?" Jenna tapped the screen of her terminal and slid whatever was on it across to his display. "A detailed understanding of digital security protocols that I have absolutely not and under no circumstance used for crime or personal gain."

"Glad to hear it," Drift said, studying the list of faces and names in front of him. "What am I looking at?"

"The proceeds of my trawling through the slicer back channels on the Spine," she told him, tucking a strand of red-blonde hair back behind one ear. "This is a rich world, which means well-educated and well-resourced kids, and that means a whole lot of people with firebrand ideals and a lack of respect for authority, be it state or Triax. It turns out there's quite a bit of information being bandied around on the quiet about who the biggest and crookedest fish are in this particular pond."

Drift scratched the skin around his mechanical right eye and scanned down the list. "Let me guess: There's a whole lot of people saying whatever the Mandarin is for 'someone should do something'?"

He expected a laugh, or possibly a snort. He certainly expected *something*. When a second or so had passed and there was no sign that Jenna had heard his comment, he glanced over at her. The young slicer was staring fixedly at her terminal, her lips slightly tight.

He frowned. "Jenna? You okay?"

"I . . . yeah. Sorry." She sighed. "You're not wrong about that. It's just that was a phrase my dad used to use. The 'someone' was never *him*, of course." Her mouth twisted. "That would have meant actually taking responsibility for something outside of his office."

Drift nodded, without quite knowing why. Jenna had never really mentioned her family and he wasn't sure why she had now—nor did he particularly care, in all honesty. Perhaps she was getting a little homesick. He made a noncommittal grunt and went back to studying the list.

"He used to say it about you."

Drift paused, uncertain if he'd heard correctly, but the query died on his lips when he looked up at Jenna. She was staring at him. Not aggressively; more like someone who hadn't been sure if they were going to say something until they'd said it, and now weren't sure if they should have done.

He licked his lips, now feeling somewhat unsure for an entirely different reason. "What?"

"We'd hear on the news about pirate attacks on shipping," Jenna said quietly, watching him. "Freighters boarded, cargos seized, crew left for dead. Gabriel Drake and the *Thirty-Six Degrees* were mentioned a lot. My father used to say that something should be done about him. About you."

Drift grimaced, trying to contain the sudden hollow feeling in his chest at the mention of the name he'd used before he'd faked his own death. "A lot of things were blamed on me that I never did; I'd just like to point that out."

"My dad never did anything, though," Jenna continued. "He never . . . I don't know, he never went off to join the star force so he could help guard ships, or anything. I don't know if it was even because he was scared to. I think it's just that he wouldn't have got paid enough. It's like, because he could do whatever he does in finance, that automatically meant he didn't *need* to care about anything else."

"Well, look at the upside," Drift said, trying a smile and to gently move the conversation on from the parts of his past he didn't want to talk about. "You got the education you did because he had that job."

"And at that posh, expensive university a friend on my course was abducted by the damned Circuit Cult," Jenna said bitterly. "And when I tried to *not* be my dad, when I tried to do the right thing and do something about it, it ruined everything, and I had to get away, fast." She sat back with a frustrated hiss and closed her eyes for a second, then sat upright again and looked at him, hard and direct.

"What are you going to do if we don't get enough money?"

"We will," Drift said, trying to project confidence.

"But what if we *don't?*" Jenna insisted, leaning forwards. "What if, this time, we don't come up with a way out? What if we can't go back to Orlov and hand him what he wants? Do we do the right thing and go back for Rourke anyway? Do we try to get her out, or do we leave her there and hope for the best?"

Drift sighed and pinched the bridge of his nose. "Honestly? Hell if I know." He held up one hand to forestall any words Jenna might have. "I don't want to leave her there, of course I don't, but as a wise man once said: You've got to be realistic about these things. It's going to be hard enough to convince Kuai to go back even if we *have* the money. Alim was Uragan's Security Chief who never took a bribe from Orlov, so he won't be popular if they realise who he is this time. Besides, if the government there find out he's alive and not on Uragan, they're going to be asking him some very serious questions about how he got away, how he let the revolution happen, and oh yeah, what happened to Governor Drugov? I can't ask him to walk into that for someone he barely knows."

"Yeah, but—"

"Yeah but nothing." He spread his hands. "If Kuai ever absolutely and truly digs his heels in, I don't know if Jia would stay on the crew without him. I know they fight all the time, but that's sort of who they are; I don't think Jia would know what to do with herself if she didn't have Kuai to annoy. Trying to get Tamara away from Orlov with just you, me, and A doesn't sound like a winning proposition to me. None of us can even speak Russian properly!"

Jenna's expression was challenging. "So what are you saying?"

"I'm saying we'd better raise the damn cash," Drift said curtly. He tapped the screen. "This woman, Han Xiuying, is apparently Zhuchengshi's Chief of Security. Based on what Alim's informant said and what your contacts have turned up, she's in the Triax's pocket. The question is, is that through greed or blackmail?"

"Does it make a difference?" Jenna asked, getting up from her seat and coming over to stand behind his chair.

"Potentially a huge one," Drift said, chewing the inside of his cheek as he thought. "She's no street-level flatfoot; if she's being bought, her price will be high. Maybe *very* high. It would be worth a lot to the Triax to have her definitely looking the other way." He looked over his shoulder at Jenna. "That would involve a lot of probably untraceable currency changing hands."

She nodded slowly. "Which is exactly the sort of thing we need. Okay, so how do we find that out?"

Drift traced down the display, highlighting names with a sweep of his finger. "These people, who are supposed to be Triax: Piotr Zhang is apparently a hotelier, Gao Dongfeng runs a . . . a private waste disposal and cleaning service?" He laughed. "Gee, can't imagine how *that* might be useful to organised crime. But anyway, all of these are the sort of 'concerned citizens' who might have meetings with the city's security chief to discuss issues of policing and their businesses, in a completely aboveboard and explainable way."

"And at those meetings they might talk about bribes, and when and how they'll be paid," Jenna said, understanding dawning. "So how do we get to listen in?"

Drift grimaced. "Still working on that part. First of all, we need to find out if it's actually happening. Is there any way you can get an itinerary for this woman?"

"You want me to slice into the computer systems of the organisation *in charge of security* here, to find out what meetings the top brass is having?" Jenna asked.

Drift thought for a moment. "Essentially, yes."

Jenna shrugged. "Sure, why not?" She went back to her terminal and activated her wrist-mounted console, something Drift knew she'd built from scratch and that included a particularly powerful processor, which happened to be illegal in most jurisdictions. "There's bound to be someone on the force with a stupidly unimaginative password, and once I'm inside . . ." She trailed off as Drift got up from his seat and headed towards the cockpit door. "Where are you off to?"

"I'm off to talk your boyfriend into doing something stupid," Drift smiled at her.

She snorted. "Doesn't this already count?"

"Fine, then. Stupid*er*." He ducked out of the cockpit before she could reply and headed towards the galley in the hope that he'd find Apirana there. Sure enough, the big Māori was cooking eggs in a pan and whistling quietly to himself. He looked around as Drift came in.

"Hey, Cap." He gestured at the light-yellow concoction. "You hungry?"

"No, you go ahead." He watched Apirana give his eggs a few more swirls around the pan before tipping them out onto a plate. "I, uh, have come to ask if you'd be interested in doing something stupid."

Apirana snorted. "Don't what we're doing already count?"

Drift stared at him for a second. "Wow."

The big man looked up, brow furrowed in confusion. "Huh?"

"No, it's just . . ." Drift scratched the skin by his eye. "You and Jenna really are a good match."

"So people keep saying," Apirana muttered, shovelling a forkful of eggs into his mouth. "Don't see it myself, bro, but I surely ain't complaining. But you were talking 'bout something else."

"Yeah. How's your ankle?"

Apirana looked down at his left leg. "Honestly? Don't really think about it much now. Still get the odd twinge, but I ain't as young as I used to be anyway. Seems to have healed fast. Wouldn't wanna run any races though."

Drift nodded. "How about punching people in the head?"

"Long as they don't move about too much first." Apirana looked back up at him, his eyes narrowing. "Oh, you got your planning face on. That wasn't a hypothetical question, was it?"

Drift pulled out his pad. "We're going to need some capital to get anything moving here, and we don't have much. So I'm looking at risking about half of it on what we *do* have on a long-odds bet that's actually stacked in our favour."

The big man set his fork down, then slowly and deliberately put his head in his hands and took a deep breath. "Go on."

Drift reached out and tapped him on the hand. "Eyes front, soldier." Apirana peeked through his fingers, and Drift held up his pad so the other man could see it. "See this? There's a fight event going down in three days, or what passes for days here. There's a few superheavy-weights on the bill, too. Now, if one of them should happen to fall ill at an inconvenient time . . ."

Apirana lowered his hands and fixed Drift with a steady stare. "Because that can just happen."

Drift shrugged. "I can walk into a drugstore on any street in this city and buy a powerful laxative. The event's in a couple of days, which means most of the fighters are probably already here, training and using gyms in this city. It's not a big-name event, so odds are they're not able to buy out a gym for private use. So it wouldn't be impossible to change up a water bottle or something. After that, well, if I was shitting my guts out a few hours before I'm due to get into a ring to fight, I'd be backing out."

Apirana frowned. "Okay. Let's say we manage that and we nobble one of the superheavies. How do we then get *me* onto a fight card in his place?"

Drift smiled. "You looked at yourself in the mirror recently, big guy? You're over two metres tall, with tattoos all over your face and upper body, and you're built like a concrete block. All a promoter's going to want at that late stage is someone the crowd won't shit over *before* the fight. You look the part, and I can talk the talk. That's all we'll need."

"Damn it, I hate it when you make everything sound so easy," Apirana rumbled. "You know we ain't gonna be able to coax a big purse out of them, right?"

"Of course not," Drift agreed. "You'll be a last-minute, no-name replacement. No, we're going to make money on the fact that you'll be a big underdog. And I'll be wagering on you winning."

CLEANING UP THE ACT

Stupid fucking Kuai.

Jia Chang was not in the best of moods. That was partly because the overalls she was wearing were a bit too tight: Seriously, couldn't the Captain have at least got the right size? It was partly because this planet's stupid day/night cycle was messing with her head, which was why she preferred being on the *Jonah* or the *Keiko*, where circadian rhythms were what she set them as. However, it was mainly because Kuai had passed some smart comment about how this would be the first time she'd actually cleaned anything. Like she hadn't had to tidy up after his mess when they'd been kids! Just because their parents had thought they were raising some sort of mechanical genius, and that meant it was *perfectly fine* for him to leave his little kits and screws and boring-ass manuals all over their little flat. No, when his mess actually started getting in the way, guess who got called on? Just their daughter, the one already acing flight simulators when she was eight, who certainly didn't have anything better to do than clear up after her self-absorbed, idiotic lump of an older brother . . .

She was still taking the injustice of it all out on her chewing gum when she walked up the steps and through the front doors of the main Zhuchengshi security station, her cleaning tools under one arm, and headed for the reception desk. The officer who at there was somehow managing to look both bored and hassled at the same time as he explained to the white-haired man in front of him that, no, Sergeant Wu wasn't on duty today, and no, he couldn't be contacted on his day off, and no, there was no one else who had those details of the robbery case he was asking about....

Jia sidled in the moment the old codger stormed off.

"Hey."

Zhuchengshi's residents mainly seemed to have speaking patterns reminiscent of the Beijing area back on Old Earth, but the city was diverse enough that she wasn't worried she'd sound too out of place. The officer glanced up at her with the glassy smile of a public-facing representative, which turned into an uncertain frown when he saw her overalls. "Yes?"

Jia smiled back at him. "So, I'm, uh, cleaning here, and it's my first day. Am I even in the right place?"

"Cleaners usually go in the side entrance," he said, jerking a thumb over his shoulder in what had to be one of the least-accurate pieces of direction Jia had ever received.

"Yeah, but like I said, it's my first day," she reminded him. "I've got my rota and my stuff, but not the access code." She glanced around, then leaned forward conspiratorially. "Also, between you and me, I'm a little late because my brother's a moron, and I had to help him find *his* uniform for *his* stupid job down at the spacedocks. If Mr. Tse catches me coming in late, I don't fancy my chances for still being here tomorrow, but if I come in this way, he won't know exactly when I came in unless he bothers to come and check the sign-in logs, and—"

"Tse?" The officer rolled his eyes. "Yeah, you don't want to get on the wrong side of him. I don't know why he still has the contract, the shit he gives people like you."

"Because he's dirt cheap and your bosses are tight," Jia snorted. She gestured at herself, taking in the ill-fitting overalls and the cleaning paraphernalia. "Think I want to be working on the breadline for him? I wanted to be a pilot! But a job's a job, right?"

"Right." He looked over her shoulder as the main doors swung open again, and she followed his glance to see an agitated-looking woman hurrying across the foyer with one child over her shoulder and another, older one scurrying along behind her. "You're meant to go in the side door, though. . . ."

The woman reached the desk, and presumably, assuming that a cleaner wouldn't actually be talking to the desk sergeant, immediately launched into a breathless diatribe about someone rear-ending her aircar but not stopping. Jia glanced down at the older kid who was looking up at her with the shameless curiosity of a child who hadn't yet been told enough times that it was rude to stare.

She glared back at him. *What you looking at, you little shit?* Then she remembered that she still had a job to do and looked up at the desk sergeant again, who was already trying to calm the new arrival down and get the pertinent details from her. Jia pulled out her pad and brought up the dummy rota Jenna had created for her using the floor plans she'd gleaned from nefarious scouring of the Spine, then waved it at the officer with an imploring look on her face. He glanced over at her, hesitated in a moment of indecision, then waved a hand irritably at the terminal at the end of the counter.

"Okay, okay, just sign in for the fire records."

"Thanks!" Jia said cheerily, not having to feign her relief as she tapped at the screen. She'd already decided to use the name Bao Jing Yan simply because the stuck-up bitch would have rather died than take a cleaning job, and Jia had never forgiven her for that stunt with the fish noodles in the playground at high school. That done, she waited for the desk sergeant to buzz the door release and slipped through into the station beyond.

Jia had to hand it to Jenna: The slicer might have been a prissy rich kid, but she was certainly good at her job, and the floor plan was right on the money. Of course, Jia could have walked through the side door as nice as you please with one of blondie's slicing devices taking care of the access code, but that might have landed her in the same place as genuine cleaners who would know she wasn't one of the crew. Coming in the front door might seem harder, but the crew of the *Keiko* had long since learned that most people were almost blind to you so long as you had the right uniform, or at least a close approximation of it.

The other advantage she'd had was that Muradov had been watching the station and seen the van of White Chrysanthemum Cleaners pulling in with their logo proudly displayed. Once Jenna had that particular detail, it had been easy for her to find out who the supervisor was, and if you had a uniform *and* the right name to drop, then the world was practically your vat-grown oyster.

Jia checked her pad and veered left. She didn't want to go near the holding cells, or anywhere that might involve other security checks. Of course, she had no doubt that the cells got cleaned, but that wasn't what she was here for. She called an elevator, trying not to fidget too much inside her uncomfortable overalls.

"Hey!"

She looked around to see three officers bearing down on her, two men and a woman. The one closest to her, one of the men, was short and stocky with a dark goatee, a mug of what was presumably coffee in his hand, and a broad grin on his face. The other man was taller, although still broad, and was eyeing his colleague with what seemed to Jia to be a mixture of misgiving and disapproval. The woman looked more Russian in ancestry, and had an odd shape to the left leg of her pants that suggested some form of augmentation.

Jia remained in place as the doors *ping*ed open beside her. *Oh, here we* *fucking go.* She'd known she wasn't in any trouble as soon as she'd seen their body language, but . . .

"Hey," the smiler repeated, looking her up and down ostentatiously, "you grease yourself to get into that this morning?"

Don't tell him to go fuck himself; don't tell him to go fuck himself. . . .

"Officer," she said instead, tucking her gum into her cheek and smiling sweetly as she stepped into the elevator, "I'd like to report a crime."

"Oh?"

"Yeah, someone's stolen all the handsome right off your face!"

The doors swept closed, cutting her off from him, but she just had time to see delighted grins spreading across the faces of the other two officers as their colleague got served. She tapped the display and the elevator began to rise towards the third floor.

"Yeah, and go fuck yourself!" she yelled happily in a general downwards direction, making an obscene gesture, then eyed what looked like a camera lens in the corner. "Not you, if there's anyone watching. Him."

She supposed cleaners probably weren't meant to swear at security officers, even from the other side of a door. Well, she didn't need to pretend to be a *good* cleaner; she just needed to not be kicked out of the building before she did what she'd come here to do. To be on the safe side, she decided to behave from that moment as if all the officers in the building were Tamara Rourke with her murderface on. No lip, no cheek, just yes-ma'am-no-ma'am-leave-me-the-fuck-alone-ma'am.

Her short elevator ride terminated a few seconds later, and the doors opened onto an empty hallway identical in layout and décor to the one she'd just left. She stepped out and looked both ways, trying to orientate herself, then checked her pad and headed right. Of course, she had Rourke in her head now, and couldn't help but wonder how the old girl was holding together.

Kuai had always maintained—quietly—that Rourke wasn't actually as tough as she pretended to be. Jia had argued against him, and not just because he was her brother. It wasn't purely a logical thing, she admitted. For her, having Tamara Rourke with you had always felt like being backed up by the biggest, baddest kid on the block. It wasn't that Jia particularly liked Rourke—well, not *that* much—but she'd never wanted that reassuring notion to be proved untrue. It was always comforting to think that no matter what problem faced them, they could call on Rourke to kick its ass.

Unless, of course, you need to sneak into a security headquarters like a motherfucking Chinese ninja. Then you need me.

Although she did kind of wish she could have brought her pilot hat.

She reached a room marked 311 and paused, checking her pad again. This was it, the room in which Jenna thought the security chief was shortly due to have her monthly meeting with a group of "concerned citizens" who were more than likely high-ranking Triax officers. Jia pulled out her antibac polisher and nudged the door open with her hip, then stepped through.

The room was a simple enough affair, nothing more than four freestanding tables that could be arranged as desired, surrounded by eight formfitting, soft chairs that would mould themselves to the shape of the occupants' posteriors and spines. The large window looking out over the headquarters' central quadrangle had a control that allowed it to be tinted into obscurity if required, and there was a refreshments machine in the corner that offered what seemed to Jia to be a ridiculously large range of drinks.

She pulled on her gloves and started working, humming under her breath as she swept the polisher back and forth over the tabletops, adding a thin veneer of antibacterial varnish as she did so. Then she got the extendable vacuum out and set to work on the carpet, crawling under the tables to reach the middle of the floor properly.

While under there, she hastily unfastened her overalls slightly and pulled three tiny electronic devices out from where they'd been nestling next to her skin. They were no larger than her thumbnail, and had been spliced together by Jenna out of commpieces bought from a local electronics store. Jia spat her gum into her hand, moulded it quickly between thumb and forefinger, then used it to attach their makeshift bugs to the underside of the tables. She took care not to cover either the tiny microphones or the slight bulge that housed the transmitters, but even so a casual glance might not have seen anything but a piece of discarded gum.

Not that anyone was likely to be casually glancing up at the underside of a table in a meeting room anyway. Which was sort of the idea. Still, every little helped.

She crawled out again, refastening her overalls so she wasn't inadvertently exposing herself. Well, that was the hard part done. Now all she had to do was maintain her cover for long enough that it wasn't completely obvious to anyone watching her on surveillance that she'd come in specifically to do something in this particular room.

Secret agent cleaner. As if I wasn't awesome enough already.

Three rooms later, and she'd fallen into an almost trancelike state of entering, polishing, and vacuuming while her brain wandered off into wondering how she could persuade the Captain to spring for a new pilot's chair. However, when she meandered out into the corridor to head for the next one she found herself face-to-face with an older woman, also in overalls and also carrying cleaning equipment. Jia's immediate impression was that the woman looked like a koi carp. She even had some straggly whiskers a little bit like barbels on either side of her wide, lippy mouth.

Jia tried a friendly, noncommittal smile. "Hey."

The other woman frowned. "Who're you?"

"Bao Jing Yan," Jia replied without missing a beat. "I'm new. Started today."

Fishface's frown deepened. "You didn't come in with us."

"Yeah, my brother made me late so I came in the front door, and—"

"You'd better come with me to see Mr. Tse," Fishface told her sternly, turning away.

"Hey, I've, like, got a rota," Jia protested to her back, "I don't have time to play follow-the-leader with you."

Fishface looked around and shot Jia a glare, her generous mouth curving downwards in undisguised displeasure. "You come with me *right now*, and maybe Mr. Tse won't fire you on the spot."

"Shit, fine," Jia groaned, setting off after the other woman. "Hey, you treat all the new girls like this, or just the pretty ones?"

If silences could kill, Jia would have been leaving in a casket. As it was, Fishface was putting extra effort into pulling the doors open as they reached them. Jia was well aware of her multitude of talents, and she knew that one of them was making people angry.

Okay, most people didn't think it was a talent as such, but that was because they had limited thinking.

What Jia truly didn't want to happen was to get to Mr. Tse, who would instantly denounce her as an imposter. That would probably get her locked up, and Jia's one night in jail all those years ago before Drift and Rourke had bailed her out and recruited her to be their pilot had been quite enough for her. And her idiot brother had said that joyriding that shuttle would be a stupid idea! It had impressed a starship captain who'd seen it and had got her a steady job, so that showed what he knew. Anyway, she didn't trust her ability to talk her way out of trouble with Mr. Tse, so it was time to fall back on what she knew.

Starting a fight.

As soon as there were a couple of cops visible in the corridor with them, she stepped up alongside Fishface as the older woman pulled another door open. There was enough force on it to hit Jia square in the face, and she fell to the floor clutching her head.

"Arrgh! Watch it, you fucking cow!"

She could see Fishface's expression through her fingers: anger mixed with consternation. The other woman knew that Jia was milking this for an audience, and furious embarrassment made her lean down and grab Jia's overalls.

"Get up, you little bitch!" Fishface hissed, trying to haul Jia upright. She hadn't counted on the fasteners on the front of Jia's overalls giving way to her tug, ripping it open practically to the waist and revealing the underwear that was all Jia had worn beneath due to the damn thing being so tight.

Well, now.

"You perverted old hag!" Jia raged, springing back to her feet and slapping the other woman's hand away. She put a little extra spittle into her words as she leaned in. "Get your filthy fucking hands off me or I'll—"

Fishface wasn't dumb and knew she'd been played, but despite this— or perhaps because of it—she apparently couldn't restrain her rage enough to prevent herself from lashing out with a slap to Jia's jaw. Well, it was actually half-slap and half-punch, but either way it was enough for Jia to sprawl convincingly sideways again just before the two officers thundered in and grabbed Fishface, hauling her away from her poor, abused victim.

"You know what?" Jia screamed, scrambling up and setting off at a furious walk that was just shy of a run. "You can shove this job! I'm going back to the agency!"

"We need you to give a statement!" one of the officers shouted after her.

"Fuck it!" Jia yelled, not looking back. "You saw what happened! I'm having nothing more to do with her!"

It turned out that even security officers would get out of the way of a cleaner with a face like a thundercloud storming down the middle of a corridor. Jia wasn't sure if this was at least partially because her face felt like it was already bruising, but she didn't care: Most people's reaction to a furious-looking stranger was to quietly step aside and let them happen to someone else, and that seemed to hold true even here.

"You didn't take long," the desk sergeant commented as he buzzed her out.

"Never should've come here," Jia snapped, hastily scrolling through the fire records and signing Bao Jing Yan out. "One of the other girls just went for me! I ain't working here." She marched out of the front doors into the sweltering desert heat, leaving a startled-looked officer and a slightly bewildered foyer of civilians behind her.

Fucking flawless.

She put her commpiece in and called the Captain, swearing at an aircar buzzing along at street level as it nearly clipped her when she dodged across the road.

+*Yes?*+

"*Done,*" she told him in English, just in case anyone was close enough to overhear.

+*Any problems?*+

"*One girl thought I didn't belong,*" Jia admitted. "*Had to start a fight to get out.*"

+*Oh, very subtle. Well done.*+

She sighed. "If you wanted subtle, why the *fuck* did you send me?"

IDLE HANDS

Tamara Rourke had been sitting in a hotel room doing virtually nothing for three weeks, and she was getting thoroughly sick of it.

She'd stretched properly as soon as she'd been left alone, to get the last kinks out of her muscles, although she'd had to strip down in front of Sacha, Andrei, and the bald man (whom she'd later learned was called Leon) before they'd given her any privacy. Once they were satisfied that she wasn't concealing any weapons or other equipment separately to her bodysuit, they'd taken it away and provided her with loose shirts and pants, all of which were too big for her.

She'd tied things up as best she could, but although she could roll up sleeves and legs, there was nothing to be done about the waists. They wouldn't give her a belt, which was sensible of them, and hadn't provided her with any underwear, which didn't really bother her. They also wouldn't give her shoes, which was no problem considering the room's carpet but which would undoubtedly cause her difficulties outside. That, of course, was almost certainly the idea: The trio weren't exactly geniuses, but they weren't stupid either.

They took turns sitting outside to guard her door. The room was only one storey above ground level, which wasn't what she'd expected, but the windows were secured with bars and could only be opened a few inches to allow ventilation. This was presumably for security against burglars, but it functioned just as well for keeping her inside. Resourceful though she might be, she couldn't conjure a laser torch out of nowhere, so if she wanted to leave the room without her guards' permission, she'd have to go through at least one of them to do it.

She picked Sacha, for three reasons. Firstly, he'd held a gun to her head. Secondly, he seemed the most overconfident. And thirdly, he wore a belt.

The hotel was clearly owned by Sergei Orlov, as the staff she'd seen had shown no visible curiosity as to why there was a North American woman under constant guard in one of the rooms: Presumably he held people here when he needed to. When they brought her food, under the watchful supervision of one of Orlov's thugs, they set it down on one side of the room without looking at or talking to her. However, each guard always sent the hotel staff in first, choosing to hover menacingly behind with one hand on the pistol holstered at their side.

It was nighttime, and the advertising holos visible from her window were blinking with the red-and-yellow of Star Cola and other less ubiquitous brands. She'd been listening at her room door and had heard the sullen exchange between Leon and Sacha as they changed over. Leon was tired, and had been in no mood to listen to Sacha's complaining about how his uncle had been trying to get his "well-connected" nephew to intercede in a squabble with local government over some form of license. In fact, he'd left abruptly before Sacha had finished his story, and Rourke had heard some muttered grumbling at the bald man's expense from the other side of the door.

Two hours later, right on schedule, the food arrived. They never bothered to knock, presumably to prevent her from setting an ambush, but they'd underestimated her preparation. You didn't need warning if your target moved to a predictable timetable.

The lock buzzed, and the room's door swung open to admit a dark-haired young woman in a hotel uniform carrying a tray of food. Rourke, who was waiting in the bathroom suite just past the room entrance, grabbed the girl by the shoulder and hauled her bodily into the bathroom before she'd even registered Rourke's presence. There was a clatter of plates as the tray spilled to the floor, and Rourke caught a glimpse of Sacha's handsome, startled face as she slammed the bathroom door shut and locked it.

She turned to the terrified maid and seized her arm, twisting it up to force the other woman down to her knees. It wasn't, in truth, a terribly painful hold, but it coupled with the girl's sudden vulnerability to produce the desired effect. The young woman screamed in genuine terror.

Sacha had been in the warehouse when Rourke had taken out two of Orlov's other thugs and had pulled a gun on the crime lord. He'd seen Orlov deal with their failure, and Rourke was banking on the fact that Sacha didn't want to become the next object lesson. Allowing his prisoner to abduct another of Orlov's employees and torture her on the other side of a locked door wouldn't reflect well on him, so he did what anyone who valued their skin would in such a scenario: He tried to get inside the small, confined space where his greater size and strength would allow him to easily subdue this nuisance.

He tried the handle first but since the door was locked, his next effort consisted of throwing all his weight at it, shoulder first, with the handle still held down. The door was solid, and it withstood his attempt. Rourke reckoned he'd give it three tries before he resorted to something more unpredictable, like trying to shoot the lock off or calling for help from someone who had a key. She waited for him to hit it a second time, then as he would be withdrawing for a third go and his weight would actually be pulling the door shut, reached out and unlocked it.

The door swung inwards easily as Sacha barged at it again, catching him off-balance. Rourke had convinced Andrei on her first day that, since she hailed from the United States of North America, she really, really needed the ability to make coffee. The fact that he'd agreed suggested that he'd never had a mug of boiling liquid with several spoons of melted sugar in it flung at him.

Sacha got the entire pot that Rourke had placed carefully on the washbasin two minutes ago, square in his face.

The scalding, syrupy mess stuck to his skin, burning on contact. Now it was Sacha's turn to scream, the full-throated howl of a man introduced to pain the likes of which he'd never felt before, but he was still in motion. Rourke dropped the coffee pot and caught his gun arm, angled it across her body so the weapon was pointing fairly harmlessly at the wall, and kicked out his near leg. Sacha's own momentum sent him face-first into the washbasin, and he collapsed to the floor making little more than a stunned whimpering.

Not good enough: Rourke twisted the gun out of his unresisting fingers—*Kobel .45, twenty-round clip, lightweight and reliable*—and struck him directly behind the ear with the butt. That knocked him out, and she used one hand to roll him over onto his back while pointing the gun at the maid with the other. The girl had gone beyond screaming and was now kneeling and watching with the wide, terrified eyes of someone who wouldn't be sleeping well for quite a while.

"*Give me your shoes,*" Rourke snapped in Russian, the fingers of her right hand unfastening Sacha's belt. The girl didn't immediately react, and Rourke deactivated the safety for a moment simply to get the distinctive buzz of arming it again. "*Your shoes. Take them off and give them to me, or I will kill you and take them myself.*"

Thankfully, this threat jolted the maid into action. She pulled off her uniform-matching flats and tossed them over before curling up in a ball, now starting to weep in apparent terror. Rourke judged it very unlikely that she was faking, and put the safety back on Sacha's gun before pulling the shoes on. The thug's belt slipped free from around him just as he started to come to, but she had time to grab his comm from his ear and snatch his pad from his pocket before he was even conscious enough to realise that his face was still burning, let alone that his prisoner was getting away.

She slipped out of her room and pulled the door shut behind her, then set off down the hall while threading Sacha's belt through the waist loops on her borrowed pants, the gun riding in a pocket and the stolen shoes a bit too big on her feet. With any luck the maid would be too terrified to come out of the bathroom without prompting, and Sacha would be preoccupied with trying to save his features. She would have really liked to tie them both up, but although she could have theoretically torn strips off her bedsheets for the purpose, she'd decided against it. It would have taken too long, for one thing, and the longer she'd spent in close proximity to Sacha, the more chance he'd have had to properly get hold of her. Besides which, throwing a potentially disfiguring liquid into someone's face and then tying them up so they could do nothing about it swung rather closer to torture than she felt comfortable with.

The stairwell down to the ground floor was deserted, but she still rode the bannisters down to make her time there as brief as possible. Instead of turning right towards the low conversations she could hear from the main reception, she slipped left into the dining room. It was deserted—she'd worked out that she got fed after the rest of the hotel had dined—with the chairs upside down on the tables. Over on the far side she could see the glow of an emergency exit sign from behind a thin gauze curtain.

She paused for a moment. Her immediate instinct was to get out as quickly and quietly as possible, and slip away into the New Samaran night. However, she suspected that the hotel would have cameras, and while her movements around inside might not have attracted anyone's attention yet, she was pretty sure that leaving through an emergency exit would.

Very well then. GIA training had drummed into her that if you couldn't sneak away unnoticed, you should create a very good reason to leave obviously, so she pulled out the gun and used its butt to smash the glass over the fire alarm activation point by her elbow.

Sirens started wailing immediately, loud enough to rouse any sleeping guests and alert everyone in the building. Rourke didn't waste any time: She stowed the gun and ran across the dining room, swept the curtain aside, and threw her weight against the emergency door. The lock had been released by the alarm, and the double doors swung open, bringing her out onto a patio area at street level with tables for guests to sit at in good weather. She paused for a moment in the fresh air, looking back up at the building as though scanning for flames, then vaulted over the rails onto the pavement and fumbled Sacha's commpiece into her ear. She pulled his pad out and hurried away, looking for all the world like someone retreating to a safe distance and calling the emergency response services.

With any luck the hotel would organise a complete evacuation, and in the corresponding confusion it would be some time before her absence would be noted. Even if Sacha had fully recovered, he'd be hard-pressed to find anyone to listen to him for the next few minutes. In the best possible scenario, he'd contact Andrei and Leon, and the three of them would hunt for her themselves, hoping to avoid any retribution from Sergei Orlov. But she held out little hope for that. More likely, the other two would feed him to the wolves and report her absence to Orlov the moment Sacha told them. As soon as Orlov learned of her disappearance, he would undoubtedly send out the kill orders for the rest of her crew.

She had to get to him before that happened.

HIGH SOCIETY

Chief Han Xiuying walked into Room 311 to find the gangsters waiting for her.

Piotr Zhang looked as smart as ever in a dark-red suit with razor creases. The hotelier had the features of a model: a strong, straight nose; a firm jaw flecked with dark stubble; and warm, almost liquid, brown eyes. He possessed a lazy self-assurance that combined with his striking good looks to make him very attractive . . . at least, to those people who didn't know what he was capable of. Xiuying knew him all too well, although she'd have been too wary to let a pretty younger man turn her head anyway.

Gao Dongfeng, in contrast, looked like his lifetime of ugliness had taken root on his face. Xiuying wasn't one to judge by appearances, but this lank-haired, broken-toothed old man looked more like a vicious old miser from a folktale than anything else, or possibly an undertaker from a horror holo. If anything, the latter was more accurate than the former: Gao had been a high-ranking Dragon Sons' enforcer long before the clan had established their base of power in Zhuchengshi, and while he might not do much dirty work himself these days, his ruthlessness was notorious amongst the people who knew about such things. He glowered at her as she walked in, his battered teeth worrying at one of his ragged fingernails.

The final member of the trio was Song Daiyu, seated between her colleagues with her back straight and her long, perfectly manicured fingers steepled in front of her. She had a line of precious stones—genuine diamonds, from what Xiuying had heard—set as subdermal implants in a half-circle around her left eye, and they glinted in the light as she raised her head slightly. The rest of her expression was nearly as hard as the gems: Song ran Zhuchengshi's Triax-owned casinos, and you didn't get or hold such a privileged position in the Dragon Sons without inner steel.

Xiuying met her stare without blinking and took a seat facing all three of them, unable to shake the recurring feeling that this was the toughest job interview ever. They never got any easier, these meetings. She always felt like she was trying to outstare three tigers at once, and if she concentrated too hard on one, then the other two would jump on her. She told hold of the underside of the table to pull her chair closer and suppressed a slight grimace as her fingers brushed against what felt like chewing gum, still slightly soft. *Disgusting. Gao's cleaning company really isn't good enough.*

"So," she said, favouring them with a thin smile and hoping they hadn't interpreted her mild revulsion as fear, "what do we need to discuss today?"

"We've got some ships coming in," Gao said without preamble, spitting a sliver of nail across the table. Not directly at her—her tolerance had limits—but she still felt herself bristling at the man's lack of respect. "You don't get to look inside them."

Xiuying raised her eyebrows. "Are your smugglers losing their touch?"

Gao glowered at her again. "I didn't ask for your smart mouth, you stinking whore."

"Dongfeng!" Zhang snapped, leaning forward and locking eyes with the older man. "Mind your language." He turned his gaze to Xiuying, all smouldering eyes and sincerity. "Our apologies, Chief Han. Please excuse my colleague. You know how he can be."

Yes indeed. Vicious, callous, and sadistic. Xiuying wanted to reach across the table and slug Gao on the jaw, but she had a greater sense of self-preservation than that. She stored the insult away instead, as she did with all such incidents. One day the game might be played differently, under different rules, and on that day she would not be above personal revenge.

Of course, it fell to Song Daiyu to bring things back to business. Gao was the iron fist and Zhang the velvet glove, but Song, it was rumoured, directed both.

"We would not normally request this level of indulgence from you, Chief Han," the younger woman said in a clipped tone. "As you say, we can usually find . . . other avenues . . . to avoid unnecessary complications with our imports. And if we lose a shipment here and there to the authorities, well, that is the price of our business." She laced her fingers together on the desk top, the long nails moving past each other like a battery of tiny blades. "However, on this occasion we cannot risk *any* intrusion. We require you to ensure that on seventhday next week our contractors are uninterrupted when they make port."

Xiuying looked at each of them in turn, trying to gauge them. No gangster was an open book unless they wanted to be, but these three in particular were hard to read. Gao was always sullen, Zhang always lazily flirtatious, and Song could have been one of the statues standing in her own premises' forecourts for all the emotion she displayed in their meetings. That said, Han Xiuying had been swimming in dangerous waters for a while now, and she had grown used to the predators there. She could see faint hints of tension at the corners of Song's eyes, in the way Gao wouldn't quite meet her gaze now, in Zhang's overly casual slump in his chair. This was big to them. Huge, perhaps.

"That's only eight days from now," she said seriously. "I imagine that the shift rotas have already been drawn up. Changing them now to ensure we only have sympathetic staff onsite would risk drawing exactly the sort of attention you're looking to avoid."

"Shifts change all the time," Zhang said reasonably. "People get dropped, people get called in; who gives a shit?"

"The people who get dropped give a shit; I can assure you of that," Xiuying snapped at him. "If you lose a shift, you lose money, and people pay attention when they lose money. Are you really so naïve that you think my officers don't know which of their colleagues are on your books? If we have to move one or two people off shift, that might be ignored. If we have to reschedule half the port staff, and people realise that there's a pattern to it, that's going to cause the kind of disruption neither of us want."

"Remind me, what are we paying you for again?" Gao sneered. "Make it happen."

"You're paying me to ensure we both make a profit," Xiuying told him coldly, "but I'm not the ultimate authority here. Have you bought off the governor yet?"

There was a stony silence. Xiuying sat back in her chair and folded her arms.

"No, I thought not. That one's an idealist, and she's got ambitions beyond this planet, which she won't get to realise if she's seen as weak or corrupt. So long as Governor Mei is in power, she can call for an investigation into me and my department, a *central* investigation with the full authority of the government. You don't want that. I don't want that. I've kept her happy with my 'efforts' so far, but if enough voices start shouting from ground level that something big is going down, and it's found that I ignored it, or facilitated it . . ." She spread her hands. "If central government comes in with their big boots on, it will be the end of me, and of our special relationship. It'll be the end of you too."

"Don't make me laugh," Gao snorted. "The government's weak, and we are strong."

"The government *here* is weak," Xiuying countered. "Your kind is

ignored so long as you don't cause too much trouble. If you get too blatant, then a bigger fish will sit up and take notice. Beijing and Moscow
don't have high tolerance levels, and they have little regard for collateral
damage. Do you want martial law on these streets? If you provoke them
enough, they'll shut this planet down and rip away all your hiding places
until they find you."

She paused, aware that she was breathing a little heavily, but she
could see that her words had made an impact. The threat of central government had always been her nuclear option, the course of action that
would guarantee her own downfall but bring the Triax down with her.
There was always the risk that they would try to call her bluff if she'd
threatened it herself, but they might be more inclined to listen to a warning that they could bring it down on their own heads.

She really hoped they'd listen. If the nuclear option ever became a
necessity, she wanted to be the one who invoked it so she had as much
time to prepare as possible.

"I appreciate your concerns," Song Daiyu said carefully. "I assure you,
none of us wish to cause any far-reaching consequences."

But . . .

"But the fact is, we do not have the authority to either cancel or
reschedule this shipment," Song continued. "We have our instructions,
which is to ensure that it lands and is unloaded without any interruption
from the authorities. Our failure in this matter would have more immediate and certain consequences for us than anything sanctioned by Old
Earth." She shrugged. "I know all about odds. We'll take our chances."

Xiuying grimaced. "That is your final decision?"

"Don't make the lady say it twice," Gao growled. "Now, are you going
to play nicely?"

It was fairly obvious what the alternative was. Gao had never directly
threatened Xiuying, but he'd skated very close on a couple of occasions.

She had no doubt that, should the Dragon Sons want to, they could kill her. She was fairly sure that, should she want to, she could ruin them. It wasn't an equal balance of power by any means, but for them to continue their relatively comfortable lives, they needed either her, or someone like her. That gave her a little leverage. Maybe not enough to affect what would happen, on this occasion, but at least to ensure she got the most out of it.

"I'll play," she assured them, "but I'll need two things from you."

"We're listening," Zhang drawled, before Gao could spit something undiplomatic.

"First of all, I'll need a sacrifice," she said. "There are going to be ramifications from this shipment of yours, whatever it is. It's been a while since my office has made any significant arrests or scored a major bust against the Triax, so I'll need something I can wave in Mei's face to prove we're still working hard. I need someone with concrete links, not a fall guy, and I'll need them to survive to trial and conviction. After that . . ." She shrugged. "Prison is a dangerous place, if you need it to be."

Zhang and Song shared a sideways glance before Song looked back at her.

"That could be . . . hard to arrange."

Xiuying smiled humourlessly. "Welcome to my world. But if you want me still sitting here moving things around to suit you, I need to convince Mei that she doesn't need to replace me. I'm not asking for the heart of your organisation, but I need someone we can shout about for a while."

Song turned her attention to Gao. "Get me some names."

Xiuying cleared her throat slightly. "And I need them by next seventhday."

Song blinked in apparent shock. "Excuse me?"

"Misdirection." Xiuying shrugged. "We launch an operation involving as many honest officers as I can manage to snag this big fish you dangle in front of us; you sneak your contraband in while everyone's looking the other way. People talk about the momentous arrest my force has made rather than some shady goings-on at the docks. I look good. You look good to your clan, because you sacrificed a pawn at just the right time to make sure we missed your big play." She circled her fingers around each other. "And so the game goes on."

Song pursed her lips, but finally nodded. "I take your point. We will find a suitable candidate." She raised her left eyebrow, causing her semi-circle of gems to shift slightly along with it. "And the second thing?"

"I want danger pay," Xiuying said bluntly. She didn't give them a chance to react, but pressed ahead instead. "If you'd come to me with this two months ago, I could have coordinated what you needed and barely lifted a finger. To arrange it now will mean I need to make calls and contact shift supervisors directly, and instruct them to make changes. That's the sort of meddling that can very easily be traced back to me, if anyone starts investigating. I'm in the system: If I get busted here, I can't do what you can and head elsewhere to start over at the same thing. I want to make sure that if I need to, I can get out before the hammer drops and not end up scratching through bins to make a living."

"What do—" Gao began angrily, but Song held up one hand and cut him off.

"Not an unreasonable request, in and of itself," the gangster said, although there was an iciness to her tone. "What sort of figure did you have in mind?"

Xiuying took a deep breath. "Four hundred grand."

She'd shot high, but not offensively high. Or so she prayed. She waited for an outburst from Gao, a smug laugh from Zhang, hard-nosed negotiating from Song.

Song looked at each of her companions in turn, then back at Xiuying. "That would be acceptable."

Xiuying could barely believe her ears. They'd gone for it. Four hundred thousand stars, and the head of the Dragon Sons' casinos had just nodded her head and okayed it. *Whatever they're planning really must be huge, if that's not going to cut in to their profit margins.*

She tried not to let her surprise show on her face. "I'm glad you agree." Time to push her luck a little. "I'll need that by next seventhday too."

Gao snorted. "You get the money *after* you pull the strings for us."

"Whatever you're doing is clearly big," Xiuying countered, "so maybe you won't need me after this. I get the money beforehand, or it doesn't happen."

Gao scowled. "Don't go thinking you're irreplaceable, *Chief*."

"Long term? Certainly not," Xiuying conceded. "By next seventhday? If I suffer an 'accident' between now and then, I'd . . . well, I was going to say that I'd stake my life on you not finding someone with enough authority to arrange what you need, but I suppose I already am." She gave them a thin smile. "A compromise, then: I get the money *on* next seventhday. You get to see that I've done what I've said I'll do. Assuming you don't stiff me, I don't need to make any last-minute calls to throw a spanner in your works and ruin everything for everyone."

"We can make this happen," Song said slowly, "but four hundred grand won't fit into your uniform pocket when it comes back from the cleaners. And I don't think a credit chip would be appropriate."

Xiuying snorted. "Hardly." Credit chips wouldn't function without bank verification. That meant a data trail, and that was something neither side wanted. "I'll take cash."

"As a lump sum?" Zhang asked. "Not much subtler."

"Then how about this?" Xiuying said. "Next seventhday evening I'll take a trip to one of your casinos." She nodded at Song Daiyu. "I'll gamble for a while, and then I'll cash my chips in. It'll turn out that I had a *very* successful evening at the tables, because I'll walk out of there four hundred grand richer. I get a receipt to explain where the money came from, and everything's aboveboard."

Song nodded briskly. "Make it the Thousand Suns."

Xiuying felt her eyebrows raise. "I didn't know that was one of yours."

"Which is why I am suggesting it," Song said, the faintest hint of a smile tugging at the corners of her mouth. "Our ownership of it isn't well-known, so fewer conclusions will be drawn about your presence there."

"Excellent." Xiuying looked down at her pad, and tapped it to bring up the agenda. "Now, unless there are any further *irregular* items to be discussed . . ."

CHECKING OUT THE COMPETITION

"I still can't believe you ended up holding a gun on the one person who might have actually been able to help us," Kuai said in Mandarin. He was sitting in a bar with Muradov and Jia, and debating whether he wanted another mijiu.

"I didn't have a great deal of choice in the matter," Muradov replied defensively. "You didn't consult me before you started your little *intervention*, if you recall, so I had to improvise."

"If the Captain or Rourke end up held at gunpoint, that's not such a big deal," Kuai argued, "because Drift can talk his way out of it and Rourke will just break their arms or something. If it happens to anyone else, we have to take steps." He looked at his sister. "Right?"

Jia glowered at him.

"See?"

Muradov frowned. "She didn't say anything."

"Yeah, but she can never bring herself to agree with me," Kuai sighed. "Right, sis?"

"Shut up, dickface."

"Mother would be so proud of you; do you know that?"

"Mother would smile and tell us that she loves us both, and never let on how fucking disappointed she was by the pair of us," Jia bit out, and knocked back a swig of whatever she was drinking. Kuai hadn't bothered to find out.

He grimaced. "Wow, you're in a good mood."

"Not wrong though, am I?"

"Yeah, actually, you are," Kuai snapped, stung into retaliating. "*I got a proper job and left Old Earth legally, unlike my bail-jumping baby sister, whom I have managed to keep in one piece like I promised our parents*, no thanks to you."

"Yeah, whatever," Jia snorted. "Wasn't you that grabbed me when I was about to get blown away into an Uragan hurricane, was it?" She nodded sideways. "That was the Chief, here."

"A decision I'm starting to regret," Muradov muttered into his flavoured water. He glanced back up at her. "Why does everyone keep calling me 'Chief,' anyway? I'm not the chief of anything anymore."

"I dunno, seems to suit you," Jia said. She levelled a finger at him. "Chief." She turned the finger to Kuai. "Dickface."

Kuai stared hard at her, seeing the signs now that he was looking for them. "You're drunk."

"Am not."

"You are." He grabbed the bottle she'd been using to top up her glass and looked at the label. "Gah! What the hell is even in this?"

"Alcohol," Jia replied. "What else matters? Besides, I'm following orders. Captain told me to get a bit drunk."

"He did *what?*" Muradov exclaimed in shock, managing to choke off the end of his sentence so it only came out as a slightly undignified squeak. The Uragan composed himself and took another sip of his water. "Why would he do that?"

"Well, okay, he told me to be ready to pull someone," Jia said with a shrug. "Same thing really."

Kuai grimaced and looked at Muradov. "You didn't know about this?"

"No!" Muradov protested, then hesitated. "Although actually, I suppose it makes a certain amount of sense. Insofar as any of this makes sense."

Kuai sighed. They were neck-deep in this scheme, and the Captain was doing his usual thing of coming up with new angles with little warning or explanation. "Drift just told me that we were to meet you here. I've been waiting for you to get to the point."

"Oh, wonderful." Muradov scratched his moustache. "Well, you see the imposing guy in the far corner with the lines shaved into his head? That's one Tommy Sanyang, who's apparently due to appear on a fight card in two days. The Captain wants him replaced with Apirana."

Kuai looked past the Uragan's shoulder. A dark-skinned man with, sure enough, lines shaved into his short hair was sitting with a couple of others under a lamp in the far corner, chatting quietly. He didn't have the face of a fighter, lacking the cauliflower ears or bent nose sported by so many, although Kuai could see a couple of faint raised scars catching the light. He was rather handsome, in fact, with high cheekbones and a strong jaw, not to mention the leanly muscled arms showed off by the sleeveless top he was wearing.

"Fit," Jia commented. "That's always a plus."

"And did the Captain say how he was proposing to make this happen?" Kuai asked, ignoring his sister to the best of his ability. It wasn't easy, but he'd had a lifetime of practice.

"I think there was originally a plan about spiking Sanyang's drink at a gym," Muradov admitted. "But I tracked him down here, so it seemed like a good time to make a play." The former security chief pulled a tiny, clear packet of white powder from his pocket. "Somehow, we need to get this into his system. I'm guessing the Captain thinks that seducing him is the easiest way to achieve that."

Kuai looked at Muradov for a moment. "And you're fine with this?"

"The Captain assures me it's merely a powerful laxative." Muradov shrugged. "There's no danger of it being lethal, or, in fact, anything more than rather unpleasant for him for a couple of days, providing he's smart enough to drink plenty of fluids."

"Cool." Jia held out her hand. "Let's have the payload."

Muradov slid it across the table to her. "Good hunting."

Kuai watched his sister palm the powder and then slide off her stool to flounce across the bar. "I'm still a little surprised that a former security chief doesn't have any objections to this plan."

"I made my call when I signed up with you," Muradov said, sipping his water. "Besides, Ms. Rourke was instrumental in getting the *Jonah* to us and saving all our lives back on Uragan. I think I at least owe her that in return. As for Mr. Sanyang over there, perhaps we're saving him from taking a beating. It could be a kindness."

"Those are the sort of flexible morals that can lead to all kinds of criminal behaviour," Kuai commented.

"The irony isn't lost on me."

"How'd you find him, anyway?" Kuai asked. He was trying not to watch Jia, but old habits died hard. Maybe he did want another drink. Watching his baby sister trying to seduce someone was never easy for him, especially when he wouldn't have minded bedding the mark himself.

"Jenna isn't the only one who can use the Spine, you know," Muradov said. "There are a lot of fighting fans in town for the event, so all I had to do was look out for people uploading pictures of fighters they've just seen, or had their picture taken with. Someone spotted him here"—he looked at his chrono—"about forty-five minutes ago, so I made the call."

Kuai nodded. Muradov had proved to be efficient and resourceful so far, which was about all they could ask for when pushing ahead with such an idiotic plan, so all things considered, Kuai was rather glad the Uragan had been added to the crew. Of course, Muradov wasn't exactly the life of the party, but then again people apparently said the same thing about Kuai.

"So what's to stop your old friend on the force from ratting us out?" he asked the other man. "I could really do without being arrested for being an accessory to assault of a security officer."

"Self-preservation, I expect," Muradov replied. "She's got absolutely no evidence to suggest I've broken the law, and even if there were any cameras covering the market, they would only show that she lured me to a public area and pulled a gun on me for no apparent reason. There's no way she can spin that to make me look criminal, and it would spark awkward questions for her."

"Yeah, but remember we're in a crooked town," Kuai pointed out. "What about all those officers she mentioned who're in the pay of the Triax?"

"Mariya's probably too principled to run to the Triax at all," Muradov said. "I think she'll actually want me to succeed in whatever it is she thinks I'm doing, even if she doesn't like me now. Besides, she's certainly too *smart* to go to them—she's not on their books, so they won't trust her anyway. If she goes to someone and says she was questioned by me, at gunpoint, they'll figure she told me everything she knows. That's the sort of thing that can lead to an early retirement at the wrong end of a bullet. Her best option is almost certainly to keep her head down and hope no one ever finds out that we spoke."

"And likewise for us," Kuai sighed. "What I wouldn't give for a solid plan right now. You ever watched any heist holos? You know, where this gang of people rob a bank or something?"

"Sure," Muradov confirmed, nodding. "Although they're usually infuriatingly inaccurate when portraying security procedures."

"Well, here's the thing," Kuai said, leaning forward and jabbing the table with his finger for emphasis. "Right now, we're in one. And all we know is that some casino has got the money we want." He sat back again, looked at the bottle he'd confiscated from his sister, then tipped a measure into his glass. "I could have told you that—most casinos carry millions every night. We've still got no idea how we're going to *get* the . . ."

He trailed off. Jia was coming back to the table, and she didn't look happy.

"That didn't take long," Muradov commented. Jia shot him a glare and tossed the packet, unopened, across the table to Kuai.

"I got nothing. The two guys he was with, yeah, eyes on my prize. Coulda walked over and plucked either of 'em, no problem. The man himself?" She shrugged. "I'm the wrong tool for the job. You're up, dickface."

Kuai picked the packet up, trying to suppress a smile. It always killed Jia to admit that someone didn't want her, and besides, he had rather been hoping for this outcome. "This is a stupid question, but you were subtle, right?"

"Oh, relax," Jia grouched, hopping back up on her stool. "I was at the bar; I got a drink"—she gestured to the glass in her hand—"I looked around a bit; I waggled my ass. I didn't walk up and sit in his lap, didn't even speak to him. They didn't see someone trying it on; they just saw a hot girl. Well, two of them did," she corrected herself.

"I'm not following," Muradov cut in, his brow furrowed.

"I know, right?" Jia said into her glass. "Hell, I'm good, but I'm only human. Some men just ain't for turning."

"No, I mean . . ." Muradov looked back at Kuai. "*You're* trying now?"

"Unless you want a go?" Kuai asked him.

"I, ah, don't think that my talents lie in that direction," Muradov admitted. "Besides, my faith would frown on it. Unless I were to marry him first."

"Lucky for everyone, the Changs are here," Jia said, perhaps a little too loudly. "If the drop-dead gorgeous pilot doesn't get you, her grease monkey idiot of a brother will. No cock is safe!"

"Shut up," Kuai told her. "It's not fair that you always get first try, anyway."

"Statistics, bitch. More men want me than want you; that's just fact." She turned to Muradov. "So, you ever been married?"

"I have not."

"So you've *never* had sex, because your faith would frown on it?!"

"Just because I wish to avoid doing something now does not mean I've always succeeded in avoiding it. . . ."

"You know what?" Kuai took a sip from his glass, then screwed up his face as he tasted what his sister had been drinking, and the pithy sentence he'd had lined up fled from his brain entirely. "Fuck his mother! *Absinthe?* Jia, you know that makes you violent!"

Jia shrugged. "Eh, what you gonna do?"

Kuai glared at her. "I'm going to seduce a muscular, handsome professional athlete and have mind-blowing sex with him *before* I spike his drink, while you piss off back to the shuttle before you get too drunk to stand."

"Fuck you. I can find someone else to sleep with now that I'm not working!"

Kuai pointed at Muradov. "Make sure she gets back safe."

The Uragan rolled his eyes. "Merciful Allah, I have been in war zones that were less hostile than you two."

"And don't you forget it," Kuai told him, then turned his back on the pair of them and headed for the bar. He looked over at Sanyang as he did so. The fighter glanced up as movement registered in his peripheral vision, and their eyes skated past each other in cursory contact. Sanyang's eyes dropped again. But half a minute later he realised that Kuai had been looking at him, and almost instinctively, he looked back up again.

Kuai made sure Sanyang saw that he was still looking, and slowed his walk slightly for a second as their eyes met for a second, longer moment.

Then he turned and headed for the bar, checking in the mirror that stood behind the rows of bottles.

Yup. Sanyang kept looking for a couple more seconds before returning to his conversation, but he'd glanced up again before Kuai had even told the barman what he wanted to drink.

Kuai allowed himself a small smile. He loved mechanics and engines, and generally didn't have much time for people. Usually he'd be quite happy just left to his own devices, making sure the *Keiko* and the *Jonah* stayed working properly, without any of the fighting, sneaking, running away, or combinations thereof that seemed to take up far too much of the crew's time. Sometimes, though, it was good to get out and meet new people.

And then take their clothes off.

TALKING UP A STORM

The Two Trees Arena was a large, double-lobed affair just north of Zhuchengshi's city centre, decorated in huge diagonal slashes of white and grey. One side held the main arena of thirty thousand seats, the other a more utilitarian leisure centre of smaller sports courts and pools. The roof housed an aircar parking lot, but the cab Drift had hired dropped Apirana and him off at ground level just in front of the low, blocky building that connected the two bigger complexes. This was where the ticket offices and centre management were situated, and was also where Drift hoped to find someone he could work a little silver-tongued magic on.

"Remember," he told Apirana as they approached the automatic doors, "business face from here on in."

"You got it, bro," the huge Māori rumbled. When Drift looked over his shoulder, he saw Apirana's features set in a stony glower, and the big man moving with a shoulder-rolling gait that emphasised his size and build. Drift nodded in satisfaction. When trying to pull the wool over someone's eyes, it was a significant advantage to have your goods looking as legitimate as possible.

He strolled through the sliding doors and sauntered over to the enquiries desk. It was staffed by a young woman who was frowning at a terminal screen and occasionally tapping at it with one finger. She had a strongly asymmetric fringe and a glistening network of silver lines on one side of her throat—purely cosmetic, so far as Drift could tell. He put on his best smile even though she wasn't looking at him yet and trusted that she would either speak English or the desk had a translation protocol, because he was damned if he was going to try and sweet-talk his way past anyone in his poor Russian.

"Excuse me, would it be possible to speak to the events manager, please? It's regarding the fight card tomorrow."

She looked up at him, her own pleasant-but-neutral smile in place, then over his shoulder at Apirana. Her smile slipped a bit, and her eyes widened slightly when they landed on the imposing presence at Drift's shoulder. She managed to tear her gaze away after a moment, but giant tattooed Māoris were obviously not an everyday occurrence for her.

"Are you . . . Do you represent one of the fighters?" she asked Drift in English, managing to regain her professionalism.

"I should soon," he replied smoothly. "I believe there's a vacancy on the card, and I can help with that."

"I see." She looked down at her terminal for a second. "Your name?"

"Rodrigo Pérez."

She tapped her terminal screen, then the side of her throat. She waited for a moment, then spoke in Mandarin that Drift's commpiece translated into his ear, via the pad in his pocket.

"*Mer, there's a Mr. Pérez here to see you. He says he wants to talk to you about the vacancy on the fight card tomorrow.*"

Drift raised his eyebrows slightly. Apparently the silver lines had a purpose after all. Some sort of subdermal commpiece? He could see some benefits, but what if you rolled over in your sleep and turned it on accidentally? Would you wake up with someone angrily shouting in your ear, demanding to know why you'd called them in the middle of the night?

"*Yes, mer,*" the receptionist said, apparently in response to whoever she'd called, jerking him from his reverie. *Mer* was a gender-neutral title, the closest equivalent his translation protocol had to the Mandarin word the woman was using. "*No, but he has . . .*" Her eyes flicked to Apirana again. "*Yes, I'd say so, mer.*"

Drift just stood there, smiling blandly, and waited for events to take their course. If he knew anything about business, then everyone involved with the show would be scrabbling around to find a replacement for Tommy Sanyang, who had pulled out of his fight that morning citing a sudden illness. An unknown man turning up at the venue with a second, huge, and menacing man in tow wouldn't normally be a promoter's first port of call . . . but under the circumstances, he was willing to bet that they'd explore any option that presented itself.

The receptionist looked up at him. "Please take a seat, sirs. Mer Chen will see you shortly."

They'd barely had time to sink into one of the comfortable maroon couches when a hassled-looking young man with a snub nose appeared through the door next to the enquiries desk. His shiny shoes clicked on the tiled floor as he hurried over to them.

"Mr. Pérez?"

Drift stood again, trying to ignore the slight twinge from his right knee. He must be getting old. "Yes?"

"If you would both like to follow me, please?" the young man said with a nervous nod of his head. Drift heard Apirana heave himself upright behind him, and the pair of them trailed after their guide as he led them back across the foyer. It occurred to Drift that nothing about this employee's nervousness seemed to stem from seeing Apirana. Perhaps this Mer Chen was in a bad mood and had a habit of taking it out on their employees.

They passed through the same door the young man had emerged

from and down a narrow corridor that was slightly obstructed by a couple of boxes stacked against one wall and a small pallet of soft drinks against the other, slightly farther along. Drift slid past with room to spare, but Apirana grunted as he turned side-on to get by without dislodging anything. A few steps more and they reached a door with a brass nameplate: The characters were in Chinese, but Drift's mechanical eye automatically translated them.

MER S. CHEN

EVENTS MANAGER

The door was wedged open slightly, and the young man gave only the most perfunctory of knocks before pushing it wider and standing back, motioning for Drift to enter. Drift did so, and found himself in a relatively small office decorated with holo-posters from prominent events hosted at the arena in the past, as well as what looked like a couple of sporting trophies that had presumably been won at some point by its occupant.

What was somewhat more concerning was the fact that he also found himself to now be the subject of three hard stares, in what felt like an atmosphere already crackling with tension. He stopped and took a second to assess, hiding behind his lazy smile.

The person standing behind the desk was presumably Mer Chen: fairly tall and smooth-cheeked, with bleached white hair artfully flicked across zir scalp in a manner that gave the impression of a cresting wave on an icy sea. Ze wore a simple but well-cut long-sleeved tunic that reached zir knees, in navy blue with white chasing, and baggy pants of the same material underneath. It was hard to get a sense of zir figure beneath the flowing clothes, but zir cheeks were plump and zir hands far from bony.

Standing closer to Drift, and therefore considerably more prominent in his thinking at this moment, were two men. The older, with some age lines on his face, had his sleek black hair coiffed up atop his head and shaved short at the sides, and a wispy moustache with a hint of ginger to it. He was considerably shorter than Drift and skinny with it, and his dark-silver suit in a Russian style seemed to hang off his spare frame. He was leaning on what looked to be a genuine wooden cane held in his right hand, complete with an ornate silvered derby handle that matched his suit, although Drift suspected it was more of an affectation than a genuine walking aid.

The second man, his head shaved near-bald, was already positioning himself between the new arrivals and his probable boss. He had heavy black boots and was clad in a no-nonsense bloodred bodysuit with a bulky, bone-coloured jacket of the sort favoured by hoverbikers worn over the top. The bodysuit would have taken care of his thermodynamic needs, so the jacket was presumably for protection: Certainly, the tough material was only a step or two down from ballistic fabrics, as it would have to be to be of any use in a high-speed fall. Given this and the man's greater size, not to mention his reaction to their arrival, Drift felt fairly safe in assuming that he was some form of bodyguard.

He tried not to let his smile widen when everyone saw Apirana. He knew it had to be a little hard on the poor guy to always be the focus of attention, but there was no denying that the big Māori made quite an impression even when he was trying to fade into the background. When he was trying to stand out . . .

"Hope we ain't interrupting anything?" Apirana said in a voice like tumbling granite. The words were perfectly polite, but there was the faintest hint in the big man's tone suggesting that no matter what you were doing, it was in your best interest to let it be interrupted. And not to complain about that too loudly.

"Mr. Pérez, my name is Serenity Chen," the events manager said in English. Zir voice was quiet, and oddly sibilant. "I am rather busy, but

I understand you wish to speak to me about the vacancy on tomorrow night's card?"

"That was my intention," Drift replied with another smile that he turned—politely—to the two men on his side of the desk. "I can wait until you've concluded your current business, though."

"Mr. Ma is the representative of the New Star Fight League," Chen explained. "He and I were discussing how to approach this situation."

Drift felt his smile widen of its own accord. "I understand that the man without an opponent is Kuang Daniu? Local boy, I believe, so far as these things go. I imagine a fair percentage of the crowd would be looking forward to seeing him fight in particular." He looked back at Chen. "I know the card is subject to change, of course, but I guess there are some things you really don't want to have to go back on, once you've advertised them."

"Spare me the bargaining talk," Ma snapped in Mandarin. *"If you have a proposition, make it, but I won't have you thinking that you hold me to ransom here. The New Star Fight League is a large organisation, and we have several possible replacements."*

"To fight a man like Kuang on a day's notice?" Drift chuckled. "You'll need deep pockets, even if there's anyone close enough. But no, sir, I'm not trying to scalp you. My client and I just saw an opportunity. You want Kuang to fight, and you want someone who looks like he belongs in there with him." He gestured to Apirana. "This is Apirana 'the Māori Badass' Wahawaha. He's big, he's tough as hell, he's covered in tattoos, and he's got a mean right hook."

Ma looked dubious. *"You just described my daughter's wife."* He looked past Drift, up at Apirana. *"Have you ever fought before?"*

Apirana snorted. "Hell yeah."

"What is your record?"

Drift saw the big man's lip twitch. "Two counts of malicious wounding. One of aggravated assault. Three of possessing narcotics with intent to supply. Two of possession of illegal firearms." His huge shoulders moved in a shrug. "Oh, and I resisted arrest, so it was three . . . no, four counts of assault of a police officer. I'm guessing you ain't too bothered about the driving without insurance."

If Ma was intimidated by the list of crimes dropped matter-of-factly from Apirana's lips, he didn't show it. The old man's eyes just narrowed. *"Are you a fighter, or a criminal?"*

"Bro, in prison everyone's looking to make a name for themselves by taking down the big dog." Apirana inhaled, swelling his chest even larger. "You put a guy who looks like me in Farport Penitentiary for fifteen years an' he either comes out a fighter or he don't come out at all."

"Look at it this way, sir," Drift cut in. "If Kuang wins, he's taken down the big, tough-looking stranger and all his fans go home happy. If he loses, you've made a new star overnight."

Ma's mouth worked briefly, as though trying to get a troublesome pip out from between his teeth. *"Five kay to show, five kay win bonus."*

Drift chuckled. "Seven kay to show. Three kay win bonus."

Ma frowned. *"Most fighters want their pay doubled if they win."*

"I know who I'm up against," Apirana said grimly. "I'll be givin' it my all, but I know the odds ain't in my favour. I'll take a seven kay basic, and if I win, then my main bonus'll be pride."

Drift watched Ma mull this over. Even with the win bonus, the price they were asking would be a lot less than half of Kuang's fee just to set foot in the ring.

Ma scratched at his nose and sighed. *"I'll give your man his shot, Pérez, assuming Kuang and his agent agree."* He focused on Apirana again and waved one thin finger in warning. *"But know this: If you turn out to be some lumbering clown who lasts thirty seconds, then you'll embarrass my organisation, and me. And if that happens, I'll make sure neither of you work again."*

"Understood." Drift beamed. "I promise you, sir, you won't regret this."

"*We'll see*," Ma replied, and looked over at the events manager. "*Mer Chen, are you happy with this arrangement?*"

"We might have had a considerable amount of unsatisfied customers if Kuang Daniu had not appeared on the card," Chen said. "So long as Mr. Kuang fights, I'm certain we will be able to continue our partnership with the New Star Fight League."

Drift tried not to smile any wider. Chen had just casually put a lot of pressure on Ma to make sure Kuang and his agent agreed to the new opponent, unless Ma wanted to risk losing the Two Trees Arena as a venue for his organisation.

"*I'll be in touch*," Ma said, his delivery just a shade too polite to be considered a snap. He turned on his heel and stalked towards the door. Apirana stood aside to let him and his bodyguard pass, while Drift called up his pad's contact details.

"You can contact me on this number," he told Chen with a smile, sliding his details over to the events manager's personal terminal. Jenna had made sure that the contact information was in the name of Rodrigo Pérez instead of Ichabod Drift, but they hadn't been able to convince Apirana to take on a false identity. The big man had said that if he was going to fight, then he was going to fight as himself, and Drift had just had to go along with it.

"Thank you," Chen said with a faint smile of zir own. "I am sure Mr. Ma will be able to make the necessary arrangements with Mr. Kuang. Please ensure that you are both here at least three hours before the first fight tomorrow."

"It'll be a pleasure," Drift replied, offering a handshake that Chen readily accepted. "Until tomorrow, then."

He went to pull his hand away, but Chen's grip was abruptly too tight.

"Mr. Pérez," the events manager said, zir dark eyes boring into Drift's.

"You are *certain* that your client will not be out of place in my arena tomorrow, I hope?"

Drift hastily recalibrated his assessment of Serenity Chen. Anyone willing to play a strong-arm card like this on him when Apirana was in the room was either incredibly stupid, or knew something that he didn't.

Drift *hated* it when people knew things he didn't.

"I assure you, Mer," he said with a smile, as though he'd never tried to withdraw from the handshake, "Mr. Kuang won't know what hit him. At least until he wakes up again, and someone explains it to him."

"I'm glad to hear it." Chen's grip relaxed, and they both withdrew their hands. "See you tomorrow, Mr. Pérez."

"Indeed." Drift turned and ushered Apirana out of the office ahead of him, propelling the big man down the corridor without another word. He nodded politely at the receptionist and gave her an absentminded smile as they went past, because smiling was one of the things he did best, and it was important not to stop doing it just because you no longer felt like it.

Okay, so Chen didn't want a joke fight stinking up the Two Trees Arena either, fair enough, but what was the deal with the intimidation?

"I think we just made a very bad call, bro," Apirana muttered from beside him as they started down the steps towards the cab rank.

"Why so?" Drift asked, pondering their problem.

"Don't-give-a-fuck attitude like that? In this town?" Apirana sighed mournfully. "I think we just booked me into a fight in a building run by the goddamn Triax."

Drift stopped in his tracks. The big man's logic ran uncomfortably true.

"*Shit.*"

HOUSE CALL

The planet of New Samara had a very stable axis, which meant that the city of New Samara had a very stable climate. Had she been walking the streets at night in a continental winter, then Tamara Rourke might have been in considerably worse shape, given her loose, thin shirt. As it was, the air was fresh without being chill, and so long as she kept moving she was at no risk of falling foul of environmental factors.

That didn't mean that she wasn't on a schedule, or potentially vulnerable. She had to assume that Orlov's people would have at least some influence in the local *politsiya*. And she didn't have time to procure a change of clothes, so she couldn't afford to be spotted by a patrol. What she really needed was an aircar.

Which was why she was lurking in the shadows of a large garbage container next to an all-night grocery store. One city was much like another in many ways, and certain things were almost guaranteed to occur.

She'd been there for twenty-two minutes, judging by the clock in the store's window, when she got what she'd been waiting for. An old Almaz A17, a few scratches down one side and the engine cover an unsprayed white instead of the burgundy red of the rest, pulled into the kerb. It was hardly the finest vehicle going, but she wasn't in a position to be choosy. She tensed, ready to move.

A youth got out of the passenger's door, his jacket unfastened and his hair a little dishevelled. He slouched across the pavement to the store, pushing open the door as he reached it. Supply run: getting the beers or the snacks, or whatever was needed for the night's entertainment. She got up from her crouch and approached the car, scanning it as she did so. The driver appeared to be the only other occupant. Excellent.

She passed around the rear of the vehicle, looking both ways as though preparing to cross the road, then darted two steps to the driver's door and hauled it open before the boy inside could do anything. There was a haze of soft narcotic smoke in the car, which probably hadn't helped his reactions. She brought the gun up into his shocked, angry face and armed it.

"Get out."

He froze for a moment, but any notion of defiance wilted in the face of the Kobel .45 a few inches from his nose. He hadn't been wearing his safety restraints anyway, so there was no delay there: He scrabbled to obey, and a hand on his collar helped to send him spilling out onto the road in a way that prevented him from making any ill-judged attempt to interfere as she was climbing into the driver's seat.

She shut the door, activated the locking systems, and quickly scanned her surroundings. Ignition card in place, no open windows, no previously unseen passengers in the rear seats . . . All in all, about as smooth a carjacking as she could hope for. She put the safety back on the Kobel, fed power to the drives, and pulled away with a whine, leaving her victim still scrambling to his feet behind her. She caught a glimpse in the mirrors of his friend emerging from the store at a run before she turned a corner and they were lost to view.

She only went three blocks before parking by the side of the road. Drug-hazed or not, she had to assume that her victims would call in her crime, and the two-tone colour of her ride made her more conspicuous than she'd have liked. She wound down the windows to get rid of the fug and bent to work on the control dash.

Higher-end makes and models would have been better designed, but the old Almaz's panel was prised loose fairly easily with the assistance of a screwdriver she found in the storage compartment. Once that was out of the way, it didn't take her long to disable the altitude limiter and the distress beacon, two tricks performed every day by joyriders on planets across the galaxy, and then she was back up and driving again.

She couldn't deny, there was a certain thrill to this. She'd been a part of the *Keiko*'s crew for so long that she'd almost forgotten what it was like to be a lone agent, deep in a mission and forced to rely solely on her own resources. However, she wasn't going to get nostalgic: The whole point of having a crew was so there were other people to pick up the slack, to watch your back while you slept, and to take over tasks that you yourself weren't an expert at. She couldn't match Jenna's level of slicing expertise, or Jia's piloting skills, or Kuai's mechanical knowledge. For that matter, although she was a more skilled fighter than Apirana, sometimes you simply needed someone with the Māori's sheer size and strength, or raw physical presence. And then there was Ichabod, with his almost uncanny people skills, disarming manner, and sometimes brilliant, sometimes ludicrous, brain for schemes and plans.

She really hoped they'd understand what she was about to do.

All aircar passengers were supposed to wear a slimline emergency parachute in case of catastrophic failure, but her quick survey of contents had showed no signs that this car carried any spares. That was going to make this harder, but she didn't have the time or inclination to purchase one. Or even the money, for that matter: For a moment she regretted not hunting through Sacha's pockets to get his wallet, but she'd been risking enough to get his pad and comm away from him. They now lay inert on the seat next to her. With any luck he wouldn't be easily able to contact anyone without them, which might give her a little more time to do what she needed to.

She triggered the ascending blinkers and pulled the Almaz upwards, rising past the storied windows around her. There was little traffic about, and she quickly pulled level with the upper floors of the high-powered business headquarters and the shiny accommodation blocks. So much of the planet's surface was given over to valuable arable land that the only place to build within the capital's tightly controlled boundaries was upwards.

She was now at an altitude reserved for the richest. New Samara was the realm of the wealthy and powerful, of course, but they needed their servants and staff. Corporation heads might meet in their gleaming offices, but people had to be employed to keep those offices gleaming. No one wanted the riffraff in their cheap bangers cluttering the upper skyways, so your car's permit dictated how high it could go. Unless you'd disabled the altitude limiter, of course, but that was an offence that carried a severe fine and possibly a custodial sentence, depending on what you did when you were up there.

For joyriders and fugitives, though, future consequences were a distant and secondary consideration compared to the needs of the present.

Rourke double-checked the homing setting on the Almaz and compared it to the holo-map of the city. If she engaged the emergency autopilot and told the vehicle to return to its registered address, it would do so, while obeying laws of altitude and traffic priority to the best of the computer's ability. It was no true replacement for a competent driver, of course, so any activation of the homing protocol would contact the authorities to alert them to the potential medical or criminal issue that had necessitated that course of action. That was why she'd deactivated the distress beacon: Once she was done with it, this vehicle would fly in a silent and hopefully safe manner back to its owner, leaving no one the wiser of where it was or where it had been.

Right now, however, she aimed it for the roof of the Grand House. The huge building was the largest casino in New Samara, and also happened to be the location of Sergei Orlov's penthouse. It loomed up out of the night like a great, dark-green ship in a sea of concrete, tarmac, and steel; not so tall as the surrounding skyscrapers, but with a much larger footprint. No name adorned its side, but it wasn't needed. If you were in New Samara and you didn't know what and where the Grand House was, you didn't belong inside it.

One end of it rose upwards into the tower of the hotel connected to the casino, where Rourke and her crew had been staying only a few weeks before, prior to the *Keiko*'s ill-fated trip to Uragan. Half of the main building's roof was taken up by a long, low structure lined with windows and studded with skylights: Orlov's penthouse flat, with his luxury aircar parked on top and presumably secured with magnetic clamps in case of high winds. The other half, at the opposite end to the hotel tower, was paved and open to the air. It had a swimming pool in the middle, a few planted areas, including two lines of short, dark conifers, and what looked like a barbecue patio near the penthouse's sliding doors.

A swimming pool. Well, that potentially made things easier.

She abandoned all pretence at sticking to the skyways and swung the Almaz into a turn that would take her directly across the Grand House's roof. Timing was critical now. She stuffed Sacha's pad and comm into her pocket, then double-checked that the Kobel's safety was on and tucked it into her belt.

Just as the Almaz passed over Sergei Orlov's swimming pool, she hammered the autopilot activation and bailed out.

Aircars were not designed to be exited in midair. The vehicle pitched to one side and threw her leap off, and instead of dropping smoothly feet-first towards the water, she found herself falling forwards. She flailed instinctively for a second, but twenty feet or so wasn't enough to have any chance of correcting her angle of entry.

It felt like a giant had swatted her with a huge, wet mattress. She was sinking, air blasted from her lungs, and her body reluctant to respond, but she managed to coax her limbs into some sort of sluggish movement. Her knees were protesting furiously—they must have hit fairly hard, and it wasn't like they were getting younger in any case—and her arms felt suddenly weak. But she needed air. For a moment she couldn't work out which way the surface lay, but then she managed to right herself and clawed upwards.

She broke the surface with as restrained a gasp as she could manage, blinked the water from her eyes, and started to stroke clumsily towards the nearest pool edge. As she did so, she silently cursed Andrei, Sacha, and Leon, and the overlarge clothing they'd provided for her. With the ballooning shirt and pants flapping around her, it was like trying to swim through a mass of wet tissue.

She seemed much, much heavier than usual as she hauled herself out, and could only manage to roll onto her side. Something dug painfully into her, which she was grateful to find was the Kobel: She'd probably have some hefty bruising where the water had slammed the metal fire-arm into the flesh over her hipbone, but at least she wouldn't have to go back into the pool to recover it.

First things first. There was no sign of movement from what she could see of the penthouse, and no shouts of alarm or challenge. An aircar was noisy, but someone like Orlov would have good soundproof-ing on his city centre home. If he had the windows and doors shut, as he might on this fresh night, he may not have heard the Almaz's thrusters or her clumsy arrival in his pool. So for now, she might still have the element of surprise.

She pushed herself up into a crouch and pulled out the Kobel, then slid the clip out and tilted the barrel downwards to drain. Most guns would fire even after being submerged in water, but it was better to be safe than sorry. Happily, it looked like the internal mechanisms were mainly dry, so she slapped the clip back in and readied it once more. Then she hurriedly unbuttoned the shirt and wrung it out, keeping a careful eye on the penthouse all the while. The wind at this height was sharp on her bare, wet skin, and there was nothing to be done about the pants, but trickles of water down her arms would make her grip even less reliable and would be distracting. Besides, she was damned if she was going to walk in on a crime boss looking any more like a contestant in an over-fifties wet T-shirt contest than she had to.

She towelled herself off as best she could with the half-dry shirt, wrung it out again, and put it back on, then ran one hand through her hair to squeeze as much water out as she could. It was longer than she liked it, having grown out to over a finger's width, but there was nothing for that now. Time to move.

She crept through the garden, hugging the lines of conifers to get as close as possible to the penthouse. Soft fronds tickled her as she pressed past, but she ignored them and focused on her goal. No windows or doors open, as she'd hoped, but that now presented her with the problem of how to get inside.

Then again, this entire plan was based around the fact that Sergei Orlov had grown too used to being unchallenged. Would a gang boss who controlled most of this system and the neighbouring ones really think he needed to lock the door leading to his private garden atop his own casino?

She darted across the last stretch of paving tiles and pressed herself up against the wall next to the door. It was a full-glass affair apart from the frame, and although the room inside—a living room, by the looks of it—was dimly lit, she could see that there was no one present. She had to hope that Orlov was at home: If he was out, then there was no telling when he would get back.

She took hold of the door's handle and applied pressure very, very carefully. For a moment nothing happened, but then it slid backwards a fraction. Perfect. She put one ear to the tiny gap she'd created and blocked the other one with her finger, trying to drown out the noise of the city at night.

Nothing at first. Then the slapping sound of flesh on flesh and a woman's yelp. Rourke paused, but it came again after a second, and then again, then rising both in frequency and in the volume of the cries. Other sounds made themselves known, too: a man's grunts, and the rhythmic knocking of what she quickly realised was a headboard against a wall.

Rourke smiled to herself. She'd never had much time for sex, but it served marvellously well as a distraction at times. She pushed the door open wide enough to admit her and slipped through, then closed it again behind her. It was smooth and nearly noiseless on its runnings, and any sounds that filtered in from the city outside didn't seem to have penetrated through to where the coupling was taking place.

The flooring inside was thick carpet, which would at least prevent her from leaving such an obvious water trail as she might have done on floorboards or tiles. She headed towards a huge armchair, pretty much large enough to be the right size for Apirana, and ducked behind it to consider her next move. She didn't want to involve any bystanders, but Orlov clearly had company. However, judging by the noises they were making, even she, amateur in such matters though she was, could take a guess that they were coming to the end of their activity.

There was a final frenzy of yelping, grunting, and banging, and then a momentary silence that was broken by a couple of heavy thumps, as though two people had slumped down onto a mattress. She heard a female voice saying something in a low, throaty chuckle, although

Rourke couldn't make out the words. The man coughed breathlessly, then responded in kind.

Rourke remained in her crouch for a few minutes, listening to the murmurs of conversation coming from the bedroom. Then there was a creak of the bed and the voices got a little louder, loud enough to be audible.

". . . *have to?*" the woman was asking in Russian.

"*I'm afraid so,*" Sergei Orlov replied good-naturedly. "*I need my sleep, woman! You'll be the death of me, although I won't deny that it would be a good way to go.*"

"*Don't say such things!*" the woman chided. It was meant to sound playful, Rourke could tell, but she thought she detected a genuine note there as well. "*What would I do without you?*"

"*Mourn me, and then find a new client very nearly as wealthy?*" Orlov suggested.

"*I am going to pretend you didn't say that.*"

"*It's true! I can only thank the stars I've managed to keep you to myself for so long.*"

"*Well, you do pay me* very *well to have a client list of only one.*" The bed shifted again, and Rourke thought she saw a movement of shadows suggesting clothes being pulled on. "*You do know that you don't have to, don't you?*"

"*No!*" Orlov's response was surprisingly sharp, although his voice softened immediately afterwards. "*What we have is business, Galina. It must be business. Were anyone to guess that you might be significant to me in some way beyond business, you would become a target for the people who would like to reach me, but can't. So I pay you generously and openly, an obvious transaction, and you are seen by others as nothing more than a . . . a contractor. No matter how you are seen by me.*"

There was a pause. Then the woman's voice came again, slightly tremulous. "*And if I am prepared to take that risk?*"

"It makes no difference. I am not. You can be paid for the time you see me, and we live apart. Or we do not see each other at all. I will have no argument on this."

There was a sigh, and a soft, wet noise that Rourke's ears interpreted as a kiss. Then the woman spoke again, sounding sad. "I expected you to say that. I understand, although I don't like it."

"Nor do I. But it's necessary."

"Very well. I'll let myself out."

"I'll see you soon."

A dark-skinned woman with hair in narrow plaits of black and white appeared in the bedroom doorway, clad in a formfitting, creaseless dress that emphasised the already generous curves of her body. She was rummaging in her bag, but still wended her way through the poorly lit living room with the casual air of someone who could probably navigate it in pitch blackness. She pressed something on the wall, and Rourke saw a door slide open, spilling warm light out across the carpet. The woman stepped through into . . . *his private elevator*, Rourke thought, remembering Ichabod's description of his meeting with Orlov.

The door slid shut. Rourke waited long enough for the hum of machinery to suggest that the elevator had descended, then got to her feet and prowled quietly towards the bedroom. She was halfway across the floor when a shifting shadow gave her a moment of warning, and she brought her gun up just as Sergei Orlov appeared in the doorway wearing nothing but a sarong.

She armed the Kobel with a buzz.

"Freeze."

THE OLD DANCE

Apirana pulled his right glove on and cinched it securely around his wrist, then repeated the action with the other hand. He wore slip-on shoes, ready to be removed when he got to the ring, a warm-up robe of plain red, and red-and-black trunks decorated with the double curl of the Tino Rangatiratanga flag. He'd had to get them custom made overnight, and Drift had protested at the cost, but Apirana had insisted. If he was going to step into a ring and fight, then he was going to do it properly.

Drift paced back and forth in front of him, nervous energy incarnate. "Remember," the Captain said, "Kuang looks to be a slow starter based on what we've seen, so your best option is probably to rush him at the bell. He's a good striker but takes a little while to settle into his rhythm; the thing is, most opponents are wary enough to give him time. His takedown defence is—"

"Bro," Apirana cut him off, getting to his feet, "we've been over this. Like, five times already. Besides, you know as well as I do that I'm gonna be outclassed in there. A game plan's all very well, but it ain't necessarily gonna survive contact with the enemy, know what I mean? I see a way to win, I'm gonna take it."

Drift stopped, a rueful grin on his face, and scratched the skin around his mechanical eye. "I know, I know. And I'd never have suggested this if I didn't think you had a chance, but—"

"But we gotta speculate to accumulate," Apirana interrupted. "How much have we got wagered on me, and what were the odds in the end?"

Drift checked his pad. "Kuai ended up putting eight grand down at twelve-to-one for a first-round finish, since . . . Well, if you're going beat him, you're probably going to do it early. So you'll nearly make the stake back just by showing up. If you win in the first round, then we've got a hundred grand to put towards what we need."

Apirana puffed his cheeks out, trying to focus his thoughts. "All right, then. Let's do this."

Drift nodded and sidled over to the locker room door, which he cracked open. A quick and muttered conversation in Russian ensued with the member of staff outside before Drift came back over and half-heartedly picked up a couple of punch mitts.

"Don't bother," Apirana told him, not unkindly. "It ain't like you know what you're doing with them anyway." He bounced on the spot, testing out his surgically repaired ankle. In all honesty, it felt no different to the one he hadn't broken a few weeks ago, and he marvelled once more at the healing technology possessed by the Universal Access Movement. "Damn, those circuitheads know their stuff."

"Just don't let Jenna hear you say that," Drift muttered, then glanced up guiltily. "Not that it's my place to . . . I mean, you know what's best, I'm sure."

"Ha!" Apirana laughed loudly and genuinely. "The whole thing's been a bit more luck than judgement on my part so far. Kinda glad she ain't here at the moment, though. I don't think either of us wants her to see me get knocked silly." He gave the air a flurry of punches, culminating in a vicious right hook that made Drift step back in mild alarm. "Wouldn't mind Rourke being about, though. Might've been able to give me a few pointers."

ANTM

"Maybe," Drift said with a nod. "But you've got to remember that Tamara's used to almost always being the smaller person in any fight. You're bigger and heavier and probably stronger than this guy, and you'll have reach on him too. What she knows might not be so relevant to you."

"Might have told me how Kuang's gonna be thinking, though," Apirana pointed out. "Ah, to hell with it." He looked up at the holo-screen on the wall, where the event's coverage was being broadcast live: This wasn't a huge, big-name show, but it was still available on the local channels, and the announcers were talking excitedly in Mandarin. At least he presumed they were excited from their tone of voice: His Mandarin was little better than the Captain's. He watched Kuang Daniu step up into the cage, jog from one side to the other, and then raise his arms and turn in a slow circle, milking the cheers of the crowd. His opponent was getting old for a fighter, although not as old as Apirana himself, but he still looked to be in good shape.

There was a knock at the locker room door and a staff member wearing a shirt with the Two Trees Arena's logo on it poked his head in. "*Shí shíhòu le.*"

"*Zǒuba,*" Apirana said, rolling his neck and shoulders. He made for the door, Drift falling in behind him, then followed the staffer's lead down a corridor towards the main arena. Apirana was almost surprised about how calm he felt, but then again, he'd been in far more dangerous situations than this over most of his life. It was only a month or so ago that he'd been dodging bullets in a revolution; a fight with rules and a doctor at ringside was practically child's play in comparison.

Of course, he reassessed that a little when he stepped out into the arena, under the lights and the gazes of thirty thousand people, and was greeted with a wall of boos.

"Think they've got a favourite?" he asked the Captain, raising his voice to make himself heard.

"They certainly seem a bit partisan!" Drift shouted back, looking around them. "Why, are you having second thoughts about knocking out the local hero?"

"You know me!" Apirana replied, focusing on the cage ahead of him. "I ain't never let someone's opinion stop me from doin' something stupid!"

He walked through the gangway, flanked by arena security and ignoring the extended hands of punters who wanted to catch hold of any fighter passing by, no matter how unheard-of or unpopular. He walked up to the checkpoint, discarded his robe, kicked off his shoes, and let the ringside referee check his mouthpiece and pat down his gloves and trunks to make sure he wasn't concealing any weapons. He turned towards the cage, taking deep breaths to psyche himself up, and looked up to see what awaited him.

Kuang Daniu was standing in the middle of the cage waiting for him, pointing downwards and shouting. The words were in Mandarin, but the meaning was fairly clear: *This is my house.* It was a blatant challenge. And, it occurred to Apirana, he knew just how to respond to a challenge.

It had been a long, long time since he'd performed "Ka Mate," but some things you learned in school stuck in your head.

He adopted a half-crouch, his forearms held horizontal in front of him. He doubted he'd be given the time to perform the full routine, and he didn't have a leader for the chant anyway, so he launched into the main refrain with all the volume his lungs could muster.

"Ka mate, ka mate! Ka ora, ka ora!"

The expression on Kuang Daniu's face as Apirana began the best-known Māori haka was priceless. Even if the other man knocked him out straight after the bell, Apirana would treasure that look of shock and apprehension for a long time.

He punched the air in front of him, bellowing in the tongue of his homeland while he did so, then tried not to grin as he realised how appropriate the chant's finale was. It referenced taking a step upwards, and then another step upwards, an account of an ancient Māori war chief climbing a ladder . . . and there just so happened to be four steps in front of him up to the cage.

"Ā, upane! Ka upane! Ā, upane! Ka upane!"

He stamped up the steps, slapping his elbows with his hands as he did so, then stepped forwards into the ring and fixed Kuang with the widest-eyed, most intimidating stare he could manage.

"WHITI TE RA!"

He stuck his tongue out for emphasis as he finished, and half a second later the crowd erupted into applause and cheers. Partisan locals they might be, but they seemed to appreciate a performance when they saw one. Apirana held his pose for a moment longer, then straightened up and allowed himself to be directed to his designated corner by a rather nervous-looking official. He took deep breaths again, trying to get his breathing and pulse under control. That was the first time he'd performed a haka in earnest, and it certainly got the blood pumping.

The ring announcer began to speak, his voice echoing around the arena and prompting a new wave of cheers from the fans. Apirana couldn't follow it, especially with the echoes, but picked up his cue as the announcer pointed towards him and raised his arms as a thoroughly mangled version of his name boomed out through Two Trees. There was some polite applause, a few cheers, and quite a few more boos.

Well. I've made an impression, if nothing else.

Now the announcer turned towards Kuang, who seemed to have recovered his composure slightly and was bouncing lightly from one foot to the other, shaking his arms out as he did so. Apirana, Drift, and Muradov had gone over all the footage they could find of the man in action and had concluded that he was a fast and efficient striker who preferred punches to kicks and was better on his feet than on the ground, but was quite good at keeping a fight standing. One thing that had stood out to Apirana, apart from his opponent's tendency to start fights slowly, was that, although Kuang was an accurate and technical striker, he didn't seem to have an awful lot of stopping power to him. He would wear opponents down over the course of a fight, and the other guy would come out looking a mess. But he didn't have many one-hit knockouts to his name.

Basically, if Apirana was willing to take some hits on the way in, he was halfway sure he could land something that would give Kuang Daniu pause without being immediately knocked into next week himself.

The ring announcer reached a crescendo, screaming out Kuang's name. He had to strain himself to be heard above the roar of the crowd, which had ceased to be mere noise and, at least from where Apirana stood in the epicentre of it, was approaching something more like a physical force. Kuang raised one hand in lazy acknowledgement, but his eyes were fixed on Apirana. The local fighter was a couple of inches shorter, but broad and well-muscled. He also didn't have much of the spare weight that Apirana was carrying around his middle. In terms of sheer athleticism, Apirana was prepared to admit that there didn't look to be much of a contest between the two of them. Or in ring experience, come to that. Although in actual *fighting* experience . . .

The ring announcer cleared out, leaving only Apirana, Kuang, and the referee. The official looked at Apirana to check his readiness. Apirana nodded. The ref looked over at Kuang. Kuang nodded too.

The referee shouted something that Apirana could barely hear thanks to the crowd noise, but the chopping motion he made with his hand could only be interpreted in one way. It was time.

Apirana sprang forward, feeling the cage floor ever so slightly sticky under his feet, the accretion of sweat from the fights that had already taken place earlier in the evening. The roar of the crowd had faded to a dull ebb in his ears, as though he'd been submerged in water. His long fighting experience instinctively focused him on Kuang's eyes as he rushed in, looking for the telltale signs that would indicate how his opponent was going to react, and he saw the other man's calm mask drop away to be replaced by the same fear he'd shown in the face of the haka.

Apirana stutter-stepped, checking his rush for the merest moment to see if Kuang would telegraph a dodge, but the other fighter seemed shell-shocked and had barely left his starting point against the far fence. Kuang threw a desperate, looping punch that grazed the air in front of Apirana's face as he misjudged Apirana's momentum, and then Apirana barrelled into him with a thunderous running kneelift to the ribcage.

It felt like he'd hit a giant sandbag, but Kuang staggered back against the wire mesh that formed the cage wall, his face screwed up in pain. Apirana stormed in after him and aimed a haymaker at Kuang's nose, but his fist only hit the fence as Kuang ducked aside. The crowd noise had gone up, if anything, penetrating through even the thumping blood in his ears as he turned on the spot, trying to get a bead on his opponent. Kuang came in low and hit him just above the waist with his shoulder, looking to take the fight to the ground: a desperation move against a man of Apirana's size. Apirana simply took a step back, then wrapped his arms around and under Kuang's chest and heaved. The other fighter's feet left the floor for a moment as Apirana threw him bodily aside with a roar, and Kuang landed hard on his hands and knees.

Apirana landed on top of him even harder.

Kuang twisted under him as he came down, trying to get onto his back where he could at least mount some form of defence, and managed to get both his arms up to block Apirana's forearm as it came down in a blow that would have surely broken the other man's nose had it connected. Kuang bucked with his hips, trying to throw Apirana off, but he couldn't generate enough power to move that much weight. Apirana steadied himself, half-straddling Kuang's body, then slammed his knee into the other man's ribcage. Did he feel something crack? He wasn't sure, but Kuang cried out in pain anyway. Apirana hammered at him with an elbow again, more effective at this range, and it smashed through Kuang's guard and into his temple. The back of the other fighter's head bounced off the canvas, and a line of blood appeared where the point of Apirana's elbow had cut him.

Kuang had never mentally started this fight, Apirana realised, as his ferocious focus began to loosen slightly; the other man had been rocked early and was simply in survival mode now. Apirana could either keep beating on him until the referee made the call to stop the fight, which would be a brave call this early in front of a crowd this partisan, or Apirana could try to find a way to win without battering Kuang to a pulp.

He wasn't just about raw power; he'd sparred and grappled with Rourke over the years they'd spent together, and he'd picked things up. He already had one leg across Kuang's chest, so he delivered one more shot with his elbow to make sure the other man didn't get any big ideas, then grabbed Kuang's right wrist as the local fighter tried to defend himself. From there it was the work of a moment to throw his other leg across Kuang's chest as well, straighten his battered opponent's arm out, and lean backwards, looking up at the arena lights.

It was an armbar, and when administered by someone who knew what they were doing, it was excruciatingly painful and could hyperextend the elbow. When it came from someone with real strength, it could break bones.

Apirana was both.

Apirana felt his opponent's body judder as Kuang tried to reach over and clasp his trapped wrist with his other hand, but Apirana had both strength and leverage on his side. He forced his own body flatter, increasing the torque on Kuang's arm and preventing him from doing anything except flailing ineffectually at Apirana's knees.

A moment later the referee appeared in Apirana's vision and waved his arms frantically. The fight was over. Kuang Daniu had submitted.

Apirana released his grip instantly and rolled up to his feet. He felt caught halfway between wanting to roar and beat his chest and wanting to laugh; the adrenaline still pumping through his veins was warring with the incandescent joy of victory, of the knowledge that he'd just won them a sizeable stack of cash to help with paying off Orlov . . . and that he'd stopped when he was supposed to. Apirana knew better than anyone that he could only bury his temper so deep, and he'd had uncomfortable visions of himself losing control in the cage. He'd never have agreed to Drift's scheme if he hadn't thought he could hold it together, but that didn't mean it hadn't played on his mind.

He became properly aware of the noise around him. The crowd was a baying animal with thirty thousand throats. The ring announcer could barely make himself heard above them, veins standing out on the side of his neck as he gave it his best effort anyway. Kuang's trainers burst into the cage the moment the door was opened, running to their fallen fighter who had rolled onto his side, clutching his arm. Drift followed more sedately, stepping respectfully around Kuang's team as he made his way across the ring, then breaking into a wide grin and clasping Apirana into a hug as he reached him.

"Knew you could do it, big man!" the Captain said with a laugh, then drew back and winked his natural eye. "Did you have to take so long about it, though?"

"Fuck you, bro," Apirana replied with a chuckle. "You think you can do better, you're welcome to get in here next time."

"Oh, *hell* no," Drift protested, making a face of mock fear. "I know my strengths, and this isn't one of them." He clapped Apirana on the shoulder as the referee came over, ready to raise A's hand and make the victory official. "You've done us proud. Let's collect your pay and get the hell out of this circus."

REPEAT PERFORMANCE

Drift felt like he was walking on proverbial sunshine as he led Apirana back to the locker rooms, despite the cacophonous boos that were still raining down from the rafters in the arena behind them. Let the locals vent their spleens! Apirana had walked into Kuang Daniu's backyard and had essentially beaten him up and taken his lunch money; it was understandable if the man's fans were a bit pissy at exactly how quickly it had been done.

"You know, I think I might have missed my calling in life," he declared expansively, pushing open the door to the room where Apirana had been getting changed such a short time ago. "Maybe I should take up managing fighters as a career."

Apirana barked a laugh. "Takin' the easy option again, I see."

"Oh, you say that," Drift smirked, "but who came up with the plan? Who managed to talk a no-name, no-record man into a bout with a local superstar? Who put down the funds for the gambling win that means we're about one-fifth towards the total we need?" He adopted an expression of false modesty and placed on hand across his chest. "I must take credit where credit is due."

"Yeah, and who actually got in the cage and beat the other guy up?" Apirana pointed out with a chuckle, pulling a towel out of his bag. "I can't

133

help but think you're missing something here, Mr. Big Picture."

Drift flapped a hand. "Pfft. Details, details. Your contribution was important, yes—"

"Important? Bloody vital, bro!"

"—but we shouldn't look past the sheer marketing genius at work here," Drift finished grandly as Apirana turned to head for the shower. He was about to continue in a slightly more serious vein when the locker rooms door slammed open to admit Serenity Chen.

And behind zir, four particularly burly men in arena security uniforms.

Drift's cheerful greeting died in his throat. The events manager's face was thunderous, and he wasn't particularly enamoured of the way the last member of security closed the door very firmly behind him and leaned against it with his arms folded.

"Mer Chen," Drift said cautiously, with a respectful nod. "Is there a problem?"

"There most certainly is," Chen said, crossing the room to glower into Drift's face. Apirana had turned away from the shower but still held the towel in his hand: ready to throw into someone's face as a distraction if a fight started, if Drift was any judge. He splayed the fingers of his right hand, hoping the big man caught the signal. *Wait.*

"I'm sorry to hear that," Drift told the events manager. "What's the issue?"

"The issue, Mr. Pérez, is that you hustled us," Chen said tightly. "You claimed your fighter was big and tough and had a mean right hook, as I recall. You didn't say anything about him being a damned berserker!"

"Bro, that weren't berserk," Apirana rumbled. "You ain't seen berserk."

Drift shot him a glare. *Not helping.* "Mer Chen, surely you can see that it wasn't in my interests to *undersell* my fighter's capabilities? Apirana's never been in a sanctioned bout before, so I gave you what I thought was a reasonable assessment of his skills. I had no idea he'd prove to be this effective." He paused for a second. "If I had, I might have tried to get a higher price out of you."

"What's the problem, anyway?" Apirana put in. "The locals ain't happy, right enough, but Kuang took the fight and lost."

Chen turned zir glare on the big Māori. "Mr. Kuang was *supposed* to lose by knockout," the events manager said acidly, "but it seems that you rushing him out of the gate shook him so badly he forgot the plan."

Everything went silent for a moment. Drift exchanged glances with Apirana and saw the big man's eyes were as troubled as he felt.

"You're telling us," he said slowly, "that the fight was *fixed?*"

"It was *supposed* to be fixed!" Chen snapped. "Your big, dumb, inexperienced man was supposed to take big swings, 'get lucky' with one, and put Kuang down, not slam him to the floor and nearly take his arm off!" Ze took a deep breath, clearly trying to compose zirself. "I will ask you a direct question, Mr. Pérez: Do you have any idea whom I represent?"

"Apart from the Two Trees Arena?" Drift asked, praying that Apirana wasn't going to rise to "dumb."

"Apart from the Two Trees Arena."

Drift glanced over at Apirana again and was relieved to see that the big man didn't seem to be on the verge of violence. He looked back at Chen. "I've got a pretty good idea, yeah."

"Then I hope you understand just what a precarious situation you are now in," Chen said coldly. "We do not like having our plans derailed. We had a large amount of money riding on the correct result of that fight."

"Oh, come on!" Drift protested. "If you'd let us in on the plan—"

"We didn't know you," Chen cut him off. "Unfortunately for you, now we do." Ze turned away from Drift and walked towards Apirana, two of the security dropping in to flank zir as ze did so. "Mr. Wahawaha. You are unhurt?"

"He barely touched me," Apirana replied warily, eyeing the two security guards. Drift would have put money on Big A being able to take them both to the cleaners if necessary, although perhaps putting money on fights wasn't a good idea right now, even hypothetically.

"Then you'll be fine to fight again a week from today, when there's another event in town," Chen said briskly. "We'll make space on the card and find an opponent. You'll accept. We'll see whether the betting lines consider you the heir to Kuang's throne or a lucky upstart who got a fluke win, and then we'll place a bet accordingly. And then you'll win or lose, accordingly." Ze paused for a second. "Do I make myself clear?"

"Crystal," Apirana said. There was a growl in his voice, but the big man didn't start throwing fists, and that was about as much as Drift could hope for at the moment.

"Good." Chen turned away from him and began to head for the door, then paused and looked over at Drift. "One more thing, Mr. Pérez. I understand that you and Mr. Wahawaha have a shuttle in dock, the *Jonah*? Please don't try to leave before next seventhday. We have low tolerance for people who interfere with our business through ignorance; we have none for people who interfere with them deliberately."

Drift swallowed. "What about Apirana's pay for tonight? We have to eat, you know."

Chen just snorted. "Don't push your luck. If you perform as required next seventhday, you'll receive the agreed fee for each appearance. If you don't . . ." Ze shrugged. "You won't really be in a position to have much use for money anyway."

The heavy leaning against the door pulled it open, and the events manager disappeared through it with zir escort. Drift waited for it to click shut again before he turned and booted the lockers behind him.

"*Me cago en la puta!*" That didn't seem enough, so he punched them as well. "Stupid! Fucking! Gah!"

"Easy, bro," Apirana said from behind him, although he sounded understandably tense as well. "I ain't relishin' this, but we just gotta go through this pantomime once more. And this time I'll know the script. It'll be okay."

Drift turned to him, trying to keep his voice level in spite of the churning in his gut. "Oh, it is not okay, A. It is a long, *long* way from okay."

GAINFUL EMPLOYMENT

Sergei Orlov stiffened, eyes widening in shock that quickly became horrified recognition. Powerful crime lord or not, he had to know things were bad when he was being held at gunpoint by a woman he'd threatened with death a couple of days beforehand.

"Please don't make any loud noises or sudden movements," Rourke continued softly. "Perhaps you'd like to sit down on your bed?" She dipped the nose of the gun a fraction to indicate that he should move backwards. Orlov obeyed, shuffling across the thick carpet and then sinking slowly onto the mattress.

"How did you escape?" he asked, licking his lips nervously.

Rourke raised an eyebrow. "Why don't you know?"

Orlov's expression of horror faded into one of confusion. "What?"

"Why don't you know?" Rourke repeated. "Why don't you know how I escaped? Judging by your shock, I'm going to take a guess that you didn't even know I *had* escaped. I was in a hotel that I presume you own, guarded around the clock by three of your men, but I've just walked into your home and listened to you having sex before you even knew there was a problem. Who were my guards?"

Sergei Orlov was looking more and more shell-shocked. "What?"

"My guards, the men you sent with me. Who were they?"

Orlov blinked a few times, apparently trying to rally his thoughts. "I . . . I don't . . ."

"There were three of them," Rourke supplied levelly. "Out of those three, Leon is probably the best foot soldier for your operation in terms of temperament, but he's drinking too much. I could smell it on him. It leaves him tired and hungover, and that makes him sloppy and disinclined to listen to his colleagues."

"His . . . his mother died recently," Orlov offered, frowning at her.

"That would explain a couple of things," Rourke replied, nodding. "Now, Andrei's cautious, but only where obvious threats are concerned. He doesn't think wider, and he can get complacent. He's too easily swayed by other people, too. Sacha, on the other hand, is just an arrogant, overconfident bully. You need bullies, but you don't need ones who get their asses handed to them by the person they're supposed to be holding prisoner."

Orlov's expression of confusion hadn't really shifted. "Why are you telling me these things, if you intend to kill me?"

Rourke took a deep breath. Drift had always been the gambler of the two of them, but desperate times called for desperate measures.

She lowered the gun. "I don't intend to kill you, Mr. Orlov. I've come to ask for a job."

There was a moment of stunned silence while, Rourke was certain, the crime boss double-checked his own translation of her words.

"You want a *job*?" Sergei Orlov finally asked in disbelief, once he was certain his ears weren't deceiving him.

"Yeah," Rourke told him, trying to maintain her relaxed demeanour. Incapacitating guards, stealing aircars, even breaking into a gangster's home: These were all variations on things she'd done many times before and had been trained to do. This part, however, was out of her comfort zone and much more Drift's speciality. It was why she'd joined up with him, after all.

"And why should I give you a job?" Orlov demanded. Some of his usual manner was coming back to him now, as though she wasn't still holding a gun.

"Why? Because I'm very, very good," Rourke said. "*But* I'm not unique. Anything I can do can be replicated by someone else, and I just broke into your home. Your operation clearly isn't up to scratch. I can help you with that."

Orlov frowned at her. She could see anger in his eyes at her temerity, but she could also see the cold calculation that had brought him to the top of the pile. He was smart enough to realise that she was telling the truth, and in sufficient control of his emotions to let rationality win out.

"But you work for Captain Drift," he pointed out.

Rourke grimaced. "Ichabod is a good man . . . mostly . . . and I have complete faith that he's going to do everything he can to honour his side of the deal with you. But I don't have complete faith that he'll succeed. And if that happens, if he doesn't come back, I don't intend to be killed slowly as an object lesson." She shrugged. "I decided I'd rather prove that I was more valuable alive and working for you."

The crime boss stroked one stubbled cheek with his thumb. "I do not negotiate with terrorists. Give me the gun, and I will—"

Rourke tossed the Kobel onto the bed beside him before he'd finished speaking. He glanced down at it in obvious surprise, then back up at her.

She folded her arms, trying to ignore the hammering of her heart. "People will promise anything at gunpoint."

He picked the gun up, ejected the magazine to check that it was loaded, and raised his eyebrows when he saw that it was. "That was very trusting of you."

"I'm confident you'll want to listen to what I have to say," Rourke told him. *Also, you're less than two metres away from me,* she added in the privacy of her own head, *and I could get my hands on you before you'd finished taking aim.*

Orlov replaced the magazine, but put the gun down on the bed beside him again. "Did you kill any of my men in your escape?"

"No," Rourke replied. "Dealing with their failures is your prerogative. Although I'll grant you that Sacha's probably not as good-looking as he was."

"He will look worse," Orlov said grimly. "And why did you decide to call on me here?"

"Your home is where you feel safest, so ironically that's the easiest place to get to you," Rourke said. "Also, I wanted to reach you before news of my escape did and you sent out a kill order for Drift and the others. And finally, if I spoke to you alone, I didn't risk embarrassing you in front of anyone else." She shrugged again. "I figured that might make you slightly more amenable to my offer."

"Very sensible," Orlov conceded, "although I do not consider myself to be a slave to pride." He looked up at her, his dark eyes weighing her. Rourke held still under his scrutiny and stared back: She wasn't going to pretend to be meek and subservient, because she knew her acting talents didn't stretch that far. The bastard could accept her as she was, just as Drift had done, or not at all.

"You have already shown great resourcefulness, and I can see that someone such as yourself could be of great benefit to me," Orlov said finally. "I also acknowledge that had you intended me harm, you could have achieved it. So I will take your intentions to be genuine."

"So we have a deal?" Rourke asked cautiously.

"I am a businessman," Orlov said. "It would be a foolish businessman who turned down a better deal for all parties when it presents itself. Here will be the new terms, Ms. Rourke: If your companions return to me by the agreed date with half a million stars, you may stay or go as you please. If they do not, but you have proved to me before that time that you will be of sufficient benefit to my organisation, you will enter my employment unharmed, and I will also not pursue Captain Drift and the crew of the *Keiko* . . . although I will still make public how they left you to your fate, not knowing what that would be. They would deserve it, I feel."

Rourke nodded, her throat tight. "And if they don't return with half a million stars and I do not prove that I will be of sufficient benefit?"

Orlov grimaced. "Then I would have to follow through with the initial terms. Although in recognition of the service you have already done me by highlighting the weaknesses in my organisation, I will at least guarantee that your death will be swift and painless."

She smiled tightly, despite his matter-of-fact discussion of her possible murder. "Better than waiting in a room to find out whether Ichabod's going to be able to save me. I never was good at being a damsel in distress. So when do I start?"

"Tomorrow morning," Orlov told her, picking up the Kobel again and getting to his feet. "Come. I think we can arrange a better class of accommodation now." He walked the two steps to the head of his bed, reached under the lip of his bedside table and pressed something, then brushed past her and strode out into the living room. His manner was once more that of the lion in his den and not just because he had the gun now, Rourke realised. He had been confirmed by her words and actions to have the power. If she wanted to keep her crew safe, she needed to win his approval.

She fell in behind him, suppressing another smile. To prove her worth, she would have to point out as many flaws as she could in what he already had in place. *Buckle up, gangsters of New Samara. The next few weeks are going to be* very *unpleasant for you.*

Orlov looked over his shoulder at her as he stopped a few metres from the door of his elevator. "You may wish to stand a little farther back."

"Sure." She backed off three steps, guessing what was coming.

The elevator's arrival was heralded by the same faint hum that she'd heard when Galina departed, only growing louder instead of fading away. The door slid open, spilling the same light across the carpet as before. On this occasion, however, it also disgorged the four armed security guards who had been summoned by the emergency alarm Orlov had just pressed.

They raised their guns to cover Orlov as the closest threat, recognised him after a split second, and hurriedly diverted their weapons away, then registered Rourke's presence and began to shift their aims once more. . . .

"*Wait!*" Orlov snapped in Russian. The guards stopped, but their eyes remained fixed on Rourke. She met the gaze of each of them in turn. *Get used to the sight, boys,* she told them silently, *you'll be seeing more of me soon.*

"*Ms. Rourke here has managed to find a way out of her captivity and into my home,*" Orlov said. His voice was level, but Rourke could hear the undercurrent of anger in it. He showed them the Kobel. "*She could have shot me dead and none of you would have been able to do a damned thing about it, but she chose not to.*"

The guards were lowering their guns now, and a couple of them were exchanging uncertain glances with each other.

"*You,*" Orlov said, pointing at one. "*You're in my garden until the morning. You*"—he pointed at another—"*find Ms. Rourke a room in the Grand House's hotel. You don't need to place a guard on her. And you two,*" he finished, "*find out what the hell went on at the Silver Star earlier this evening, and get Sacha, Andrei, and Leon rounded up. Take whoever you need and don't bother being gentle. If those three aren't where I can lay hands on them by the time I wake up tomorrow, you can kiss your jobs good-bye.*"

"*Can I get some clothing that is the right size, too?*" Rourke called. "*Even my old bodysuit would do, if I can wash it.*"

Orlov looked around at her and snorted in wry amusement. "*But of course, you can speak Russian.*"

Rourke shrugged. *"I would not be much use to you otherwise, would I?"*

"And you choose to let me know this now . . . why?"

"So you know what I do and do not understand, and can decide what to say around me accordingly," she said simply, walking forward. *"An employee should be honest about these things, surely?"*

Orlov nodded approvingly. *"As you say. In the morning then, Ms. Rourke."*

"In the morning," she replied. She walked through the guards and into the elevator, which galvanised them into action: Three of them got in with her, sealing off the doors and sending it humming smoothly downwards, while the other remained behind to guard Sergei Orlov's garden.

She'd started the evening with no shoes in a second-string hotel, under armed guard, and with the very real threat of a gruesome death in a couple of months. It wasn't even midnight on New Samara's twenty-six-hour clock yet, and she was going to be sleeping the rest of the night in the most luxurious hotel on the planet, with shoes, and with no armed guard outside her door: She was prepared to chalk that up as a win. Tomorrow, she'd set about taking her fate into her own hands. Granted, that would involve helping someone who was by any reasonable definition a bad man, or at the very least thoroughly amoral.

Then again, it wouldn't be the first time.

LAUNDRY RUN

Kuai blinked, barely able to comprehend what the Captain was telling them. "*So the Triax knows this is our shuttle?*" he asked in English.

The crew of the *Jonah* were sitting in the galley again, as was standard for their meetings. Apirana was sunk in his armchair, as usual, and Jenna was perched on the arm of it, as had also become usual. Muradov was staring into his coffee at the table, Kuai was sitting far enough away from his sister that she couldn't kick him, and the Captain . . . well, he was pacing up and down with a grim expression on his face.

"*They know that it's my shuttle, or mine and A's,*" the Captain said, "*They might not have been paying attention to the rest of you, or just think you're crew. But we've got a bigger problem than that.*"

"*The timing,*" Muradov spoke up, without raising his gaze.

"*Precisely,*" Drift said, snapping his fingers and pointing at the Uragan. "*The big payoff to Chief Han is supposed to take place next seventhday, and you can pretty much guarantee that she's going to be gambling her way into money at about the same time that A and I are supposed to be at the Two Trees Arena doing a little dance for the Triax.*" He threw his hands up in frustration. "*So first of all, that means that the rest of you are going to need to get the money without us. Secondly, it means we're going to have to*

145

be even more careful about everything, because there's no way to be sure of when we're all going to be able to take off."

"Perhaps we need to prioritise," Muradov said. "If we manage to secure the funds but there is a risk of us being apprehended, should we not leave the planet? You and Apirana could follow us on commercial shipping and meet us at a prearranged rendezvous."

There was a moment of silence while everyone, Drift included, looked at the former security chief. Kuai had to admit, the suggestion made a certain kind of sense: Supposing the rest of them had managed to pull off the job and get the money—and exactly how they'd do that he'd no idea, especially without Drift and Apirana—he didn't want to be sitting around in the spaceport waiting for the security forces to show up and arrest them. The trouble was, Muradov was still a relatively unknown quantity, and neither Kuai, Jia, nor Jenna were exactly fighters. If the Chief decided he wanted to commandeer the *Jonah* and the *Keiko*, along with the half a million stars they were hoping to have raised, Kuai wasn't sure they'd be up to stopping him. Of course, there was no saying that Muradov would be able to pilot either ship, but there was also nothing to say he couldn't. The crew knew he'd been a security chief on Uragan and a sniper in the Red Star armed forces, and that was about it.

Besides, from what Kuai understood, interstellar travel was actually relatively simple since it just involved programming the navigation console. You needed a bit of training to do that, certainly, but it only required some study. Jia's unusual level of talent lay in manual atmospheric shuttle flying, both in terms of delicate close manoeuvring and the sort of breakneck, hair-raising, and often downright illegal stunts she had to pull to get them into places unnoticed, and out of them fast and in one piece. If Muradov waited until they'd docked with the *Keiko*, and knew how to program the nav console to get to a void station or waystation somewhere that had an assisted docking system, then he'd never have to take the *Jonah* down into atmosphere. . . .

"Fine," Drift said with a grimace, breaking the silence. "*I don't like it, but it might be the only option. We're going to be cutting it fine to get the money back to Orlov anyway, since we have to wait until next seventhday before we can make the score. It could be that you just have to head for New Samara and meet up with A and me once Rourke's back with you.*" He scratched at the skin around his mechanical eye for a second. "*Jenna, you're in charge of making that call.*"

"I . . . What?" Jenna looked stunned, which Kuai couldn't blame her for. "Why me?"

"*Because I know how badly you want to get Rourke back, but since I don't imagine you want to leave A behind, I think you should be able to take a balanced view of things,*" the Captain answered with a shrug. "*Besides, the Chief is new, Kuai's a coward, and Jia's insane.*"

"Hey!" Kuai shouted, getting to his feet and glaring angrily at Drift. "I am not a coward!" How dare he? Kuai wasn't a good fighter, and he wasn't a good shot: He recognised that and didn't try to get involved when there was violence in the offing, but that was just good sense. Just because he did most of his work in the engine room didn't mean he was a coward!

"You're not?" Drift asked, looking skeptical.

"Damn right I'm not!" Kuai snapped. "*You want to think what would have happened to me if that damned superheavyweight fighter had found out I was trying to dope him? He'd have pounded me!*"

"I thought he pounded you anyway," Jia laughed in Mandarin.

"Envy is a terrible thing," Kuai said, leering at her. "Also, shut up. Also, you're insane!"

"Who the fuck are you calling insane, you damned asshole?" his sister demanded, getting to her feet in turn.

"He called you insane!" Kuai shouted in frustration, pointing at Drift.

"He did? Huh. I wasn't listening." Jia turned a suspicious glare on the Captain and switched to English. *"Hey, idiot, I'm not insane!"*

Drift had been watching their exchange in apparent bewilderment, and now sighed. *"You're not insane?"*

"No!"

The Captain looked at Kuai. *"And you're not a coward?"*

"No!" Kuai snapped. Drift smiled in response, and suddenly, Kuai got the nasty feeling that he'd been suckered into a trap.

"Good," the Captain said, *"because in that case I've got a very important job for both of you. The sort of job I couldn't give to anyone who was insane or a coward. . . ."*

And that was how Kuai found himself sauntering into Northside Laundry as though he owned it, with his sister trailing behind him doing her best impression of a Triax enforcer. Guangming Alpha had dipped below the horizon a couple of hours ago. That hadn't had much effect on the businesses in Zhuchengshi, but the streets outside were at least a bit darker than they were in daytime despite the presence of artificial lighting and Guangming Beta in the sky. Kuai took what comfort he could from that, since if they ended up having to run for it, there might at least be a few more shadows to hide in.

Northside Laundry had some public-use machines that were churning around, providing a useful amount of covering noise, but so far as the *Jonah*'s crew knew, the contract work—such as security uniforms that might need an additional packet in the pocket—was done in the back. The shop was empty when the Changs entered, barring a bored-looking male youth in his late teens behind the counter wearing a much-washed and slightly faded uniform, and an old woman near the door who appeared to be defying the background noise by sleeping in her chair.

"Good evening," the kid said, barely glancing up from whatever he was scrolling through on his pad as Kuai approached. "Can I help you?"

Kuai leaned in close, a little closer than was really necessary for him to be heard clearly. The kid took notice of this and automatically moved his head back a little. Kuai saw his eyes flicker slightly to the side where, judging by the chomping sounds, Jia was aggressively chewing her gum.

"Question for you, friend," Kuai said in a low voice. "You know who Gao Dongfeng is?"

The kid's face froze. "Uh, yeah?"

Thank the heavens for that. "You ever met him?" Kuai continued. He'd never really done this before, and he'd been desperately trying to work out how to go about it. He didn't have the physical presence of Apirana or the freewheeling charm of the Captain, so in desperation he'd plumped for trying to imitate Rourke's ice-cold demeanour. *If getting her back means I don't have to do this again, that's worth half a million.*

"Uh, no?" the kid said, his eyes widening slightly in apparent alarm.

Kuai moved his lips in a way that he hoped looked like the sort of smile Rourke gave when something wasn't particularly funny. "Do you want to keep it that way?"

The kid's mouth opened to frame another "uh," but then he stopped without making a noise as his eyes were drawn sideways. Kuai frowned and followed his gaze to see that Jia had pulled out what looked to be a switchblade and was casually cleaning under her nails with it.

"Will you put that away?!" Kuai hissed desperately, and entirely genuinely, he cast a glance towards the shopfront. There didn't seem to be anyone walking past, but that could change at any moment, and there was also the sleeping beauty by the door to worry about. The blade might be hidden from the street by Jia's body, but what the hell was his sister thinking?

"You wanted to try talking." Jia shrugged without looking up. "So talk to him."

Kuai glared at her, trying to get across without words exactly how aggravating her impromptu and undiscussed method acting was, then turned back to the counter. If the kid had any sense, he'd have probably bolted, but he seemed to have been rooted to the spot by the joint threats of Gao Dongfeng's name and Jia's blade-based antics.

"Look, this doesn't need to go badly for you," Kuai said, trying to sound as earnest as possible. He dug into his pocket, and as smoothly as he could, brought a roll of notes into view. It was one thousand stars, ten bills of one hundred each, and the kid's eyes locked on to it like the Captain seeing a bottle of whiskey. "We just need a favour from you."

"What sort of favour?" the kid said immediately, apparently transfixed. *It seemed that night-shift workers in a laundry didn't get paid well. Who'd have thought it?*

Here goes nothing. "The sort of favour," Kuai said, dropping his voice even lower, just in case the woman by the door had woken up and had some sort of supernatural hearing capability, "where a couple of security uniforms go missing."

"Go missing . . . in what way?" the kid asked, tearing his eyes from the money for a moment to look up at Kuai's face.

Kuai shrugged. "Don't know, don't care. Maybe a machine shreds them. Maybe they get bleached to fuck. Maybe they just simply go missing. But you tell your boss some story about why there're two less uniforms than there should be, and what *actually* happens is they come to me."

The kid cast a fearful glance at the door behind him that must have led to the back rooms where the rest of the staff would be. "I dunno, man. That's kind of big."

Kuai snorted. "These cops—they've each got however many uniforms so they can wear a clean one every day. So the laundry messes one up; what's the big deal? It's going to happen sometimes. All I need is two: One to fit my sister, and one to fit me. More or less: I don't need exact measurements." He'd already decided not to pretend that he and Jia weren't related, since apparently, it was pretty obvious from their faces. He couldn't see it himself.

"Mr. Song'll take it out of my pay," the kid whined. Kuai knew he was angling for more money, and was sorely tempted to reach over the counter and slap the kid around the face. But that wouldn't help them. Instead, he pulled the roll of notes back into his fist.

"Listen, friend, I'm trying to make this easy for everyone," he said sternly. "You know who runs this place, right? Really runs it? And don't give me any of this 'Mr. Song' crap."

"Yeah, I know," the kid muttered, looking down.

"So ask yourself, why aren't I talking to Mr. Song about this?" Kuai said, then continued before the kid could get a word in. "I'll tell you why: He's unreliable. He talks too much. And he's *greedy*."

The kid looked up at the emphasis on that last word, and Kuai was pretty sure the message hadn't been lost on him.

"So here's what I'll offer you," Kuai said, pulling two more rolls of notes out of his pocket. He set them down one at a time on the counter, along with the original, trying to look casual but feeling like a vein was about to burst in his forehead, because if one of the other staff came out of the back now, then this was all going to go to hell. "This is for doing me the favour. This is to cover what'll get taken out of your pay. And this is to make sure that you don't tell anyone what actually happened to those uniforms," Kuai said, pointing to each in turn. "Are we clear?"

The kid looked at the three thousand stars in used notes laid out on the counter, his expression an agony of indecision.

"And don't you go bragging about this," Kuai added, as though it was already a done deal. "Anyone who needs to know how you helped us will know. If it turns out you suffer from a loose tongue, you'll get to find out exactly how quietly my sister can sneak up behind people."

The kid swallowed, swiped the notes off the counter, and crammed them into his pocket, stealing a glance over his shoulder at the staff door as he did so. "Okay, look, I'll take some garbage to the Dumpster out back before I finish my shift, and I'll leave the uniforms on the ground beside it, wrapped up in something. I don't know exactly when I'll be able to do it; it'll be whenever I get a chance, okay?"

Kuai nodded, trying not to collapse in relief. "Good call, friend. Don't worry; this won't be a regular thing. And we'll remember you helped us."

Beside him, Jia folded her blade closed again with what sounded like a genuine sigh of disappointment.

NEW DAWN

The knock at her room door brought Rourke awake. Old habits bred into her in the GIA and maintained during her years of life on the edge of the law with the *Keiko* meant that she rarely struggled through the haze of post-sleep confusion that snared so many people, and she immediately slipped out of the wide, too-soft bed and into the clothes she'd cast off the previous night. She cinched the pants as tightly as she could, pulled on her stolen shoes, and padded to the door. The holo-screen in the back of it activated at the touch of her fingers, shimmering into a full-length, full-width display of the corridor on the other side, as though the door itself had simply ceased to exist. However, the bellhop standing on the other side was still looking at an opaque, wood-effect surface. The Grand House disdained such archaic concepts as spyholes, and instead, every suite's door had tiny fibre-optic threads embedded in it to give the guest a clear picture of the area outside, should they need it.

She looked the bellhop up and down. There was no sign of any weapon bulges beneath his tightly buttoned uniform, and both his hands were clutching an irregularly shaped bundle in white plaswrap. She didn't really think Orlov would send someone to kill her having put her up in his best hotel for the night, but she hadn't lived this long by being overburdened with a sense of trust. Still, the bellhop seemed harmless, so she pulled the door open. *"Yes?"*

"Mr. Orlov sends his regards," the man said, proffering the bundle, *"and requests you meet him in fifteen minutes in the foyer."* His tone was neutral, but his face unmistakeably curious at what his boss could possibly want with this small North American woman in the oversized clothes.

She took the package. *"Thank you."* She shut the door on him and turned the holo-screen off. Bellhops normally wanted tipping for the slightest thing, but he'd just run a message for the hotel owner. And besides, she had no cash.

She tapped the control unit next to the bathroom door, and the external wall faded out, replaced by the majestic view across New Samara. Rassvet, a star with a slightly blue tinge, was rising, and the tall buildings of the capital city threw long shadows over the streets. Here and there between the glittering towers, she could see distant splashes of green: New Samara's almost endless crop fields, a globe-spanning patchwork of agriculture that left only the baking deserts and the howling polar regions untouched.

She tore the plaswrap open and found familiar, dark-green material beneath. It was her bodysuit, freshly laundered. She found herself surprisingly relieved that it had been kept: She had others back on the *Keiko*, of course, but right here and now, she welcomed the chance to dress in something familiar, not to mention the right size. Further investigation showed that her boots had also been returned to her, and she shucked off the maid's stolen flats gratefully.

First things first. Orlov had requested that she meet him in fifteen minutes, and only a fool would take it as an actual request. He would expect her to be on time.

She dialled a protein bar from the room's dispenser, pulled off her clothes, and headed for the shower suite.

Twelve minutes later, feeling clean and refreshed and with her hair still slightly damp, she was taking the elevator down to the main foyer along with two respectable-looking women in their midthirties. They were dressed sensibly and somewhat soberly, their clothes nothing at all like the flamboyant sartorial pieces worn to the Grand House's casino in the evenings by the well-to-do, and certainly a world apart from her utilitarian bodysuit. Rourke amused herself for a moment as they stepped out into the foyer together by imagining that they were her bodyguards.

It didn't last, of course. The couple veered to the left, towards the restaurant where the paying guests would be served freshly cooked breakfasts prepared from Samaran ingredients, instead of the prepackaged snack she'd just finished chewing. Rourke kept straight on, heading for the comfortable chairs spaced around the lobby, where she could see two figures in dark suits. One of them, his head shaved bald, casually intercepted her before she could approach too close.

She eyed him briefly. *Six feet tall, two hundred pounds, firearm under his right armpit, so almost certainly left-handed. Smart enough to keep me at enough of a distance that I can't grab his gun without warning, even though I'm supposed to be employed by his boss now. Finally, someone who knows what he's doing.*

She nodded to him, one professional acknowledging another. "You must be Roman," she said in English.

His brow furrowed. "We have not met."

"No, but Ichabod mentioned you from when you escorted him to see Mr. Orlov." She glanced over at the other guard, a stocky woman with short hair that was a fiery red and spiked outwards, as though to give her the appearance of a small explosion. *Five foot eight but probably weighs more than Roman, mostly muscle by the looks of it. Right-handed. Weightlifter's shoulders. Almost certainly strong, but the mass would probably slow her down.* "And your partner?"

"Larysa," the woman volunteered. The top of what looked like a spiderweb tattoo was just visible above her collar on the left side of her neck, and she had a curved bar through her septum.

Sergei Orlov rose into view out of a chair and turned to greet her. He was wearing a dark-green suit the same shade as the exterior of his building, and he'd shaved his chin smooth that morning. "Ms. Rourke. Thank you for being so prompt."

"Under the circumstances, sir, I think we can dispense with the 'Ms.,'" Rourke told him crisply. "My first or last name will do fine."

"Very well." Orlov straightened his cuffs and turned towards the doors that connected the hotel to the casino. "Come with me."

Rourke fell in beside and half a step behind him, leaving the other two to position themselves as they wished. Roman took up a similar position on Orlov's other side, while Larysa trailed a couple of paces behind. Orlov pushed open the heavy rosewood door that admitted them into the casino's reception area, and two liveried attendants equipped with portable scanners stepped forward automatically. They hesitated when they saw Orlov, and once they'd seen him, they ignored the two bodyguards, but their eyes lingered on Rourke.

She sighed and extended her arms. "Go ahead, knock yourselves out."

The attendants looked at Orlov, who nodded, and they quickly swept their wands over Rourke's body. They apparently didn't find anything—Rourke recognised the model as one that vibrated instead of beeped, for added discretion—and she was waved through.

"I hope you didn't mind," Orlov said, a slight smile tugging at his upper lip as they walked past the chip counters.

"It was an effective demonstration that you don't fully trust me yet," Rourke acknowledged. "And nor should you."

"So tell me," Orlov said, ignoring her statement, "what measures would you suggest I take to keep myself safe?"

"First of all," Rourke replied as an attendant opened another door for them on to the main floor of the Grand House casino, "you need to accept that there's no such thing as 'safe.'"

The Grand House wasn't deserted, even at this hour of the morning. The sort of guests who had the money to gamble here were not, by and large, the sort who needed to pay much attention to minor concerns such as night and day: They tended to have people to do that for them. It was quieter than in the evenings, however, and the nearest few tables— blackjack, by the look of it—were empty.

"Explain," Orlov said, frowning slightly as he turned to look down at her.

"To begin with, there's the universe to consider," Rourke stated simply. "Humanity has been living on this planet for, what, a couple of hundred years? Even with today's science, tectonic activity is virtually unpredictable. We have very little information about the history of New Samara: For all we know, a fault line could open up beneath our feet tomorrow, and this entire city could be swallowed before you could even reach your aircar on the roof." She shrugged. "Then there's the possibility of some sort of catastrophic solar flare from Rassvet, dumping more radiation onto us than the magnetosphere can handle. Unexpected pathogens generated by some as-yet-unknown reaction between Terran crops and bacteria and the native soils . . . The potential threats are virtually endless."

Orlov pursed his lips. "I see."

"Then there's human threats that are completely incidental to who you are," Rourke continued as they walked. "A stray bullet that was never meant for you: a low risk, I'll grant you, but still a risk. Perhaps the Free Systems commit some terrorist atrocity here, or the USNA opens hostilities in a new interstellar war by dropping a couple of nukes on one of the Red Star's main agriworlds. You'd go down as an incidental civilian casualty, but you'd be a casualty nonetheless.

"And that's without the fact that shuttles go up and down from a spaceport only a few miles from here every day. Flight and guidance systems are theoretically foolproof these days, but fools are surprisingly ingenious. And of course, maintenance of a craft still comes down to the captain. Once something goes awry, you've essentially got a few hundred tons of mass packed with high-explosive fuel in the sky over your head. If that crashes anywhere near here, you're as good as dead."

"And I could choke on my food, or the drive system of my aircar could fail catastrophically," Orlov growled. "I am aware of this."

"So what about human threats that *aren't* incidental to who you are?" Rourke asked, looking sideways at him. "I was pointing a gun at you yesterday. You could have died. The only thing that saved you was the fact that I didn't want Ichabod or myself to die as well. If I hadn't cared about my fate, or his, you'd be in a morgue."

"The fact that we are having this conversation suggests that I judged you correctly," Orlov replied, skirting a potted fern.

"Perhaps," Rourke acknowledged, "but sometimes you won't get that chance. My example of the shuttle wasn't chosen at random. If someone in control of one decides they really, really want you dead, then all they have to do is aim it here, at your home, or your business. And they'll probably get you. Your influence is far-reaching. You might not even know who they are, let alone what you've done to make them willing to sacrifice their life just to take yours. If you don't know that, you can't make that judgement."

Orlov's mouth tightened, but he said nothing.

"It doesn't have to be someone with that many resources, of course," Rourke continued. "An aircar aimed at your penthouse might get lucky. A small group of people in this casino could rush you, if they weren't too bothered about the consequences for them afterwards. I'm sure your guards are very proficient," she added, nodding at Roman and Larysa, "but even a small advantage of numbers might be able to force a brief opening. And that could be all that's needed."

Orlov snorted. "You just walked through the weapons scan, Tamara. They'll be coming at me with their bare hands. I think we could hold them off long enough for hotel security to assist." He nodded at the other men and women scattered around the room, burly and serious-looking, with commpieces in their ears.

"Perhaps. Perhaps not." Rourke stopped and turned to Roman. "Do you have a pen?"

The bald guard reached into his inside jacket pocket and produced one. Rourke had assumed that he would: He might need to take notes for his boss, some people still found it faster to use a pen than a pad, and voice notes could be distracting or corrupted by background noise.

Roman's pen was sleek and grey, and made of some metal alloy. Rourke held it between her thumb and the first two fingers of her right hand, then looked Orlov in the eye.

"I could kill you with this."

The crime boss smiled a little, as though uncertain if she was joking. "You mean if it contained some hidden blade?"

"Certainly, but in this case, just because it's a pen." She extended the nib. "It's a pointed metal object. I could stab this into your jugular or your windpipe and cause you some major problems. I might be able to get it through your pants and into your femoral artery, and then you've got about a minute and a half to live. I could go right through your eye socket with it and hit your brain: That might or might not kill you, depending, but you wouldn't enjoy it much regardless." She tapped the back of her neck. "Where your skull meets your neck, that's brainstem territory. A stab wound there might damage all sorts of vital processes."

Orlov had been looking more and more uncomfortable as her list of targets lengthened, but now his expression was bordering on the incredulous. "You are suggesting that I should ban pens from my casino?"

"I'm suggesting nothing of the sort," Rourke told him, handing the pen back to Roman. "I'm just pointing out that there are an awful lot of ways you can die. Humans surround themselves with the methods to kill other humans all the time, but a combination of evolution and social conditioning means that we rarely even think about it, let alone act on it. What that means is that when someone deranged or determined enough *does* recognise those possibilities . . ." She shrugged. "Well, then bad things happen. So if you want to make yourself safer, you need to think about which possibilities you want to spend the most resources guarding against."

Orlov studied her, his dark eyes unreadable. Then he inhaled, nostrils flaring slightly. "I believe you may be correct. Do you have any suggestions?"

Rourke deliberately suppressed a small smile. She might not be able to charm her way into someone's good graces like Ichabod could, but when it came down to logic and facts, she was on far more solid ground. For a moment she'd even had a flashback to those eight months she'd spent tutoring at the GIA academy before she'd decided that teaching definitely wasn't for her.

"I think your personnel would be a good place to start," she told him. "Do you have anywhere I could assess all your people who you ever use as bodyguards?"

SOME ALTERATIONS NEEDED

"How did you do?" Drift asked urgently as the Changs walked up the ramp into the *Jonah*'s main cargo bay.

"Let's see," Kuai replied, opening the nondescript canvas satchel he was holding.

"You mean you didn't check?!" Drift fought the impulse to put his head in his hands or, failing that, clip his mechanic about the ear. Still, at least they were back in one piece and hadn't been arrested, or stabbed by genuine Triax thugs.

"What were we going to do?" Kuai demanded. "Go back in and ask for a refund if we didn't get what we wanted?" He pulled out a set of security blacks and held them up against himself. "Hey, that's not a bad fit."

"What about mine?" his sister demanded. Kuai reached into the bag and retrieved another set of clothes, then whistled as he shoved the shirt none-too-gently against his sister.

"Heh. Looks like you've got six days to get good with a needle and thread. That or gain about twenty pounds."

"That burger place round the corner looked good," Jia said, turning on her heel. "I am *on* this shit."

NEW FRIENDS

"*That,*" Larysa said in her native Russian as she accompanied Rourke away from the small conference room where they'd spent the last hour, "*was highly entertaining.*"

Rourke looked sideways at the other woman. "*You don't think I made too many enemies?*"

"*Oh, you certainly did that,*" Larysa laughed, "*but it was necessary. When you reached into Nicolai's jacket and pulled the trigger on his gun before he even knew what you were doing, to prove that you could use it to shoot someone behind him? I thought he was going to die of embarrassment, but he needed to learn.*"

"*Hmm.*" Rourke had discovered what she'd expected from the impromptu session: that some of Orlov's so-called bodyguards knew what they were about—Larysa and Roman, particularly—but the rest had more enthusiasm than proper training. They were tough, certainly, and knew how to use their weapons, but they had little idea of how to watch for threats or even prevent their own weapons from being used against them. "*I have to say, this may take some time.*"

"*The boss has stayed alive so far.*" Larysa shrugged. "*I'm sure he'll be fine for a little while longer while you train us up.*"

"*What brought you into this, anyway?*" Rourke asked as they turned

left towards one of the casino halls. A cross corridor brought her a whiff
of food, and her stomach growled to remind her that she'd only had a
protein bar that morning.

"*I've studied martial arts since I was a child,*" Larysa said. "*You know how
it's meant to promote discipline and self-control?*"

Rourke nodded.

"*Yeah, well, your mileage may vary,*" Larysa said with a snorted laugh. "*I
was kind of a tearaway; I was just also a tearaway who happened to be very
good at kicking people in the head. Which I didn't do. Much. It was mainly
theft, stuff like that.*" She shrugged again. "*When I got a bit older, I found
that my history made it hard to get a job, so I thought I'd focus on what I was
good at. Went and got actual training and qualifications in protecting other
people, but the old convictions were still hanging over me. Of course, Mr.
Orlov doesn't mind too much about a criminal record.*"

"No, I imagine he doesn't," Rourke agreed, trying not to sniff the air
too obviously.

"*Oh, are you hungry?*" Larysa asked, apparently noticing. "*Hang on
a second.*" She motioned Rourke to follow her, and cut back down the
corridor they'd just passed, pushing her way through a pair of double
doors and then turned off into an area marked STAFF ONLY. Rourke
trailed behind her and inhaled deeply as they entered a room of polished
steel surfaces and gleaming floor tiles that was clearly a kitchen. Several
kitchen staff looked up as the two of them appeared, and a raw-boned
man crossed his arms at Larysa.

"*I thought I told you to stay out, glutton?*"

"*Piss off, Tomas,*" Larysa said easily. She jerked a thumb over her shoulder, indicating Rourke. "*This is Tamara; she's working for the boss now.
Give her some food.*"

Tomas sighed, although Rourke got the impression from his manner
that the animosity between them was nowhere near as pronounced as

they were pretending. *"Why you goons can't find your food elsewhere I don't know."* He twitched slightly, as though recalling something, then turned to address Rourke, looking slightly ashamed. *"Pardon me, Tamara. I don't mean anything personal to you. Just to this gorilla."* Here he jabbed Larysa with a nearby ladle. *"And her cronies."*

"Don't make me throw you across your own kitchen, Tomas," Larysa said levelly. *"Or I could ask Tamara to do it. She's been training us this morning. I'd wager she could tie me in knots if she wanted."*

Rourke cast a sidelong glance at the other woman. She had faith in her own technique, but she still wouldn't want to get into a grappling match with Larysa. Technique could only do so much against sheer brute strength, and that was without factoring in Larysa's own training.

Regardless of its truthfulness (or perhaps in spite of it), the statement seemed to impress Tomas. The cook raised his eyebrows, nodded to Tamara respectfully, and waved a hand. *"My kitchen is yours."*

It was mainly snack food, such as would be served in the casino rather than the hotel restaurant, but it was well-prepared and tasty. Rourke and Larysa each availed themselves of a plate before Tomas grew protective of his supplies once more, and chased them out.

"Am I actually working for Mr. Orlov now?" Rourke asked as they wandered down the corridor, munching contentedly.

"Officially? Probably not," Larysa admitted, *"but Tomas doesn't need to know that. We get free food while we work on-site here, so I don't see why you shouldn't as well. The way I understand it, you will be working for the boss if you impress him, so you might as well get a taste of how it'll be."*

"Much appreciated," Rourke said, nodding.

"So, we've all heard the rumours," Larysa said, popping something wrapped in pastry into her mouth, *"but I'm dying to know: How did you escape from those three clowns and find your way into Mr. Orlov's apartment?"*

"*I could tell you,*" Rourke replied, keeping her face smooth, "*but then I'd have to kill you.*"

Larysa barked a short laugh around her pastry. "*Like Sacha, you mean?*"

Rourke felt her stomach tighten. "*I didn't kill him.*"

"*Not directly, perhaps,*" Larysa agreed, "*but you've seen what happens to the people who severely disappoint the boss.*" She lowered her voice a little, although there were no customers nearby. "*He, Leon, and Andrei were dragged in a few hours ago. I understand Sacha won't be leaving.*"

Rourke grimaced. Still, perhaps it was best for her. A scarred, vengeful Sacha might have caused her considerable problems down the road. The story tasted a little bitter in her mouth now she knew that Sacha had been made a fatal example of as a result of it, but she wanted to build on this budding camaraderie with Larysa. So she told it anyway. The other woman seemed friendly, and although Rourke suspected that Larysa had been told to pry, she really had nothing to hide.

She did, however, leave out her past with the Galactic Intelligence Agency. She also didn't mention everything she'd overheard with Orlov and his mistress. She didn't think he'd appreciate any of those details being shared with his other staff.

"*Damn.*" Larysa was looking at Rourke with even greater respect once she'd finished her tale. "*That's all true?*"

"*My hand to any god you care to name,*" Rourke replied, holding up the palm that wasn't still supporting a plate.

"*Well, I've decided: I want to be like you when I grow up,*" Larysa said with a smile. Rourke wasn't particularly offended, since she estimated that the other woman was a good twenty years younger than her and the compliment seemed genuine anyway.

"*So what now?*" she asked. They'd reached one of the casino's main halls, which was a long way from crowded at this hour but still had a fair few gamblers scattered around.

"*Take a walk around; see what you think of the setup,*" Larysa replied, waving an arm vaguely. She took Rourke's empty plate from her. "*I'll get these back to Tomas before he goes spare. When you've finished taking a look, just ask one of the reds to give me a shout, and I'll come to find you.*" She gestured around, taking in the casino's regular security staff who stood at intervals around the room in their pristine red jackets, looking like some cross between waiters and regimental guards. They were doubtless there to deal with the more mundane incidents of drunken or rowdy punters, rather than being specifically entrusted with the well-being of the casino's owner.

"*I'll do that,*" Rourke assured her. She didn't mention the fact that the Grand House's interior was undoubtedly covered by surveillance cameras, and that someone, somewhere would surely know where she was at all times. This was probably another test, to see what she would do when left to her own devices.

Well, she would do exactly what she was supposed to do: take a walk around and look at any obvious security risks. As to whether she'd tell anyone about what she found . . . well, that might depend on whether or not she thought she might need to exploit it at some point in the future.

COUNCIL OF WAR

It was 1100 hours on fourthday, Zhuchengshi local time. Drift was getting sick of this planet and its stupid day/night cycles, but at least he could try to adapt to it. Alim Muradov wasn't so lucky: The Chief had an atomic timepiece set to the clock of Mecca, back on Old Earth, and observed his daily prayer routines in line with his religion's holiest city. It was the only option, he'd explained seriously, since the prayer times were linked to the passage of a single sun across the sky over twenty-four hours. On a planet with two suns, or underground where the sun had no meaning like on Uragan, or in deep space where there were thousands of nearly identical stars, Muslims were forced to ignore their own experiences and follow the lead of their ancestral home planet.

In Drift's personal opinion, those sorts of arbitrary impositions were just another reason to ignore religion. He'd been raised a Catholic at his grandmother's insistence, but neither of his parents had been particularly devout, and he'd never really seen the point of the whole thing. His main interaction with Catholicism these days was to blaspheme at it, other than the occasional momentarily sincere prayer he'd fire off when he felt particularly close to death.

He'd been praying more often lately than he felt comfortable with.

He surveyed his crew. It still felt weird not having Rourke around, and he was left with a permanent nagging doubt that he'd missed something important that she'd have picked up on. Nonetheless, they had to push ahead. Otherwise he'd never have her on the crew again.

"We're going to go through this one more time," he said, glancing from face to face, "to check that everyone knows what's supposed to happen and when, and to make doubly sure that we've got everything we need. So, to begin: A and I make our way to the Two Trees Arena at about this time on seventhday. We don't yet know what the result of his fight is supposed to be," he said with a rueful glance at the big Māori, "so we can't place a bet on it. But if all goes to plan, we won't need to."

"I got all my fight gear, and I win or lose depending on what we're told," Apirana said calmly. "When we're done, we get out of there and make our way back here, quick as we can."

Beside him, Jenna looked up. "I'm in the Thousand Suns casino, watching out for Chief Han to arrive. When she does, I signal Kuai and Jia, and leave to get back to the *Jonah*."

"You've got a dress?" Drift asked. He'd stressed to Jenna how important it was that she looked the part in the casino, to avoid drawing suspicion. Luckily, Zhuchengshi had plenty of shops that catered to the stylish rich.

"Oh, she's got a dress, bro." Apirana chuckled with a sly sideways glance at his girlfriend. "Looks like a million dollars in it, too."

"Shut up," Jenna muttered, blushing furiously and studiously not meeting anyone's eyes. Drift pursed his lips.

"Jenna, I'm being completely serious here, but I need to know you're comfortable with what you've got. You're a pretty young lady," he added, "and you'll probably turn some heads. If you can't handle some attention from interested parties, then you might get distracted, and that means you might miss Han's entrance."

"We could always put A in the dress instead," Kuai spoke up. "That'd solve the problem."

"I can't be in two places at once," Apirana pointed out.

"But you'd wear the dress?"

"Bro, you find a dress that'll *fit* me, I'll wear it." The big Māori shook his head. "I ain't wearin' heels, though. Don't think this ankle of mine'd like it."

"*Anyway,*" Drift said loudly, trying to drag them back on track. "Jenna: Are you comfortable with your role? We've got the Chief keeping watch too, but I really want a body inside so we've got as much warning as possible."

"I'll be fine, Cap," Jenna said, straightening up and giving him a firm nod. "I can deal with lecherous randomers."

Drift nodded in reply, and turned his gaze on the Changs. "Good. And . . . ?"

"Me and Dickface are dressed up as cops," Jia said around a mouthful of burger. She had made adjustments to her pilfered uniform, but seemed to consider it an excuse to eat as much as possible anyway. "When Han is coming out with her money, we go up to her and tell her that the Triax have decided to bump her off and she's to come with us for safety."

"And we do it while sounding professional," Kuai added, glaring at his sister, "so she doesn't suspect."

"Fuck you, *lǎo tóuzi,*" Jia sniffed. "I'm as professional as the day is long."

"Every day here's really short."

"Shut—"

Drift slammed his hand down on the table and both Changs jumped a little, then settled down again. Kuai looked back at Drift.

"We act professional, so she doesn't suspect."

"Glad to hear it," Drift said dryly. He turned to look at the last member of the crew. "Chief?"

"I have found a vantage point overlooking the entrance of the Thousand Suns," Muradov said, scratching his moustache. "I take a shot near

Chief Han while she is talking to Jia and Kuai. I take care not to hit anyone, including her, but it should hopefully give their story enough credence to persuade her to go with them."

"We get her to come with us to the side of the casino, where we've parked the aircar we're hiring tomorrow," Jia said. "Then we tase that bitch and take her money."

"And what don't you do?" Drift asked.

"We don't pull our guns," Jia sighed, rolling her eyes, "because they're only there to complete the costume, and we can't shoot for shit."

"Maybe you guys should look into correcting that sometime," Apirana put in mildly.

"Maybe you should fuck off?"

"Not helping!" Drift snapped. Apirana was grinning, but even a good-natured slanging match was beyond Drift's patience levels right now. "Next?"

"We take the car, pick the Chief up, and dump Han," Kuai said. "We only take her away from the casino conscious if we absolutely have to, because the longer she knows what's going on, the more likely she is to cause problems."

"And she may recognise me," Muradov added. "I only met her once, but she will have seen as many pictures of me as I have of her. Besides, anyone involved in the level of corruption that she is will be paranoid. Although we seek to play on that to deceive her, she could wise up at any moment."

"Like I said," Jia commented, making a jabbing motion with one hand. "Tase the bitch; take her money. We pick up the Chief, dump Han, and get back to the *Jonah*."

"I'll be keeping as close an eye as I can on what's going on across the city," Jenna said, "and keeping everyone updated. Hopefully, the fact that the Triax are going to be unloading their contraband means that the spaceport staff aren't going to be bothering to pay much attention to *anyone* coming in or out."

"We can't bank on that," Drift pointed out. "They might think they need to be seen doing something. But hopefully, yes."

"If you get back first, we take off when we have the money. If the money gets back here first, we wait for you and A to get back after his fight, then take off," Jenna continued, biting her lip briefly. "If we get the money back first but there have been . . . *complications* . . . I make the decision on whether to wait for you or not."

"That you do." Drift smiled at her encouragingly. "If you leave without us, A and I book our own flight to New Samara and meet you in the capital. We'll contact you when we touch down."

"And if we have to leave you behind, I take the ransom to Sergei Orlov," Jenna added, clearly trying not to look nervous. Drift couldn't blame her: He thought the gangster was likely to honour his side of the deal, but you could never be sure. He certainly wasn't relishing the thought of coming face-to-face again with the man who'd had him trapped in a shipping container for hours on end and threatened him with death. The simple fact was, though, that Jia couldn't be trusted to hold her tongue, Kuai couldn't be trusted to actually do it, and Muradov might be recognised. In the absence of him or Apirana, Jenna really was the only choice.

"Hopefully it won't come to that," he told Jenna with a smile. "Everything will be fine, we'll all get off here together, and I'll deal with Orlov myself."

I just hope Tamara is okay.

GOING FOR A WALK

Rourke sniffed the morning air as she stepped out of the corner store, and smiled. For all New Samara's faults—such as being the place where she was currently held captive—there were certainly worse places to spend time. This might have been the longest period she'd ever spent on any planet with a naturally breathable atmosphere, and certainly since she'd joined the *Keiko*. Recycled air was fine for staying alive, but it didn't compare to the real thing. It was much like the preprocessed food that was the mainstay of ship rations: adequate for what they were but never really able to match up to fresh ingredients, such as they used in the food at the Grand House. Now, for the first time, she'd been allowed out of that building, and she'd used the opportunity to go and get some supplies so she could cook for herself. Tamara Rourke would never make a chef, but she was still looking forward to it.

She felt her smile take on a slightly ironic tilt as she hurried back towards the Grand House. She had no doubt that this concession of free movement and a glimpse of independence had been calculated by Orlov, in the same way that captors anywhere would try to manipulate the perceptions and emotions of their captives. However, just because she was aware of the likely root of these new privileges didn't mean that she didn't enjoy them.

The lobby security eyed her warily as she came back in. Word had got out, and most of the Grand House's staff now seemed to know that she'd been locked up somewhere but had somehow shown up in the casino in the middle of the night, and the boss had instructed that she be put up in one of the hotel suites. What very few people seemed to know was how or why, and from what Rourke could gather, this was a topic of considerable, quiet speculation. Roman seemed to be staying aloof from it, but Larysa was apparently enjoying lording her superior knowledge over the rank and file. Rourke was just waiting for someone to pluck up the courage to flat out ask her, but for now everyone seemed content to watch her with sidelong glances and whisper amongst themselves.

It wasn't too dissimilar to being back at high school, although from what Rourke dimly remembered of those days, this was actually less stress-inducing.

She was halfway across the lobby when she noticed a tall, curvaceous woman with long black-and-white braids coming the other way, striding towards the exit with an easy, fluid grace: Galina, the woman Rourke had seen in Orlov's apartment that night while she'd been hiding behind an armchair.

Rourke watched Galina cross the lobby and noted with mild amusement how many of the staff's heads were also turning. She was just wondering idly whether they knew that they were ogling their boss's squeeze when something caught her eye: a white man and woman in the corner, seated on comfortable chairs as though waiting for someone, had clearly also noticed Galina's presence but were reacting differently from everyone else. The man took one look at Galina and then shut down the pad he'd been idly studying, putting it into his pocket. The woman kept her eyes on Galina for a moment longer and said a few words, her lips barely moving. The man didn't react to her, and there was no one else within earshot. And Rourke could see a commpiece in her ear.

Rourke bent down, pretending to refasten her boot but keeping the pair of them in view. Galina didn't seem to have noticed them or given them any signal, but as she passed out of the doors. They both got to their feet and, with unhurried but deceptively swift gaits, headed after her.

Rourke cursed under her breath. It was always possible that Orlov had assigned two of his staff to keep an eye on his moll, but to Rourke's eye it looked more like Galina had just picked up a pair of tails. It was a fairly standard trick to use two: Many people would start to suspect that they were being followed if a single person behind them seemed to be silently mirroring their route, whereas an apparent couple could voice desires to stop or change direction and make the whole thing seem more organic. The question was, what was Tamara Rourke going to do about it?

The easy thing to do would be to pretend that she'd never seen it, head back up to her room, and get on with her day. She'd never met Galina and owed the woman nothing . . . except that wasn't exactly true. Galina was affiliated with Orlov—in fact, he genuinely seemed to care about her—and Rourke was working for Orlov now. Only as a temporary measure, perhaps, but her continued survival might come down to how valuable she made herself. Certainly, Orlov might never know that she'd had the chance to help Galina and hadn't taken it, but if Rourke managed to foil what looked like a hostile activity, then he'd have no choice but to take notice.

Besides, Galina might well be about as innocent as anyone involved with Orlov could be. She wouldn't be the first person to have fallen in love with someone of whom it was probably advisable to steer well clear, and Rourke very much doubted that she'd be the last.

Rourke didn't have a comm, didn't have a pad, and certainly didn't have much time, so she simply walked up to the main foyer desk and swung her bag up onto the counter. The two receptionists stared at her in shock.

"Call Roman Verenich; tell him that Galina is being followed and the

American is going after her," Rourke said briskly in Russian. "*Tell him to bring a car and drive her route home until he finds us.*" She turned and headed for the main doors, then looked over her shoulder as an after-thought. "*Also, look after my groceries!*"

She dashed out of the Grand House again and cut left, the direction she'd seen both Galina and her tails take. Sure enough, the man and woman she'd noticed in the foyer were about thirty metres ahead of her, walking down the pavement hand in hand, as though they hadn't a care in the world. Perhaps twenty metres beyond them was Galina, looking a little out of place in her figure-hugging dinner dress at this hour of the morning but walking with enough self-confidence to give the impression that she was attired normally and everyone else simply hadn't put enough effort in.

That could work in her favour, Rourke thought. Galina was a striking sight and likely to attract stares. If the tails meant her any harm, they'd need to make sure they were alone on the street unless they wanted to risk someone looking at their quarry exactly when they made their move. In that case, all Rourke had to do was follow them as casually as they were following Galina and simply make sure they knew she was there.

Of course, it could be that the tails were just there to act as spotters, and any actual threat was going to come from elsewhere. In which case, Rourke would be able to do nothing except watch as whatever was going to go down went down. She didn't have a gun, so would have no real way of influencing anything from this distance.

Rourke sighed. Once you'd decided on a course of action, you really did have to commit to it.

She momentarily considered trying to take a shortcut through side alleys and head Galina off, but her knowledge of New Samara's street layout wasn't good enough, and she didn't actually know where the other woman was heading. Besides, she wanted this to look as natural as possible, and sometimes that meant being blatant. So she broke into a trot and jogged past the two tails, running on the road for a few steps as she did so, and kept going until she pulled up alongside Galina.

"*Hi*," Rourke said, pleased to note that she wasn't even remotely out of breath.

The younger woman looked sideways and down at her, heavily made-up eyes widening in surprise, but she didn't stop walking. "*Hello?*" Her eyes narrowed again in recognition. "*You were in the Grand House lobby, coming in.*"

"*Distinctive, huh?*" Rourke snorted. New Samara was a fairly cosmopolitan place, but you still didn't get many petite, middle-aged black women in bodysuits wandering around. "*My name is Tamara Rourke. I've just started working for Mr. Orlov.*"

Galina managed to keep her expression neutral. "*The casino owner?*"

"*Yes, and your boyfriend, or whatever you want to call it,*" Rourke said. Galina opened her mouth, probably to frame a denial, and Rourke raised a hand to cut her off. "*Don't bother: I know; Orlov knows I know. I haven't told anyone else. The point is that I think someone else knows anyway. Don't turn around and look, whatever you do, but a man and a woman started following you the moment you left the Grand House's lobby. Did you know that?*"

The other woman's expression tightened, but to her credit she didn't turn her head. "*No.*"

"*Shit. And here I was hoping that I was just getting paranoid about a protection detail.*" Rourke sighed and reviewed her options, which were frustratingly limited given that Galina wasn't dressed for running or hiding. "*Please call Mr. Orlov; tell him what's going on and that I'm with you.*"

Galina nodded and tapped her wrist console, but shook her head after several seconds. "*Damn the man; he cancelled the call!*" Her lip twisted. "*I'm less important than business, obviously.*"

Rourke grimaced. "*Can you keep trying?*"

"If I do, he'll simply block me until he is ready to talk to me," Galina said, a note of bitterness entering her voice. "I've been down this road before."

Rourke exhaled in frustration. "Fine then: plan B. You're heading back to your house?"

"I was intending to," Galina said, swallowing nervously as she looked ahead of them. "Should we change that?"

"Does Roman Verenich know where you live?" Rourke asked her.

"Yes, I believe so."

"Then we stick to your route," Rourke said firmly. "I left a message for him to come with a car and pick us up, and he can't do that if he can't find us."

"And in the meantime?" Galina demanded. "I live several blocks away, and I presume these people aren't following me for my health!"

"Hey, I'm improvising here," Rourke told her, trying not to snap at her. "Just keep everything looking as natural as possible. If anyone tries anything, keep behind me: I might not look like much, but I can fight. However, I'm hoping that my presence will throw people off long enough for Roman to get here."

"Why?" Galina asked. "No offence, but as you said, you don't look like much."

"If someone's set tails on you, then this has been planned," Rourke said, "and I'm not part of their plan. If whoever it is thinks that I'm just here talking to you naturally, then they'll hopefully pull a rain check and plan to try again another day when there's no unexpected variables."

"And if they don't think that you're here talking to me naturally?" Galina asked.

Rourke grimaced. "Then they might try it anyway, because if they know they've been made, they've got to think that they won't get another chance."

"So tell me," Galina said as they kept walking, Rourke taking one-and-a-half paces for every click of the taller woman's heels on the pavement, "why aren't you just calling back to organise a rescue?"

"*I don't have a comm,*" Rourke said shortly, then became aware that Galina was staring at her as though she'd said she didn't have a heart. "*Well, fine, I have a comm, but I don't have it on me.*"

"*Why in the stars not?*"

Rourke tried out one or two sentences in her head, but couldn't find a way to satisfactorily word the fact that she was technically a hostage and not actually fully trusted by anyone in Orlov's operation. The last thing she wanted was for Galina to decide that Rourke was actually in on whatever was going on and make an ill-advised dash for it: They needed to keep everything looking normal for as long as possible.

Something about their surroundings suddenly sprang out at Rourke, and a nasty suspicion crystallised in her stomach. Instead of answering the younger woman's question, she nodded to where a narrow side road joined the main concourse just ahead of them. "*Do you turn left here?*"

Galina frowned. "*Yes, why?*"

There was a truck grumbling down the street towards them, not moving particularly fast. By Rourke's calculations it would reach the mouth of the alley just when they did, and if she were a betting woman, which she certainly was not—she'd have put money on it coming to a halt right across the alley and blocking anyone's view down it.

She bent down to fiddle with her boot again, bringing them to a standstill. "*That truck ahead of us. Is it slowing down?*"

"*Uh . . . ,*" Galina paused for a moment. "*Yes.*"

"Shit!" Rourke hissed in English, taking refuge in one of her birth languages for a moment. She cast a casual glance down the street behind them as she pretended to refasten her laces. The tails were still there and had paused while they looked in a shop window. Rourke accidentally met the eyes of the man as he glanced sideways at her, and she looked away hurriedly, her heart starting to beat faster. She couldn't stall for much longer: They were going to have to either deviate from Galina's usual route, which would risk tipping their observers off and forcing their hand, or play this out and hope that forewarned would be sufficiently forearmed.

An aircar buzzed by overhead, a black Takagi Sunrise with, judging by what Rourke could see from her crouch, tinted windows. She heard the sound of its engine change a little, recognised the reflection of noise caused by it entering a narrow space such as an alleyway, and a three-dimensional model of the next few seconds jumped into her head.

The Sunrise would set down a few paces into the alley, while the truck would come to a halt across the mouth of it just as Rourke and Galina turned the corner. The Sunrise's doors would open to disgorge three or four armed men or women while the tails would probably hurry into the alley from behind, likely drawing weapons themselves. Rourke and Galina would be either shot on the spot or, more likely, taken at gunpoint either into the Sunrise or through the side-loading door of the truck and kidnapped. Galina would then be used as leverage against Orlov, while Rourke would, in all probability, be killed as soon as clearance was received from someone important enough to make that decision.

Going into the alley, then, was not an option. The question was whether the hostiles had a backup plan that involved shooting dead Galina and anyone with her if the plan didn't work out once it had been set into motion.

Rourke straightened up again. Right now, playing those odds looked to be their only chance, unattractive an option though it was. She eyed the truck, which was crawling towards the alley mouth slow enough to begin drawing attention to itself. At any moment, someone was going to realise that they weren't playing ball.

"*Get ready to—*"

There was the thrum of a powerful engine and a blast of air brakes, and a midrange Excelsior roared to a halt next to them. The rear passenger door snapped open, and Roman's bald head peered out at them.

"*Get in!*" Orlov's bodyguard snapped, motioning impatiently.

Rourke moved first, pulling Galina with her and doing her best to shield the larger woman's body with her own from the two tails, while the Excelsior's door performed the same function from the other direction. Galina clambered into the car commendably quickly despite her dress and heels, and Rourke swung herself in after her. She'd barely dragged the door shut behind them when the Excelsior kicked off from the ground again, veering up into the sky with a roar of its engine and accompanying horn blasts from startled fellow drivers. Rourke looked up and wasn't particularly surprised to see Boris behind the wheel.

"*Explain,*" Roman said shortly, hauling her into a seat. Rourke buckled herself in and obliged, describing the behaviour of the tails and outlining the setup of the truck and Sunrise that they'd just avoided. To her relief, Roman nodded grimly as she spoke.

"*It could all be coincidence, but it doesn't sound like it,*" the bodyguard said when she'd finished. He activated his comm and waited a couple of seconds, then spoke again. "*Sir, it's Roman. I think we need to discuss the security arrangements of your, ah . . . personal friends.*"

He looked at Rourke again, weighing her with his eyes.

"*I recommend consulting the American.*"

PLACE YOUR BETS

Jenna sipped at her glass of white wine as she leaned on the railing of the Thousand Suns gallery area and adjusted the straps of her shoulder bag. It was a snazzy black thing, designer fashion apparently, and had been chosen to compliment the figure-hugging cream dress she was wearing. Not chosen by her, mind you: She'd never had much of an interest in fashion, and none of the crew were much better. She'd simply found a suitable shop and an assistant with some time to spare, and explained her predicament: She had a fancy party to attend, where she'd be expected to hobnob with high society, and didn't have a thing to wear.

The assistant had been helpful, as was common with sales staff who can see a profitable transaction at the end of it. Jenna hadn't gone for all their suggestions—the antigrav heels had looked interesting, but were strange to walk in and hideously expensive—but she'd come away with a suitably dazzling outfit and only the lingering sensation that she'd been burning money.

Besides, it wasn't like she was going to wear something like this every day, or would want to, but she didn't think she'd dressed up like this since her bachelor's graduation ball. It felt nice to wear clothes chosen specifically for how they looked instead of comfort or practicality. Of course, it had also been nice to see A's face when she'd shown him this outfit, but she'd have enjoyed wearing it regardless.

She glanced up at a holo-screen on the wall. The Thousand Suns was broadcasting the fight event taking place at the Two Trees Arena tonight, and every now and again she'd see a still picture of a familiar, tattooed face glaring down at her. She tried not to pay too much attention to it and keep her mind on the job, but it wasn't easy. Apirana was supposedly going into a fixed fight, so there shouldn't be a high risk of him getting hurt no matter what the outcome was, but that was only theoretical. He'd be going up against someone roughly his own size, and humans that big could do serious damage to each other with one wild punch. And what if A were told to lose, but the other fighter was told to beat him up as punishment for ruining their last attempt at a fixed fight?

She tried not to think about what might happen if A were told to lose but then got hurt. She knew very well that his gentle demeanour hid a berserker-like rage that could spill forth in moments of pain or stress. She had no concerns about him turning it on her—she'd once slapped him on the jaw when he'd been in the grip of it, and he'd still managed to control himself—but in a fight, against someone he didn't know? He might lose control, and then only God knew what might happen. It was certainly unlikely to lead to a smooth exit for him and Drift afterwards.

She became aware that someone was looking at her, and she glanced to her left. A man stood there, possibly a few years older than her, in a slate-blue suit that had clearly been tailored to his aesthetically pleasing figure. Most of his scalp was clean-shaved, but he had a low line of black hair that ran diagonally over his head from above his right eyebrow to the back left-hand side of his neck. He also had warm brown eyes, and cheekbones she could have practically shaved with.

Oh my.

She looked him up and down, trying not to be too overt about it, and gave him a small smile. "Can I help you?"

He smiled back and spoke in Mandarin, although her comm and pad combined to translate it in her ear. *"I would like to buy you a drink."*

"That's very kind of you," she said, "but this is a casino." She raised her glass slightly for emphasis. "The drinks are free."

"Then perhaps I can persuade you to accept the company of someone who would like to buy you a drink, if it were necessary?" He took a step closer as he spoke. Damn it, he *was* very attractive, but she had a job to do, and idle flirting wasn't on the cards.

"Sorry," she said, trying to look vaguely apologetic. "I'm flattered. But I'm waiting for someone, and I don't need any other company. Thank you, though."

He didn't take the hint. *"Oh, who are you waiting for?"*

She let her smile slip as she glanced across at the entrance hall to check for any sign of Han's arrival. "I really don't see how that's any of your business. Good-bye."

Annoyingly, he only smiled more widely. *"Oh, come on, a lovely lady like you? If you're not waiting for someone where there's some romance, that's just a waste."*

Jenna gritted her teeth, fighting the urge to punch this entitled idiot. What she really wanted to do was lay into him—verbally, at least—but that would be just as much of a distraction as flirting with him would have been. She considered complaining to the casino's staff that he was harassing her, but that would take time and would involve her having to move from her vantage point, so she went for blatant intimidation instead.

"I'm waiting for a friend," she told his annoying smile, as mildly as she could. "My *boyfriend* is fighting at the Two Trees Arena tonight." She gestured at one of the holo-screens where, as it happened, they were showing clips of Apirana's demolition of his previous opponent. Given how short the fight had been, the clips covered pretty much all of it.

"*Huh, right,*" her unwanted admirer snorted. "*Bullshit.*"

Jenna sighed, tapped her pad a couple of times, and held it up so he could see the screen. It was a picture of her and Apirana, their arms around each other and grinning at the camera, with the imposing rings of Medusa II in the background. They'd been on a waystation with an impressive viewing window in orbit around the huge gas giant, and Jenna had decided she couldn't resist. Jia made retching noises even while taking the picture, Jenna recalled. Of course, a few hours later they'd been ambushed and kidnapped by Sergei Orlov's thugs.

The man's smile abruptly vanished, and he hastily backed away, then turned and disappeared into the steady flow of punters without another word.

"'No' means 'no' the first time, dickhead," she muttered in the general direction of his departing back, then turned to watch the main entrance again. All visitors came into the central hall first, then either chose their pursuits from those available on the main floor or scaled the grand, sweeping staircases on either side to reach the balconies where she was currently waiting, and one of the smaller, quieter (and nonoverlooked) rooms that led off them.

Her comm crackled and disgorged Alim Muradov's voice. +*Jenna, I believe I have just seen her.*+

"Okay," she murmured, concentrating on the comings and goings around the entrance a little more. "What's she wearing?"

+*Black dress that sparkles, from what I saw under the coat, low shoes, and her hair is done up in a bun of some sort.*+

"Let's see . . ." Jenna waited, sipping idly at her wine. The seconds dragged into a minute, and then towards two. She wanted to ask if the Chief had been certain, but she supposed it would take time for Han to check her coat in, change her cash into tokens, and so on. Then, just as she was starting to fret, she saw someone matching Muradov's description. She checked around her to ensure she wasn't being watched, then quickly brought the woman into the viewfinder of her pad and kicked up the zoom, wishing momentarily that she had a mechanical eye like Drift's that could do this far more surreptitiously. The face that expanded into view matched the images that she'd found of Chief Han on the Spine: a severe mouth, a mole on one cheek, a blunt fringe of near-black hair that contained strands of grey.

"That's her," she confirmed, blanking her pad again. She eased away from the rail she'd been leaning on and began to walk casually towards the stairs, finishing her wine as she did so. "Okay, Tweedledum and Tweedledee, you're up."

+*Tweedlewhat and Tweedlewho?*+ Jia's voice replied. Jenna sighed, and did her best to impersonate the Captain's tone.

"Does *no one* appreciate the classics anymore?"

THE PAST AND THE PRESENT

It was early afternoon in New Samara, and Tamara Rourke was doing one of her regular sweeps of the Grand House. Orlov had made it clear that Roman and Larysa should take Rourke's security suggestions seriously ever since her intervention in the incident with Galina, and she had no intention of passing up this opportunity. So far as Rourke was concerned, any and every improvement she could make or potential hazard she could spot increased her value, and therefore her likelihood of staying alive if Drift and the rest couldn't succeed in raising her ransom.

Nothing seemed out of place, and she took a seat at an unused blackjack table to sip at a glass of water she'd taken from a passing robotic waiter and consider how she was going to respond to Larysa's inevitable jibes about paranoia and obsessiveness when she returned with nothing to report. Larysa had a tendency towards good-natured mockery, Rourke had found, but seemed to take as much pleasure in being put down herself as she did in delivering put-downs. While Rourke knew well enough that it would be Sergei Orlov who would have the final say in her fate, it couldn't hurt to foster good relationships with the other staff, and Larysa was far more overtly friendly than the somewhat reserved Roman.

Her musings were interrupted by a flicker of movement in her

peripheral vision, and she turned in time to see a tall, wiry man of probable Chinese heritage seating himself next to her. He was perhaps in his
early thirties, with a thin moustache, a suit that wasn't quite of the sort
of quality she'd have expected from the Grand House's normal clientele,
and a wide smile on his face.

"*This table isn't being used,*" she told him, sizing him up. He didn't
appear obviously inebriated, in that she couldn't smell alcohol on his
breath and there was no sign of pupil dilation, but it surely wasn't normal
behaviour to sit yourself next to a complete stranger at an empty casino
table and grin at them.

"*I know,*" he replied, leaning a little closer. Rourke didn't lean away in
response, but was already working out where to move, where to strike,
and how to disengage if he proved to be a threat.

"*Then what are you doing?*"

He grinned more widely. "*I'm pretending to flirt with you, of course.*"

Rourke hesitated, caught off guard. "*What do you mean?*"

"You don't remember me, do you?" the man said quietly, and this time
he spoke in English with an accent from the North American planets.
Rourke tried not to let her surprise register on her face, but she lowered
her voice in response and played for time.

"You're going to have to help me out here."

The man winked. "I'll show you mine if you show me yours." He
turned his left hand over where it rested on his leg so his palm was
visible to her, although thanks to the table it would have been hidden
from anyone else. A moment later an insignia flashed momentarily into
view as he activated an electat. Rourke knew it intimately: An identical
one was still lurking unseen beneath the flesh of her own left hand.

It was the symbol of the GIA.

She fixed him with a glare that could cut hull metal and tried to think
about exactly what cameras she'd seen that would be covering them and

from what angles. "Who the hell are you, and what the hell do you think you're doing?"

"Like I said, you don't remember me." His wide grin was still there, but his tone of voice was serious: She doubted that anyone watching from a distance would see anything other than an overenthusiastic guy hitting on an uninterested woman. "Danny Wong. I took your unarmed combat training classes for a while."

She blinked. But that would mean . . . "At the academy?"

"Bingo."

Rourke tried to keep a grimace from her face. Of all the times she could be recognised by someone from her old life, now was about the worst. "You've got ten seconds to tell me what you want from me before I bail. I'm retired."

"So I heard." Wong nodded eagerly, as though she'd said something that was encouraging his fictional flirting. "But I saw you here a few weeks ago with your friend with the metal eye, although I didn't get a chance to speak with you. He's a better poker player than he lets on, isn't he?"

Rourke frowned. She remembered Ichabod recounting his heroic poker win at the tables here, and his description of his opponents. He'd focused mainly on the attractive women—of course—but she did recall him mentioning a Chinese man who looked out of place and dangerous. Her business partner was sometimes more perceptive than she gave him credit for: Wong was wiry rather than physically imposing, but he did have a certain tension to him that a trained observer might pick up on.

"Five seconds."

Wong sighed. "We're trying to find a way to remove Sergei Orlov: That's why I've been coming here and losing the government's money week after week. I've seen you with him when he's walked the floors, and you were with his girlfriend a couple of weeks ago. You seem to be in with him. You can help us."

It had been a long time since Tamara Rourke had truly felt the world drop away from under her feet, but this was unquestionably one of those moments. She took a sip of her water and tried to slow her suddenly racing heart. "You're insane."

"It only makes *more* sense now Uragan's declared for the Free Systems," Wong said earnestly. "Orlov unofficially runs most of this system and has a huge influence all around. If he goes when the status of one of the Red Star's most important ore planets is still up in the air, we could destabilise half a sector."

Rourke had to concede; it made sense. If you looked at it from the point of view of the permanently meddling GIA, at any rate. And it wasn't like she'd turned against her old government, far from it . . . but she'd grown weary of taking immutable, morally questionable orders from arrogant superiors ten years ago. That was why she'd struck out on her own and why she'd taken up with Ichabod. Perilous though their career together had sometimes been, she had some control over where they went and what they did, and the man had at least some sense of ethics.

If Tamara Rourke did anything morally questionable now, at least she did it on her own terms and for her own reasons.

Something Wong had just said struck her. He'd said that Rourke had been seen with Orlov's girlfriend, which had to be when she'd followed Galina out of the Grand House. No wonder the setup had seemed familiar to her and set her internal alarm bells ringing: She'd stumbled into the middle of a goddamned GIA kidnapping attempt.

Rourke took another sip of her water. The simple fact that Wong was talking to her meant that her old employers hadn't cottoned on to the fact that she'd deliberately sabotaged their scheme, but she'd have to play this very carefully. There was an old saying about the first time being happenstance, the second time being coincidence, and the third time being enemy action, but from Rourke's experience the GIA didn't believe in coincidences.

"Okay," she said, trying to keep her voice level. "You can't be working alone. You've got a field team, right?"

"Sure." Wong nodded.

"And do they know you've made contact with me?" Rourke asked him. "Has this been cleared up the line?"

"No," Wong said, shaking his head slightly. "I haven't called it in yet. They're a bit by the book, and I wasn't sure if I'd get another chance to speak to you alone unless I approached you now."

Translation: You're looking to get some serious cred with your superiors by single-handedly coming up with the solution to their problem. I can use this. "Okay," Rourke said again, thinking fast and checking the room over while trying not to be too obvious about it. "Here's what we're going to do. You go to that bar over there, see it? Get yourself a drink and try to look dejected because I just gave you the brush-off. I need to work out how we're going to coordinate this, because we sure as hell can't continue this conversation here and now."

"Right," Wong said, looking serious. "So how do I contact you?"

"You don't," Rourke said shortly, "not unless you want me dead. I'll contact *you*. What's your cover?"

"Galactic Exports office," Wong said, pulling a slim but sturdy piece of plaspaper from his pocket and handing it to her. She glanced at it: It looked like a standard shipping company letterhead with an address and a comm code. "If you can't reach me, call this number"—he pointed at one at the bottom of the card—"and ask for Jhonen in Finance. He's my superior."

"Okay," Rourke said. "I don't know if I'll be able to contact you—I don't have my own comm, for one thing—but I'll try. If I haven't called by this time tomorrow, come back the day after at 2000 hours. If I don't come to you, keep coming back at the same time for as long as your chief will let you. If I don't see you here two days from now, and I haven't been able to get in touch by any other means, I'll assume that my involvement hasn't been green-lighted by your higher-ups." She fixed him with a glare. "Do *not* come back to me unless this is cleared. I'm not getting involved in some goddamn vigilante operation that your own damn team isn't on board with. Are we clear?"

"We're clear," Wong said. He looked a little like he'd just chewed something bitter. Perhaps he hadn't been counting on his miracle ace in the hole taking command of the situation quite so completely.

"Good," Rourke said. "I'm bailing." She got up and walked away without a backwards glance, trying to look like someone who'd finally had enough of an unwanted admirer. She crossed the room to the far doors, pushed her way through them, and then broke into a run that didn't stop until she found a member of hotel security in their red coat.

"*I need to speak to Larysa urgently. Mr. Orlov's bodyguard,*" she added impatiently in Russian, when the woman just stared at her.

"*One moment,*" the woman said, clearly wondering exactly what was going on, and turned away slightly to mutter into her commpiece. Her eyebrows went up a few seconds later, and she wordlessly unhooked her commpiece and passed it to Rourke.

"*Larysa?*"

+*What's the problem?*+ Larysa's voice came through, a little tinny until Rourke had wrestled the earpiece in properly. +*Don't tell me you've found a dent in a door or something.*+

"*A little bit more important than that,*" Rourke replied grimly. "*There's a guy at the bar in the Orchid Room: midthirties, thin moustache, bad suit. He's GIA, and he just tried to recruit me to help kill Mr. Orlov. I've stalled him for now, but you can't let him leave. Tell whoever you send to be careful: He'll be well-trained, and he'll try to fight his way out if he thinks his cover's truly been blown.*"

There was a stunned pause from the other end. A couple of feet away from her, the hotel security officer was wearing an expression of utter astonishment.

+You're being serious?+ Larysa asked.

"Yes, damn it, I'm being serious!" Rourke hissed. "I don't know what he actually wanted me to do. I just fed him enough bullshit to get the hell out of there without him suspecting."

+Okay,+ Larysa replied, and now her voice was grim too. +I'll trust you on this one, but I hope you're right.+

"Oh, I really wish I was wrong," Rourke said fervently.

+Roger that. Stay nearby in case he moves and we need you to pinpoint him.+

The comm clicked off. Rourke let out a shuddering breath and didn't look back towards the Orchid Room. She didn't like to think what was going to happen to Wong, but she knew it wouldn't be pleasant and would almost certainly be ultimately fatal. If he was good, then he wouldn't spill the location of his teammates even under torture—she had no allusions that the sensitive work and personnel would be based at the address on his business card—they'd work out he'd been compromised and would get off New Samara without further unpleasantness. He would probably let slip that she was ex-GIA, of course, but she hoped that Orlov would simply view that as an asset to his operation. Especially after she had so obviously demonstrated where her loyalties lay by handing over poor Danny Wong on a plate.

Was betraying an agent of her government to a gangster morally reprehensible? Possibly. Would it have also been morally reprehensible to assist in the assassination of a man she'd promised to serve as an employee? Possibly, although the identity of that man and exactly why she was serving him would have to be considered. But then again, would she have enjoyed dying painfully had that attempted assassination failed, or if it succeeded and the GIA hadn't pulled her far out of the fire after-wards? No, most certainly not. Would she have enjoyed the knowledge that, should her crew have come back with the money for her ransom, they would then have also been executed as punishment for her treach-ery? Once again, no.

Tamara Rourke had made her choice. The only way to get out of this with everyone she valued remaining in one piece, including herself, was to be the best employee to Sergei Orlov that she possibly could. If that meant making a present of an overtrusting GIA agent she'd once trained . . . well, she owed him nothing other than the bond of the electat they shared, and every GIA employee knew that field agents were ulti-mately expendable.

"There's a reason you're supposed to clear things with your chief, kid," she muttered darkly.

DOUBLE DEALING

Song Daiyu nodded as the voice in her ear told her the news she'd been expecting, then ended the call and looked up.

"Han is here."

"Good," Gao Dongfeng grunted from the other chair in her office. The vile old man had his feet resting on her edge of her desk and was worrying at his nails again with his teeth. "You still want to go through with this farce?"

Song sighed inwardly. Gao Dongfeng's personal brand of brutality had been necessary when the Dragon Sons were getting established in Zhuchengshi: The wars against their rivals had been bitter and bloody, and the old man's tenacity and sheer ruthlessness had been pivotal. These days, however, he was a crude tool in a role that required a precision instrument, and if anything, he was getting cruder. Song looked forwards to the moment that Gao could be disposed of and someone subtler appointed instead— someone who understood that violence was a means, not the end; someone who didn't act without the approval of the clan, and when they were called upon to act, didn't argue about it; someone who recognised that a threat could be veiled and that a threat was sometimes more effective than an act.

Someone who wouldn't rest their damn feet on my desk would be a good start too.

She gave Gao a cool stare. Challenging him openly at this stage would be unwise, not to mention unnecessary. So rather than protest his conduct, she simply ignored it and tried her best to indicate that it didn't bother her. "Farce?"

"You're throwing money at a corpse," Gao snorted, not looking up. "We could have killed her yesterday, or the day before, or—"

"Han is no fool," Song interrupted him. "We don't know what counter-measures she'll have taken, and we *cannot* have the shipment interrupted. She knows we can kill her; I wouldn't have put it past her to have a file ready to transmit on her person at all times, maybe even linked to a heart monitor so it's sent automatically if her pulse stops." She shrugged. "We need a few days to get the shipment in and dispersed, that's all. After that, her usefulness may be outweighed by her potential to cause us trouble—especially now she's starting to grow a backbone, even if it is only born out of self-interest."

"I've got a couple of squads in the area," Gao offered. "We can off her the moment she steps out of these doors and take the money back. Zhuchengshi's a harsh city: Street crime happens all the time, especially to stupid rich folk."

"I am *not* having a prominent public figure gunned down on the steps of my casino," Song snapped at him. "We're not invulnerable, no matter what you might think. That damn governor's not for turning, and she thinks Han is her friend."

"You heard Han," Gao argued. "The governor doesn't want anyone thinking she can't control this place, or she'll never get a better posting. She won't call in the big guns; it'll be proof she can't cope."

"It's too risky." Song shook her head. "Especially tonight, the shipment hasn't even arrived yet."

"Too risky, or you don't have the balls to make the call?" Gao said, scorn dripping from his tone. "You'd rather throw four hundred grand at this woman and let her stash it somewhere, or maybe just make a run for it and throw open everything she knows about us?"

"It's a small loss compared to what we'll make from the shipment," Song snapped at him. "It's not about 'balls,' Gao; it's about brains!" The old man's brows lowered, but Song was angry now and she carried on regardless. "And I'm not just talking money! Governor Mei isn't the only one who wants to improve her position: If we make this happen, our names will be gold!" *Yours only very briefly, if I have any say in it,* she added silently.

For a moment she thought Gao was going to snarl back, maybe even get physical, but then the fire in his eyes faded a little and was replaced with a sullen expression. "So play it safe and hope for the best, that's your genius plan, is it?"

"That is *the* plan, not just *my* plan," Song told him coldly. "Zhang agrees with me."

"The girl-faced idiot," Gao muttered.

Song spread her hands on the table, trying to signify an end to that topic of conversation. "Everything's ready for our sacrifice to the security forces, I take it?"

"Huh? Oh, yeah." Gao nodded dismissively. "They've been given the tip-offs they need and enough evidence to make them move. They should be getting ready to make their arrest right now."

"And you're certain ze won't be too great a loss to us?" Song asked. It wasn't her side of the operation, but she wanted to get as much of an overview as possible. She hadn't been lying when she said she wanted to improve her position.

"Not a risk of that," Gao laughed nastily. "The fool can't even fix a fight properly anymore, it seems: We lost a lot of money last week because ze decided some rookie fighter didn't need to know the plan and all our betting went haywire. No, Serenity Chen has definitely outlived zir usefulness."

A LOSING PROPOSITION

Drift watched as Apirana fired off a couple of quick left jabs, then a lunging elbow smash. The big man shuffled his feet, moving sideways, then delivered a kick with his right leg.

"You'll tire yourself out," Drift observed. They were back in the Two Trees Arena's dressing rooms, and Apirana was shadowboxing.

"I'm loosening up," the big Māori grunted.

"For what?" Drift asked. "It's not like you're actually going to be fighting."

"To make sure I don't pull a muscle or something an' get the fight stopped by a doctor," Apirana said, turning round to address him. "I ain't as young as I used to be, so if Chen wants this fight going to the third round or whatever, I'd best be ready."

"Fine, knock yourself out," Drift sighed. "Not literally," he added after a second.

Apirana didn't return to his warm-up and instead placed his hands on his hips. "Bro, you look tense and you ain't even getting in a ring."

"Can you blame me?" Drift demanded, suddenly aware of exactly how on edge he felt now that Big A had verbalised it. "You and I are stuck here in this . . . this *charade* while we're relying on three kids in their twenties and a guy we met a couple of months ago to make the score we need to ransom Tamara back." He held his hands up. "No disrespect to Jenna, you understand that, right? But I'm used to being in the middle of a scheme like this, being involved. Besides," he added, "this kind of thing isn't really the strong suit for any of them."

"You gotta have a bit more faith, bro," Apirana said calmly. "Jenna got me an' Rourke outta Uragan City when I had a broken ankle an' Rourke was running on fumes. Jenna might not be good in a fight, but mentally, she's as strong as anyone I've ever known. You did good, putting her in charge."

Drift looked at the big man, a strange sensation tugging at his chest. "You actually do love her, don't you?"

Apirana sighed, and chuckled ruefully. "Maybe? Hell if I know, bro, I ain't ever been in love before!" His eyes grew slightly unfocused, as though looking at a scene Drift couldn't see. "I know I trust her, deep trust. You know? I could tell her anything, an' I don't think she'd judge me for it. She accepts who I am, an' who I *was*. An' I sure as hell know I wanna keep her from harm, but I know she's an adult. An' I can't protect her; I don't have the *right* to protect her. She'll do what she wants to do, or what she feels she has to do, an' I'll just try to help her an' support her, an' maybe try to talk her out of something if I think it's a bad idea." He laughed again. "Then again, she's that much smarter than me that I'm more inclined to trust her judgement than mine."

Drift grunted noncommittally, somewhat nonplussed by this level of revelation from the big man.

"Plus, she's hot," Apirana added, grinning suddenly. "I don't like to think of myself as a shallow man, but I gotta admit that the fact that she's hot kinda helps." He paused, his big face taking on a thoughtful expression. "You don't have to answer this, bro, but: You ever been in love?"

"High school, maybe," Drift said dismissively. "If you could call it that."

"Was just wondering," Apirana said, shrugging. "Dunno what you had with that girl we met back in Old New York, for example."

"Mai?" Drift snorted a laugh. Maiha Takahara had been the first mate of an old rival in his privateer days, and their brief-but-furious sexual encounters had taken place whenever both ships had been in the same port at the same time . . . providing they could dodge the rest of their respective crews. "No. Don't get me wrong; we got along okay, but it was always a purely physical thing."

"Huh. So nothing since high school?" Apirana grimaced. "Hey, guess maybe it's just not for you. I mean, Rourke don't even like sex, so—"

"Once. Maybe. I don't know." Drift shook his head, not certain why he was even saying this. "I was still young, and it didn't last long enough for me to be sure. But perhaps."

"Damn," Apirana grunted. "One of you break it off?"

Drift looked down at his hands, trying to fight down an unexpected memory of them covered in blood: a doomed attempt to staunch the flow from a stab wound, without adequate medical supplies available.

"She died."

"Ah, shit, bro," Apirana said sorrowfully. "I shouldn't have asked. Your business, I din't mean to bring up—"

The changing room door opened without warning, and Serenity Chen walked in. The events manager nodded briefly at Apirana as ze walked past him, then came to a halt in front of Drift. "Mr. Pérez."

Drift got to his feet, pushing the past to the back of his mind as he did so. Rodrigo Pérez was unlikely to be feeling much different to Drift himself right now—on edge, frustrated, and rather apprehensive—so he didn't feel the need to put too much effort into the persona.

"Mer Chen," he acknowledged neutrally, glancing past the other person towards the door, which had swung shut again. "Any final instructions?"

"The bookies and the punters were impressed with Mr. Wahawaha's performance against Kuang Daniu," Chen said, looking between the two of them before zir gaze settled on Apirana. "Lukas Ivanovic will be beating you in the first round, by submission." Ze paused for a moment, zir jaw working. "*Don't* fuck this up."

Apirana just nodded, his face a blank mask. "You got it."

"Provided we get paid now," Drift added. Chen looked back to him, zir eyes narrowing.

"Out of the question. You'll get paid after the show, like everyone else."

"We still didn't get paid for the *last* show, or did you forget?" Drift demanded. "C'mon, we're here; we've showed up. You think we're going to turn around and walk away now? We'll go out there, Apirana will do what he needs to, and then we'll be on our way. But we want our damn money now."

"An' if that don't happen," Apirana put in mildly, "maybe I'll do my best to punch Mr. Ivanovic's teeth right down his throat."

"That would be a very unwise move," Chen bit out.

"Sure." Apirana shrugged. "But when they interview the winner afterwards an' I start talking about how I was told to throw the fight, what do you think'll happen then? Bad news for both of us, I'm guessing. So I'll play your game an' keep your racket sweet, but you pony up first, got it?"

Chen glared at him, then exhaled in frustration, zir nostrils flaring. "Very well. You have an account here?"

"No," Drift replied with a shake of his head, "but he'll take plastic." A universal credit chip would be perfect: Given that Apirana's fight fees were a legitimate expense, there was no risk to either party from a data trail, and the bank coding would mean Chen couldn't take it back off them like ze could have theoretically done with cash.

Chen nodded curtly. "Fine. Accounts will have it ready in the next fifteen minutes." Ze turned for the door, then paused to look back over their shoulder. "You do understand that if you cross me on this, you are unlikely to survive the night?"

"We're not looking for trouble," Drift said wearily. "We just want to get paid."

"So long as we understand each other," Chen snapped, and exited into the corridor outside. The door banged shut behind zir.

"We'll only be getting fifteen grand for both, won't we?" Apirana grunted into the momentary silence that followed. "Seems to me like if I'm gonna throw a fight, I should get more."

"Don't even start," Drift told him. He had an urge to berate the Māori for playing hardball too soon with Chen, but he supposed it had worked out. Besides, they'd be getting off this planet as soon after the event as they could manage, so Chen was welcome to come looking for them later if it gave the events manager any pleasure. "And . . . don't go public about the fight-fixing, will you?"

"Bro, gimme some credit," Apirana told him, looking hurt. "I ain't stupid. You know I don't want no complications here."

"Good." Drift took a deep breath and let it out again. Everything would be fine. They'd get the payment from Chen and go out into the arena, Apirana would commit a short piece of what would hopefully be fairly painless sports fraud, and they'd disappear into the night. No reason for anything to go wrong.

Just so long as everything else went to plan, of course.

A VOTE OF CONFIDENCE

"Good," Tamara Rourke said, looking over the four bodyguards surrounding Roman, who was playing the part of Sergei Orlov for this exercise. *"You've got the spacing about right, I think. Close enough to protect, not close enough to crowd him or limit his mobility."* She stepped up to one, a man called Grigori. *"If you just—"*

Her hand whipped towards his armpit holster midsentence, but he snatched her wrist with his right hand and drew his left back for a punch. They both froze for a second, then Rourke gave a satisfied nod and stepped back. *"Very good."*

She'd realised over the last two weeks that several of Orlov's security team had a habit of becoming complacent, of only being ready to react when they thought they needed to be. That was, of course, not the point of being a bodyguard: You had to be ready at all times, at least while you were on duty. So far as Rourke was concerned, while she was training them, they were on duty, and if they could learn to jump out of the mind-set of an attentive trainee and into that of a vigilant protector in a split second, then they would be as ready as she could make them for the real world.

"They're getting good," Larysa commented, stepping up beside her.

"They're not bad," Rourke agreed. She'd never felt that training was

her forte, but trying to avoid being killed by a mob boss was a powerful motivator. *"How long has Leon been in the car?"*

"Seventeen minutes," Larysa replied with a glance at her chrono. *"Time for a drive failure?"*

"I think so," Rourke said, nodding. The other woman tapped a button on her pad, and an alarm went off on the other side of the gymnasium hall that Rourke had commandeered for their training sessions. A genuine limo aircar sat on the floor there, albeit with some modifications. One of them was an alarm system that could be remotely triggered, indicating to the person inside that the antigrav drive had failed. Since it was easy to react to something if you were ready for it, now they'd gone through the initial drill, the bodyguards would sit inside for randomly determined lengths of time before they were required to act. Occasionally, it wouldn't go off at all, just to mess with them.

One of the doors flew open, and Leon leapt out, dragging a weighted dummy with him. He smacked a red button on the dummy's chest and then a corresponding one on his own, simulating the release of a parachute and stopping the clock.

"2.34 seconds between drive failure and parachute activation," Larysa said, her eyebrows raising as she looked at her pad. She raised her voice. *"Well done, Leon! The boss is almost certainly still alive! And you probably are too."*

Leon gave them a thumbs-up, although he didn't quite meet Rourke's eyes. He and Andrei had suffered from the reflected ignominy of Sacha's failure, and he was quite clearly uneasy around her. Rourke wasn't sure if that was due to resentment towards her over Sacha's fate, embarrassment at the knowledge that she'd played all three of them, or simple fretting over the fact that it could have quite easily been him going face-first into a washbasin. However, she couldn't fault his application in the training sessions.

The hall door opened, and she looked around to see Orlov walking in, with Andrei and Nicolai at his shoulders. Everyone stopped what they were doing and turned to watch the boss, with the exception of Roman. He let out a groan and collapsed: Much to Rourke's approval, two of his "guards" threw themselves down to cover his body with theirs, while the other two drew their weapons—not loaded, of course—and scanned for theoretical threats. Roman tapped the two on top of him on their shoulders a second or so later, and they helped him back up again.

"What was that?" Orlov asked, crossing the hall to stand beside her.

"They were reacting to you collapsing as though you had been shot," Rourke told him. "Roman was being you."

"But I'm here," Orlov pointed out, with a slightly puzzled smile.

"In this context, sir, you're a distraction," Rourke said briskly. "They need to be ready to protect the person they're guarding at a moment's notice, in spite of distractions."

"Even when I'm somewhere else?" Orlov asked.

"They could be protecting a body double," Rourke said with a shrug, "so they'd have to look convincing. Getting them focused is the main thing."

"You seem to have done an admirable job," Orlov remarked. He looked over at the limo and the weighted dummy, and frowned. "And that?"

"Getting you clear of a midair drive failure," Rourke explained. "We work on the basis that you may not be able to get out by yourself."

"*Fascinating,*" Orlov murmured in Russian, then raised his voice and returned to speaking in English. "When you have finished here, come to my office. There is something I need you to do."

Rourke nodded. "Yes, sir." She'd left the Grand House several times now on various errands and trips with Roman, Larysa, and on one occasion Orlov himself. She was still living out of the same hotel room at the moment, but if she ended up working for the gang boss, then she'd have to find her own accommodation. She suspected it would come as something of a shock after living in a luxury hotel for six weeks.

Assuming Ichabod doesn't come back with the money. Her stomach tightened. There were two weeks left before Orlov's deadline, and no way of knowing if the rest of her crew would be back in time unless and until they actually turned up. She was working on the basis that they wouldn't: She hadn't been lying when she'd told Orlov that she had every faith that Drift would do his best, but wasn't entirely sure he'd succeed.

Something occurred to her. "You didn't come here just to ask me to come and see you later, did you, sir? You could have called me for that, or sent a message through someone else."

"No," Orlov admitted, and gestured at the room. "I wanted to see what you were doing. If you're going to such lengths to ensure my safety, I felt I should find out what measures you are employing."

Rourke looked at the dark eyes studying her and nodded slowly. *He still doesn't completely trust me. Nor would I, in his position, but that doesn't help me live for longer than another two weeks.* "I hope you're satisfied with what you've seen, sir."

"Very much so," Orlov said with a nod. "But we shall discuss this further later." He turned and walked away, flanked once more by Andrei and Nicolai.

"Somebody's in trouble," Larysa murmured in a singsong voice from beside Rourke. Her spoken English was broken, but the other woman could understand the language well enough.

Rourke shot her a glance, her pulse suddenly jumping. *"What?"*

Larysa blinked, then laughed. *"Oh, calm down. I'm just joking."*

Rourke glared at her. *"Yes, well, don't forget that I'm still living on borrowed time right now. I think I can be forgiven for being a bit jumpy."*

"The day I see you actually jump at something is the day I eat my own foot," Larysa said with a grin. She jerked a thumb over her shoulder at the sparring mats. *"Come on, you said you'd show me that shoulder lock."*

An hour later, when the training session had ended and Rourke and Larysa had left each other aching and exhausted, Rourke grabbed a shower and then made her way to Orlov's office. Unlike his penthouse, the casino owner's office was on the middle floor of the building, albeit in a section only accessible to casino staff. That still covered quite a lot of different people, of course, but Orlov was adamant that he wanted to be able to walk out of his office and access the casino quickly instead of being shut away behind a private elevator. Still, Rourke had convinced him to have two guards on his door at all times.

It was Nicolai and Andrei, at least both of them nodded cautiously to her as she approached. Andrei had tried to exact some not-too-subtle revenge for Sacha in the unarmed combat sessions, and Rourke had needed to choke him unconscious twice before he realised exactly how stupid an idea that was. Since then his attitude to her had been sullen but respectful.

"*Gents,*" Rourke said to them. "*Is Mr. Orlov available?*"

"*He said for you to go straight in,*" Nicolai said, pressing a button on the wall behind him. She noticed that he angled his body as she walked past so she wouldn't easily be able to reach the gun in his armpit holster. Good: He'd learned his lesson well.

She pushed the door open and entered the office. It wasn't huge, but was easily spacious enough for one person. "Sir?"

"Ah, Tamara." Sergei Orlov looked up from his desk and gestured to the seat in front of him. "Please, sit down."

She sat in the chair and waited while he closed down whatever file he'd been working on at his terminal. He killed the screen with a swipe of his hand and sat back, looking at her over steepled fingers. Rourke had a sudden image of him as some middle manager in a company some-where, and her as a ground-level employee. She imagined what it was like for a normal person to be called into the office by their boss. Probably nerve-wracking, depending on the boss and the situation. But probably unlikely to be potentially fatal.

"You've made several suggestions since you began advising me on security matters," Orlov began. "I must admit, they have all made sense, and I have decided to enact most of them. Some of them I've ignored, because as you once pointed out, I will never be *truly* safe. And I felt they would overly limit my ability to enjoy my life."

"That's your prerogative of course, sir," Rourke said.

"I've noticed a difference in my security staff as well," Orlov said. "I can see that the training you've been delivering has had an effect. I've been getting reports of what you've been doing with them, of course, but I wanted to drop in today to take a look for myself. It was impressive."

"I'm glad you think so, sir."

Orlov studied her for a second. "I've noticed that you've never asked after the GIA agent we . . . apprehended."

Rourke kept her face smooth with the ease of long years of practice. "Not my business, sir."

Orlov sighed, looking down at his desktop. "He was not, sadly, particularly informative. We didn't even really get anything that my contacts in the *politsiya* could act on."

Rourke nodded. With any luck, Wong hadn't dragged the rest of his team down with him. They didn't deserve to suffer for his hotheadedness. Or her cold-bloodedness.

"Tell me," Orlov asked, looking back up at her. "Did he give any indication as to why he chose to approach you? Surely it can't have been simply because you were a fellow North American?"

Here we go. She'd already decided that telling the truth was the best policy if this situation arose, but couldn't pretend that she was completely calm about the possible ramifications. She raised her left hand and willed her electat into visibility.

"Because it appears that he studied under me at one point, sir."

Orlov didn't react to the sight of her old GIA badge, which told her all she needed to know about his motivation for asking. Wong *had* let slip about her identity, and this had been a test of her honesty.

"You didn't mention your previous career with the GIA," Orlov said mildly, those dark eyes watching her closely.

"I don't make a habit of it, sir," Rourke replied quietly, closing her hand again and dropping it to her lap. "I flew with Ichabod for a decade before he found out."

"And was he angry about you keeping this information from him?"

"He took it surprisingly well, sir." *Mainly because we were all neck-deep in shit at the time, and it gave us a possible way out.*

"You must admit," Orlov said in that same mild tone, "it seems a strange coincidence that an agent trained by you would *just happen* to make contact with you here."

Rourke tried to keep herself focused, and alert for the slightest noise. She didn't think that Orlov would be stupid enough to confront her in his office and then try to get Nicolai or Andrei to jump her from behind, but you never knew.

"Not particularly, sir. I trained a lot of people in combat techniques in a fairly short time at the academy, and they were all to be agents working in Red Star space. That's where I was stationed for most of my active career, and all our training sessions were conducted exclusively in Russian. The students needed to learn to use the correct language even when under physical or mental stress, in order to maintain their cover."

Orlov raised his eyebrows. "The sort of thorough approach I would expect from you, having seen you at work. So your GIA career in the field consisted mainly of protecting dignitaries and the like?"

"No, sir," Rourke said, "not really. You might say that I've reverse engineered most of this."

"So you were an assassin?"

"I needed to know how to eliminate hostile elements on occasion," Rourke said carefully, "but no, sir, I wasn't a dedicated assassin." She didn't mention her time spent destabilising governments, just in case Orlov decided that she must have had a part in the chaos on Uragan.

Orlov nodded slowly, as though considering. "So if I were to tell you that there is an element who is hostile to me that I need eliminating . . . what would your response be?"

Rourke looked at him, her throat suddenly tight. "I'd tell you to hire a hitter." She pushed down an unpleasant memory. "The Laughing Man, if you can find him. He's the best at what he does."

"I thought he'd killed one of your crew a few months ago?" Orlov asked.

"He did," Rourke said grimly, trying not to think of Micah van Schaken bleeding to death from a pair of throat wounds in Glass City's street market. "He's still the best at what he does, my personal opinion of him aside."

Orlov nodded. "And if I asked you to take care of this element yourself?"

Rourke straightened in her chair and took a deep breath. "I'd say no."

Orlov's dark eyes seemed to turn colder. "And why would you do such a thing?"

"I left the GIA because I was tired of being told where to go and what to do, and who needed to die to make it happen," Rourke said honestly. "I told you that I would help you identify the failings in your organisation, to keep you safe. I never said I'd play assassin for you. I'm not stupid: I know that if I help you stay alive, other people will die." She shook her head. "But I won't go after them in cold blood myself."

Orlov frowned. "I'm not used to being disappointed, Tamara."

"Then I suggest you stop asking me to do something that I won't do." Rourke folded her arms and stared back at him. "I think I've proved that I'm valuable. We can both still benefit from this arrangement."

Orlov studied her for a moment more, then, to Rourke's surprise, he abruptly smiled. "Good. Good."

Rourke allowed herself to frown slightly. "I'm sorry, sir, I don't understand."

"I have few rivals on New Samara," Orlov explained easily, pressing a button on his desk. A few moments later a whirring noise began, just on the edge of hearing. "Removing a hostile element was likely to require leaving this planet. Had you been eager, I might have thought that you were seeking a chance to get away from me. Instead you stuck to your guns, as it were, and also chose the option that would keep you here." The whirring stopped, and a panel in his desk slid aside to allow a cup of coffee to rise into view. Orlov took it and sipped, keeping his eyes on Rourke. "You will forgive that one last test of loyalty, I hope?"

"Certainly, sir, I—" Rourke's brain caught up with her ears. "Wait. One *last* test?"

"Tamara, you are without doubt a valuable asset to my organisation," Orlov said, putting his drink down. "We still have a little time before your colleagues may or may not be returning with the fee I demanded of them, but that is of little consequence to me now.

"As of this moment, I am offering you employment as my personal security advisor. You would continue to be responsible for the training of my bodyguards and would work with Roman and Larysa on all aspects of security with regard to me and my organisation. You would not be expected to take direct action yourself unless I or my employees come under attack in your presence."

His dark eyebrows twitched upwards. "You may have some time to consider my offer, of course. Let us say . . . until the deadline I set for Captain Drift expires?"

TO PROTECT AND SERVE

Their problems had started, Jia reflected, when they hadn't been able to find parking within sight of the Thousand Suns' entrance.

Well, to her mind their problems had *actually* started when the Captain had put her and her idiot brother together for this part of the job. She sort of understood why he'd done it, given that Jenna couldn't speak Mandarin and Muradov might be recognised, but it still sucked. And the fact that Kuai hadn't been able to get a parking spot in the right place didn't help.

The Thousand Suns was a huge building: roughly rectangular, Jia supposed, with various embellishments at the corners and lumpy architectural bits she didn't know the names of added on for appearance's sake. It was built mainly out of the light-grey rock that was apparently local, presumably in an attempt to give the place a feel of somewhere from Old Earth. Jia had grown up on Old Earth and hadn't seen a damn thing that looked like this, so that was just a piece of idiocy so far as she was concerned.

Of course, the corner of Chengdu where her parents lived wasn't exactly the sort of place where you got enormous casinos that had a city block all to themselves, but that was beside the point.

There was a parking lot the next block over, connected to the casino by an enclosed, elevated walkway that hummed with repulsors to ensure no aircar could collide with it no matter how inattentive the driver, but that would have been useless for Jia and Kuai. They needed to be somewhere they could reach the entrance quickly, not a couple of minutes after Han had already departed. The main street at the front of the Thousand Suns was a wide, six-lane affair, albeit with speed restrictions that kept the traffic at a sedate pace. They were still in the middle of Zhuchengshi, after all, and the casino owners wouldn't have wanted their precious piece of pretentious rock to look like it was sitting next to a freeway. There was on-street parking down both sides of it, but it was completely full. The Changs had needed to park on one of the narrower streets running off the main thoroughfare, and walk back to a point where they could keep an eye on the entrance.

The casino's side of the street wasn't an option: The front of its plot had a wide, curving driveway for taxis and other vehicles to drop punters off and pick them up, with sprinkler-watered lawns and drooping palm trees, and ornamental fountains connected by gravel walkways. It was pretty, but there was nowhere to lurk unobtrusively. Jia was certain that casino staff would get suspicious if there were two cops just hanging around out front for ages. They needed to approach as though they'd just arrived when Han was leaving, which was why they'd wanted to be sitting in a car on the other side of the street. Since that wasn't an option, they were both standing in a shadowed, recessed goods entrance for another massive building—a hotel, Jia thought—a few metres down a side street from where the traffic growled or hummed its way along the road.

"*See anything yet, Chief?*" she asked quietly. All comm traffic was to be in English, so Jenna could get a better idea of what was going on as she listened in back at the *Jonah*. A translation programme was fine, but it was of limited use if you didn't know who was saying what: not a problem when dealing with a spaceport controller, potentially a large problem if one of your crew had run into trouble but you didn't know which one.

+*I promise, Jia, I will tell you the moment I see her face,*+ Alim Muradov's voice replied in her ear.

"*And you're not gonna get bored and go to sleep up there?*" she said.

+*Oddly enough, the ability to stay awake and focused is an important one for military snipers,*+ the Chief's voice said dryly. +*I have stayed alert for hours at a time watching a single piece of ground.*+

"*Yeah, fine, whatever,*" Jia said. "*Just make sure you don't shoot me in the back of the head when we get over there, yeah?*"

+*How about in the back of the leg?*+

Jia blinked. "*What?*"

+*I am stuck up here on a rooftop after dark in an elevated desert city, and I am freezing. I think I should be allowed some* fun.+

Beside Jia, Kuai snorted with laughter. She glared at her brother, then cast a dark glance upwards in the vague direction of where she thought Muradov was.

"*That's not funny, you know that?*"

+*Sorry, Jia,*+ the Chief said, although Jia didn't think he sounded particularly contrite. +*Soldiers' humour is a strange thing, and snipers are the darkest of them all. Being up here must be putting me back into the mind-set.*+

+*Would you lot mind cutting the chatter?*+ Jenna's voice broke in. +*I'm trying to keep tabs on what's going on where, particularly at this spaceport, and it's not easy with you bickering in my ear.*+

+*You heard her, Jia,*+ Muradov admonished. +*Keep the noise down.*+

"*Don't make me come up there and kick your ass, copper,*" Jia snapped. Jenna started to say something, and Jia hissed in frustration. "*Yeah, yeah, we'll be quiet! Keep your pants on.*"

+*I have no idea how the Captain copes with you all,*+ Jenna sighed.

"*Whiskey, I think,*" Kuai suggested.

+*Okay, that's enough! Everyone shut up!*+

Jia stuck her tongue out at her brother, who looked like he might snap something back at Jenna but instead muted his comm, signaling for his sister to do the same, and, in Mandarin, addressed Jia. "Stop that. We're supposed to look like security officers."

"Yeah, whatever," Jia told him absently, peering across the road again. "If anyone sees us hanging around here for however long then we're gonna look suspicious anyway. So long as we look professional when we get over *there*, that's all that matters."

The night dragged on, and traffic continued to grumble past. Across the way the twin spotlights of the Thousand Suns danced over the sky in their choreographed display, forming two long, narrow cones of light as they caught minuscule specks of dust in their beams, while well-dressed patrons got in and out of cabs on the front drive. The doors to the warmly lit entrance hall were permanently open, and after another half an hour Jia had to concede that it looked a hell of a lot more welcoming than standing out here freezing her ass off.

"If you'd asked me when I was eighteen, I never would have thought that a life of interstellar crime would involve so much waiting around in uncomfortable places," she remarked to her brother, rubbing her arms with her hands. Her stolen uniform wasn't anywhere near as thick as she would have liked, and she was starting to gain some sympathy for the Chief. It was probably even more exposed up where he was.

"I don't recall you asking me anything about getting involved in a life of interstellar crime," Kuai grunted. "I seem to remember you jumping bail for that flying offence at the first opportunity and giving me an hour to sort out getting my things to come with you."

"Never asked you to," Jia told him huffily. They'd had this conversation a dozen times, and it had not ever varied. But Kuai never seemed to tire of bringing it up. "You're just lucky Rourke and Drift needed a mechanic at the same time."

"Lucky?" Kuai nearly spat. "I've been beaten up, abducted, imprisoned, and shot at, not to mention *actually shot*." He slapped his leg, where he'd taken a bullet on Hroza Major. "I don't count that as *lucky*. I could have a nice safe job working as a mechanic back on Old Earth if I weren't out here trying to keep you out of trouble."

Jia sighed, trying to keep her temper. "Think of the things we've *seen*, though. New Shinjuku's oceans, the House of the Redeemer, the Great Mosque on Akbar II . . . Jörmungandr! Biggest damn void station ever built. You wouldn't have seen any of those if you'd stayed behind."

"And I'd be perfectly happy with that," Kuai muttered. "It would have been safer."

"You know, mum and dad were fine with me leaving home," Jia said, turning away from him to look over at the Thousand Suns again. "They trusted me."

"They didn't know you like I do," Kuai retorted.

"Yeah?" Jia said. "Well, you haven't exactly done a good job of keeping me out of trouble, have you? Maybe they knew me better than you did. Maybe they understood there was no point trying to make me be anyone other than *me*."

She heard an intake of breath as though Kuai was going to respond, but then her comm crackled and Muradov's voice spoke into her ear.

+*Jia, Kuai. She's coming out.*+

Jia squinted. Sure enough, a small figure that looked to be dressed in the right clothes had just appeared in the entranceway of the casino. "*Got her.*" She set off at a run, without waiting for her brother. Speed was everything now.

The traffic was slow-moving enough that running out in front of it wasn't the most foolish thing she'd ever done, although she had a pretty big back catalogue of stupid acts to compare to, so perhaps that wasn't the best yardstick. Thankfully, however, the sight of a uniformed security officer darting into the road with one hand held up to ward off vehicles led to several screeches of brakes and one blast of retros from an aircar, and she got across the first two lines of traffic fine. A Xióng Z4 in the third lane didn't stop, and she had to kill her momentum to avoid being hit by it. The bus behind braked sharply, though, and she made it to the central reservation of hardy, drought-tolerant desert plants.

"Jia!" her brother shouted from behind her. "Wait, damn it!"

"No time!" she yelled over her shoulder, and plunged into the next lanes. Chief Han could have exited the casino because a cab she'd booked had arrived, for all they knew: It was vital they reached her as soon as possible to convince her that the only car she should get into was the one they'd brought with them. . . .

A horn blared as something large, red, and metallic skidded to a halt only a couple of feet away from her. Jia didn't even bother to swear at the driver, instead dashing across the next lane. A car braked sharply in front of her in the third lane of traffic and was rear-ended by the one behind, jerking forward that bit farther: Jia simply jumped and slid over the hood instead of breaking her stride to go around it, fighting the urge to grin as she thought of what Rourke would say if the older woman could see her now. Rourke had once pointed out that what slowed most people down when they were on foot in an urban environment was their own preconceptions. Once you started viewing the city as an assault course instead of things that you shouldn't climb on or over, things became a lot quicker.

Jia reached the pavement on the other side and sprinted over it onto the grass that made up the Thousand Suns' front lawn, ignoring the shocked looks she received from a couple who stood arm in arm, admiring one of the fountains. A pair of the casino's security staff had started to descend the steps down to the driveway, presumably in response to a desperately running intruder, but slowed down in confusion once they recognised her uniform.

"*You still with me, Chief?*" she panted.

+*Loud and clear, Jia.*+

"Chief Han!" she yelled, waving one arm furiously. The security chief was already watching her in astonishment, and Jia was sure she saw the other woman's eyes widen in surprise, and possibly fear. Han had presumably just taken a huge payoff from the Triax, after all; she might well be scared of being arrested by her own colleagues on charges of corruption.

The casino security stood aside, and Jia pounded up the steps to where Han stood, frozen in uncertainty and clutching her bag. A couple of seconds later Jia heard running footsteps on gravel and knew that her brother was just behind her.

"Chief," she puffed, momentarily glad that her lack of breath would probably be a suitable excuse for avoiding procedural language she didn't know and getting straight to the point.

"*What is the meaning—*" Han began, but Jia took a couple of steps closer and took her arm.

"*Chief, we've had a tip-off,*" she explained in a breathless whisper, "*the Triax are going to kill you.*"

Han's eyes widened in shock and flickered past Jia to the nearby casino security. "What?"

"*It's true, ma'am,*" Kuai added, appearing at Jia's elbow. "*We need to get you away from here right now. We have a car—*"

"*This is ridiculous,*" Han protested, but Jia could see the fear in her face and could tell that the other woman thought it might be true. "*Who sent you? Why haven't I been—*"

An ornamental terra-cotta plant pot just behind Han, at least three feet high and nearly that across, fell apart with a bang and a crack. Half a second later the faint sound of a gunshot reached them, just audible over the growl of traffic and the hum of background music from the casino's entrance hall.

"Fuck!" Jia barked, not needing to act: Even knowing it was coming, she'd still nearly jumped out of her skin. Everyone around had instinctively ducked and raised their hands, as though that would help.

"Come on, Chief!" Kuai shouted, grabbing Han's other arm and propelling her away towards the road where their hire car was parked. *"Let's get out of here!"*

+*Nice gun Rourke has here,*+ Muradov's glacially calm voice said into Jia's ear as she bolted after the other two. +*The sighting seems a little off, though.*+

A SELF-FULFILLING PROPHECY

"*Gao!*"

Song Daiyu stormed out of her office into the management suite. Gao Dongfeng looked up from where he'd been coaxing the drinks dispenser into providing him with something that might have made a fair attempt at being coffee, and the sneer on his lips faded when he saw her face.

"What?" he said, far more cautiously than usual. Song stormed up to him and jabbed him in the chest with one finger, feeling the fabric of his jacket give beneath her long nail.

"Security just called up! Han cashed in her chips and took the payoff, and then as soon as she gets outside, two cops come running up! One of my people heard them tell her that we're trying to kill her, and then there's a fucking *gunshot*! What the hell are you playing at?"

"How do they know it was a gunshot?" Gao demanded. "It could have been—"

"Because one of the damn planters exploded!" Song nearly screamed at him. "You've gone too far this time! I specifically told you that we were not to touch Han until—"

"I never told anyone to take a shot at her, you stupid bitch!" Gao snarled, pushing her away. Song readied herself to go for his eyes with her nails if he followed up after her, but instead the old man paused, his face screwing up into a grimace. "Two cops?"

"Yes," Song snapped, "a man and a woman, and Han's running off with them now. Why?"

"I haven't told anyone to kill her, so the cops can't know about what hasn't happened!" Gao growled, shaking his head. "This doesn't make any . . . Wait."

"What?" Song demanded when he froze, his eyes wandering as though trying to remember something. "Don't you go senile on me now, you old bastard!"

"Two cop uniforms went missing from one of my laundrettes this week," Gao said slowly, looking at her. For once his gaze was direct and open, instead of being shrouded in disdain. "Some stupid kid on the night shift had lost them: I told the manager to fire him and be done with. But maybe they weren't lost."

Song gaped at him, astounded. "What are you saying?"

"I'm saying there's another player in this game," Gao snarled, snatching his commpiece out of his pocket and settling it in his ear, "and I don't know who it is, but I'd bet my life that those two aren't real cops." He pulled his pad out and jabbed it angrily.

"What are you doing?" Song asked warily.

"I'm calling in my squads," Gao replied, not looking at her. "Come on, you son of a dog, answer me!"

"No!" Song snapped. "That's is unacceptable; we need to—"

"Shut up, girl, and get back to minding your gaming tables," Gao snorted. "The game has changed, so now we play things my way. If she thinks we're after her blood, she'll call in on the shipment, and then we're all fucked. We have to get to her before she thinks to do that." He turned away from her, pressing the commpiece farther into his ear. "Wei, get your boys ready. Chief Han's on the run with a man and a woman wearing cop uniforms.

"Kill them all."

BYCATCH

Lukas Ivanovic was smaller than Apirana, but not by much. Drift watched him bouncing up and down on the balls of his feet and swinging his arms back and forth across his hairy chest. The big fighter was apparently in his late thirties, and his face certainly bore testament to the fact that he'd spent much of his adult life involved in violent pursuits, with a nose that was bent right over on one side and two cauliflower ears, not to mention a few choice scars. Drift couldn't work out if Ivanovic had never had the money to have the damage repaired, or simply couldn't be bothered. Perhaps there wasn't much point while you were still fighting, Drift mused: Wait until you retired, then get everything fixed up at once.

"Go get him, big man," he told Apirana quietly as the ringside official checked the Māori's mouthguard and gloves. It was meaningless noise, of course, but both of them were used to playing a character to work a scam. It was just that this was someone else's scam.

"You got it, bro," Big A replied with a grin, then imperiously waved aside the official and faced the cage. Drift stepped back as well and watched as the big Māori dropped into a crouch and began bellowing his war chant.

He stuck his hand into his pocket as Apirana began slapping his arms and felt the reassuring presence of the credit chip Serenity Chen had begrudgingly handed over a few minutes previously. Apirana had checked it in his pad, and the money was good: seventeen thousand stars, just as promised. What with the money from their original win betting on Apirana, and the big score his crew was hopefully securing from Chief Han any moment now, it was enough to bring them over the half a million mark despite the various bribes and expenses they'd had to lay out to make this venture work.

Assuming, of course, that Jenna, Muradov, and the Changs weren't having any troubles with what was admittedly a somewhat thrown-together plan. It all relied on Han being taken in for a minute or so, and Jia or Kuai being able to tell one end of a Taser from the other. Drift thought that both those things were likely, but knew all too well that there were never any certainties in life.

He had to believe that they could pull it off. The alternatives if they couldn't were so dire that they didn't bear thinking about until there was no other option.

Of course, he reflected, if it *did* work out, this was an object lesson for all of them. This was a hugely ambitious job, but it came with a big reward. His crew was capable of pulling off some truly remarkable feats when they stretched themselves: It was just a shame that the motivation for such things normally had to be the threat of imminent death. Perhaps if they could get that level of motivation in normal circumstances then they might have a better chance of turning a profit out of the galaxy. . . .

Apirana stormed up the steps into the cage and bellowed something in Māori at Ivanovic. The other fighter stared him down, but Drift could tell that Ivanovic wasn't quite as calm as he'd like to make out. Was he even in on the result? He had to be, Drift assumed: Chen was unlikely to chance zir arm twice, and there was no guarantee that Ivanovic would even go for a submission in the first round otherwise. Perhaps Apirana's pre-match routine hadn't reassured Ivanovic that his opponent was going to go along with the plan?

You just do your job, and A will do his. And then we can get out of here and leave Serenity Chen and this stupid building behind us.

Apirana finished his routine, to the cheers of some of the crowd (and the jeers of several more, who apparently hadn't forgiven him for despatching Kuang Daniu so quickly), and walked over to his starting position against one side of the cage. Drift made his way around so he was standing behind the big man on the other side of the cage and hopped up onto the lip that the ring boys and girls walked around.

"Ugly bastard, isn't he?" he said conversationally as the ring announcer began his introductions and a camera drone buzzed down into the ring to focus on the man's face.

"Gotta say, bro, I kinda wish that one of these was real," Apirana replied quietly. "Woulda been nice to test myself, know what I mean? Only if it made sense to, though. I ain't gonna jump ship and sign up to a fight gym somewhere now, try to make a new career out of it."

"Glad to hear it," Drift told him. The ring announcer screamed something virtually incomprehensible and gestured at Apirana, who responded by walking forward and throwing up his right hand, thumb, and little finger extended. The crowd responded again: something of a mixed reaction, certainly, but definitely a reaction.

"Five minutes, big man," Drift told Apirana as the Māori retreated back towards him while the announcer shifted to introducing Ivanovic. "Five minutes or less, and we're walking out of here."

"So long as he don't try some sort of leg lock on my bad ankle," Apirana muttered back. "Otherwise I might be hopping."

Drift grimaced. "Yeah, well, hopefully not. Okay, uh . . . good luck?" He hopped down as the announcer pointed at the referee and then made a beeline for the cage door. Apirana bounced a couple of times, the huge muscles of his calves flexing as he did so, then the referee made a chopping motion with his hand to indicate the start of the bout. Apirana advanced towards his opponent.

The crowd made some noises of discontent almost immediately. Perhaps, Drift thought, they'd been hoping to see another raging charge and another opponent demolished almost immediately. If so, they were in for a disappointment: Apirana fired off a couple of loose jabs, range finders that fell short, then began circling. Ivanovic didn't seem to be in any hurry to close the distance either, as he tried a kick to Apirana's left leg that the Māori almost casually stepped back from.

"C'mon, c'mon, c'mon, c'mon," Drift muttered as the two behemoths circled cautiously. "Just get *on* with it, will you?" He glanced up at the fight clock and was startled to see that only ten seconds had passed. It already felt like half a minute had ticked by.

The people in the other corner were shouting something. Drift looked over at them for a moment, then decided he should probably join in just to keep up appearances. He cast his mind back to the dim days long ago where he'd briefly trained for this sort of thing at high school back on Soldevalle.

"One, two! One, two!"

Apirana jabbed with his left fist, then lunged forward with his right. Ivanovic blocked the shot with his left hand, but it made an ugly smacking sound, and he retreated a few steps to the cage wall before making his way in again.

"Good!" Drift shouted insincerely. Seriously, why was Ivanovic making such a meal of this? Get in there, go in low, get the big guy off his feet, and do some sort of armlock or choke hold or something. Job done, everyone would be happy except anyone who'd bet on Apirana, and to be honest, if they bet on an unknown fighter with one win to his name in this crooked town, more fool them.

He glanced over at Chen. The events manager was seated at ringside with a look of stony calm on zir face, but seemed to feel Drift's gaze and looked back at him. One eyebrow raised in query, and Drift returned his eyes to the ring, where nothing seemed to have happened since he'd last been watching. *Damn it, they can't hold us responsible if Ivanovic just stands there all round.*

He looked up at the fight clock again, big red numbers counting down on a four-sided screen suspended far above the ring . . . and frowned as something caught his eye, high up in the crowd on the far side of the arena. He closed his natural left one and kicked up the zoom on his right.

Black uniforms: the local security force. There was a group of them, two standing silhouetted against the light from the entrance and exit, two more now making their way down the steps that led between the rows of seats. They were a way off yet, but seemed to be heading for the ringside area.

His heart suddenly racing, Drift brought his mechanical eye back into line with his left one and looked around. There, there, and there as well. . . . Suddenly, the Two Trees Arena was crawling with cops.

"A!" he shouted in alarm, without thinking, and looked back at the cage. Apirana must have heard something in his voice, some indication that things weren't right, because the big man's head jerked towards him. His inattention only lasted for a split second, but it was long enough for Lukas Ivanovic to make his move.

The other fighter lunged forward, a far cry from his previous plodding inactivity, and lashed out with a thunderous right hook that caught Apirana on the jaw. Blindsided and off-balance, the Māori began to stumble sideways as his legs abruptly failed to follow instructions.

Ivanovic followed him, reaching out his hands to grab Apirana and, presumably, throw him to the mat where he could end the fight according to Chen's wishes.

What actually happened was that he collided with a suddenly rallying Apirana who thrust one arm between the other fighter's legs and hoisted him clear off the ground with a combination of leverage and sheer brute strength, held him almost horizontal for a second, then jumped forward to slam Ivanovic to the mat and land clean on top of him in the same motion.

The crowd leapt to their feet almost as one, and a massive cheer erupted in praise of what they'd just seen.

Serenity Chen leapt to zir feet as well and opened zir mouth to yell something, then apparently thought better of it and glared murderously at Drift instead.

Drift felt sick. He could hear Apirana bellowing, and realised as one of the Māori's fists rose and then descended again that the unexpected blow to the head had hurt Apirana just enough for his self-control to snap. Drift had been on the wrong end of one of Apirana's murderous rages once, and he would have undoubtedly been throttled to death if Jenna hadn't intervened. Lukas Ivanovic was much bigger and stronger than Drift, and a trained fighter to boot: Drift simply had to hope that he could weather this storm and then maybe pull something out of the bag to get a win and stop him and Apirana from being gunned down by Triax thugs the moment they stepped outside the Two Trees.

Wait. The security officers . . .

Drift remembered what had sparked his initial shout and looked around himself again, just in time to see two black-clad figures push their way through protesting officials and grab Serenity Chen by zir arms. The events manager's face was apoplectic for a moment as ze felt hands on zir, but then zir expression shifted into sudden uncertainty as ze saw the uniforms.

The crowd was shouting louder and differently now, as the disturbance at ringside became more and more widespread. Officers were everywhere, arresting officials wherever they found them. A woman with dark hair cut into short bangs and wearing a suit—presumably a detective—was showing the timekeeper and ring announcer her badge and saying something urgently. Moments later the klaxon sounded, way before the end of the round was due, and the ring announcer raised his microphone. This time he didn't draw out his words, and Drift's translation protocol on his comm was able to make sense of them as they boomed out across the arena:

"*Ladies and gentlemen, we . . . The Two Trees Arena regrets to announce that this event is suspended . . .*"

The detective snatched the microphone from him and spoke through a squeal of feedback.

"*This event is suspended due to allegations of match-fixing. Please vacate the building.*"

Drift stared around him in horror, then realised that the referee in the cage was trying to pull Apirana off Ivanovic. He wasn't having much luck.

"Shit." Drift hopped up and pulled himself directly over the cage into the ring, then lunged for Apirana and heaved on the big man's arm. "*Madre de Dios*, A! It's over! *It's over!*"

For a long moment or two it was like trying to shift a truck all by himself. Then Apirana stopped resisting and allowed himself to be hauled backwards. Drift ended up in a sitting position, with the big man half-sprawled next to him.

"Ah, shit," Apirana said softly, looking over at Ivanovic. The other fighter was moving, Drift was relieved to see, but his already-battered face had taken a severe pounding in the last few seconds: He had a long cut on his forehead that was leaking blood, a couple of new welts, and one eye that was already swelling up. Ivanovic's team were making their way into the cage in a more traditional manner than Drift had, flooding in through the door and surrounding their fallen man while casting several dark looks in Apirana's direction.

The referee appeared in front of them, yelling in Mandarin.

"Oh, shut it," Drift snapped at him, gesturing at the chaos outside the cage. "Haven't you got bigger things to worry about?"

The referee looked around uncertainly, perhaps only just now realising exactly what was taking place. Drift couldn't really blame him. Being in the cage with these two beasts would mean having to concentrate hard on what was going on simply to not get squashed, let alone try to officiate. If the ref had been busy trying to pull Apirana away when the klaxon went off, then he might not have heard the stuttering announcement over the public-address system afterwards.

"Okay," Drift said into Apirana's ear as officers started to make their way towards the cage door. "Well, none of this has gone to plan, but they can't really doubt that you were trying to win that one, right? I mean, look at the other guy. So we're just a fighter and his agent, trying to make a name for you. It's the guys throwing fights who'd be in trouble, not the ones winning them. . . ."

"Ah, *shit*," Apirana muttered, now sounding less sorrowful and rather more agitated. "Bro, we might be in trouble after all."

The detective was approaching them with two officers in tow. She looked down at them, then motioned them to get up.

"My name is Detective Li of the Zhuchengshi Security Forces," she said. Drift noticed that she frowned in Apirana's direction for a long moment before continuing. "You are both being detained for questioning in relation to allegations of match-fixing."

WHAT A LOVELY DAY

One of New Samara's seasonal deluges had just passed, and the bruise-coloured clouds were receding into the northern sky, leaving Rassvet relatively unobscured once more. The star's heat was already beginning to evaporate off some of the standing water, and the moist air seemed to stick in Tamara Rourke's throat a little when she inhaled.

She looked around, a little startled, when a bird started calling somewhere to her left. Roman snorted in mild amusement.

"It's a recording."

"Really?" Rourke looked at him curiously. *"Why is it playing?"*

"They tried to bring some native species here when the planet was first settled, apparently," Roman told her, shifting his shoulder as though trying to get his slimline parachute to settle better. They were standing outside the staff entrance of the Grand House, waiting for Sergei Orlov, and for Boris to bring an aircar round. *"It didn't work in most cases: not enough of an ecosystem. But the government still thought people might feel more at home if they had some familiar noises, so there are speakers in the city that play birdsong at dawn and dusk, and every now and then after a storm."* He gestured with one hand in the direction the whistles had come from. *"We get a mistle thrush."*

"Huh. Every day is a school day." There were some planets where an

almost Earth-like ecosystem had been achieved, Rourke knew: Franklin Major and Minor in Jenna's home system were two, and she knew there were a couple of planets in the galaxy where a breathable atmosphere had been used not to grow crops but to make giant game parks for the super rich to go hunting. However, in general, humanity had viewed that it was better to only take what they needed from Earth, which tended to boil down to a lot of plant seeds and some bees.

"*So what's today's trip?*" Rourke asked, changing the subject.

"*Today the boss goes to see one of his new developments on the east side of town and puts the fear of God into the contractors who are behind schedule,*" Roman said dryly. "*One does not simply tell Mr. Orlov that his new two-hundred-bedroom luxury hotel and leisure complex has encountered 'unexpected delays.'*"

"I bet one doesn't," Rourke muttered. "*I assume that no, ah, examples will be made there and then?*"

"*Good God, no,*" Roman replied, looking momentarily appalled. "*No, I'll be doing that later. Grab the assistant foreman on his way home, and bang!*" He punched one hand into the other. "*Good-bye, kneecaps.*"

He held Rourke's gaze for a moment, then burst out laughing. "*Ha! Your face!*"

Rourke eyed him steadily. "*And here was me thinking that it was Larysa with the lousy sense of humour.*"

"*Oh, it is.*" Roman chuckled. "*But you shouldn't take things so seriously. That kind of thug work . . . that's not usually necessary anymore. Anyone who does business with Mr. Orlov knows what could happen if they displease him, so it rarely has to actually happen at all.*"

Rourke thought back to her abduction from Medusa II. "*I might disagree with that assessment.*"

Roman shifted uncomfortably, and Rourke got the impression that he had at least briefly forgotten exactly how she'd come to be standing with him. *"Yeah, well. 'Rarely' isn't the same thing as 'never.'"* He looked up, apparently grateful for the distraction, as the familiar whine of an aircar became audible. *"Ah, here comes our ride."*

The limo glided to a halt in front of them, and Boris threw the vehicle into neutral, then wound the window down and looked over the top of his glare shades at them both. *"Afternoon, folks. Are you going my way?"*

"Sadly," Roman sighed. *"Have you learned how to fly that thing yet?"*

"You sound like my father, Roman," Boris said, twisting his gravelly voice into one with a lisp and what sounded to Rourke like a stereotypical rural accent. *"'How long has it been since you passed your test, Boris? You know they advise retesting every three years, don't you, Boris? Isn't it time you got a proper job instead of being behind a damn steering wheel, Boris?'"* He spat on the ground. *"Parents, eh? They never let a thing like making a mess of their own lives get in the way of telling you how to live yours."*

He looked like he was going to say more, but cut himself off as brisk footsteps from behind Rourke announced the arrival of Sergei Orlov, with Nicolai at his shoulder. Roman stepped up smartly to open the limo's rear door, and the gang boss boarded the car without having to break stride, with Nicolai following him in. Roman shut the door behind them both and skirted the rear of the vehicle to enter on the other side while Rourke did the same at the front, climbing in beside Boris, who gently fed power to the drive and pulled away smoothly. Regardless of whatever criticisms his father might have to offer, Boris certainly seemed an excellent driver to Rourke.

"The construction site, sir?" Boris asked as they climbed into the air and headed towards the public air routes.

"Yes," Orlov replied. *"Roman, call ahead. I don't want to be kept waiting around."*

Rourke heard the faint beeps as Roman activated his comm, presumably to call a site supervisor, and took the opportunity to look out of the window. It was the first time she'd flown in an aircar over New Samara that hadn't been in a stolen vehicle at night, and you always got a different perspective looking at the streets from above. Her training had drummed into her the importance of knowing your location as well as you could from all angles, but that had fed into an interest in simply seeing how a city had been put together. Some places had grown organically, whereas others had been planned in their entirety from the start, and it didn't usually take a great deal of observation to work out which. In the case of New Samara, it was fairly self-evident that the Red Star government had always known exactly how big they were going to let the planet's one temperate city get. However, from what she'd heard, they had made some concessions to expansion recently, one part of which was Orlov's new development.

It didn't take a genius to work out how it was that Sergei Orlov had managed to get that concession; Larysa had been known to say that the boss had so many politicians in his pocket that he walked with a limp, although even Larysa had better sense than to use that wording within Orlov's hearing.

It was while looking out of the window and taking in the layout of the streets that Rourke noticed the black Takagi Sunrise pulling out of a side lane. Nothing remarkable in and of itself, of course: There would be more than one black Takagi Sunrise in New Samara; in fact, there were probably at least a couple of hundred. However, her experience with Galina meant that she'd paid very close attention to every single one she'd seen since, and this one was accelerating so that it was pulling directly underneath them on the flight lane below.

"*We've got someone beneath us*," she said to Boris, pressing her head against the window in an effort to keep tabs on the other car. "*Change la—*"

There a loud, metallic bang from beneath them, and the limo's drive abruptly cut out.

"*Bail!*" Rourke yelled as the car's nose began to dip. She opened the door beside her and threw herself heedlessly into the rushing air, slapping her chest as she did so to activate the parachute.

Of course, while being in a plummeting aircar when it hit the ground probably wasn't a good idea, jumping out of one was not without its problems. Boris had been flying in the third lane up, which was probably the worst place to be: too far to fall safely, not far enough for the parachute to provide much assistance. Rourke's leap took her clear of the air lane but directly into the side of the building, and she grunted in pain as she slammed into the unyielding surface. She caught a confused glimpse of images: Roman and Orlov falling together, their parachutes unfurling as they did so; the limo careering towards the ground; other aircars veering or braking sharply to avoid the chaos; another chute, probably Nicolai's, getting caught on the front of another vehicle in a different lane. Rourke didn't see what happened in the last instance because she was spun away by the force of her own impact, but it would almost certainly be fatal for someone.

The pavement, which was mercifully wide, rushed up at her. She thought for a horrible moment that she was going to hit facedown, but then her parachute opened enough to catch some air and arrested her momentum slightly. While not enough to slow her much, it did jerk her upright, and she was able to get her feet under her to drop and roll instead of landing in a way that would probably have broken her arms and knees. Even as it was, she felt a spike of pain up her right leg from the impact, and she winced as she got back to her feet and hurriedly detached her chute.

She looked around and caught sight of Roman and Orlov, a little farther up the road. Orlov was pushing himself backwards out of the road with his arms, but Roman's chute had become entangled in an ornamental cherry tree, and he was reaching up, trying to disconnect it while still a few feet off the ground. Rourke hurried to them, trying to ignore the pain in her leg. "*Sir! Are you hurt?*"

"*My ankle,*" Orlov replied through gritted teeth, gesturing at his leg. "*I think it's sprained.*"

Rourke hissed in frustration and scanned the traffic around them, searching for the Sunrise. The limo was some way farther down the street, lying on its side, and their crash had clearly caused various other more minor accidents as vehicles had swerved or braked to avoid the chaos and hit each other. Aircars were landing, drivers were gesticulating at each other, and horns were sounding. She caught a glimpse of a dark-suited figure lying in the road with people starting to cluster around him. Nicolai or Boris? She couldn't tell from here, but probably Nicolai. She suspected Boris was either still in the limo or crushed beneath it.

"*Sir, we need to move,*" Rourke said firmly. "*It was the GIA: They'll have seen us bail out, and they'll be coming back for you.*"

Orlov looked up at her sharply. "*You're sure?*"

"*A Takagi Sunrise came underneath us just before we went down,*" Rourke said grimly, reaching down. Orlov took her hand, and she pulled him upright with some considerable effort, then steadied him as he staggered. "*I didn't see the plates on either occasion, but it's too much of a coincidence given the car I saw when I was with Galina.*"

"*They'll come back, in front of all this?*" Orlov asked, gesturing with one hand and taking in the chaos on several levels of the street.

"*Taking a car down in broad daylight isn't subtle,*" Rourke said. "*It looks like they want you dead, by whatever means necessary.*" She looked over at Roman as the bald bodyguard finally managed to get himself free and dropped to the ground. "*You okay?*"

"*I'm fine,*" Roman answered shortly. His hand was already inside his jacket and gripping his gun. "*What* was *that?*"

"*Overload bolt, probably,*" Rourke said, scanning their surroundings.

"*It's like a shockbolt, but for aircars rather than people: overloads the electronics and shorts out the drivers.*" Being in the open and surrounded by people wouldn't help them now, she doubted; they needed to get Orlov out of sight.

Or did they?

For a moment, Rourke hesitated. The GIA, her former employers, were making a direct bid to kill Sergei Orlov, the man currently holding her hostage. In most circumstances that would be a good thing. She didn't even have to lift a finger; all she had to do was stand around and wait for the Sunrise to come back, then watch them blow the mobster away. It sounded like an ideal scenario.

Except that it wasn't. Rourke knew better than most that the GIA would view her as expendable at best, and that was only if Danny Wong had actually told anyone who she was before approaching her. Even if he had, his subsequent disappearance might have been blamed on her. The odds were that the GIA now considered her to be part of Orlov's team, and therefore in this situation she'd be regarded as kill on sight. The operatives certainly weren't likely to include her in whatever extraction plan they had, assuming they even had one.

More importantly, Orlov dying right now didn't help her any. His death and her survival wouldn't look at all good to whomever might be left in Orlov's organisation, and she had no resources to get off-world. Even if she did, she had no idea where Drift and the others were, and it still left her with the problem of them coming back and stumbling into a situation where she was gone and they'd take the fall for it.

Besides which, this was exactly why she'd grown weary of her active service. Orchestrating an aircar accident that endangered the lives of civilians to kill one man, and not even because he was an interstellar criminal. No, this was simply to try to destabilise a sector, to bring economic and political uncertainty to the lives of billions as companies foundered and new predators arose in the murky, all-pervading world of organised crime to try to replace the suddenly absent big fish. The *status quo* of Orlov's dominance would be gone, and with him would go all the protection rackets and clear demarcations of territory. There would be blood in the streets and back alleys as different organisations tried to bite off pieces of his former empire, and ordinary people got caught in the middle.

Besides, she'd rather liked Boris and couldn't help feeling slightly responsible for Nicolai. He'd been a conscientious student and eager to learn.

She held out her hand to Roman. "*Give me your gun, call for backup, and get him out of here.*"

Roman's brow wrinkled. "*What?*"

"*His ankle's hurt, and I'm not big or strong enough to support him properly for long,*" Rourke said briskly. "*If you're helping him, then you won't be able to shoot straight, and I'm the better shot anyway. We can't stagger around waiting for them to come back and finish the job. Give me your gun and go. I'll take care of them here.*"

Roman looked to Orlov for guidance, and Rourke felt the gang boss nod.

"*Do it, Roman,*" Orlov said, his voice tight. "*She's talking sense.*"

To his credit, Roman didn't hesitate once he'd been given an order. He pulled out his gun and handed it to her, then ducked in to replace her under Orlov's left arm as she slipped away. Rourke armed the weapon with a buzz, holding it in both hands with the barrel pointing at the ground.

"*Now go,*" she told them. "*Head back to the Grand House. I'll meet you there if I can't catch up with you.*" The GIA agents would know they didn't have long before emergency services responded to the pileup, including the police. If they were coming back, they'd be coming back now.

Orlov and Roman began to move away, and Rourke considered her next course of action. Their chutes were an obvious marker and would be where the agents would surely look first, which provided her with obvious bait for a trap. A somewhat improvised trap, to be sure, but a trap nonetheless.

She stepped out into the road, weaving her way through the ground-level traffic that had now slowed to a crawl due to the congestion caused by the accidents up ahead. She made it across the two lanes on her side to the vehicles going the other way, which were moving a little quicker, then picked her way past the first of those as well.

As she was looking down the second lane of ground-level traffic, waiting for a gap, she saw a black Takagi Sunrise heading in her direction, slowing a little more as it glided past the wrecked limo on the opposite side of the road.

She couldn't stay where she was, so she took a chance and darted out in front of a sleek red wheeled coupe. It slammed on its brakes but didn't sound its horn, possibly because the driver had caught sight of her gun, and she made it to the other side of the road where she ducked between two large garbage bins outside a shop and peeked back out again.

The Sunrise came on.

Rourke scrubbed the palm of each hand in turn down the legs of her bodysuit and took a firm grip on Roman's pistol. There was a chance that the car was protected in some way with bulletproof glass or the like, but she just had to hope that wasn't the case. Besides, they'd need to have an open window if they were intending to shoot anyone. The question was, did Rourke want to shoot first? Was she confident enough that this car, this fairly common make and model, definitely contained GIA agents that were intent on killing Sergei Orlov and anyone else who got in the way?

The Sunrise began to indicate, pulling into the inside lane now it was around the congestion caused by the crashed limo. That meant there were only two lanes of traffic—the ones travelling eastwards—between it and the discarded parachutes. Its windows were open, but it wasn't so cold a day that this was at all remarkable.

Rourke watched it, keeping as much of her as she could in cover, hoping that it would just drive on by and not show any interest, but the Sunrise slowed for no apparent reason as it came alongside the discarded parachutes. Rourke had a split second to make her call and wrestled with indecision. Was this innocent rubbernecking, or were the two figures she could see in the car assassins in the employ of the North American government, looking for their quarry?

The pale face of the passenger turned towards her, scanning her side of the road. She met a pair of blue eyes that widened in shock and rec-ognition, saw the shape of a gun being brought up, and knew that her suspicions had been borne out.

The agents had probably been expecting their targets to be recover-ing from their emergency skydive, and still with their parachutes. Even when checking the other side of the road, they certainly hadn't antici-pated that they'd driven into a trap. They were presumably expecting dazed, disoriented gangsters who thought their drive had failed natu-rally and didn't even realise they were being targeted.

Their mistake.

There was only a momentary difference in their reaction speeds, but it was enough. Roman's pistol barked twice, and the gunman's head jerked back, the rear window and windshield abruptly coloured with red spatters. The driver's instinctive flinch caused the Sunrise to swerve aside, but then he regained control and began to climb without warning, causing other aircars to swerve and blast their horns.

Rourke couldn't let him get away. He was more mobile than her and might come back for her when she didn't have the element of surprise and before she'd regained the relative safety of the Grand House. Also, there weren't many—or indeed, any—other petite black women who were seen in the company of Sergei Orlov. Right now she might be nothing more than a side note, but the only way to avoid drawing massive attention to herself as the killer of one GIA agent was to take care of the other before he could report back.

She straightened up to get the best angle of fire possible and began emptying the clip of Roman's gun at the Sunrise.

Metal sparked as bullets ricocheted off, her low angle shots deflected by the car's bodywork, and for a moment she thought her efforts would be in vain. Then a bullet caught the rear windshield, smashing it. The Sunrise kept rising, but its sharp ascent was nose first, and for one second, Rourke had a clear view up through the inside of the vehicle.

She managed to get three shots off before the gun clicked empty. The Sunrise was still climbing away from her.

And it kept going.

Rather than veering away when it reached the top lane of traffic, the Sunrise continued rising towards the clouds, spinning gently as it did so. It would presumably carry on until it reached its altitude limit, and hang there until the fuel cell gave out and the lifters died or—more likely—the emergency services that would even now be hurrying to the scene of the limo's crash retrieved it before it could fall on anyone. The driver was either dead or incapacitated enough to be unable to control their vehicle.

Rourke didn't waste time watching any further. She could do nothing more in any case, and that little exchange had taken place in far more of a public view than she was used to. She needed to ditch Roman's gun before someone caught her with it, and get back to the Grand House as soon as possible.

She turned and broke into a run. Running was suspicious, but she wanted to get away from the immediate vicinity and the sirens she could hear on the air. Once she was a couple of streets removed, she'd slow down into a walk.

Overall, she was rather glad that she'd been taking an interest in how the city was laid out.

BROTHERLY LOVE

Chief Han was, in Jia's personal opinion, a bit too fucking slow for her own good. Not in terms of intelligence—you probably had to be pretty smart to become security chief, even if you were taking bribes from the Triax—but simply in terms of covering ground. Jia was never going to claim to be athletic, since she spent most of her time in a spaceship's limiting confines and kept her weight down mainly by drinking coffee and chewing appetite suppressants, but she was pretty sure that if she thought someone was shooting at her, she'd be moving a damned sight faster than Han was now, even in slightly impractical shoes.

She briefly toyed with the idea of asking Muradov for a second shot to encourage her along a bit, but decided that Han might hear her and so kept her mouth shut.

"Where are we going?" Han demanded as they ducked between palm trees and ornamental shrubs. The edge of the casino's front plot was coming up, bordered with a low hedge at roughly knee height. Beyond it was the pavement, and a side street off the main boulevard with a line of parked cars down each side. Kuai had parked theirs in a space farther up the street, on the far side.

"Just over here!" Kuai puffed. Jia could see that he was in pain and guessed that running was aggravating the old bullet injury in his leg.

Then again, he'd always been a crybaby. "We've got an unmarked car parked on this street."

"An unmarked car?" Han was still with them, but she seemed less and less certain as they ran. "Where did you get that?"

"Just following orders, ma'am," Jia said, hopping over the hedge and holding out her arms to half-pull, half-lift Han over after her. She and Kuai managed it, but the security chief wrenched herself away from them both.

"*Whose* orders?" she demanded, one hand clenched into a fist and the other tightly gripping the handles of her bag. "Who sent you here? Who gave you this information?"

Jia exchanged looks with her brother, wondering whether they could get away with Tasering Han now and grabbing the cash. They were supposed to wait until they had her in the car, but it looked like that might not be an option any longer.

"That's an order!" Han snapped. "You'll tell me right now, or—"

"Oh *shit!*" Jia cut her off, pointing over the security chief's shoulder. Farther up the side street, pretty much opposite where their rental car was parked, a large metallic door in the casino's side marked STAFF PARKING was whirring upwards. Ducking out of the entranceway, in ones and twos, were people who didn't look like anyone the Thousand Suns would normally employ. In fact, they looked about as much like an archetypical street gang as it was possible to get outside of a low-budget action holo, and several of them had already drawn handguns.

"Run!" Jia barked, grabbing Han and almost throwing the security chief into the street. She followed her, pushing the older woman towards the questionable shelter of the line of cars on the far side. "Go!"

A gun barked once, and then it sounded to Jia's terrified ears as though a veritable battery of weapons had opened up when the others joined in. She and Han leapt desperately through the gap between two cars and hit the pavement on the other side of the street, with Kuai barrelling in after them a second later. Jia glanced over at him to make sure he hadn't been hit, but he was already crawling away from the gap and into cover beside her.

"Shit, shit, shit!" Jia hissed. She yelped in fright as a car window shattered above her and the bullet knocked a few chips out of the far wall.

"They're insane!" Han hissed, rooting around in her bag desperately. "To do this now, in the middle of the street . . ." She looked up and fixed both of them with a momentary stare. "Aren't you going to shoot back at the pig fuckers? They'll be on us in seconds otherwise!"

Jia blinked at her in surprise for a moment, then clumsily unclipped her gun with fingers that suddenly felt too large. She scrabbled along the pavement, cutting her hand on broken glass, then reached the car's hood. She tried to think for a moment of what Rourke would do in this situation.

Probably be somewhere else.

Not helpful. She took a breath with a whimper and swung up over the hood, desperately searching for a target. Something moved on the far side of the street, little more than a blur against blurs to her panicked eyes, and she squeezed her trigger: The gun kicked in her hand and a shooting pain took hold of her wrist, but she fired twice more and then ducked back down. Return fire came half a second later, and the wall above them puffed more chips of concrete as bullets hit home.

Suddenly Muradov's voice was in her ear. +*Jia? Kuai? I can hear gunshots; what's happening?*+

"It's all gone tits up!" Jia hissed at him. "*The fucking Triax are trying to kill us!*"

There was a clang in the background, and Muradov's breathing got louder, as though he'd started moving quickly. +*What are their numbers and dispositions?*+

"Six or seven of them, and pretty fucking pissed off, Chief!" Jia continued in English.

A grunt, and then Muradov was speaking in Russian. +*I meant, where are they in relation to you? Can you get to the car?*+

"No!" Jia looked up the street as Kuai threw himself up, shooting at their antagonists. He ducked back down a moment later, shaking his head grimly to indicate that he didn't think he'd hit anyone. "They're on the other side of the street, but the fuckers are level with our car. And there's a gap in the cars on this side before that! We'd be dead meat if we tried to make it across there!"

+*Do what you can. I'll be with you as soon as possible.*+

Han grabbed Jia's arm. "Who are you talking to?"

"Someone who might be able to help," Jia replied back in Mandarin, shaking the other woman off and firing blindly twice over the car hood. If she remembered correctly, these guns had a magazine of twenty, which meant she'd gone through a quarter of the ammunition in there already. She had two more on her belt, as was standard security force procedure according to Muradov, but even so she suddenly felt woefully under-equipped, not to mention underskilled. Thankfully the Triax thugs didn't exactly seem to be sharpshooters: They were hitting the cars, but not much else.

"Have you even called in for backup?" Han demanded. She hadn't drawn a gun, but Jia supposed you couldn't get away with carrying one into a casino, no matter how paranoid and corrupt you were.

"You want to do that, you knock yourself out," Jia snapped, leaning down to see if she could see feet moving underneath the cars. No such luck: The light cast by the streetlamps wasn't strong enough to show anything conclusive.

"You're not even cops, are you?" Han said grimly, looking from Jia to Kuai and back again.

"Give the lady a medal," Kuai snorted. "But if it makes you feel any better, right now *we* don't want you dead, and *they* do!"

"This is intolerable!" Han spat, fumbling with her comm. Whoever she was calling clearly answered quickly, because a moment later she was speaking again. "Xiulan! The Triax are trying to kill me! I'm at the Thousand Suns casino, and I want reliable units here *now*!"

"Reliable units?" Kuai said from the other side of her. "Didn't think you had many of those."

"I assure you, I am *very* aware of which officers are on the take and which aren't," Han bit out at him, covering her comm for a second, then took her hand away and resumed speaking to the person on the other end. "No, of course I'm not okay, I'm being shot at! Just get people here on the double! Anyone who's not coming here goes to the spaceport! The Triax are trying something big, I know it!"

Jia shot a glance at Kuai, her stomach churning. That could prove problematic, even if they got out of this.

"Just *do* it!" Han yelled into her comm. "If it proves to be nothing, then fine; I'll take responsibility, and I'll resign or whatever the governor wants. But I'm not letting them get away with this!" She tapped her comm to cancel the call and then glared at Jia.

"So what's your plan, other than not hitting anything with that—*gnnggghhhhhh*!"

She spasmed for a moment, then fell forward with a moan. On the other side of her, Kuai was holding his Taser.

"Are you out of your fucking *mind*?" Jia snarled at him. "What the *fuck* did you just do?!"

"They want her, right?" Kuai said, his eyes wide and hard and desperate. "Her or the money, whatever. Both. So we stuff the money into our shirts, we throw her and the bag out there, and we run for it."

"And let them kill her?" Jia asked in horror, looking down at Han. She didn't owe the woman anything, of course, and they needed the money to save Rourke. But to throw a stunned human being out to where she'd be riddled with bullets in three seconds flat just didn't sit well with her.

"They're going to kill *all* of us in a second!" Kuai snapped at her. "This way we at least have a—*shitshitshit!*"

A shape lurched into view over the car's trunk, backlit by the street-lights: a Triax thug, gun already swinging down to point at them. Jia jerked her own weapon up, but Kuai was quicker, for once, and raised his pistol to fire repeatedly upwards at point-blank range.

The bullets tore holes in the thug's face and blew the back of his skull right out. Jia's own shot thudded into the man's shoulder, but did little more than knock the newly made corpse slightly sideways as it slith-ered grotesquely out the car and landed in a wet, suddenly boneless heap half-on and half-off the pavement.

"Fuck!" Kuai panted, desperately wiping his face where the man's blood had spattered down onto him. He turned his red-smeared fea-tures towards Jia, and his eyes widened in horror. "Jia, get down!"

He leapt for her as more gunshots went off, hideously loud even over the blood thundering in her ears, and Jia found herself crushed to the pavement underneath him, even as she turned to see what he was looking at. She caught a glimpse of another Triax gang member, now on their side of the street—so they no longer had the cars as cover—and pointing his gun at them. She shrugged her brother off her and brought her gun up, braced it in two hands, and squeezed the trigger once, again, and again.

Her aim was true this time. Blood spouted from his thigh, his stom-ach, and then his chest, and he began a slow collapse, his gun falling from his hands.

"Yeah, that's fucking *right*, you son of a whore!" she screamed, pushing herself up into a kneeling position. "You fuck with me, that's what you get!"

Kuai was still sitting on her legs. She turned to tell him to get the fuck off her, but the words froze in her throat.

"Kuai?"

Her brother was on his back on the pavement, staring blankly up at the desert sky above them. The black of his uniform couldn't get much darker, but there was a ragged tear in the fabric just over his heart that was already wet with blood. Another wound, where his neck met his shoulder, was turning the pavement beneath it red.

"*Kuai?!*"

MAN DOWN

More gunshots rang out on the night air. Alim Muradov gave the magnetic grapnel he'd attached to the building's ventilation shaft a good tug, and it seemed to hold firm.

"Do what you can," he said into his comm, trying to calm Jia with just the tone of his voice, "I'll be with you as soon as possible."

Of course, that meant abseiling straight down ten stories with Tamara Rourke's Crusader 920 slung across his shoulders. He hadn't had time to disassemble the gun and pack it into its carry bag, so it would just have to hang loose. Besides, it would hardly make him much more conspicuous, and he had the feeling he might need it.

For just a moment, Alim wondered what he was doing. He hadn't abseiled off anything since his army days, and as a tunnel rat by birth, he'd never had much of a head for heights. But he'd joined this crew of his own free will, knowing full well that they were prone to straying to the far side of the law, and he'd be a poor man indeed if he backed out when they needed him. His self-esteem hadn't fared well in the wake of the Uragan debacle: He didn't think he could live with himself if he turned out to be as poor an outlaw as he had a lawman.

Besides, if he wanted to get off this planet, he really needed Jia Chang to stay in one piece.

He threw himself backwards without allowing himself any longer to think it through. The grapnel had a universal attachment that neatly gripped the tac belt on his uniform, which was now divested of rank markings but still unmistakably the clothing of the Red Star Confederate's security forces. It was the only clothing he'd had to his name when he first joined the crew, and Drift had persuaded him to keep it. Presumably for just this sort of purpose.

Alim gripped the grapnel's main body—a metal tube about the length and circumference of his forearm, with twin handles either side of it—as the alarmingly thin steel-composite wire rapidly unspooled out of it. He knew very well that his tac belt would easily be strong enough to take his weight, and this grapnel that he'd appropriated from the *Jonah*'s storage lockers looked standard issue and in good condition, but the last thing he wanted was an unpleasant surprise when he was twenty metres above a concrete pavement. That wouldn't help anyone.

He kicked off the wall, deliberately not looking down. Instead he counted off the windows as he descended past them to get an idea of how much farther he needed to go. His first bound took him two stories; the next one lowered him by three. Halfway down already.

More gunshots. He had to assume that someone would call the police immediately . . . or would they? Anyone watching would see the Changs' uniforms and probably presume that they were calling in their own backup. The casino employees almost certainly wouldn't raise the alarm since it sounded like the Triax were behind this hit attempt. Even allowing for Jia to have misidentified their attackers, it didn't make sense for anyone else to be trying to kill Han Xiuying.

That meant that, unless Han called them herself, it was possible that the police wouldn't even be aware of this until long after it had played out. That might give Alim and the Changs the time they needed to get away.

His last bound touched him down onto the pavement, and he breathed a sigh of relief as he felt solid ground underneath him again. He debated over the grapnel for a second, then unclipped it from his belt and pressed the retract button to send it whizzing upwards out of sight. It would have taken too long to deactivate it and wind it back in, not to mention the potential damage of magnet and cable falling on top of him. The *Jonah* could get another grapnel: They couldn't get another Jia or Kuai.

There was no one in this side street, and although traffic continued to pile past on the main boulevard, it seemed that no one had stopped to gawk at the man in black clothes bouncing down the side of a building. Well, he was probably about to draw a lot of attention anyway, but there was nothing for it. Holding the Crusader as close to his body as he could, he broke into a run.

His sniper's vantage point had given him an excellent view of the front steps of the Thousand Suns, but the casino's palm trees and the corner of the building itself had blocked his view of the street where the Changs had parked and where they were even now sheltering from hostile fire. He needed to get to the next intersection to draw a proper bead on their attackers.

And then what?

Alim had told Captain Drift when he'd joined that he wouldn't kill anyone unless crew members were in danger. And yes, the Changs certainly were in danger, but did that mean Alim had to take a life, or lives? Could he perhaps disable the attackers somehow? Shots that might cripple, but not kill?

More gunshots, and then a scream rent the air: He thought he recognised Jia's voice, albeit distorted by emotion. That didn't bode well.

He reached the intersection and stopped his own momentum by grabbing a lamppost, then hammered the button that would stop the traffic so pedestrians could cross. On the other side of the main boulevard, through the press of vehicles, he could see three—no, four shapes—crossing the street with guns drawn. He couldn't see the Changs, or Chief Han, but he could make out their positions from the focus of the Triax thugs.

The Changs weren't shooting. They'd be overrun in a couple of seconds, if they were even still alive.

The lights changed, and the traffic ground to a halt, leaving a clear stretch of tarmac between Alim and his victims.

"Allah forgive me," Alim muttered, although despite the boundless nature of Allah's mercy, he wasn't sure he still warranted any. Then he raised his borrowed rifle to his shoulder and focused through the scope.

They jumped into view immediately. Barely a hundred yards away, and given that they were on the same elevation as him, they were actually closer than the shot he'd made from the top of the building he'd been perched on. An untrained person might have struggled to hit them: Alim didn't really need the scope.

The idea of winging them had gone from his head. He would need to get over there, and allowing any of them the ability to shoot back at him, however unlikely that might be, was too risky. So he lined up on the skull of the man farthest away and pulled the trigger.

The gun punched back against his shoulder, but long practice prevented it from throwing his aim off. The side of the man's head exploded in a cloud of red, and he dropped to the ground in the middle of the road. His fellows stopped in their tracks and turned to look at him, which given the victim's position meant that for another crucial second they weren't looking at Alim.

Which was, after all, the idea.

The next man got hit in the back of the head while still turning to see what had happened to his friend, and slumped forwards. Alim could hear a couple of shouts and car doors opening as drivers realised that a man was aiming a rifle directly across their path and decided to flee on foot, but he ignored the distraction.

The last two were now looking back to face where their ears told them the gunfire was coming from. This time Alim targeted the closest man, the one who had—at least statistically—the best odds of hitting him with return fire. The shot took the thug in the shoulder, and he fell with a scream audible even over the traffic noise. The last man had managed to raise his handgun and shoot back: Alim didn't bother to duck because he was already squeezing his own trigger again. The man collapsed like a puppet with its strings cut as Alim's bullet took him between the eyes.

Alim let out his breath, then tracked across and down to where his third victim was lying on the ground. His scope showed him the man's face: eyes screwed up, teeth gritted, one hand clamped to his wounded shoulder, and sweat beading on his brow already, visible even under the streetlights. Alim could just hear his low, ululating moans of pain.

The safest thing to do would be to pull the trigger again. The man worked for the Triax and would make his living inflicting violence or the threat of violence on others. This was a corrupt city where he might never face justice.

But he'd also dropped his gun and showed no inclination to move from his protective, foetal position. And Alim couldn't bring himself to do it.

"Idiot," he breathed, breaking into a run across the main boulevard. The lights were still red and holding back the traffic because only a handful of seconds had passed since they'd changed in the first place, so his dash across the intersection was uninterrupted. He got to the other side, well aware of the many sets of eyes that must have been glued to him as he sprinted past the vehicles while carrying a large rifle. He supposed that pictures or video of him might have been taken, but it didn't matter now: Either this mad gamble would still pay out and they'd flee the planet before the security forces got themselves organised, or something would go wrong and it would fail totally. One way or another, he doubted he'd be in a situation where his face was plastered over advertising screens as part of a massive manhunt while he was still on this planet.

He ignored the mewling Triax enforcer and dodged between two parked cars to get onto the pavement, then nearly stopped in his tracks at what he saw. Beyond where Han Xiuying was on her hands and knees, one black-uniformed shape was bent desperately over another that laid on its back on blood-soaked paving slabs. It was a sight he'd seen too many times in his previous career, and it filled him with dread automatically. Now, though, in this place . . .

"Jia?" He was disgusted with himself, but he was relieved to see that the girl appeared unhurt. A well-maintained shuttle could surely fly for a while without attention, but without a pilot it was essentially useless. He picked up his pace again, dashing the last few steps past Han to end in a crouch beside her.

He opened his mouth to ask how bad it was, but the words dried up as his eyes met the blank, glassy stare of the body that used to be Kuai Chang.

His experienced gaze took in the damage automatically, without any prompting on his part or any desire to truly see what had happened. The chest shot had at least clipped the heart, but that wouldn't have killed the little mechanic so quickly on its own. The bullet that had hit his neck, though: That had torn the carotid artery wide open.

"Where were you?" Jia screamed at Alim, rounding on him. She grabbed for his shoulders, and he knocked her hands aside with self-defence moves so ingrained he didn't even have to think about them. "Where the *fuck* were you?!" Her burst of frenzied action lasted only a second before she collapsed back onto her knees, sobbing as though she intended to drown herself in her own tears.

The front of her tac vest was undone, Alim saw, and tugged partially apart. He guessed that she'd been trying to remove her shirt to apply pressure to the wound, but her haste and the unfamiliar fastenings had foiled her. She'd tried to use her hands instead, unsuccessfully.

"Jia," he said urgently, "we need to go." She didn't respond—he hadn't really expected her to—but out of the corner of his eye, he saw Chief Han rise unsteadily to her feet, still clutching her bag.

Something snapped inside Alim Muradov. This was supposed to be an officer of the law, but instead she'd allowed a culture where gangs ran riot and controlled entire cities. Now one of Alim's new crew was dead because of her greed, because of her actions that had led the Triax to believe that they could order the killing of a high-ranking public servant and two uniformed security officers with minimal consequences. The fact that they were right, that there would be no consequences, just tasted even more bitter to him.

It would be very, very easy to put a bullet into Han Xiuying and be done with it. If anything, she deserved it more than the men Alim had just shot down in the street. They were street thugs, probably poor as such things were measured here, maybe drawn into the gang by family or by connections through friends. Their actions might have immediate and drastic impacts on those they encountered, but they weren't big-picture criminals. Han Xiuying, on the other hand, had made choices that made life more miserable for an entire city and had done so while being paid to do the opposite.

Alim took his hand off his gun and gripped his Taser instead. He still had morals, damn it all, even if others didn't.

He stepped up behind Han and blasted her in the back. She let out a strangled gasp and fell: Alim grabbed her bag from her hand as she collapsed and opened it hurriedly. Roll after roll of tightly wadded, high-denomination currency met his gaze. He had no time to count it, and didn't really have any options if it wasn't the amount they were hoping for, but it seemed that at least this part of their plan had worked out. The bitterest pill of all would have been if Han had taken a credit chip, leaving the money untouchable, but it seemed that she didn't want it to be traced at all. Had Alim Muradov been a betting man, he would have placed a wager that Zhuchengshi's security chief had been planning to take her money and run, leaving her corrupt dealings with the Triax as far behind her as she could.

He saw his chance. He'd hoped to be able to do this when the Changs had picked him up in the aircar and they dumped Chief Han, but he hadn't discussed it with Drift. Now, his anger removed any remaining doubts about the wisdom of it. He dropped to one knee beside Han and leaned down until his mouth was nearly level with her ear, then whispered into it in Russian.

"Tell the Dragon Sons that Sergei Orlov sends his regards."

He got back to his feet and turned away from the incapacitated woman who would have been his peer only a few weeks ago. The notion faintly disgusted him now, but he needed to focus. He could hear sirens, still far away at the moment but getting inexorably closer. They weren't going to have as much time as he'd hoped.

"Jia!" He grabbed the pilot by the back of her tac vest and shook her. He didn't have time to be gentle, so he fell back on his military training. Get them up; keep them moving. "Jia! We need to go, *now!*"

"I'm not leaving him!" Jia bawled. Every inch of the young woman's blustering shell had cracked and fallen away; at exactly the wrong moment, Alim couldn't help but note.

"Then we take him with us!" He grabbed Jia's tear-streaked face and turned it towards him. "Do you have the car keys?" She stared blankly, so he slapped her. He'd apologise later. "The keys! Do you have them?"

She shook her head unsteadily. "Kuai . . ."

Of course, the brother had been driving: He'd claimed that Jia couldn't drive an aircar in a way that wouldn't have garnered attention, and after seeing her piloting, Alim was inclined to agree. He plunged his hand into Kuai's right pants pocket and was rewarded with the fob that would activate the aircar.

One task at a time. No reasoning, no cajoling, just instructions. "Jia, get his legs."

Shakily, the girl took her brother's ankles. Alim grabbed the body under its shoulders, trying to ignore how the blood-soaked uniform felt under his fingers. "To the car. Lift!"

They hoisted Kuai up and carried him the thirty yards or so to the rental car. He wasn't a heavy man, thankfully. Other people were now clustering around the bottom of the street, coming to gawk now the shooting had stopped. Alim hoped they stayed away, but he suspected that two security officers carrying an apparently dead third one to an unmarked car and leaving was likely to cause comment, especially when sirens were on the way.

Nothing for it.

He pulled the rear door open with one hand and hoisted Kuai onto the back seat, then took his legs from Jia and swung the body into what was broadly a sitting position. Jia stood there dumbly, so he grabbed her shoulder and pointed towards the other side of the car.

"Get in the back, and strap yourself in."

She didn't nod, but moved to do as he'd said. She was in shock, but responding to clear instructions: something to be thankful for, at any rate. He opened the driver's door and dropped into the seat, then slotted the fob into place and fired up the engine. He had always been much more used to wheeled vehicles than aircars, but he'd flown a few times, and he managed to lift up out of the parking spot at the second try.

"*Jenna,*" he said in English, activating his comm. "*Jenna, are you there?*"

+*Chief? What's been going on? Is everyone okay?*+

"No," Alim said grimly, lowering his window. He'd have to do his best to evade the sirens based on sound and direction, which wasn't an attractive prospect, but at least they hopefully weren't actively looking for this vehicle. Yet. "*Kuai is dead.*"

+*Oh my God. Oh my God. How?*+

"*It seems the Triax were planning a hit all along,*" Alim said. "*But I do not have time for explanations. We have the money, but I could not get Jia to leave her brother, so I have a dead body in the back of this car. I believe the Two Trees Arena is practically on the way back to the spaceport. Should I attempt to pick up Apirana and the Captain and risk discovery, or are we leaving them here and taking off without them?*"

He didn't add that he had no idea if Jia would even be able or willing to fly the *Jonah* out of the atmosphere. McIlroy was an intelligent woman, and would be able to work that much out for herself.

There was a pause.

"*Jenna?*"

+*I was watching the fight broadcast,*+ McIlroy said, her voice flat and drained. +*The entire thing has been busted by the cops for match-fixing. And then the feed was cut, and the show went back to the studio or whatever. But the last thing I saw, there were police all around the ring when A was fighting.*

+*Chief, I think they've been arrested.*+

SITTING TIGHT

"Are we under arrest?" Drift demanded, mustering his best Russian since he had no idea if the security officer he was talking to spoke English or had a translation program running.

"No, just don't try to leave the building," the officer told him in Mandarin, barely even glancing up from her pad. Drift's own pad provided its coolly neutral translation, but he didn't need it to hear the boredom in the woman's voice. *"The detective will get to you."*

"And if we try to leave?" Drift asked, figuring he may as well find out.

"Then we'll arrest you," the cop replied with a shrug. *"Just wait where you are, and the detective will work out whether we need to question you further at the station or whether we can let you go. It's not hard, is it?"*

Drift didn't trust himself to answer as civilly as would be wise in the circumstances, so he settled for a grunt and turned away. Apirana looked up as he approached. The big man was swaddled in his warm-up robe, since now that the Two Trees Arena had largely emptied of people, the ambient temperature was dropping noticeably.

"We're staying put?" the Māori asked, his resigned tone indicating he already knew the answer.

"Sì," Drift muttered, slumping down into a seat beside the big man. He looked around, trying not to appear too furtive, but the security officers

were all busy elsewhere. So far as they seemed to be concerned, none of the various fighters, coaches, and officials gathered in the hall was going anywhere, so it wasn't necessary to eavesdrop on every word. "The local feds picked a fine time to get efficient," he said, not bothering to hide the bitterness in his tone. "Why couldn't they have just continued to look the other way?"

"Easy, bro," Apirana said softly. "Remember, we don't know anything was crooked. I mean, I sure wouldn't have fought in this arena if I knew anyone was fixin' fights."

Drift glanced sideways at the big man, then nodded. Apirana was right: To play the role convincingly, he needed to be playing it at all times, not just when confronted with a cop asking him questions. Of course, that didn't mean that Rodrigo Pérez wouldn't be annoyed that his client's fight had been stopped prematurely—especially when said client had been pummelling his opponent—but motivation was vital: It would dictate which way the performance went.

"We got a bigger problem, though," Apirana continued in that same soft tone. "That detective: I can't be a hundred percent sure, but I think that's the Chief's old friend."

Drift bit the inside of his cheek in lieu of swearing out loud. "Her name was Li, wasn't it?"

"Yup," Apirana confirmed, nodding. "Li ain't exactly an uncommon name, and the Chief didn't mention her rank. But she looks about the same. O'course, I only really saw her from behind."

"And if she's not on the take, it would make sense to send her as part of a team to arrest a Triax member," Drift muttered. "Please tell me she didn't get a good look at you when you grabbed her in the market."

"I ain't a fool, bro," Apirana said reproachfully. "I know I'm distinctive. Had the mask on and my hood up, an' we were in the shadows. Nothing to be done about my size, o'course, but we got a few big men in here. If she'd seen me on my own, I wouldn't fancy our chances. As it is, I might have a bit of camouflage. Plus, it was a month ago, or whatever."

"Fingers crossed," Drift said. He was desperate to know what had gone on with the rest of the crew, but the *Jonah*'s transmitters couldn't penetrate the Two Trees' walls, and the security forces had disabled the internal routers to prevent anyone from calling out on Zhuchengshi's network. He'd rarely felt so cut off and isolated. Had the heist gone ahead? Had they got the money? Was everyone okay? He couldn't shake the feeling that trusting such an important piece of deception to Jia and Kuai was tantamount to foolishness, but they'd apparently bluffed the kid in the laundrette well enough. Besides, there weren't any other options: Even if Muradov hadn't been at risk of recognition, he was the only logical choice for the sort of sharpshooting the plan had required.

He really, really hoped that Jenna wouldn't call time and take off without Apirana and him onboard, but at the same time they couldn't afford for the ransom to be delayed. If that meant that the pair of them had to help the police with their enquiries and stick around, then that was a price he supposed they would have to pay, but it was an absolutely last-ditch option.

A movement on the far side of the fighting cage caught his eye, and he nudged Apirana. "Eyes front, *amigo*. We've got incoming."

Detective Li was skirting around the raised structure with two uniformed officers trailing behind her. She was heading straight for them with a brisk stride, and didn't look to be in a particularly good mood. He studied her as intently as he dared: She had an athletic build and the sort of brisk step he'd expect from an ex-military type. He was almost certain this was the same woman Apirana had grabbed in the street market after she'd pulled a gun on Muradov, and that was bad news however you painted it.

"Rodrigo Pérez?" Li asked, coming to a halt in front of them and looking Drift up and down. It was the second time she'd scrutinised him, and she didn't seem much more impressed than the first, briefer time in the cage.

"Yes, ma'am." Drift nodded. He'd debated whether to admit that it wasn't his real name, but then that left the way open for possible allegations of fraudulent business practices. His pad was currently programmed to Rodrigo Pérez thanks to Jenna, so he'd decided to keep up the pretence and hope for the best.

Li shifted her gaze to Apirana. "And . . ." She looked down at her pad, then up at the big man again, and her brow wrinkled.

Apirana just sat and waited, his expression blankly polite. At least, that was how it looked to Drift, who'd long ago learned to see past the moko worked across his features. To those unfamiliar with Apirana, the markings almost certainly gave him a more fearsome aspect.

Li's patience cracked after about two seconds. "Your name, sir?"

"Apirana Wahawaha," A replied smoothly, although his expression darkened ever so slightly. Drift knew that the big man found it annoying when people couldn't pronounce his name, and he couldn't blame him for it.

"You were contracted to fight this evening?" Li asked him.

"I was."

"And when did this happen?"

"Seven days ago," Apirana replied calmly.

Li frowned. "You fought on that evening too, I believe."

"I did."

"And you were booked to fight again only seven days later?"

Apirana shrugged. "The fight didn't really take very long. It seemed a shame to waste the preparation, an' the arena here seemed to think there was money to be made from me since I'd just beaten the local boy."

Li tapped something into her pad, then looked up at him again. "Were you offered money to throw this fight?"

Apirana's eyes narrowed. "I suggest you go ask my opponent tonight how confident he felt that he was gonna win."

Li folded her arms and glared at him. "I asked whether you'd been offered money, Mr. . . . ." She trailed off again, then continued as though she'd never paused. "Not whether you'd accepted."

"Ma'am," Drift broke in, "are you accusing my client of being complicit in fight-fixing?"

Li looked at him with what was little short of a glare. "I'll come to you, Mr. Pérez. But no, as I said, I'm simply asking your client if he was *offered* money to throw a fight."

"And if he was offered it and refused it, but didn't report it to the authorities, that would make him complicit, would it not?" Drift said. "Because he would have been aware that there were dishonest practices taking place?"

Li glowered at him, and Drift hoped he'd stayed the right side of showing he was no fool without antagonising the detective.

"I never even got *offered* money to throw a fight," Apirana said firmly, matching her emphasis. He folded his arms and glared at Li. "Seven to show and then three to win, both nights. So you comin' in when you did cost me three grand that I won't be seeing now."

Drift supposed that, actually, the big man was telling them the truth. Chen had never offered him money to throw a fight: Ze'd just demanded that it happen. However, Drift was fairly sure that Li wouldn't appreciate the semantics if Chen came clean about zir recent botched attempts and implicated the pair of them.

"Ma'am," he said respectfully, "we really have nothing to tell you. My client has had two fights; he won one and was on his way to winning the other. We'll be happy to assist you if you feel it's necessary, but might we at least make a call first?"

Li's face immediately took on a suspicious cast. "Someone you need to talk to, Mr. Pérez?"

"I need to call my girlfriend," Apirana rumbled. "She don't watch the fights, and she'll have been expectin' a call from me to say how I got on. She'll be gettin' worried that I've been badly hurt or something." He looked slightly shamefaced, and his next sentence came out slightly mumbled. "I forgot to call her when I should've, last time. She went *ballistic.*"

Drift tried not to smile. The notion that Jenna might go ballistic at Apirana was an amusing one in and of itself, but bless him, the big guy was doing his best to distance himself from any notion that he might be the type to abduct security officers off the street.

Li frowned. "I'll need a contact address before I can even let you out of this building." She looked at him expectantly.

Drift swore inwardly. They didn't have any lodgings booked in a hotel, and he had the nasty feeling that Li would check any details he might give her to determine whether they were genuine. That left him with an honest disclosure about being based out of the *Jonah*, but that would draw its own questions of why a no-name fighter and his agent had their own shuttle. Not to mention the fact that if Li checked it out and found Alim Muradov there . . .

"*Ma'am!*"

The shout came from the uniformed officer Drift had spoken to earlier, who was now running towards them. Li looked around irritably.

"*I'm in the middle of—*"

The officer clattered to a halt and began speaking urgently, fast and quiet enough that Drift's translation program couldn't pick up more than the occasional word here and there. What he did manage to make out didn't make a great deal of sense to him, so he sat quietly and tried to look as though he wasn't listening at all. He did keep an eye on what he could see of Li's face, though, and watched as the detective's expression changed from impatient to shocked, and then to uncertain.

"*And you're quite sure of where this came from?*" she demanded.

"*Yes, ma'am,*" the officer said, apparently too surprised by the question to keep her voice down anymore, "*straight down the wire.*"

Li's jaw worked for a moment, then set pugnaciously. "*Right, then.*" She raised her head and her voice, shouting out to the rest of the arena. "*Fang! Yun! Your teams take details and follow on as soon as you can. All other officers, with me! Everyone else . . .*" She looked around the hall at the various civilians still gathered there, and finished with her eyes on Drift and Apirana. "*None of you here are under arrest, but don't leave town until cleared to do so by someone from my department!*"

Drift gave her what he hoped was a firm nod and tried not to look too relieved as Li swept away, black-uniformed officers conglomerating around and behind her like the tail of some sort of inversely coloured comet. One of the few remaining ones sauntered over, pad in hand.

"*Names and contact details.*"

"Rodrigo Pérez," Drift said smoothly. He had a feeling this officer wasn't going to bother double-checking his story here and now, so he took a gamble and named a hotel he'd seen on his way to and from the Jonah. "Room 214, Cho Palace."

"Apirana Wahawaha," Apirana added, "room 220, same place."

The officer looked up at him. "*How do you spell that?*"

Apirana gave him a level look, but spelled his name out. The officer dutifully tapped it in, then grunted. "*Huh. Cho Palace is on the other side of the spaceport, isn't it?*"

"Uh . . ." Drift racked his brain for a moment, hoping he wasn't going to be asked further questions about the place. "Yeah, I think so. Haven't been there long."

"*Word of advice,*" the officer said, turning away, "*give it a while before heading back.*" He walked off to where the timekeeper and ring announcer were sitting, and left the pair of them alone.

"What do you suppose that meant?" Apirana asked, his tone decidedly uncertain.

"I don't know," Drift admitted, getting to his feet and trying to fight down the wave of apprehension about Jenna, the *Jonah*, and the entire viability of their scheme. "But I think we should get outside and find out as soon as we can."

TOUGH CHOICES

". . . so I'm up in that crawlspace, trying not to put too much weight on the panels and thinking I shouldn't have had such a big dinner, when I hear the other two shouting," Larysa was saying, drawing a card and making a face. They were sitting in three nonmatching chairs around the coffee table in Larysa's apartment, and the night was wearing on. *"Now, bear in mind that I couldn't see down into the corridor at all. Then I just hear their feet go clattering off the other way, and I'm left up there with no idea what's going on or why they've run off."*

"I take it they weren't just playing a prank on you?" Roman asked, putting down the two of spades. *"Pick up two, Tamara."*

"Huh." Tamara Rourke frowned at him, then placed the three of spades on it. *"I don't think so. Pick up five, Larysa."*

"No, it wasn't just a prank." Larysa chuckled, laying the three of diamonds. *"Eight, Roman, and last card."*

"Son of a . . . !" Roman glared at her, then grudgingly drew eight cards from the deck. *"I swear you're some sort of card witch."*

"And yet you keep playing with me."

"Chance would be a fine thing," Roman commented mildly. Larysa made a comical gagging sound in response.

"So what was it, then?" Rourke asked. She didn't have a diamond or a three, so she picked up what turned out to be the jack of hearts.

"It was the security guard, of course," Larysa snorted. "The other two saw him coming through the door and ran off. They claimed afterwards that they'd shouted up to me, but I didn't hear a single word clearly. So I'm left up there waiting, no idea he's right below me, and then I think that I might as well do what I came here to do. So like a fool I lift up one of the panels and drop through on the other side of the door they sent me up there to unlock, and damn me if the bastard isn't there waiting for me! Nearly twists my arm off, then calls the police. And that," she finished triumphantly, "was how I got kicked out of my second school."

"Are you playing, or reminiscing?" Rourke asked, raising an eyebrow.

"Hmm? Oh, yeah." Larysa casually dropped the five of diamonds onto the discard pile. "Out."

Roman groaned and laid his cards down, revealing more than enough points to eliminate him. "I'm out. And I need a drink. I'll see you two in the morning."

"I have drink!" Larysa protested, pulling a bottle out from underneath the table.

"I said a drink, not to drown in drink," Roman replied, getting to his feet and pulling his jacket on. "I've drunk with you too many times before. It never ends well." He nodded at Rourke. "Tamara."

Rourke sighed and laid her cards down as well. "Wait up. Larysa wins again."

"You just don't want to drink with me either," Larysa said, pulling a face that Rourke guessed was supposed to indicate hurt feelings.

"Guilty," she admitted. "But I also need to get to bed. I don't think Mr. Orlov will be very impressed if I'm hungover."

"You're assuming that he'll notice," Larysa said with a snort. "I still have a job, don't I?"

"Well, I don't actually have a job yet," Rourke reminded her, "so I don't intend to risk it."

"*Spoilsport,*" Larysa sighed good-naturedly. "*Fine, you two run off and have fun without me.*"

"*I had fun once,*" Rourke deadpanned. "*I hated it. See you in the morning, Larysa.*"

"*And don't drink all of that,*" Roman told his colleague sternly. Larysa stuck her tongue out at him.

"*Hey, pull the door shut properly this time!*" she called after them as they navigated past a small but genuine wooden sideboard—an heirloom from her grandmother, apparently—and an airer loaded with washing. "*The damn thing sticks.*"

"*Yeah, yeah,*" Roman grunted. He ushered Rourke through ahead of him, then stepped out into the corridor beside her and tugged the front door shut. It did indeed take a fair bit of effort from him to get it to close fully. "*Damn, that's stiff! Why hasn't she got that fixed?*"

"*You know how strong she is.*" Rourke shrugged. "*She probably only thinks of it as a minor annoyance.*"

"*You could be right,*" Roman said. He turned and headed for the elevator, and Rourke fell in beside him. "*You dodged a bullet by leaving when you did, by the way.*"

"*I can imagine,*" Rourke replied, nodding. "*Larysa doesn't strike me as the type to go half-speed at drinking. Or anything, really.*"

"*She needs to watch it,*" Roman said bluntly. "*It's not like she's got a problem, or anything like that, but Mr. Orlov isn't as oblivious as she thinks. You probably did her a favour by leaving too.*"

"*You think so?*"

"*Almost certainly,*" Roman said. "*I'm sure she'll have one or two, but not as much as if she were trying to impress you.*"

Rourke couldn't help but chuckle. "*Impress me?*"

Roman's eyebrows raised as he looked sideways and down at her. "*You hadn't noticed? She tries to hide it behind . . .*" He waved one hand vaguely.

"*Well, being Larysa, basically. But behind the bravado and the jokes, I think she's on the verge of hero worship. Mr. Orlov doesn't employ many women.*"

"*I'd noticed that,*" Rourke remarked. In truth, aside from her and Larysa, there were only a couple of women in all of the security staff that ever had personal contact with the mob boss.

"*So you can imagine Larysa's face when she hears that this smuggler woman comes out of a crate after however many hours and manages to pull a gun on the boss. And then, after being shut up in a grotty hotel for a couple of weeks, that same woman hands Sacha his own ass when he's armed and she's not, disappears, then waltzes into the boss's apartment and pulls a gun on him again.*" They'd reached the elevators, and Roman pressed the button to call one. "*And then the boss employs her simply because she's that damn good.*"

"*It's not a career choice I would recommend,*" Rourke said as the doors hissed open and she and Roman stepped inside. "*If Mr. Orlov had been a little less rational and a bit more emotional, I could have quite easily died twice. But my hand was somewhat forced.*"

"*I have to admit, I couldn't work out if I was more angry or impressed by what you did,*" Roman said as the doors shut again and the maglev plate began gliding upwards. "*Larysa just went for impressed. You certainly have an admirer there.*"

Rourke nodded thoughtfully, then narrowed her eyes at him. Russian might not have been one of her birth languages, but she'd been speaking it long enough for something in Roman's voice to tip her off. "*Admirer?*"

Roman shrugged noncommittally. "*Larysa's had relationships with, if you'll excuse me, older women before. She hasn't said anything to me about you, but that's the history. She's not secretive about her past, so I don't think it's unfair to tell you.*" He shrugged again. "*Do with that information what you will.*"

"*That's an odd thing to say,*" Rourke said as the elevator's doors opened again and they stepped out into the tiled lobby of the apartment block. It stretched up for many floors above them, but those more spacious homes belonged to richer, more influential people. Folk like Larysa tended to live belowground, in a windowless world of artificial light.

"*I like my life to be kept as simple as possible,*" Roman replied, nodding a greeting to the night porter sitting behind her desk. "*If Larysa's opinion of you is more than just professional admiration, then that could complicate our work, but there's no help for the heart. So if you're prepared, at least you can have an answer ready if she asks a question. That seems better than her possibly taking you by surprise, and you maybe hurting her feelings if she's not your type and you haven't had time to consider a response, and then . . .*" He waved both hands vaguely this time. Rourke was coming to the realisation that this was the man's default gesture to replace the verbalisation of emotions that he found confusing.

"*You seem to have considered this in some detail,*" she pointed out as they passed through the block's entrance door and into the cool night outside.

"*Experience,*" Roman grunted. "*There was a kid a year or so ago who turned out to have some interest in Larysa: young guy called Dimi. So he would strike up a conversation with her, and you know what Larysa's like; she'll tell her life story to most people and drink with anyone. Then he started wanting to spar with her.*"

Rourke winced. "*I can see where this is going.*"

"*Huh? Oh, no, nothing like that,*" Roman assured her with a grin. "*The young fool knew better than to cop a feel on the mats; he'd have left minus an arm. I'm quite sure she thought there was nothing out of the ordinary going on, but then he blurts something out one day. And she just stares at him for a couple of seconds, like she's been smacked between the eyes with a saucepan, then starts laughing.*"

Rourke winced again. "*Ow. I'm not sure that's better.*"

"*I think he'd have preferred to lose the arm,*" Roman agreed. "*I'm certain she wasn't laughing at him as such, more at both of them each getting the wrong end of the stick, but that's the sort of reaction you can't really explain away after the event."

"And I'm sure that everyone else was sympathetic and understanding, and didn't mock him in any way," Rourke said dryly.

"However did you guess?" Roman snorted. "No, he got no end of grief about it. Sacha ended up taking it a bit far, as Sacha usually did, and then Larysa threw him through a table."

"That must have helped wonderfully," Rourke commented.

"Oddly enough, no." Roman sighed. "In the end I persuaded the boss to send Dimi off somewhere else without telling him that it was all because the idiot had got lovestruck over the wrong girl and then everyone else had behaved like imbeciles." He shook his head. "Humans are so stupid, I sometimes wonder how we managed to ever leave Old Earth in the first place."

"You might have a point," Rourke conceded. They'd reached a junction, and she nodded towards where the dark-green bulk of the Grand House and its attached hotel tower could be seen in the distance. "This is my turning. I'll see you tomorrow . . . and thanks for the heads-up."

"Don't mention it," Roman said, turning his jacket's collar up against the cool breeze. "Like I said, I just want things to stay as simple as possible."

"Well, it's appreciated anyway," Rourke told him honestly. "Night."

"Night." Roman turned and walked away, his hands buried in his pockets and shoulders hunched to tuck as much of his bald scalp as possible into shelter behind his collar. Rourke looked around for traffic and, seeing none, hurried across the road to the opposite sidewalk and set off for the Grand House.

It was strange how easily she'd settled into a new routine, she reflected. During the day she trained Orlov's security guards, trying to make them more alert to threats and better at neutralising them. In the evenings she tended to spend time with Roman and Larysa and found that she actually enjoyed their company. Neither of them had pasts that were squeaky-clean, of course, but the full details of hers would almost far outweigh both of theirs put together. Even leaving aside the things she'd done personally, once you started to take into consideration the turmoil, strife, and death toll involved in the revolutions she'd been involved in at the behest of the GIA . . . Well, it didn't really bear thinking about.

In fact, Rourke realised, she was almost feeling relaxed. She was about as certain as she could be that Orlov honestly intended to employ her, and if he planned to double-cross her at some point, then there was very little she could do about it anyway. She might be able to turn the tables on whoever he sent, maybe even kill Orlov himself, but his instructions would live on and she'd have his entire outfit searching for her. Leaving the planet would be out of the question, going to ground in New Samara was equally unfeasible, and fleeing to one of the small farming communities elsewhere would hardly provide her with any shelter. Barring her former crew showing up with a miracle in the form of half a million stars in the next four days, she was pretty much stuck here. Perhaps it was simply time to come to terms with it and accept Orlov's offer?

The thing was, that didn't sound like such a bad deal these days. She had respect from her employer and her colleagues, she would have steady pay instead of a cut from whatever latest shenanigans the *Keiko*'s crew had turned a profit from, and she'd be able to get somewhere to live that might even be larger than either of her cabins on the *Jonah* or its mothership. She'd miss Ichabod, of course: They'd been business partners for a decade now, and although he could be positively infuriating at times, he had a certain vitality to him that in some way also defined her. She was sensible, reserved, and cautious by nature, but part of that was because she was always measured against his flamboyance. She'd gotten so used to being the yin to his yang that it was strange to think of just being Tamara Rourke without setting that against Ichabod Drift. She'd miss

Jenna too, and Apirana—the Changs not so much—but Drift might actually leave a hole in her life.

Still, she wasn't too old to find herself a new place in the world. She'd worried about that after she'd left the GIA, and she'd proved herself wrong then, so there was no reason she couldn't reinvent herself once more. Yes, she'd be working for a gangster, but one whose primary focus seemed to be on mainstream business interests. Orlov was certainly ruthless—the fates of the three of his men she'd embarrassed testified to that, not to mention the threats he'd made to her and Ichabod—but she'd already got the impression from Roman that the direction of his boss's operation had been changing. Orlov had enough money that he could leave his criminal empire further and further behind, or at least bring it into legitimacy with him. In ten years' time, perhaps the man would be no more of a criminal than any other captain of industry.

Of course, there was still the issue of leaving the crew to cope without *her*. But she was sure that they'd be fine.

DESPERATE TIMES

The walk through the Two Trees Arena seemed achingly long to Drift, but they were very nearly on the heels of the departing security forces, and to run headlong would surely invite comment and attention. As a result, he and Apirana kept to a brisk walk and tried to look like they wanted nothing more than a breath of fresh air.

They reached the main lobby, and he tried his comm again. To his delight, mixed with apprehension, he found that he could once more make contact with the *Jonah*'s transmitters.

"Hello," he tried, hailing any of his crew who could hear him. "Anyone out there?"

There was a moment of silence, then—

+*Captain!*+

It was Jenna, and she sounded about as relieved as he'd ever heard her. Drift felt a smile creep over his face and saw a matching one on Apirana's.

"Good to hear your voice," he said truthfully. "Don't worry, your boyfriend's still in one piece. How are we doing?"

+*We got what we needed, but we've got* big *problems,*+ Jenna said, the tension in her voice ratcheting up as she spoke. +*Chief?*+

Muradov's voice cut in. +*Captain, are you at the Two Trees Arena?*+

"Just coming outside now," Drift answered, exchanging a worried glance with Apirana as they passed through the main doors. The last of the security forces aircars and road vehicles were leaving, packed with black-uniformed personnel, and they did indeed seem to be heading in the direction of the spaceport. "Where are you? What are these problems? Has something kicked off at the spaceport?"

+*Not to my knowledge,*+ Muradov said in alarm, raising his voice slightly to make himself heard over a strange noise in the background. +*Why?*+

"Because pretty much every officer who was here has just left for it," Drift said grimly. "What's that noise I can hear, anyway?"

+*That is the sound of Jia mourning her brother.*+

Drift stopped in his tracks, feeling like he'd been punched in the stomach. "What?"

+*I am coming to collect you, Captain, and will explain further then. I would rather not get in the way of the security forces anyway.*+

"Hang on a second, bro," Apirana cut in, "what do you me—"

"A," Drift said, putting a restraining hand on the bigger man's arm. "Not now. Not over the comms. We'll find out in a moment in any case." He activated his again, fighting down the taste of bile in his throat. "Jenna, any sign of what's going on at your end?"

+*I can't see anything,*+ the young slicer replied, +*and there're no alerts posted. That doesn't necessarily mean anything though. I can try to, ah, find out.*+

"Do it," Drift said firmly. By "find out," Jenna meant slicing into the security forces' private frequencies to listen in on their instructions. He didn't know how much information she'd be able to glean as a non-native speaker using a translation programme, but anything would be better than nothing. He forced himself to concentrate: There was nothing to be done for Kuai, if Muradov's testimony was to be believed, so he had to focus on how best to get the rest of them out of here. "Chief, is there any possibility that all this ruckus has been sparked by your little shopping trip?"

+I consider that unlikely, Captain.+ Muradov took a moment to mutter a curse in Russian, which Drift presumed was aimed at the aircar the Uragan was apparently piloting. +My best guess would be that our . . . host . . . decided to take revenge on her . . . secondary employers.+

Drift's growing apprehension wasn't so severe that he couldn't appreciate Muradov's ability to adapt on the fly to talking about nefarious actions over a channel that might just be eavesdropped on. All the same, the possibility Muradov had raised was truly alarming.

"Jia, do you know anything about this? Did you hear anything?"

+She is not wearing her comm, Captain,+ Muradov replied, +and she does not respond when I talk to her. Admittedly, I am somewhat preoccupied as I have not driven one of these for several years.+

"Shit." Drift looked up at the skies. "How far away are you?"

+You should see me momentarily.+

Sure enough, in only a few seconds, the whine of an individual aircar became audible over the background hum of the city, and Drift turned to see the rental vehicle they'd hired the day before descending towards them as he turned off his comm. He noted absently that even under the current circumstances, Muradov was still using the indicators correctly. He wasn't sure whether that was a result of the Chief's long-standing respect for the law, a desire to avoid attention from it, or both.

"Get ready," he said to Apirana as the vehicle swung down and he saw a familiar shape slumped against the window. "This isn't going to be pleasant."

"Never is," Apirana agreed apprehensively.

Muradov rotated the aircar somewhat clumsily just before landing, so the passenger side was facing them. Drift slapped Apirana's shoulder and pointed at it. "Front."

"Got it," the Māori replied, and they pulled their respective doors open to climb in. Drift braced himself.

The smell of blood assaulted him immediately, sharp and metallic, even as he squeezed into the seat next to Jia. The pilot's shoulders were shaking, and she was sobbing as she clung to Kuai's body. Drift saw Apirana crane his head around from the seat in front, then close his eyes in an expression of nauseated horror and turn away again.

Drift looked past Jia and grimaced in turn. Kuai's neck was ruined from what must have been a gunshot, and the front of his stolen uniform was also wet with blood. The little mechanic's face was composed, but there was no mistaking his lolling head for someone who was merely asleep.

Drift had a sudden flashback to a day on Old Earth. . . . How many years ago now? The *Jonah* had landed in Chengdu in China, and he and Rourke had been forced to part ways with their then-pilot over an argument about pay. They were trying to find a replacement when a broadcast had come up on the local news holo about a girl in her late teens who had apparently somehow stolen a shuttle and joyridden it with an equal degree of skill and recklessness. That girl had of course been Jia, and he and Rourke had found where she'd been remanded and immediately stumped up her (fairly sizeable) bail on the grounds that talent like that shouldn't be allowed to go to waste in a prison cell. Of course, that had meant jumping her bail, but Jia had never been overly concerned about rules or laws. The potential fly in the ointment had been her older brother, who'd been there when Drift had made his offer and had flatly promised to report all of them to the authorities unless he was hired as mechanic so he could keep his little sister out of trouble.

"That never really worked out quite as you planned, did it?" Drift muttered sorrowfully. He wouldn't miss Kuai's relentless negativity, or his shameless passive-aggressiveness, but he'd been a part of Drift's life for longer than anyone else on the crew except Jia and Rourke. The sudden void was a bit like having a leg that kept aching and playing up, but then one day waking up to find that it wasn't there at all.

He felt the aircar lurch under him as Muradov took off once more, and snapped back to the present. "Chief, report."

"The Triax must have actually been planning the hit on Chief Han that we thought we were bluffing about," Muradov replied grimly. "I could not get an angle to cover the front of the casino and the Changs' parking spot, so I was unable to intervene quickly enough when it broke down. I am sorry, Captain."

"Nothing to be done now," Drift said wearily. He weaved his arm through Jia's and felt for her hand. She clasped it, but gave no other acknowledgement of his presence. He didn't push it. They'd all need Jia soon enough, or all of this would be for nothing, but he could let her grieve in peace for the moment. "Tell me that we at least got what we came for."

"So far as I know," Muradov replied, reaching under his chair and tossing an expensive-looking handbag into Apirana's lap. "I have not had time to count it, but there is a lot of money there."

"A? Count it," Drift ordered.

"Cap?"

"Do it," he reiterated, "now. If we're short by a little then we *may* be able to make up the difference on the way back to New Samara, but we need to know as soon as possible."

"Gotcha," Apirana muttered, and dug into the bag with one big hand to pull out tight rolls of banknotes.

"Jenna?" Drift said, activating his comm again. "Anything?"

+One second.+

Drift bit back an unhelpfully vitriolic retort. "We're kinda on a time-scale here, Jenna."

+*I'm* listening, *Captain.*+ There was a pause for a few moments, in which Drift attempted not to grind his teeth, before the slicer spoke again. +*Okay, it sounds like the Chief was right. We've got an all-units out, centred on the spaceport.*+ A note of dread touched her tone. +*They must be coming for the shipment.*+

"Me cago en la puta!" Drift spat. "Have we got any indication that they know what ship they're looking for?"

+*Not that I can tell, Cap.*+ Jenna's voice was apologetic. +*I mean, they might, but it's so jumbled—*+

"Never mind," Drift cut her off, trying to think. A large chunk of Zhuchengshi's security forces were even now converging on the spaceport where he, Ichabod Drift, was heading, and since they didn't seem to have a target, they'd presumably lock down every single shuttle there and search them all until they found what they were after. What was more, Drift was heading there in the company of a freshly made corpse in a security uniform; two other people wearing security uniforms who technically had no right to be doing so; a fighter suspected of involvement in match-fixing who'd been ordered not to leave town, let alone the planet; and four hundred thousand stars in cash that had just been stolen from the city's security chief.

What was more, the corpse was his mechanic, and his pilot was virtually catatonic with grief as a result.

"This," he said aloud, "is not one of our better days."

DESPERATE MEASURES

Jenna peered nervously out of the *Jonah*'s viewshield. She could see flashing blue lights in the distance now, just visible against the ever-present, multicoloured background of Zhuchengshi's streetlights, signs, and advertising boards.

She couldn't help but notice that there seemed to be an awful lot of them.

"Captain?" she said into her comm. "What's the plan?"

+*The simple answer is that I don't have one,*+ Drift's voice replied, somewhat tetchily, +*so we're going to be making this up on the fly. The one thing we can't do is allow them to pin the* Jonah *down and search it. We need to be leaving as soon as possible if we're going to get back to New Samara in time.*+

"Is Jia even going to be able to fly?" Jenna asked, finally voicing her fears. She knew that Rourke had some ability at flying a shuttle, although it was basic next to Jia's expertise, but Rourke was light years away. And as for the rest of them . . .

+*One thing at a time,*+ Drift snapped. +*We can't get to you as we are. Even if spaceport security was half-asleep and you weren't about to be flooded with uniforms, there's no way we'd get past them. We're going to have to cause a lot of chaos, very quickly, so that even if anyone sees us, they're too busy to try to stop us.*+

"Normally I'd suggest calling the emergency services," Jenna said, taking another worried glance out of the viewshield, "but under the circumstances I'm not sure what other options we have." She scanned the cockpit, looking for inspiration.

Then Apirana's voice came through. +*How about the engine overload warning?*+

Jenna stopped still. "Oh. Oh, you beautiful man. That's perfect." A shuttle's engines were, by necessity, powerful things, and there was always the possibility of an explosion. That would be bad enough for the crew in vacuum, and far from good news for them or anyone beneath them if flying in atmosphere, but truly disastrous if it happened when the shuttle was docked at a spaceport or waystation. In such close proximity to other equally powerful engines, there was always the possibility of a chain reaction. An engine overload warning was broadcast immediately on all bandwidths, and the standard response was to take off as soon as possible and get to a safe distance, leaving behind any crew members who didn't happen to be on board.

Needless to say, the activation of the beacon in anything other than a genuine emergency was considered to be a criminal offence and punishable by stiff fines or possibly jail time, not to mention full culpability for any and all costs or damages caused by other people's responses. However, Jenna supposed that they weren't exactly planning to stick around and be answerable to charges.

"Captain?"

+*Do it.*+

"I'll need the ship's access code to engage the manual override," Jenna told him, settling down into the pilot's chair where Jia's buttocks had formed two distinct indents from her long hours at the helm. She flipped up the protective casing over the keys and entered the digits as Drift rattled them off to her, one after another. She pressed the final key, and the main helm console lit up as she felt the main engines quiver into life, ready to fire up the thrusters and take her skywards had she the inclination or knowledge to do such a foolish thing. Instead she reached down to a small panel next to her right knee and flipped open another panel to reveal a large red button.

Jenna distinctly remembered being shown it by Jia on her first full day on board the *Jonah*, once she'd recovered from the truly epic hangover she'd been suffering. The pilot had pointed at the button and declared calmly, "You see this? You ever touch this, I break your face. We clear?"

"We clear," she remembered, and pressed the red button with her thumb.

Klaxons began hooting throatily and immediately, while honest-to-goodness red lights began to flash in the cockpit and, she presumed, in the rest of the ship as well. Ship manufacturers didn't like to leave any of their customers remotely in the dark about the fact that they were about to die in fiery oblivion, it seemed. More to the point, she saw answering warning lights blink into existence on top of the distant spaceport towers, all around the containing walls, and even in the few cockpits of other shuttles that she could see from where she was. It truly was a genuine emergency broadcast that would automatically override everything else in the vicinity.

"We're good!" she shouted into her comm. "I guess, anyway!"

+Good.+ Drift's voice came back to her. +*Are they buying it?*+

Jenna took another look out of the viewshield. She could already see people running hither and thither: ground staff or shuttle crew who'd realised they were caught in the open and were seeking the nearest cover, without knowing which of the many metal behemoths around them might be about to explode. No ships were moving yet, but it had only been a matter of seconds. Even Jia, skilled and somewhat reckless though she was, would have struggled to get the *Jonah* into the air in much under half a minute, even if she were already sitting in the pilot's seat, unless the thrusters were powered up and she'd been about to take off anyway.

"The signal's certainly gone out!" she told the Captain. "Everyone on the ground looks to be panicking, but I can't see any . . . Hold on." There, the blue glow of a thruster starting to fire. It would be several more long seconds for the crew on board before they'd be able to lift off, but they were clearly about to attempt it. Then she saw another ship flicker into life, and then a third. "They're buying it, Cap; they're buying it!"

+Good.+ Drift's voice seemed tenser than she'd have expected. But then he said his next sentence, and the bottom dropped out of her stomach.

+You're going to need to get her into the air.+

"What?!"

+I'm serious, Jenna!+ Drift was firm and strong, which was quite easy for him. +I'm not asking you to fly her anywhere, just get her off the ground with everyone else and open the main cargo bay. The Chief can fly us straight in, and we'll take it from there.+

"Captain, you must have lost your *fucking* mind!" Jenna all but screamed at him. "I'm a *slicer*, not a goddamn *pilot!*"

+And very shortly, unless you do what I say, you're going to be a slicer sitting in the only grounded shuttle with a whole load of security officers wondering why you haven't exploded yet,+ Drift bit out. +I said we were making this up as we went, Jenna!+

+Jenna,+ Apirana's voice cut in. +You got this. Me an' Rourke managed to fly that boat on Uragan, an' if it hadn't been for the storm, I reckon it would've been pretty simple.+

"You're a lying asshole, Apirana Wahawaha," Jenna told him bitterly. "You said afterwards that you nearly threw up, you were so scared."

+Well, yeah. But you're a helluva lot smarter than me, so I figure it'll be easier for you.+

"I am *not* smarter than you," Jenna said, but she found herself sitting back and looking at the controls in front of her nonetheless. They didn't make any more sense than they had done a moment ago, but the Captain was right about one thing: Shuttles were preparing to lift off all around her, and she watched one actually began to rise from the ground.

"Oh, to hell with it," she said into her comm, her stomach fluttering so hard it felt like she was going to lose her dinner. "Fine, I'll give it a try. Any chance of Jia talking me through it?"

+I'll see,+ Drift replied, sounding uncertain. +But don't wait.+

"Sure," Jenna muttered, trying to keep her breathing steady. "No pressure." She unfastened her wrist-mounted terminal and placed it on the dash, then accessed the Spine. Zhongtu was a rich planet with a rich populace, which meant the local datastores would have an awful lot of information readily available. Including, for example, control layouts for a *Carcharodon*-class shuttle. And, she noticed, a "Learn to Fly" instructional video that was supposed to be used with a flight simulator and *definitely* not with the real thing.

"Here goes nothing," she grimaced, then paused. On the corner of the dash, on top of what the holo-display from her terminal assured her were the trim controls, was a hat. It was a browny-grey colour, lined with some synthetic approximation of fur, and had tied-up flaps at each side that could be let down to cover the ears if necessary.

Jia's pilot hat, which the temperamental and somewhat superstitious woman was adamant was necessary for difficult manoeuvres, for reasons that she'd never been satisfactorily able to verbalise.

"Can't hurt," Jenna said to herself and jammed it onto her head. It immediately made her head too warm, not to mention a little itchy, and she wondered when Jia had last washed it. However, she had no more capacity to procrastinate, so she gingerly reached out and began to feed power to the lift thrusters.

There was no immediate effect, not even a change in the pitch of the engines so far as she could tell, although with the klaxons still going, they'd have had to be on the verge of genuinely exploding before she'd actually be able to hear them. She moved the lever a little farther, then a little farther . . .

"Shit!" she barked as the *Jonah* lurched upwards, and her opinion of Jia's piloting skill instantly rose a few notches. Jenna had barely moved the lever, yet it had felt like she'd thrown it to full. How did Jia manage to make their takeoffs so (usually) smooth? "Captain, I'm off the ground!"

+*Good work! How high are you?*+

"Uh . . ." She scanned her instruments desperately, looking for the altimeter. "Two . . . metres?"

There was a momentary pause, then the Captain spoke again with the tone of someone trying to remain patient. +*We'll need you to go a little higher, Jenna.*+

"Oh God." Jenna tried to peer up through the *Jonah*'s viewshield, but the flashing red lights made it hard to see what was going on. Somewhere there would be a readout of the chaos that was now in full swing around her, but she doubted she'd be able to make head or tail of it in any case, so she'd just have to hope for the best. She grabbed the thruster lever again and jammed it forwards some more.

"Craaaaaap!"

The *Jonah* jumped upwards like her brother when he'd accidentally sat on an imported bee back on Franklin Minor when they'd been kids, only somewhat farther and quicker. She pulled back a little, not wanting to go too high, she'd apparently overreacted, and the shuttle began to sink again.

"Fucking machine!" she raged, trying to edge the control forwards again enough to arrest her descent. "Why won't you—"

+*Jenna?*+

"What?!" she screamed at Drift.

+*Open the door!*+

She looked up desperately as the *Jonah* seemed to settle rather unsteadily into place in midair. The flashing lights of the security forces had reached the spaceport but were slowing uncertainly, probably due to the warning signs indicating that something large and destructive was going to happen at any moment. However, weaving through and over them was another pair of headlights, a pair that had to be carrying the rest of her crew.

"The door! Right!" She scanned the dash furiously. She knew where the switch was for the damn doors; she'd used it countless times. But right now her head was full of unfamiliar flight controls, and she couldn't see the wood for the trees.

+*Jenna!*+

There! Jenna slammed her hand down on it and felt the *Jonah*'s balance shift ever so slightly as the main cargo ramp began to lower. She reached out for something to try to bring the nose up a little, then decided against it, just in case she flipped the entire craft onto its back or something equally disastrous.

"Uh," she said uncertainly as their rental car ploughed on towards her, veering around a rising *Georgia*-class shuttle as it did so, "aren't you coming in a little fast?"

+*If anyone has anything valuable in the cargo bay,*+ Alim Muradov's voice said seriously, +*I apologise in advance.*+

Then he threw the car into a flat spin for 180 degrees and threw the main drive to full. The aircar's forward momentum abruptly became backwards momentum, and dropped just as abruptly as its thrusters fought against that momentum. Jenna saw the aircar disappear out of view beneath her cockpit and winced, fully expecting to see a fireball blossom out and feel the *Jonah* buck under her. Her crewmates' still-active comms broadcast a terminal-sounding metallic noise a second later, and she bit her knuckles in horror.

+*Madre de Dios!*+ Drift's voice barked. +*I thought you said you hadn't flown one of these in a while?*+

+*If I had, I would never have tried that,*+ Muradov replied, sounding rather shaken. +*Is everyone well?*+

+*The fuck you playing at, báichī?*+ a voice shouted in the background, quieter than the others but instantly recognisable.

Jenna breathed again. Not only were her crew still alive and unexploded, the Chief's recklessness had apparently roused Jia enough for her to start swearing again, albeit still with the sound of tears in her voice.

"A?" she asked hopefully.

+*It'll take more than the Chief's piss-poor driving to kill me,*+ her boyfriend replied. +*Uh, d'you mind shuttin' the door, though? Don't want any cops following us in.*+

"Got it." Jenna flicked the appropriate switch and just barely felt the main cargo door begin to grind closed again. "Guys, I would really appreciate it if someone who knew what they were doing could get up here. I get the nasty feeling that we're going to get caught in someone's backwash in a minute, and then we're as good as toast."

+*Working on it,*+ Drift's voice was tense. +*The important thing is that we're airborne, which means nothing the local cops have got can tie us down now. Just get to your station, and be ready to do anything you can to keep people off our backs.*+

Jenna muted her comm furiously, wrenched Jia's hat off and nearly hurled it at the controls before catching herself in time and dropping it gently somewhere it wouldn't nudge anything important. Get to her station, indeed! She'd just got a genuine shuttle off the ground with no training whatsoever, and did she get any thanks for it? She grabbed her wrist terminal and threw herself into her seat, then crossed her arms and scowled at the cockpit door.

She heard Jia before she saw her. Which, given the cockpit door was designed to have an airtight seal, was pretty impressive.

"—*give a fuck!*" Jia was shouting as the door slid open. The pilot backed in, her eyes red and her cheeks tearstained. The Captain followed her, hands out in a placating manner but seemingly unable to get a word in edgeways. Behind him came Apirana, who stopped in the doorway. He was trying to look casual, but Jenna knew he'd placed himself there to make sure Jia couldn't leave.

"You think I give a shit about this now?" Jia raged at Drift. "You think I care? My brother's fucking dead!" She flew at the Captain suddenly, hammering her fist into his chest. "He's fucking *dead!* This is your fault! Your stupid, fucked-up plan!"

"I know!" Drift yelled back, trying to fend her off. "I know it's my fault!" Jia could only see his mechanical right eye from where she was sitting, but the corner of his mouth was quivering as though he was on the verge of tears too. "I fucked up, Jia! But now I need *you* to make sure that my fucked-up plan doesn't kill you, and Jenna, and A, and the Chief as well! I need you to get us out of here!"

"And how's that gonna help Kuai? Huh?" Jia demanded. She was clenching and unclenching her fists apparently unconsciously, and Jenna braced herself for what might happen if Jia launched herself at the Captain again. If they struggled and knocked the flight controls . . .

"It's gonna help him because it means you can get him home," Apirana spoke up, his voice booming out and filling the small cockpit, momentarily drowning out even the still-wailing alarms. Jenna jumped: She'd forgotten how loud he could be when he tried.

"It means you can take him back to Chengdu," Apirana continued, taking a step forward. "It means you can go back to your parents and give him a burial, or a cremation, or whatever your family does, Jia. If we get taken here, by the cops, we'll all be arrested, and you won't see him again until they let you out for some faceless ceremony, maybe. Get us out of here, and you can take care of him."

Jia glared at the Māori, but her rage seemed to have abruptly burned out, leaving only bitterness. "I am *done* with this fucking ship. And with all of you."

Jenna felt the other woman's words land like a punch to the gut. The pilot was arrogant, foul-mouthed, and generally abrasive, but she was not given to idle threats, except perhaps to her brother. Jia Chang was the choreographer of the beautiful, sometimes desperate, dances the *Keiko* and the *Jonah* pulled across the cosmos. Losing her would be like stripping away part of the ships' souls.

"If that's what it takes," Drift said, and now Jenna could hear the hitch in his voice, because the Captain recognised what had just happened. "Just get us somewhere I can find a new pilot to take us to New Samara, Jia. Just do that for us, and be on your way, if that's what you want. We need the ransom for Rourke, or this has all been for nothing. But every cent that we have left over—that is yours, to get you home. To get you both home."

Jia stared at him for a few seconds. Then her mouth twisted. "Get out of my cockpit."

Drift nodded once and turned away. Now Jenna saw his natural eye, and saw the tears sparkling in it. Then the Captain slipped past Apirana and was gone, his long stride heading towards the cargo bay where, presumably, Muradov was moving Kuai's body to the mortuary compartment most ships had in case a crew member died unexpectedly on a voyage.

"I'll need someone in the engine room," Jia said, eyeing Apirana challengingly. He nodded in his turn.

"I'll do what I can." He turned to Jenna and bent down, and suddenly, she had been enveloped in his huge arms. She hugged him back, fighting the feeling she always had that she might as well be trying to encircle a mighty oak with her arms.

"Thank you," Apirana breathed into her ear. "That must've took real guts."

"It was only a few hundred tons being held aloft by controlled explosions," Jenna murmured back, trying to take refuge in humour. "No big deal."

He snorted. "Show-off." Then he withdrew and ducked through the doorway, heading aft towards the engine room that, until now, had always been Kuai's domain. A flashing light on her terminal caught Jenna's attention, and she looked down at it.

"We're being hailed," she told Jia, trying to keep her tone businesslike. "Security frequencies."

"Fuck 'em," Jia retorted, taking three steps to the pilot's seat and dropping into it. She reached down and did something with the emergency panel, and suddenly, the alarms cut out as sharply as they'd started. The sudden quiet seemed almost ominous.

Jia reached out and picked up her hat. Then she spun her seat around and hurled the hat with a snarl at where the Captain normally sat, before swivelling back to place her hands on the drive levers.

"Fuck 'em all," Jia Chang said into the silence. Then she rammed the levers forwards, and the *Jonah* leapt away, climbing faster and harder than Jenna could remember it every doing before, into the sky towards where the *Keiko* sat in orbit overhead.

HOMEWARD BOUND

Drift had half-expected Jia to spend every waking moment she wasn't actually flying the *Keiko* beside the cryo-cabinet that held Kuai's body. Instead the pilot had almost literally walled herself off in the cockpit, snapping at anyone who'd entered and only leaving for food or comfort breaks. She'd even been sleeping in her chair, and certainly hadn't washed: After a couple of days, Drift didn't even want to enter the cockpit simply due to the smell. As a result, he hadn't been too sure of exactly where they were until the *Keiko*'s klaxon sounded and he felt the shudder as his freighter powered down its Alcubierre drive and began moving under its thrusters again.

He looked at his chrono. Five days since they'd left, more or less: not long enough for them to have got back to New Samara, no matter how hard Jia had pushed it. That presumably meant she hadn't had a change of heart, and Drift's sank a little further in response.

"Where are we?" he asked Jenna. The two of them had been sitting in companionable silence in the *Keiko*'s common room while the Chief had been fiddling around trying to fix the holo–chess board, prodding at circuits and muttering under his breath in Russian.

"Hold on, just recalibrating," Jenna told him, checking her wrist terminal. "Okay, we're at the Stranno Bazar; it's a Red Star waystation." She looked up at him. "It looks like it's not far off the straight route between Zhongtu and New Samara."

"Thank God for that," Drift muttered, pushing himself up out of his seat. "Any idea how long before we dock?"

"You're better off asking Jia," Jenna said apologetically.

"Let's assume I don't want to do that."

Jenna grimaced. "Fine, but this isn't exactly a fine-tuned locator." She studied her wrist for a moment. "Maybe half an hour? Depending on exactly how eager Jia is to get shot of us and how bothered she is about being pulled up for dangerous flying."

"So call it twenty minutes then." Drift nodded. "Chief, with me: We're getting Kuai ready. Jenna, you get the cash, and sort out what we need to ransom Tamara. Anything over that goes with Jia. I made her a promise, and I'm damn well keeping this one."

"You're sure she's leaving?" Jenna asked in a small voice.

"We don't need fuel, we don't need supplies, and we're on a tight schedule," Drift said, trying to ignore the bitter taste in his mouth. "There's no reason for Jia to have us stop here unless she intends to take her leave. She's kept her side of the bargain when I'm sure she'd have much rather flown us into a star or something. I don't want to see her go, but if she *is* going, then we don't have time to waste. We get everything ready for her, then she either leaves or stays. It's her call."

He made his way to the door and palmed it open. Muradov hurried up behind him and followed him through, and they set off for the infirmary together.

"I don't suppose this has been the best introduction to your new career," Drift commented as they headed for the elevator.

"It could have run more smoothly," Muradov conceded. "Overall, however, I still prefer this to being in the army."

Drift looked at him in surprise. "Really? I'd have thought it had all been a little . . . chaotic."

"I cannot dispute that," the Chief snorted. "But there is an important difference, Captain." They reached the metal doors, and he pressed the button to call the maglev car up. "The military would abandon an element of their force left in a predicament such as Tamara Rourke is. They would cut their losses and press on. You and your crew did not."

"We haven't got her back yet," Drift said darkly as the doors slid open in front of them. "And we lost two more in the process."

"I did not say we have her back," Muradov corrected him gently. "Simply that we have not given up on her. And I was sad to lose Kuai, but Jia leaving is her choice, and cannot be laid at your door. I recall that she was most determined to help Rourke. In fact, she shouted her brother down even though he was very clear what he felt the risks were. I suspect her desire to leave is just as much due to guilt on her part as it is anger at you, or the rest of us."

Drift raised his eyebrows as they stepped into the elevator. "You know, I hadn't actually thought about that."

"I suspected as much," Muradov said. "But it is another reason why I am glad to be on your crew, Captain. I know better than many that life can be brutal and short in this galaxy. I am happy to have companions who show each other loyalty and are quicker to blame themselves than others."

Drift grunted something noncommittal and scratched at the skin around his right eye, not quite sure what to say for a moment.

"I must confess," Muradov added quietly, "I am not without my own guilt. Had I acted quicker, Kuai might still be alive."

Drift opened his mouth to tell the Chief that it was his plan that had been at fault, then shut it again. Competing to take the blame wasn't much more useful than trying to place it elsewhere.

"I think we can all take lessons from this," he said instead as the elevator doors opened and they stepped out. "None of this would have happened if I hadn't taken that first job from Sergei Orlov, but it seemed like a sound prospect. Still, I should have known better. So from now on, I steer clear of his type, no matter how appealing the work may be. Way back when, I set out to make an honest career for myself. It never seemed to pay enough, but maybe I just should have tried harder or stuck at it for longer. Besides, it's not like these get-rich-quick schemes have ever worked out that well."

Muradov cocked an eyebrow at him as they opened the door to the infirmary. "You are 'going straight'?"

"Again," Drift said, and sighed. "Let's see if I can stick to it, this time." He crossed the infirmary floor to a contoured metal wall and activated the release. A part of the wall about two feet square detached with a *click* and slid out smoothly, revealing itself to be one end of a cryo-casket that could keep a body preserved more or less indefinitely, assuming you remembered to replace the power source every month or so. He checked the readings—all okay—and activated the maglev so he and Muradov could easily steer it to the docking hatch where Jia would connect them to the waystation.

He didn't activate the viewing plate to see Kuai's face, not even for one last time. He'd prefer to remember him in life.

"You are certain this will work for her?" Muradov asked dubiously. "The last thing I would want is for Jia to be arrested due to an irregularity over the body she is transporting."

"Jenna's cooked up the best fake documentation she can, with your help," Drift reminded him. "Anyone who checks this should find all they need to tell them that Kuai's death has been officially recorded and registered and that the body has been released to the family."

"Then let us pray that will be good enough," Muradov said soberly. He took the other end of the casket, and they began to manoeuvre it around the two sickbeds set in the middle of the floor. Drift had often wondered about the mind-set behind setting the morgue in the wall of the infirmary, but economy of space was always a concern on vessels like this, and he supposed practicality had won out in the design process.

"So what now?" Muradov asked a few seconds later.

"Hmm?"

"Jia leaving presents us with a problem," Muradov said, "if you will forgive my understatement. We have somewhere we urgently need to be, and no means of getting there."

"Waystations are a good place to hire pilots, so Jia's done us that favour at least," Drift said. His mind briefly wandered back to a fateful meeting on the Grand Souk, many years before. "I'll have to go recruiting and hope I can find someone who isn't a rank amateur, or just lying about what they can do."

The infirmary was near the docking hatch, on the basis that patients might need to be transported from it to a more advanced medical facility with a minimum of delay, so it didn't take them long to get there. As a result, Drift found himself standing with Muradov, and Kuai's casket, in awkward silence, trying not to look at his chrono too often but unable to prevent himself from wishing that time would just hurry up so they could get this over with.

They were joined a few minutes later by Jenna, holding a small money pouch that she handed to Drift, and Apirana, with bags containing both Jia and Kuai's possessions from their quarters, stacked up on another maglev bed. The big man looked pensive, and Drift got the impression that the arm Apirana placed around Jenna's shoulders was as much for his own comfort as hers.

That was good, at least. Even if most of his decisions had been flawed in some way, even if he'd made bad calls at many, many other points, Jenna and Big A were happy together, and they'd never have met each other without him. He had to focus on the positives, such as they were. If he allowed himself to get dragged down by guilt and negativity, then that wouldn't help anyone. He owed it to his crew—what was left of it—to provide a direction. They could then choose to follow him, or not. He could do nothing more.

He tried hard to remember that when he felt the slight jolt as the *Keiko* docked with Stranno Bazar, then heard the cockpit door slide open. Jia's footsteps echoed for a couple of seconds, then the pilot turned the corner and came to a dead stop.

She looked a mess. Her face was dirty, her hair was dishevelled, and her flight suit was stained. She had at least changed out of the security blacks she'd been wearing when she came back aboard, but that looked to be about all she'd done since Zhongtu. Drift couldn't really blame her.

There were tear tracks down her cheeks from when she'd been crying, but at the moment her eyes were hard and dry, and they focused on Drift.

"You this fucking eager to get rid of me?"

"No," Drift said honestly. "I don't want to lose you. You're the best damn pilot I've ever met, and you're my friend. But I figure you brought us here because you want to leave, so . . ." He gestured to the pile of bags and Kuai's casket. "We tried to make it easy. If you want to go, you can go. No delays. If you want to stay, I'll be a hell of a lot happier."

Jia's gaze held him for a moment, her face unreadable, then switched to the bags. "That my stuff?"

"Yours an' Kuai's," Apirana rumbled. "I bagged everything in both your cabins, an' all his stuff from the engine room, careful like."

Jia nodded once, her jaw visibly working. "Right."

There was a moment of silence and stillness. Then Jia stepped forward, holding her hand out.

"Give it here, then."

Apirana wordlessly tugged the maglev bed out so Jia could take the handle. She didn't look at Drift as she did so, and he tried to fight down the hollow feeling in his chest. He'd thought he'd been prepared for this moment, but he'd been wrong.

"Do you need a hand with anything?" he croaked.

"Think you've done enough, don't you?" Jia replied flatly, turning away from him. She paused for a second, then reached out, and grabbed Jenna in a one-armed hug. The taller girl froze for a moment in apparent surprise, then hugged her back a trifle awkwardly.

"Uh, I've got your money here. Should help get you home . . ."

"Take care of yourself, *báichī*," Jia muttered, letting go and taking the proffered money pouch, then turning away. She took a deep breath and laid her hand on Kuai's casket. Drift nodded over her shoulder to Muradov, who activated the air lock.

"Thanks, Chief," Jia said quietly. She stepped out into the docking corridor without a backwards glance. Muradov didn't close the air lock behind her, and so they watched until she got to the far end, where she opened that door as well and stepped out into the flow of foot traffic beyond. She turned left, and the Chang siblings disappeared from Ichabod Drift's life.

The far air lock door slid shut, and then it was just the remaining members of the *Keiko*'s crew.

"So what now?" Apirana asked heavily.

Drift exhaled and tried to compose himself. "We keep going. We need a pilot. Chief, with me: Between the two of us, we should be able to find someone who can fly a ship that at least one of us can understand. A, Jenna, see if you can sort the cockpit out so it's a bit . . . fresher, and more welcoming. If you get what I mean."

Apirana nodded. "I getcha."

"Good luck, Cap," Jenna said, squeezing his shoulder.

Drift didn't trust himself to answer.

UNFORESEEN CONSEQUENCES

Rourke woke up to the sound of her alarm, and the light of Rassvet streaming in through her window. She'd left the glass untinted, because she liked the sunrise. Besides, New Samara's twenty-six-hour daily cycle allowed for a slightly more leisurely routine than on planets or ships that adhered to the twenty-four-hour standard clock humanity had carried with them from Old Earth. She could get to bed late and still sleep for long enough to rise fully rested.

She'd grown used to operative hours when young, and smuggler hours when older, but that didn't mean she didn't enjoy a good sleep when she could catch one.

A couple of seconds after waking she realised that she had not, in fact, been roused by her alarm. Instead, it was her comm's call tone. She reached out to the bedside table and plugged it into her ear. She didn't look at her pad to see who was calling: It was almost certainly Larysa.

"Hello?"

+Good morning, Tamara.+

Rourke felt her eyebrows raise slightly. The voice in her ear was that of Sergei Orlov.

"Good morning, sir."

+How are you finding your new accommodation?+

Rourke looked around the apartment, which she'd picked herself and moved into only the day before. The furniture was rented, but it was perfectly serviceable. Besides, she could pick up pieces more to her taste in time. For now, it was simply nice to have a place she could call her own. It wasn't as luxurious as her room at the Grand House had been, and she had to cook her own food, but it was larger, and no one else had a key to the door.

Well, theoretically. She knew that Orlov's thugs—or her colleagues, as she now had to think of them—could realistically come through that door whenever they wanted. However, she at least knew that if any of them came to her flat with bad intentions, they would be very, very cautious about it.

"Very much to my liking, sir. I appreciate you extending me an advance on my wages so I could secure it."

+*It seemed a worthwhile investment at the time.*+

Rourke stiffened slightly, feeling herself abruptly becoming hyper-alert. She eyed the apartment door, then the window. Orlov surely wasn't fool enough to give *her* warning before he sent people after her—and why would he do that, anyway?—but there was no mistaking his words. "'At the time,' sir?"

+*I've just received a message from an incoming vessel that I believe you know, Tamara.*+

She sat bolt upright in bed, her stomach jumping. "What?"

+*It simply reads 'I have your money.' And it's signed off by Captain Ichabod Drift.*+

Rourke swallowed, not trusting herself to speak. For two months, she'd walled herself off from this moment. She knew that Ichabod and the others could be ferociously competent, of course, but Orlov had set them what had surely been an unattainable target. She didn't dare think that they would succeed, so she'd taken matters into her own hands. She'd escaped as much as was feasible, she'd approached Orlov on her own terms, and she'd proved her worth. She'd made the best of the hand she'd been dealt, and that had turned out not too badly at all.

She wasn't sure what she'd expected from Ichabod and the others. A gutsy, almost-certainly doomed rescue attempt, perhaps? A return, bearing some money and a desperate plea for more time? In the darker moments, when even she had struggled to sleep at night, she'd wondered to herself whether Drift really would leave her to her fate and slink off into the galaxy. Even Sergei Orlov could only reach so far, after all, and a two-month head start would be a trail so cold as to be virtually useless. The crew might have reasoned that they could do nothing for her except to die along with her, and therefore decided to save themselves. As the deadline had grown closer with no sign of her crew, she'd started to accept that this was the most likely outcome. She'd actually already forgiven them for it.

Of course, that had probably been helped by the fact that she had no longer been facing death. If a band saw to the face were the only thing she'd had to look forward to, then she might have been less charitably inclined. Even the hangover she'd endured the previous morning, after Larysa had finally convinced Rourke and Roman to drink with her in celebration of Rourke officially accepting Orlov's offer of employment, was probably less painful than that.

Probably.

+Tamara?+

She realised with a start that Orlov was still awaiting her response. She moistened a mouth that had abruptly become dry. "Sorry, sir. That somewhat startled me."

+And me. However, I need to know your thoughts on this.+

She played for time. "Sir?"

+I made a deal with Captain Drift, Tamara,+ Orlov said, and now his voice carried the slightest tone of impatience. +*If his message is to be believed, he has fulfilled his side of the deal. I need to know your intentions.*+

"Sir," Rourke said evenly as she slid out of bed, "I am now officially your employee. I signed—"

+*I am well aware what you signed,*+ Orlov snapped. +*I am also well aware, as are you, that you are here because I abducted you and that you felt compelled to offer me your services in light of my threat to unlawfully end your life. Any contracts you may or may not have signed can be held laughably void under those circumstances. Only one thing matters here: the agreement I made with Captain Drift.*

+*I am, as I told Captain Drift two months ago, a businessman. I honour my deals. Should you wish to return to his crew, then you are free to do so. The money he will provide me with will more than recompense me for the advance of your wages, and I consider the services you have done for my organisation to have cancelled the debt incurred by your crew's failure to perform the job for me on Uragan.*+

Rourke found herself consumed, just for a second, by a pure, irrational hatred of the man. Well, hatred might be rational for Sergei Orlov, for many people and for many reasons, but not for this one. She found herself abruptly and violently resenting the fact that he'd given her a choice.

If Orlov had laughed at his own promises and turned Drift away, that would be one thing. Assuming he hadn't hurt the *Keiko*'s crew, Rourke would still have worked for him. She already knew that the man was dangerous and could never be trusted completely: It had always been a case of playing the odds. But this apparently genuine offer? Giving her the chance to turn her back on this new, comparatively stable life she'd just managed to forge for herself, the result of her second major reinvention since leaving the GIA?

She hated him for it, because she already knew the answer she was going to give him.

"I will be staying in your employment, sir." She tried to muster a hint of levity in her tone, but it sounded weak even to her ears. "I think I'm getting a little old for jaunting around the galaxy."

There was a brief pause.

+I am a little surprised, I will admit. But I am also very pleased. I believe that Captain Drift will be landing in approximately two hours. Please be at my apartment in ninety minutes.+

Rourke froze. "Sir . . ."

+Yes?+

She squeezed her eyes shut. *Please don't make me face him. Please don't let me see his expression.* She took a breath and opened her eyes again. "Are you sure that's wise?"

+Far wiser than telling Ichabod Drift that his business partner has elected to remain with me, but forbidding him from seeing her. I imagine your former crew have worked very hard to acquire that money, and it's proof of how highly they value you. Captain Drift would likely think that I had already killed you and would probably seek to return the favour. I cannot guarantee that he could be restrained in a way that would not lead to him being badly hurt.+

Orlov was right, of course. She could just imagine Ichabod doing something stupid out of friendship, out of loyalty . . . basically out of all the things that she was sacrificing to remain here. But she couldn't eat friendship, and couldn't live in loyalty, and she'd been through one too many jobs where all of the crew's savings had to go on a desperately needed ship part or some other unexpected expense.

Like her ransom, for example.

When it came down to it, she *was* getting old. She was edging towards sixty, no matter what her appearance might suggest, and she wasn't going to be able to choke inconvenient security guards into unconsciousness forever. Live simply, earn money, save up for a retirement. It wasn't a grand dream, but it was one that had never quite come to fruition on the *Keiko*, no matter how carefully she and Ichabod had planned things. And at some point, she was certain, something was going to give. She'd dropped the ball a couple of months ago on Uragan, and only Jenna's quick thinking had prevented the crew's long-standing rival Ricardo *fucking* Moutinho from potentially killing both of them, plus Apirana as well. Rourke had actually collapsed moments after getting back onto the *Jonah* following that draining, drawn-out run through the war-torn capital city.

Maybe some of those arguments might persuade Ichabod that she hadn't lost her mind. With a huge slice of luck, perhaps she would even manage to convince herself that she wasn't betraying him.

"I understand, sir," she said, trying to keep the heaviness she could feel in her heart out of her tone. "I'll be there."

She ended the call and reached for her bodysuit. Old habits died hard, and she supposed she should at least *look* like herself when she ended her business partnership.

BLOOD MONEY

+*Captain?*+

Drift's head snapped up as the unfamiliar tones came over his comm, but it was only Spark. Their new pilot had only been with them for a few days, and he hadn't yet got used to zir voice.

"Drift here," he said, trying to sound as crisp and professional as possible. It wasn't the kid's fault that ze'd signed on with a battered crew on their way to pay off a debt, which was, in fact, all Spark knew of their current job. Drift had no idea how good a pilot ze actually was, but at that point, all he'd been interested in seeing was zir licence.

+*We've been assigned a bay,*+ Spark said. +*Should be touching down in just under five minutes.*+

"Roger that," Drift replied. He looked up at Apirana, who was lurking nearby. "You know what to do?"

"I know," Apirana said, although his face was troubled.

Drift clenched his jaw. "Tell me again."

The Māori sighed. "We give you two hours from when you leave the ship. You don't come back or contact us in two hours, we take off."

"Good." Drift nodded grimly, straightening the jacket of his suit. It was the same one he'd worn to the Grand House originally, and he was wearing it now for the same reason: Without a suitable outfit, he was unlikely to make it past the front door. "Make sure that you do. I don't want any heroic rescue attempts. Orlov's either going to deal with me squarely, or he won't. If he doesn't, he'll be ready for anything you can bring at him."

"Gotta tell you, Cap, I'm thinkin' the Chief kinda wants to take a shot at the bastard anyway," Apirana said, lowering his voice.

Drift shrugged, trying and failing to muster some sort of emotion. He felt burned out. "Whatever. He can if he wants. But you and Jenna, at least; promise me you'll get out of here. Spark seems able to plot a course, and it doesn't feel like we're going to crash-land. So ze must know something of what ze's doing. Take the ships and go make a living with them. Or hell, sell them if you want to," he added, trying to swallow a lump in his throat at the thought. "It's not like they'll be any use to me."

"Won't need to, Cap," Apirana rumbled, shaking his head.

"You don't know that," Drift said firmly. "But do this for me, yeah? If you sell them, give the big girl a new name before you pass her on."

"The *Keiko*? Sure thing, Cap," Apirana said with a frown. "But like I said, we won't need to."

"Here's hoping," Drift muttered. He slapped the big man on the shoulder. "Okay, get back to the engine room. I'm heading up to the bridge for the last part."

"Best of luck, Ichabod," Apirana said soberly, squeezing Drift's shoulder in turn. "Go get 'er back for us." He turned away and headed aft, and Drift climbed the stairs that led up towards the cockpit.

The door slid aside, and he stepped in, trying to hide a grimace at the unusual sight that met his eyes. Instead of Jia's straight, dark hair—or often, her hat—the back of his new pilot's head was shaved so close that he could see zir skin, and the thin dusting of hair that remained was bleached blonde.

"Captain," Spark acknowledged, looking over zir shoulder briefly. Ze had starburst tattoos beside each of zir surprisingly large, liquid eyes, and if Drift had to guess, he'd have said that zir ancestors hailed from somewhere in Old Earth's Middle East.

"No problems?" he asked, trying to keep his voice normal.

"A-OK, sir," ze replied, turning back to zir instruments. "Smooth system they've got here; it's almost like port control knows what they're doing."

Drift nodded, although Spark wasn't looking anymore, then frowned as ze started to hum to zirself. It was oddly atonal, wandering high and low without much inclination towards an actual tune, and it wasn't the first time he'd heard their new pilot doing it. Drift couldn't help but wonder if the odd mannerism was at all related to the circuitry in zir head. Spark had apparently purchased an implant that meant ze could go without sleep for a long time due to resting one half of zir brain after another. When Apirana had expressed dubiousness about that, Spark had loftily informed him that it was how dolphins slept while swimming.

Drift had actually swum with dolphins once, off the Baja California coast when his family had taken a boating holiday to Old Earth during his teenage years. The sea mammals had struck him as laughing at a joke he didn't know about, and he'd harboured an intense dislike for the species ever since.

"Any word?" he asked Jenna, who was seated at her terminal as usual.

"I was just about to call you," the slicer replied, frowning at her screen. "A message just came through, apparently from Orlov. It says that he's arranged for an aircar to pick you up at the edge of the spaceport to take you to the Grand House." She looked up at him, brushing a strand of red-gold hair back behind her ear. "It also says that he'll understand if you'd prefer to make your own way."

Drift chewed the inside of his cheek for a moment, thinking. "So, get in a car and risk getting disappeared behind tinted windows? Or walk across the city and risk a 'random' mugging?"

"You think he's looking to screw us over?" Jenna asked.

"He's screwed us over already," Drift laughed bitterly. "But there's nothing for it. I'm walking into his power base. Even if I get there safe and unmolested, there's no guarantee I'll be coming out again."

Spark looked around curiously. "You people make many enemies like this?"

"I try not to make a habit of it," Drift muttered, although he was aware that just because he tried not to didn't mean that he had a great success rate. Kelsier, Orlov, Ricardo *fucking* Moutinho, quite possibly Marcus Hall the Laughing Man . . . The list of people his crew had had potentially fatal disagreements with just in the last year was an alarming one. Thinking about it only made him more determined to stick to legal shipping jobs in the future.

He watched the spaceport of New Samara grow beneath them, the shuttles laid out in its grid of bays expanding from what looked like a child's toys into vessels as big as or bigger than the *Jonah*. He kept an eye on Spark as ze brought them down, making minor corrections to their angle or rate of descent. Ze certainly appeared competent, even if ze seemed to need to concentrate more than Jia had. Which wasn't necessarily a bad thing, Drift supposed; that young woman had been positively cavalier at times.

Finally, the *Jonah* settled gently onto her landing rests in their designated bay, and Spark powered down the drives, then swivelled around in zir chair and threw Drift a salute. "All yours, Captain!"

Drift nodded back, unable to muster much enthusiasm at the prospect. "Acknowledged, pilot. Now go and get some *proper* sleep, if you can. We'll wake you if we need you."

"Aye, sir." Spark grinned, slide out of zir chair, and squeezed past him. "No rush on my account."

Drift waited for the cockpit door to slide shut again, then turned to Jenna. "I've already talked to A, but I need to know—"

"I know, I know," Jenna protested, raising her hands. "You don't come back, we leave. Although what makes you think I'm going to follow the orders of a man I'm supposed to be treating as dead, I don't know."

Drift glared at her, putting as much force into his natural eye's stare as he could. "I mean it, Jenna. Don't tangle with Orlov any further."

"Then make sure you come back," she told him fiercely. "Because if that gangland bastard decides to play games, then I'm making no promises."

Drift closed his eyes for a moment in frustration, his mechanical one blanking out in response to the mental stimulus. "Jesus, Jenna. I just don't want anyone else I care about to die because of stupid decisions I've made. Can you understand that?"

"Yes," the slicer said, nodding soberly. "But I've got no intention of dying. And if I *do*, it'll be for me, not for you. So take this, and go get our badass back."

She reached under her seat and pulled out the pack that contained Rourke's ransom. Drift took the pack and shouldered it, searched for further words, and couldn't find any. So he gave Jenna what he hoped was a purposeful nod, turned to palm the door release, and began walking towards the cargo bay.

The fresh air of New Samara was welcome, despite the sharp petrochemical and ozone edges that were inevitable around a spaceport. Drift could get used to the smell of recycled air, since that was all he sometimes got for weeks or months at a time, moving between ships, waystations, and hermetically sealed habs on planets or moons. However, there was nothing quite like a planet's worth of breathable atmosphere, especially when he'd only recently left one.

He made his way through the designated pedestrian walkways between the ships, dodging the loading trucks and passenger buses that crawled back and forth. He was just heading for the customs checkpoint when a sleek, dark aircar with—of course—tinted windows whispered up beside him. The front passenger window slithered downwards, and he found himself looking at the face of Sergei Orlov's bald bodyguard.

"Captain Drift," Roman said. "Mr. Orlov would like me to offer you a lift."

Drift stared at him for a moment, then nodded wordlessly. At least it would get this over with quicker, whether or not Orlov was planning to double-cross him. Roman opened his door and got out, then gestured.

"Arms out, please."

Drift glowered at him, but allowed himself to be patted down. He wasn't armed, of course: He'd had no allusions that he'd have been able to get any sort of weapon into Orlov's presence anyway. However, he resisted when Roman tried to take the pack from him.

"That's for your boss," he ground out between clenched teeth, "not you."

Roman stared at him, unblinking. "Then let me check it is not a bomb, and we can get on with this."

Drift reluctantly let the bodyguard take the sack, but all Roman did was peer inside and root around with one hand, then pass it back to him and open the rear door. "Get in."

Drift obeyed. There was another of Orlov's thugs on the far side, of course, with long hair tied back into a ponytail, and it got decidedly uncomfortable when Roman squeezed in on Drift's right instead of going back to his seat in the front. Drift kept the pack on his lap and his eyes facing forwards, all the way out of the spaceport and through New Samara's streets, studiously ignoring his escort until the dark-green bulk of the Grand House hove into view.

He started to breathe a little more easily once he saw the giant casino. He'd been half-expecting to be taken back to somewhere like the abandoned slaughterhouse, where he and Rourke would be put to death, assuming his business partner was even still alive. If Orlov wanted this meeting to take place at the Grand House, then possibly, just possibly, the mobster might be keeping things aboveboard.

The driver parked outside, and Drift walked in flanked by Roman and the other thug, for all the world as though *he* owned the casino. He certainly got a few puzzled glances from the staff, who appeared to be wondering why this tall, thin Mexican with the brightly coloured hair was being escorted by Mr. Orlov's personal bodyguards. The door staff on the casino itself seemed to want to check him over with their scanning wands, but Roman just rolled his eyes and made a shooing motion until they backed off.

"I'm all for the staff being thorough," he confided to Drift in a low voice as they made their way around the edge of the main room, "but I would have hoped they'd have credited me with the ability to check you myself."

Drift blinked. That had almost sounded . . . conversational.

They reached the elevator bank on the far side, which Roman opened with a pass. He motioned Drift to step inside, and took up station next to the controls.

"Where are we going?" Drift asked as he followed the other man in. The long-haired guard remained outside, taking up station outside the doors.

"We haven't changed the route," Roman said mildly, thumbing the button to close the doors. "You're going to see Mr. Orlov, of course."

"In his apartment?" Drift asked, puzzled.

"You'd prefer the slaughterhouse?" Roman asked, his thumb hovering over the button that would tell the elevator to start rising.

"Uh, no," Drift said. "No, we're good."

"Good." Roman jabbed his thumb at the control panel, and they began to move upwards, as smoothly as silk. "I have some advice for you, if you're willing to hear it."

Drift frowned, and looked sideways at him. The bald man was staring straight ahead at the doors, his face betraying nothing.

"Go on, then."

"Just . . ." Roman hesitated for a moment, then turned his face and met Drift's eyes. "Don't overreact to anything. That's all."

"Well, that's encouraging," Drift muttered. He felt the elevator slowing to a halt, and a moment later, there was a *ping* to announce they'd arrived. The doors slid open and, sure enough, the luxuriously carpeted entrance hallway of Sergei Orlov's apartment stretched out in front of them. Roman stepped out and jerked his head for Drift to follow him.

"Roman!" Orlov's voice boomed out. "Did he come?"

Drift raised his voice in response. "How about we quit the games and get this over with?"

"As you wish, Captain," Orlov replied, sounding slightly amused. "By all means."

Drift gritted his teeth and followed Roman around the corner into the apartment proper . . . and came to a dead halt.

Sergei Orlov was sitting in a chair behind a glass coffee table and was scribbling something on an official-looking form in front of him. He looked up as Drift appeared, nodded with apparent satisfaction, and set his pen down to clasp his fingers in front of him.

At his left shoulder was a bulky, short-haired female bodyguard dressed in a suit much like Roman's. Drift could tell from her build and her shoulders that she could probably overpower anyone on the *Keiko's* crew except Apirana, but he didn't waste much time looking at her. Instead, his attention was drawn to the person standing behind Orlov's right shoulder.

Tamara Rourke was wearing the same bodysuit she'd had on when they'd been captured, so at least Orlov had allowed her that comfort. Drift looked her over quickly, searching for signs of mistreatment. She didn't seem to be bound or restrained at all, but of course, the lives of her entire crew had been dependent on her good behaviour. Orlov could have subjected her to anything, because Tamara had known that if she resisted, that might be enough to doom Drift and the others. That might explain why she looked well.

"Tamara," he said, trying to keep his voice steady. He was looking for a response, something to say that she was okay.

"Ichabod," she replied, but it wasn't the calm, dry tone he'd always associated with her. It sounded choked, like she was struggling to get the words out. He didn't like to think what Orlov or his goons might have done that could have made Tamara Rourke exhibit anything other than glacial defiance in the presence of enemies, but his brain persisted in flashing up suggestions, each worse than the last.

"Captain," Orlov said seriously, "I am glad you adhered to this agreement. I was beginning to wonder if you would disappoint me again."

Drift nearly threw the pack at him, but caught himself at the last moment and tossed it carelessly onto the table instead. It scattered papers, knocking some to the floor.

"Count it."

Orlov raised his eyebrows, apparently unperturbed by the disruption in front of him. "I feel I should inform you, Captain, that the situation has cha—"

"*Count it,*" Drift bit out. He didn't want to hear about situations changing. He just wanted Orlov to check the damned money and hand Rourke over, before Drift lost his temper and did something stupid.

Orlov shrugged and opened the pack, then tipped the money out. Roll after roll of notes tumbled onto the table. The mobster picked one up, frowning. "Some of these appear to be a trifle . . . bloodstained."

Drift manage to restrain himself from launching bodily at the man. "That's because my mechanic bled to death near them, you smug bastard."

He hadn't meant to say it like that. He shouldn't have said it like that. He should have waited until he and Rourke were clear, if indeed they would have got clear, and broken it to her gently. It wasn't fair on Rourke to be told as a side effect of him flinging some vitriol at Sergei Orlov, but the words were past his teeth before he could bite them back. His eyes flicked guiltily to Rourke, and her devastated expression was nearly enough to break his heart.

"Kuai . . . ?" she whispered, barely audible.

He nodded, blinking moistness away from his left eye. "I'm sorry, Tamara. I shouldn't have . . . I'm sorry."

"Hmm." All expression had dropped from Orlov's face, even the faint condescension, as he continued to apparently study the notes in his hand. "Well, that is a pity. You have my condolences."

"I don't want your *fucking* condolences," Drift spat. "Just let my business partner go!"

"As I was trying to say, Captain, the situation has changed . . ." Still holding that particular roll of notes between thumb and index finger, Sergei Orlov looked up at Rourke.

". . . Tamara?"

BACK IN THE SADDLE

Rourke stared at the money on the table, momentarily unable to believe her ears. Kuai, gone? How? What had happened? What about Jia? For that matter, what about the rest of the crew?

Orlov was speaking again. She blinked, trying to get her thoughts in order as he craned his neck around to look up at her.

"Tamara?"

Orlov's dark eyes were fixed on her expectantly. She glanced up and saw Ichabod was looking at her too, his natural brown eye burning fiercely in his face alongside his blank mechanical prosthetic. Drift was vibrating like a piano wire, taut and almost ready to snap. He'd clearly been through hell to get this money.

And now she was going to tell him that she didn't need ransoming. That she didn't *want* ransoming. That she wanted to stay here and make a new, stable life for herself. If that meant playing guard to a gangster, well, that wouldn't be the worst thing she'd done in her life. Not by a long shot.

But she could tell from looking at Drift that it would break him.

A couple of hours ago, Rourke had made one of the hardest choices of her life to date. Now she had to make it all over again, in a split second, based on new information. Nothing about the situation had changed for her; it was simply about the impact her choices would have on the people she cared about.

Orlov opened his mouth again, presumably to frame his question once more.

Rourke snatched the pen off his table and plunged it into the gangster's eye socket before he could react.

Orlov let out a strangled cry that cut off almost immediately, but Rourke didn't wait to see exactly how much damage she'd done. She lunged for Larysa, hoping to take her out of the equation quickly. Rourke had noticed that Larysa was hungover as soon as she'd walked into Orlov's apartment, and was counting on that to slow the other woman down by a critical fraction. She just prayed that Drift would react quickly enough and could keep Roman busy, at least for a few moments.

Larysa was still gaping and groping in her armpit holster for her gun when Rourke collided with her and ripped the comm from her ear. Sloppy; she should never have tried to draw with a hostile at this close a range. Larysa managed to pull the weapon clear as Rourke's momentum propelled her backwards, but Rourke lashed out desperately and knocked the gun from her hand.

"What are you doing?!" Larysa screamed in Russian, trying to fend Rourke off. She hadn't made the mental switch, Rourke realised, hadn't fully processed that Rourke had just tried to kill Orlov and had possibly succeeded. Maybe it was the hangover, maybe it was the sense of camaraderie that had developed over the last few weeks, maybe some part of it was even as Roman had suggested and Larysa genuinely had some romantic interest in her. The other woman was, momentarily at least, seeking to immobilise Rourke instead of striking back properly.

Rourke might have been smaller, weaker, and older than Larysa, but one thing she could never be accused of was an unwillingness to act with conviction. She lowered her shoulder and drove it into Larysa's sturdy midsection, trying to get the bigger woman off her feet.

However, even taken off guard, Larysa still had excellent balance, and all Rourke managed to do was knock her back a few steps into the wall. She heard something smash—glass in a picture frame, perhaps—then something clubbed into her back, and she lost most of her breath. A fist: Larysa had wised up and was fighting back properly now. Rourke felt the other woman's weight shift and braced herself for a knee to the ribs.

It came with a force that nearly lifted Rourke off her feet, but she wrapped one arm behind Larysa's knee and pivoted sideways, hooking one of her legs around Larysa's standing leg as she did so. The combination of factors left the bodyguard with nowhere to go except down, and she thudded onto her back with Rourke on top of her. On her way to the floor, the back of Larysa's head smashed into a decorative vase, one of several pieces of decoration boasted by Orlov's apartment; the vase exploded into pieces, but the impact didn't seem to do much beyond angering Larysa, who reached back to grab one of the large, jagged shards before driving it at Rourke's face.

Rourke twisted desperately and grabbed for the hand holding the improvised weapon, feeling the sharp porcelain scrape along her temple as she was unable to quite get out of the way in time, then caught Larysa's other wrist as the bodyguard's left hand grabbed for Rourke's throat. She leaned back, but Larysa had the floor to brace against, and her strength was telling. The other woman could easily bench-press her own weight, let alone Rourke's relatively small frame, and Rourke had no chance of outmuscling her. From here, Rourke could either let Larysa grab or cut her, or she could let her upper body be pushed far enough upwards and backwards for Larysa to get her legs between them. From there the bodyguard could push Rourke away and get back to her feet, and then Rourke didn't fancy her chances.

Rourke leaned back as far as she dared and frantically slammed her left knee into Larysa's ribs, over and over. The first few blows bought her nothing but grunts from the other woman, but then Larysa's furious mask spasmed in pain, and her right arm jerked involuntarily downwards in an attempt to protect herself.

Rourke released Larysa's right wrist and lashed out with the best punch she could muster, striking the bigger woman square in the temple. Larysa didn't go fully limp, but her body abruptly lost much of its strength, and her left arm faltered in its quest for Rourke's throat. Rourke dropped Larysa's other wrist, kneeling on the bodyguard's right arm as she did so, and lashed out twice with her right hand. The punches struck home almost undefended, and Larysa's eyes started to roll back in her head.

Rourke grabbed the shard that Larysa had been trying to lacerate her with from the other woman's unresisting fingers and stabbed it into the bodyguard's throat, then rolled clear of the gout of blood.

There was a thud, then a gunshot, quickly followed by two more.

Rourke came up in a crouch and saw Drift on his back on the floor, and she tasted bile in her throat. Then she saw the gun in his hands, pointed upwards at Roman, who had apparently just thrown him there. The bald man's shirt was abruptly flooding with red, and he staggered sideways on suddenly unsteady legs. He managed to focus on Rourke, his face twisting in incomprehension as he struggled for a word in Russian.

"*Why . . . ?*"

Then his foot caught something, and he collapsed, unable to keep his balance. Rourke got to her feet and noticed Larysa's gun was still on the floor where she'd knocked it: Drift must have wrestled Roman's from him in their struggle.

She crossed to Ichabod's side and knelt down. "You okay?"

"Yeah," the Mexican puffed. "Just winded." He turned to look at her, struggling for breath. "What the hell . . . was that for?"

Rourke gritted her teeth.

Everything.

But she couldn't say that. She couldn't explain to Drift how she'd given her word to Orlov that she'd remain in his employment, and that she had no idea if he'd let her go back on that word. That the only way she could be sure of her and Drift both getting out was to strike first, and strike hard, before Roman or Larysa had any notion that things weren't going to go down the way they'd thought.

She couldn't explain that she was angry at herself for agreeing to work for Orlov in the first place, and also at herself for going back on the decision that was best for her. She couldn't also explain that she was angry at Drift for coming back and putting her in this position. She certainly couldn't explain that she was irrationally, unfairly angry at Kuai for dying and being the source of the guilt that had caused her to change her mind.

"For Kuai," she said levelly, holding Drift's gaze. "If Orlov hadn't forced you into this deal, he'd still be alive."

She turned to look at Sergei Orlov. Her initial blow had been decisive, apparently: The most powerful man in the Rassvet system was slumped in his chair, drool running from his mouth while blood and vitreous jelly leaked down his right cheek. The pen was still sticking out of his eye socket.

"You should have listened to me," she muttered under her breath.

"Huh?" Drift grunted, propping himself up on his elbows.

"Never mind," Rourke told him, grabbing him under the arm and hauling him to his feet. "Come on, we need to get out of here." She eyed the apartment's entrance warily. "Did Roman manage to call anyone?"

"Give me some credit, please," Drift said, holding up a comm in his left hand. "I might have been able to take him out quicker if I hadn't needed to worry about him calling for backup."

Rourke nodded, thinking quickly. "Good. Even so, someone might have heard those shots. I know there's good soundproofing here, but you never know. We'd best move."

"Yeah, about that," Drift said. He spread his arms, gesturing at the walls around them. "Move *where*? If we take the elevator down, I think people might start asking questions about why we're unaccompanied and why we look like we've been in a fight."

"Simple," Rourke said, crossing to Orlov and rooting in his pockets. "We don't go down; we go *up*. Orlov's aircar is parked on the roof. All we need to do is get to street level, and we can go on foot from there." She retrieved the gangster's car fob, then eyed the money spread out over the table and began raking it back into the pack Orlov had tipped it out of. Drift hunkered down wordlessly next to her and scooped more up, passing it to her.

"Ichabod," she said.

"Yeah?"

"It means a lot." She moistened her lips and went on. "It really does. That you came back for me. Even though you didn't know what he was going to do. Even though you'd . . . though *we* lost Kuai."

"And Jia," Drift said heavily, dumping another double handful of notes into the pack.

Rourke felt her chest constrict again. "What?"

"Not . . . no," Drift said hastily. "Not like that. But she's left the crew. She's taken Kuai back to Old Earth. We had to hire a new pilot on the fly, as it were. Kid called Spark." He cleared his throat, as though he was having trouble speaking. "Seems sound enough."

"Oh." Rourke stared at the pack for a moment. Jia had been infuriating at times, and Rourke hadn't thought she'd really miss her when she'd been planning to stay on New Samara. However, the notion of flying around in the *Jonah* or the *Keiko* without Jia at the helm was just . . . weird. What exactly was she going back to?

She'd have to find out. She'd made her bunk, and she'd lie in it.

"Okay." She swept the last of the notes in and closed the pack. "Let's get out of here."

"Wait."

She turned to look at Drift, who was eyeing Orlov's body with an ugly expression on his face.

"What?" she asked, anxious to just be gone.

Drift straightened up, took two steps, and plucked the pen loose from Orlov's eye socket. It came out with an ugly sucking noise. He held it out to Rourke, who recoiled slightly.

"Ichabod, what the hell?"

"Write down 'revenge' in Chinese," Drift instructed, proffering the pen again.

Rourke frowned. "What? Where?"

"On a piece of paper! I don't care which one."

Rourke took the pen from him, trying not to grimace, turned over one of the pieces of paper Orlov had been dealing with, and scrawled two characters on the blank back of it. "Okay, *now* can we leave?"

"One more thing." Drift took the paper and pen from her, then placed the paper over the left side of Orlov's face and, to Rourke's astonishment, pinned it to him by ramming the pen into the former mob boss's *other* eye socket. "Yeah, now we can go."

"Do you mind telling me what that little display was about?" Rourke asked as they headed for the doors that led to Orlov's rooftop garden and, indirectly, up to where his aircar was parked on the penthouse roof.

"We got the money by interfering in a Triax payoff to a crooked security chief," Drift said, following her. "It seems Muradov took it into his head to tell the woman in question that she could blame the little incident on Sergei Orlov. He said he thought it would help throw the Triax off our scent, although personally, I think it's more likely he just fancied sending some trouble Orlov's way."

Rourke nodded as she pulled open the doors, and the winds of New Samara whipped around them. "So when word reaches Orlov's outfit that the Triax blame him for interfering in their dealings, they assume that the 'revenge' was the Triax."

"And with any luck the two outfits gun for each other indiscriminately instead of focusing on us," Drift said as they started up the steps to the penthouse roof. "It's not perfect, but it's the best I could come up with on the spur of the moment."

Rourke laughed humourlessly. "I think you've just summed up both our lives in one sentence."

"I just might have, at that." They reached the top of the steps, and Drift whistled in momentary appreciation as he took in the sleek lines of Orlov's private aircar. "Nice. Want me to drive?"

Rourke knew what was supposed to happen here. She was supposed to snort derisively and insult his driving abilities, then pilot the car herself. It was a routine they went through nearly every time they needed to get somewhere via vehicle, and Drift had initiated it through a desire for some sort of familiarity in a turbulent time.

It was a routine she currently had no real stomach for, because things weren't the same between them anymore. But she couldn't let him know that.

She snorted. "I've seen your driving, remember? Get in, Captain Drift."

LOOSE ENDS

The *Jonah* was climbing high into the New Samaran sky, heading back
for the *Keiko*, where it lay at anchor at a waystation, and Tamara Rourke
was alone in her cabin. The new pilot, Spark, did indeed seem perfectly
competent, if a little odd. Then again, Jia Chang had hardly been normal.
Come to think of it, most of the career pilots Rourke had met had been
odd in one way or another. Perhaps it was something about the job, or
more likely, about the sort of person who wanted the job.

She'd seen Apirana and Jenna, of course, both of whom were
delighted to have her back safe and well. She was glad to see them, too,
and was also glad that their relationship appeared to have deepened
and strengthened while they'd been away from her. Hopefully they
could take comfort in that to get them over the loss of Kuai and, in a
different way, of his sister.

Muradov had greeted her professionally and courteously, and had
given her rifle back with apologies for using it without her permission.
She'd waved the apologies away and had retired to her cabin shortly
afterwards, asking not to be disturbed for a while.

She plugged her comm into her ear and opened her pad up, then
dialled a number from memory. They were still close enough to the surface for the *Jonah*'s transmitters to patch into New Samara's network and

get her signal to where it needed to go, albeit with a second or so delay due to transit time.

+*Hello, Galactic Exports.*+

"Hello," Rourke said levelly. "Could I speak to Jhonen in Finance, please?"

+*One moment, transferring you now.*+

There was a brief snatch of hold music, and then a new voice came on. It was an older voice, with a slight rasp to it.

+*This is Jhonen. How can I help you?*+

Rourke licked her lips. "My name is Tamara Rourke. I was approached by one of your employees called Danny Wong about an account held at the Grand House."

There was a pause, longer than could be accounted for by signal delay.

+*Go on.*+

Rourke swallowed.

"Please inform our superiors that I have now closed this account."

She terminated the call before Jhonen could reply, if he indeed would have done at all, then lay back on her bunk and stared at the ceiling. Eventually her heart rate calmed, her eyes closed, and Tamara Rourke fell asleep.